THE LIGHT AT THE END OF THE WORLD

THE LIGHT AT THE END OF THE WORLD

A NOVEL

SIDDHARTHA DEB

First published in the Indian subcontinent by Context, an imprint of Westland Books, a division of Nasadiya Technologies Private Limited, in 2023

No. 269/2B, First Floor, 'Irai Arul', Vimalraj Street, Nethaji Nagar, Alapakkam Main Road, Maduravoyal, Chennai 600095

Westland, the Westland logo, Context and the Context logo are the trademarks of Nasadiya Technologies Private Limited, or its affiliates.

ISBN: 9789357762885

10 9 8 7 6 5 4 3 2 1

This is a work of fiction. Names, characters, organisations, places, events and incidents are either products of the author's imagination or used fictitiously.

Typeset by SÜRYA, New Delhi

Printed at Thomson Press (India) Ltd

For all ghuspetiyas everywhere, real and imagined, near and far.

For Carl Bromley, who asked me what I was smoking when I wrote this.

And for Ranen, who was always there.

CONTENTS

CITY OF BRUME

The angel would like to stay, awaken the dead,
and make whole what has been smashed.
But a storm is blowing from Paradise …

WALTER BENJAMIN

India is not a nation. It is a prisonhouse of all possible nations.

POLITICAL PRISONER

The city is shrouded in fog. Days of winter grey, grounding flights at the airport and leaving trains stranded on tracks hashtagged over burnt, stubbled fields. Night-time traffic in the city becomes a jittery crawl, yellow headlamps and blinking hazard lights creeping in slow motion along empty avenues. After days have passed, maybe even years, Bibi thinks, the fog lifts. The queues begin.

Men, women, the elderly proceed in zombie shuffle along separate lines to get new currency in return for the old, discontinued banknotes. Handwritten signs flap in front of ATM machines. 'Out of Order,' some of them say. Others, simply: '*NO CASH.*' Bibi, who has not stood in line to turn in her expired money and who does not possess the new magenta banknotes, the ones with images of the piloted Mars Mission on the back, uses her credit card to buy groceries and milk from the DLF Promenade mall. Then, because she doesn't have cash for an autorickshaw, she walks back to her flat in Munirka Village, past the endless walls of the university, her backpack heavy with supplies.

THE QUEUING ENDS, the surgical strikes begin. Special forces make raids across the border, targeting jihadi camps deep inside Pakistan. On the primetime television show, *The National Interest*, the glossy-haired news anchor asks experts whether beheading enemy soldiers is a suitable riposte to the martyred torso found along the Line of Control. The anchor is wearing a Western suit, and his face takes up half the screen. A couple of Pakistani politicians—stereotypical, bearded maulvi faces—are among the seven guests squeezed into the other half, men and women sitting in remote studios who look utterly bored until they start shouting. As #BrahmAstra crawls in fluorescent orange across the bottom of the screen, the anchor's voice rises in pitch. 'We are going to finish you off. You are done,' he screams at the Pakistani guests. They try to respond, but the microphone cuts them off. The volume is turned up on the voice of the anchor as he rants, the ticker now flashing in glorious, multicoloured fury—#SuperWeapon #NuclearOption #FinalSolution—as India unites behind him against jihadis, against foreigners, against anti-nationals.

Eventually, for reasons as mysterious and opaque as those that started off the chain of events, the surgical strikes end. The killings by the cow vigilantes begin. Muslims suspected of transporting cattle to slaughterhouses are pulled out of trucks. They are beaten to death with iron rods and metal pipes while the cows look on, bony haunches caked in their own shit, bovine eyes glazed with horror.

A Muslim migrant worker is set on fire by a local man while his cousin films the death and uploads it on to social media. An eight-year-old girl is raped and murdered, a teenager is raped and murdered, women are raped and murdered. They are raped and murdered inside police stations, on buses, on trains, in taxis, in temples, in forests, in fields, in huts, in hotels, in ashrams and in offices.

An anonymous number shows up on Bibi's WhatsApp and sends her a series of messages. '*I want …*' '*I will …*' '*You are …*' She blocks the number. The profile picture is a mask, made up of the trimmed white beard, gold-rimmed Gucci glasses and holes for eyes popularised in an election campaign many years ago. It could be anybody.

THROUGHOUT THESE TURBULENT months, Bibi sleeps. The end of the year comes and goes, the new year begins, and still she sleeps. She sleeps like a fairytale princess with a spell upon her. She sleeps like everything—the fog, the money queues, the killings—has happened many times before and will happen many times again, an unending cycle of the present, a loop to be broken only by some apocalyptic rupture.

An elongated figure standing upright at the tiller of a boat surfaces in her dreams. Without a face, without eyes, it somehow still observes her. Around the boat, the tops of buildings raise their heads above rushing water, trees sprouting from their faded cladding, creepers tangled around wires and satellite dishes.

Bibi cannot understand what the boatman wants. She is as useless in these dreams of hers as she is during her waking hours, unable to respond to the demands that shadow her, helpless in the face of an unending stasis. She ignores the deadlines piling up at work. She has done nothing about the task urged upon her by the farmhouse people. She is unresponsive to her mother's needs and pays no attention to her flatmate, Moi, who is caught up in her own fantasies of a perfect husband and emigration to the West.

All Bibi does is sleep and dream, especially enjoying the ones where strange, unknown lovers propose to her, even if the relationships always end before she can luxuriate in a single one's embrace. Sometimes, there are children in her dreams, as if she has jumped all the possible queues of partner, pregnancy or adoption and has abruptly become a mother. When she wakes up, she can recall two children a few years apart, a boy and a girl, their cheeks chubby with baby fat, clinging to their tiny cricket bats with desperate intensity as they wait for Bibi in the dreary corridor of a government office.

In these encounters, Bibi is never in Delhi, city of demonetisation and brume. Sometimes, she moves through places she does not know, does not recognise, where a balcony opens out to a glittering sea. There are dreams where she walks down tunnels and the tunnels lead into corridors and she is forever opening doors to small rooms heavy with grief. In others, she is saying heart-rending goodbyes to her shadowy beloved in what looks like her lost hometown, Shillong. The streets are lush with pines and firs, the stone walls thick with moss, the air heavy with the smell of tea and pungent kwai, kerosene and regret. Lightning flashes above the hills, and the umbrellas and raincoats make it impossible to kiss the beloved properly one last time. Bibi can never finish bundling the children up, is still adjusting the mufflers around their necks when she wakes up and knows that she is not in Shillong and that she has never had that other life.

In the streets and the parks of her lost hometown, she is always late for a rendezvous with her beloved and it is always raining.

1

Not that long ago, on the Monday after Diwali, Bibi finds herself running late for work. It is November. Winter fog, troubling situations and disorienting dreams are yet to come as she skips breakfast, rushing helter-skelter along the alleyways of Munirka. Buildings jostle around her like men at a queue, leering at the tiny courtyards edged with refuse. Dark, intestinally tangled electrical lines loom overhead. The stores that are open are small, mean and dimly lit, the eyes of a young Jat shopkeeper blank as they follow the clothes spinning endlessly in the washing machines set up in his tiny laundry.

The magenta line of the Delhi Metro is down for undisclosed reasons, and so she must take an autorickshaw to the Hauz Khas station and then the yellow line to Rajiv Chowk. Already, there is a text from SS, her boss, sitting on her phone. *Where u at? Need to talk ASAP*. Bibi keeps going, tall even without heels on, tall even though she has a tendency to stoop. A half-built wall materialises where there was a short cut just the day before. Hastily, she backtracks. A test subject in a labyrinth, a rat in a maze.

When she emerges from the village into the messy sprawl of businesses that is Rama Market, it is hard to spot an autorickshaw. The air around her is yellow, an uncanny haze dense and heavy with the smoke of Diwali firecrackers, brick kilns, steel furnaces, power plants, carbon-fuelled automobiles and distant fields that have been burnt to clear land for a winter crop that will still not save the farmers from destitution. She finds an auto, its dashboard festooned with plastic Hanuman stickers, sitting exactly in the middle to avoid the cold drafts attacking down both flanks.

'Hauz Khas?' she asks.

The driver shakes his head. 'Too much traffic.'

His face projects indifference and exhaustion in equal measure as he bargains, asking her if she's willing to take the auto farther, up to the Dilli Haat stop on the yellow line. She has no choice but to agree.

The names of the roads around her evoke the twentieth-century ruins of non-alignment, of Third Worldism, of Bandung, as the auto adds its emissions to the yellow haze. Behind her sprawls Jawaharlal Nehru University or JNU, a dying bastion of leftism wrapped in the embrace of Nelson Mandela Marg and Aruna Asaf Ali Marg. In front of her stretches Olof Palme Marg and then, as they turn left, Africa Avenue. Children with bloodshot eyes cluster around her auto as it stops at the traffic signal near Bhikaji Cama Place, an agglomeration of hideous concrete buildings named after the woman who, at the Second Communist International, raised a new flag, designed for a future nation called India.

The auto takes forever, crawling past endless, unpainted, unnamed flyovers that add to the claustrophobia, bullied by hulking SUVs with tinted windows and yellow licence plates all the way to the metro station. There are more traffic lights, more emaciated, glue-sniffing children holding up glossy magazines encased in transparent plastic sleeves. On their covers, Bibi sees faces replicating themselves like viruses. Men in suits and men in saffron robes. The occasional woman, light-skinned, power dressing, leaning in. Men with Gucci glasses and men with knotted ties. Men with rudraksha beads and men with dead eyes. It is only when Bibi is underground, waiting for the northbound train on the yellow line, that she finally feels that she has some air.

AKANKSHA, THE BABY-FACED receptionist, begins babbling as soon as Bibi walks in. Something about Bibi's time sheets, something about the man from accounts wanting to talk to her. Bibi is unable to give her attention to Akanksha, a girl from small-town Meerut carrying on a deliriously happy affair with Veer, the staff artist who commutes from the suburban township of Dwarka and who shares his lunch, packed in a stainless steel tiffin carrier by his wife, with Akanksha. Everything in Veer's lunch—the parathas folded into little triangles, the collage of mixed vegetables, the lumpy dahi, the pickles in their fiery red oil slick—is home-made, or, as Bibi should really say, *wife-made*. After Veer and Akanksha have finished eating the wife-made lunch at Veer's desk, he teaches Akanksha to draw, holding her small, soft hand in his as he guides it over the sketchbook he has bought for her from the stationery shop downstairs.

Not so different from her, Akanksha, apart from her youth and her excitement with love. Just one more provincial afloat in the big city, trying to contain in her shifting, sliding self those terribly opposed realms—loneliness against attention, work versus art. Bibi has been there herself, in Calcutta, in Delhi, in all these years of drift punctuated by brief, concentrated moments of joy. She remembers, if only faintly, what it is like when, in the constant flow of strangers indifferent or hostile, in the maddening flow of atomised traffic and fragmented presences, amid the overwhelming sense that this life is going nowhere and that all options have been foreclosed, someone arrives, someone whose fingers intertwine with yours, someone in whose company the city tilts on its axis.

It is the city then suddenly become different, housed on a planet in whose sky float two crescent moons, where the sun, every day, rises in the south and sets in the north. Then, one morning, the beloved is gone, and it is the same old city once again, squatting on an aged, abused planet spinning along a shop-soiled, familiar axis, a city that seems more worn and rundown than ever.

2

Bibi's boss is called S.S. Chakravarthy, which makes him sound like a ship, but he goes by his initials. No one knows what the initials stand for. SS is guarded about it, as he is about many things. It isn't clear, for instance, why, after working at the biggest media houses in the country, he has ended up at Amidala. Nor is it entirely certain to Bibi what Amidala's business consists of, or what she herself does in return for the monthly pay cheques deposited to her account.

There are frequent consultations involving corporations, think tanks and government agencies. Reports are produced often, massive files uploaded to the web and blitzed to media organisers and influential individuals. The titles have a distinct pattern, a primary colour usually paired with an abstract word: 'Green Justice', 'Blue Economy', 'Red Planet'.

Well, no, maybe not 'Red Planet'. Like messages in glass bottles, the reports sink into the internet ocean, the tides and waves of data carrying them who knows where. Amidala claims to shape the world with its reports and its rota of global thinkers who have interpretations for everything: the rising tide of authoritarianism that they believe represents a revolt against nanny states; the sudden popularity of gurus that showcases the religious freedom that can flourish only in a democracy; the hysteria over a skewed sex ratio that is an alarmist misreading of sovereign individual choice, and which, if left to market forces, will inevitably produce a self-correction.

Events are organised constantly, independently as well as in association with other similar organisations, producing a regular outflow of promotional material that it is Bibi's task to edit. Often, though, she is no more than a glorified secretary, putting together hotel bookings and travel itineraries for men with expensive suits and sharp American accents who are scheduled to speak at leadership summits and cultural festivals being held in suitably exotic locations, her emails and calls hurrying after their busy lives to make sure that the flower bouquets, mineral water and AV equipment are in place during the talks, that the airport pickups and hotel drop-offs have gone smoothly, that the bills for entertainment and extras have been paid off quickly.

Bibi is competent at these tasks, but only she knows that her projection of efficiency is a lie. She has perfected the art of doing the bare minimum and withdrawing into the background, of being invisible even when required to be physically present. The day she is gone from Amidala, she will leave behind no memories, no traces. They will wonder, if they are given to wondering, whether they missed something fundamental about her. Was she a spirit, a ghost?

SHE KNOCKS AT the door, goes in. SS looks momentarily puzzled as she enters. He is seated on a Swiss ball in front of his adjustable desk, clutching a biography of the latest American president like he is required to swear an oath on it. When he registers that the visitor is Bibi, that he himself has called her for this meeting, he puts the presidential biography down. He sucks in his stomach, adjusts his posture on the ball and pushes forward a beige folder. It is labelled with the name of the client, *Vimana Energy Enterprises*.

'Remember this?' he asks.

Bibi sort of remembers it. A client meeting, bright lights in the conference room bouncing off the shiny shirts of two men who have introduced themselves as Vikas and Vinay. The rest is something of a blur. As usual, she is distracted, not really listening to what the men are saying. Something about start-ups, seed funds, venture capital, commodities, oil, renewables, something about key investors and the Vibrant India Summit coming up in February where the prime minister will make a speech. Mineral sand deposits to power a string of thorium nuclear reactors. Futuristic technologies that will reduce pollution and India's dependency on oil imports, that, in conjunction with nuclear plants, dams, pipelines and ports, will create a grid of self-contained energy, choking China's oil route through the Indian Ocean and backing Pakistan into a fuel crisis from which it will never recover. A superplan for a superpower, in keeping with the Mars landing and the superweapon being fine-tuned in the Ombani defence labs, the one the media has taken to calling the Brahmastra—Brahma's weapon.

Bibi's attention switches on fully only when familiar place names begin to crop up in this conversation. Rivers in northeast India, tides and currents in the Bay of Bengal, mineral-rich hill ranges and mountains. She hears the interesting but perplexing sentence, 'The island is our unsinkable aircraft carrier.' But she has been too slow in focusing her mind upon what is being said. The conversation is already aiming in a different direction, with a dull discussion of the promotional material to be produced, in particular how the owner of the company, a bland-looking man with the bland-sounding name of Shekhar Gupta, should be featured. A suitable speech, to be delivered at the Vibrant India summit, will have to be ghostwritten for him. Yoga, ancient Vedic science and solar panels must be mentioned in this speech, which will argue that the super technology of the future has been developed only by harnessing the super technology of the past; the ape who piloted the Mars probe was none other than a descendant of the monkey-god Hanuman, just as the superweapon being finished in the Ombani Labs is only a modern manifestation of the weapon made by Brahma, creator of the universe, a weapon so terrible that even the gods have always shirked from its use.

Bibi, alert now, takes dutiful notes. She has the impression of something vital missed, but the meeting is already coming to an end, Vinay and Vikas holding her hand for far too long in the clammy handshakes insisted upon to mark the conclusion of business.

That is all she recalls of Vimana Energy Enterprises. A leftover, niggling feeling that she should have been paying more attention, that a previous version of her would have registered every detail. A feeling buried easily enough under a purposeless job dedicated to appearances. Illusions masking the bone, events and promotional material churned out like mirages and client companies flickering in and out of existence like sand dunes in a vast, windswept desert.

SS opens the folder and begins talking.

A MAN WHO didn't give his name arrived at the Vimana office in Gurugram on Saturday, the day before Diwali. The office was more or less shut, with some construction work going on. The man, who had no appointment, told the receptionist that he had information about Vimana's involvement in tax fraud and offshore accounts. He had proof that their invoices were faked and their customs clearances misleading, that instead of importing parts for solar panels and windmills, as claimed in their paperwork, Vimana had purchased electronic equipment, mobile phone jammers and bars of Rand gold.

Vikas, who was in the office, came out to meet the man making these accusations. He assumed the man was a small-time hustler trying to make easy money, maybe a sting reporter sniffing around for sensational news, someone most certainly in the pay of a business or political rival. He sat the man down in the reception area and asked to be shown some proof. The man said he had links in the chain of evidence that extended beyond Vimana, that implicated other, bigger companies, that went right to the top.

SS leans forward. 'He mentioned the names of our biggest political leaders,' he says in a hushed voice. 'He may have referred to the events of 1984, of 2002 and 2020. He may have called them genocides.'

A faint, greyish light filters through the window behind SS, so that noon feels like dusk. Bibi can hear the ebb and flow of afternoon traffic on the Outer Circle of Connaught Place, the sudden acceleration of a bus going down Sansad Marg, towards the sandbagged security barriers encircling the parliament.

SS continues his story. There was something off about the man. Nondescript in the beginning, he now appeared fantastically dirty to Vikas, as though he had undergone a gradual transformation while making his accusations. Wild, unshaven and with a foul smell emanating from him, he radiated such a crazed air that Vikas was astonished that the stranger had been able to make his way into the office at all. He signalled the receptionist to call security. The receptionist picked up her phone. Vikas stood up and was knocked to the floor by the visitor. The man straddled Vikas, hands in a chokehold. Both the receptionist and Vikas later said that the visitor seemed possessed, producing a guttural noise from the back of his throat that was barely human and with some device in his shirt flashing red and blue. The coffee table was knocked over, a flower vase shattered. As security guards clustered in a confusion of uniforms, batons and walkie-talkies, the man got up, sprang past the receptionist and ran inside the office to hide.

'What happened then?' Bibi asks.

SS gets up from the Swiss ball and paces around before he returns. 'The office isn't completely finished because the company has been waiting for their vaastu expert's opinion. How desks and plants and lights should be arranged, how pools of bad energy might be eliminated. There are some dead corridors, a few unused store rooms, places where the wiring is still going on. Quite a few spots where one can hide, in other words, but the only entry and exit point is through the reception area, which was crowded with security guards. When the police showed up, they searched everywhere. It took them a while to check out all the corridors, clear every room and cubicle. The office was empty, except for a deaf old man, a Muslim painter, who had seen and heard nothing as he applied primer to a wall in the conference room. In the kitchen, a window was open. But the window was small, perhaps big enough for a child. The office itself is on the thirteenth floor of a high-rise, right behind the Civil Hospital. There were people below, drivers, servants, the usual hangers-on clustered around the hospital, who said that they saw a monkey sneak out through the window, that it leapt from ledge to ledge, from building to building, before it disappeared into the hospital. But no one saw the man without a name come out of the Vimana office. He vanished, like he had never been there at all.'

'How freaky,' Bibi says. 'But what does any of this have to do with us?'

'That's the thing. The man left a USB drive behind as he fled. Vikas claims it fell out of the man's pocket, or that he might have grabbed it from the man during his tussle. I personally think it was left behind deliberately.

'But why, and by whom?'

'We don't know that yet,' SS says. 'The drive turned out to have a bizarre assortment of files on it. Lists of names, random video footage, articles and blog posts about detention centres. A treasure trove of conspiracies. Mutant creatures, engineered viruses, experimental weapons involving Artificial Intelligence and alien wrecks discovered in remote mountain areas. Hundreds upon hundreds of pages of stuff that had no logic. Nothing that added up to anything at all.'

Bibi can see the Vimana logo on the client folder. A stylised rendition of Hanuman, the monkey god, tail curled in an upward flourish, carrying a mountain on one hand. Like a surfer, he stands on what looks like a flying temple. She assumes it is a Vimana, a Vedic aircraft. She tries to remember the story in the *Ramayana* and why monkeys and bears are co-opted into a human war that involves the invasion of a distant island.

'Among the files,' SS says, 'there were articles written by you. From your stint as a journalist. From before Amidala.'

SS displays a series of smudged printouts. The story on the detention centre, the one on the abandoned Union Carbide factory, that piece on the odd antiquities uncovered by geologists prospecting for minerals in the mountains. Articles heavy with black text overrun SS's desk, obscuring the American president's shiny face. She can see the accompanying pictures: the weeds and flowers blooming around the chemical tanks, the elderly villager pointing across desiccated fields to the site of the dig and, of course, the businessman connected to the detention centre in Assam. A 'Greatest Hits' compilation from Bibi's past.

'Old things,' Bibi says, taking a sharp breath. 'From a lifetime ago.' Outside, police sirens ebb and flow, like signals pulsing from a distant, long-dead star. Bibi thinks she hears a crowd chanting, but what are they saying?

She forces her attention back to the papers in SS's hand. She still remembers the trouble with the detention centre story, the rumours that had to be sifted through, beginning with stray remarks by a very drunk army officer at a Delhi five-star hotel, someone who mistook her interest in his story for an interest in him and who had to be persuaded into relinquishing his sudden grip on her wrist, but whose account led her eventually to military bases in the Northeast, the walls topped with barbed wire and signposted by watchtowers that looked over the watery fields to where the land dissolved into the sinewy curve of the Brahmaputra River. But it is no longer her story, and those are no longer her memories. She is no longer the person who had that byline, did that work, fought those battles.

'Old things, exactly. If it was up to me, I'd ignore it all. I think the man without a name was just trying to hustle Vimana. I think he ran out through the front door during the brawl. I think Vikas and these other jokers made up the story about him vanishing in order to save face with their boss. Really, I don't give a shit about any of this and the whole thing sounds ridiculous to me. I was told that the file name of the USB drive is KEY DRIVE, which suggests that we're not exactly looking at Ed Snowden or WikiLeaks level whistleblowing here.'

SS stops, struck by his own eloquence. When he speaks again, he is more in control, his voice soothing and conciliatory as he addresses Bibi. 'It's just that Shekhar Gupta got worried, had one of his people look up your old work, and then spoke to our owners about it. He should have talked to me before he went to the owners, but he didn't. Now, our owners are really laid-back, totally hands-off folks. But things have been sensitive recently, you know. The overall political atmosphere. The trade wars, the border incursions, these things. So they decided that a face to face meeting with you was the best thing. Just to clear up the air.'

There is a knock on the door. SS pauses as a man comes in holding a tray with his left hand, propping it against his chest for extra support. It is Mohinder, the new security guard. A red tea towel hangs rakishly down his right shoulder, draped over the arm that ends in a smooth, conical stump just above the elbow.

SS irritably refuses the mug held out towards him by Mohinder, who retracts it hurriedly. The pile of photocopies is knocked over. 'For fuck's sake,' SS mutters. 'What makes a security company hire a guy with one arm as a guard? And why is he doing double duty as office peon?'

Mohinder gives no indication that he has heard or understood what has been said. He picks the papers up with his left hand, putting them back on the desk a few sheets at a time. Bibi joins him in the task, trying not to look at the words before her. When they are done, the papers stacked up, order restored, Mohinder retreats with the tray. His feet make no sound as he leaves. One can barely hear the door closing behind him.

'When do the owners want this meeting with us?'

'With just you. Tomorrow at eleven.'

Bibi's phone buzzes as SS texts her the address. A farmhouse in Chhattarpur, on the outskirts of the city. It is a long way from the office. It's all right if Bibi doesn't come in to work after her meeting, SS says.

3

Something is wrong with the eyeball in the sky as Bibi gets into the auto. It hovers behind a filter of pollution, a whitish, phlegmy disc so indistinct that Bibi does not know whether she is looking at the sun or the moon. Everything else has a sepia tinge to it, the present acidifying into a distant past, into some kind of warped, alternative nineteenth century that just happens to include mobile phones.

It makes Bibi think of her final reporting trip all those years ago, the rented four-wheel drive bouncing along the road snaking through the mountains towards the river valley, the windows open to the characteristic smell of the highways of the Northeast, diesel-spiked rain and the occasional, ghostly whiff of coal fires, tobacco and potatoes. She is more than a thousand miles east of Delhi, back to the corner of the subcontinent where she grew up. But even though she has just left Shillong, the town she was born in, even though she is so familiar with this part of the country, she is gripped by a sense of weightlessness. All around her is the border slicing through the highlands and the rivers, an imagined line but one that bristles with guard posts, security cameras and electronic sensors, the angled upper edges of the chain-link fences topped with coiled razor wire. It has sectioned up this in-between, nowhere realm and its in-between, nowhere people, demarcating them as belonging to India, or to Bangladesh, or to Burma, or as undocumented, paperless, 'D for Doubtful' individuals who belong to no government at all. India doesn't want those it calls Bangladeshis, and Bangladesh doesn't want them, because Bangladesh, wracked by a century of famine, genocide, and authoritarianism is now at the forefront of climate collapse, its people dispatching themselves wherever they can to find a livelihood, to the Gulf states, Greece and New York, but sometimes also just across the border, to India. Bibi is aiming for one particular edge of that border, travelling all morning past faded signboards advertising government loan schemes that no longer exist and chemical fertilisers that, apart from their toxic byproducts, ceased to be effective decades ago. She is searching for a detention centre that officially does not exist but rumours of whose presence ripple far away in Delhi and surface in the murmurs of people back in Shillong. It is hidden inside an army camp, or is near an army camp, on that everyone agrees. All other details are contradictory, the detention centre changing shape with the teller: sometimes it looks like a factory, with guard towers and isolated structures; sometimes it resembles a vast municipal hospital built in colonial times, connected by covered bridges and endless corridors; at other times it is a palace crumbling slowly into ruins. Clandestine trials are carried out inside this shape-shifting complex, she has been told, and yet prisoners have been known to inexplicably escape. The inside of the rented SUV reeks of sweat and fuel as it eats up the miles, but when Bibi steps out for a roadside tea break, the air is cold and the sky clear, the trees cascading in dark waves down the slopes of the hills. Bibi follows the driver past hunched miners, mostly undocumented, some no more than teenage boys, all of them drinking themselves into a liberating stupor with pale, milky liquor served in plastic cups. She enters the tea stall chosen by the driver and is struck by what she can only think of as a *dimness* to the people, all on the verge of fading away. The dimness is in the poor lighting of the stall, in the greying patina of the clothes worn by the customers and in the blurred outline of the faces around the rough-hewn, unpainted, wooden tables, everything feeling like a slightly unfocused memory, as if Bibi has travelled back in time but been unable to sync fully with this version of the past. Nothing, not the sweet tea and damp biscuits served in a chipped cup and saucer, not the barely legible newsprint pasted over the bamboo walls, and not the meagre possessions of the people around her suggest that the world has moved much beyond a sooty, early industrialisation. For all she knows, the British are still at their colonial outposts, meticulously recording the Mon-Khmer and Tibeto-Burman languages of the region after putting down the Sepoy Rebellion in the plains. The only moment of dissonance comes is when a mobile phone reveals itself in the blackened, calloused hand of a miner boy at the next table, a plain, grey Nokia, the cheapest and most common of mobile phones, but that glows in that tea stall with magic, that suggests a collision of different realities and trajectories, Bibi, these people, the Nokia, all shifting, sliding elements falling through a hole in time.

The auto sputters on in harried, laborious progress, Bibi's memory of the highways of northeast India giving way to the reality of an overhead stretch of the Delhi Metro. A row of gunmetal carriages sits on the tracks, waiting to enter Chhattarpur station, dimly silhouetted in the November haze.

THE AQI IS 689 and rising. The driver is possibly only in his fifties, but he has been battered into old age, the scarf around his head like a makeshift bandage. He breaks into a series of wretched, hacking coughs and reaches for a dented Bisleri bottle wedged under his seat, its plastic casing wrinkled and translucent from repeated use.

South Delhi gives way to a cluster of temples, a giant Hanuman staring down through the mustard haze like someone who has been tear-gassed, his monkey cheeks distended, his mace raised in a retaliatory strike. There are high walls along both sides of the road, topped with broken glass and barbed wire. Traffic thins out into a scattering of SUVs and military trucks as they drive past hotels and weekend resorts and management schools, past mansion after mansion that goes by the Delhi name of *farmhouse* even though none of them have anything to do with farming. A white Hummer comes bursting out from some invisible driveway and is upon them before they even see it, the driver's face a mask behind gleaming wraparound sunglasses. The auto driver curses and coughs as he's forced to swerve. His engine stalls and he pulls at his gear shaft again and again, the rattle of the engine matching the rattle of his chest.

When he is unable to start his vehicle and slumps over, wheezing with the effort, Bibi pays him and proceeds on foot. The sound of her boots is her only companion as she walks past walls that get ever higher and increasingly more forbidding, the expanse of the properties unending, stretching all the way to the edge of the smoky world.

WHEN SHE REACHES her destination, she gives her name to the men at the guardhouse. Crackling walkie-talkies, interrupted by hacking coughs, attempt to find out whether Bibi is expected. Eventually, a guard opens the gate and shouts at her to proceed, forced to raise his hoarse voice because the haze cuts off sound as well as sight.

The approach to the farmhouse is not meant for walking, and Bibi feels that she is barely making any progress. The haze blankets her surroundings, giving her approach a dreamlike quality as images come into focus like memories and dissolve like dreams. Slashes of moss-green lawn, the sharp, blue inhalation of what is perhaps a swimming pool. Bibi wonders why swimming pool floors are always painted blue and if this has anything to do with the sky and the ocean. She wonders what it would be like to swim in the ocean and look up at a blue sky.

The farmhouse, or mansion, or whatever it is, looms in front of her, like a sunken ship raised for salvage. Dwarfish men, their uniform caps worn in an abject, servile way, are polishing shiny cars that tower over them. There is a European-style angel in black stone at the centre of the portico. The angel's wings are raised in anticipation of flight, its face pensive as Bibi approaches the glazed double doors, rings the bell and waits.

A LIVERIED SERVANT leads Bibi inside. Photographs line a staircase sweeping up one wall. On the other end, a picture window looks out to the back, at a second swimming pool glowing from underwater lights. Framed by that glass wall, seated at a round, wrought-iron table with a lacy white tablecloth, a woman taps at a phone. Two other phones lie in front of her, next to a laptop and a scattering of brochures in dark, restrained colours.

Outside, the haze has cleared slightly. A man shrunken into his uniform swabs the pool deck on his knees. A peacock struts on the lawns behind him, psychedelic feathers held out in a dance no one is interested in, a counterculture figure arriving far too late to a different kind of party.

Bibi becomes conscious of a great many other things as she joins the woman at the table and introduces herself. The rings glittering on the woman's fingers as she texts, the reddish highlights in her hair. The wintry smell of freshly squeezed sweet lime juice. The woman's name, Preitty, which Bibi thinks must be a made-up word, the end product, perhaps, of numerological calculations carried out by an astrologer. This room, this farmhouse, the smoothly pumping heart of a vast machine of which the office Bibi works in is only one node.

As Preitty rises and asks Bibi to come along, Bibi is assailed by two contradictory impressions. She senses the impregnability of the wealth and power on display, so secure and smooth that nothing will ever threaten it. And yet, there is also a fragility to it all—it will take no more than a single rock hurled against that sheer glass window for everything to come crashing down.

4

Up the staircase they go, past the sweep of the balustrade, floating high above the lit chandeliers. Giant panoramic photographs line the wall: a thin, two-dimensional woman with colourful bangles up to her elbows sorting through incense sticks in a dusty slum yard: a man rushing to board a tram on a Calcutta street, pursued by another man; red-coated colonial soldiers eating an elaborate meal at some remote mountain pass. The staircase turns sharply right, towards the back of the farmhouse, disorienting somehow. Bibi cannot make out Preitty's table below, but she can see the blue of the swimming pool outside.

It is perhaps after they have climbed two flights that the farmhouse begins to shrug off the five-star aesthetic of its lower levels. Shorn of polish and glitter, the house is palpably older. The pictures on the wall are now portraits, small black-and-white studio photos of men related to one another, dressed in the same way, all individualities airbrushed out so that it looks like it is the same man appearing many times over, his eyes constantly fixed on Bibi as she passes by.

Walls of unpainted stone, damp and cold, close in as they progress farther. Bibi sees blind stairwells and windows opening abruptly on to other, apparently abandoned, rooms. Landings reveal sudden glimpses of the smoky sky above.

They pass another of the many uniformed, baseball-capped minions, this one cleaning the floor of a panic room. The door is made of reinforced steel, the interior equipped with a refrigerator, a treadmill and a bank of monitors. Another floor and another chamber, darker than the others, its marble floor slick with damp flower petals. The features of the deity are obscured in the gloom, but a man sits next to the idol, bent over the sharp glow of a smartphone. He looks up as they pass, his eyes little discs of red, grey hair cascading down to his wide shoulders.

Then they reach a level that is organised more rationally. All the doors now have to be opened by Preitty with an electronic keycard. The flooring is no longer marble or granite but shiny and plasticky, made for easy cleaning. A row of unmarked doors mark one side of the corridor, small, square windowpanes set in each door.

A lobby area opens up before them. It is small and utilitarian, with a sofa facing a television set mounted on the wall, the sound on the television muted. A man, small, pale, like a mouse in a children's book, is sitting on the sofa, hunched in on himself. The glossy-haired news anchor eyes the man, jabbing his fountain pen for emphasis. His lips move at a frantic rate, outpacing the glittering ticker in which the most prominent letters spell out #AntiNational #Conspiracy #BrahmAstra.

The pale man stares at Bibi. He is perhaps Kashmiri. Head cocked to one side, tongue moving frantically, he is muttering away. Sounds that are almost words, but he keeps tripping up, stumbling like a drunken man trying to find his footing, the words decomposing into a random sequence of noises. Two fingers are missing on his right hand.

'I am un ram,' he says to Bibi as she passes. 'Eadlines am India mam.'

ANOTHER FLIGHT OF stairs is visible ahead. It is impossible, Bibi thinks, for this house to be so large, for it to have so many floors, for it not to have a lift to negotiate the floors. But they have reached their destination. In contrast to the rest of the upper floors, the study they enter is airy, with large windows on one side that look down at the swimming pool and the gardens at the back. A swing is suspended from the branch of an eucalyptus tree. It feels like the distance has been reduced again, the study only a few flights up from the ground floor, all the levels passed in between like scenes from a fever dream.

Inside the study, everything is expensive, from the heavy wooden desk with a green top to the Rolex on the wrist of the man sitting behind the desk. Because he is sitting well back from the overhead light, Bibi can't make out his face. A distinct smell lingers in the air, an aroma of ginger and bay leaves and cardamoms. A cup clinks in the shadows. Bibi realises she is smelling freshly made tea.

'That person who went to the Vimana office knew little of importance,' the man says. 'The question is, what do you know?'

HE IS A thin man, this speaker in the shadows. His face moves into the light, and Bibi can see some of his features. With those ears sticking out from a bald head, he looks harmless, even comical. If someone were to put a pair of pince-nez glasses on him, he would have just the slightest of resemblances to Gandhi. Yet, as soon as Bibi registers the resemblance, it is gone, leaving her faltering like she was expecting to find a step where there is none.

'Sit,' he says sharply and is overwhelmed by a dry cough that goes on forever. Preitty makes no move towards the man but waits stonily as he takes out a handkerchief and hacks into it. When he has recovered, he sips his tea and clears his throat. Then he leans forward and addresses Bibi.

'This is not the first time something like this has happened to our interests. A stranger coming out of nowhere with unhinged accusations. A blog post or social media thread exposing transactional details not meant for the general public. An internal policy document sent to a black-box site. Leaks everywhere, so many that any distinction between the false and the true becomes blurred, and always at a time most delicate for us.'

'I really don't understand what any of this has to do with me,' Bibi says.

'You will,' the man replies. 'By the time you leave, you will have understood a great many things. When we went through the drive, we paid careful attention to the material on it. We noticed the presence of your article, and we noticed, among the other documents, articles written by a man you once worked with, who came from the same obscure town as you. How could this be a coincidence?'

Before Bibi can say anything, he breaks into another coughing fit. Something he cannot get rid of is stuck in his throat. A hair, or the subtlest of fishbones. Spasms shake his body and tears stream from his eyes as he punches viciously at a button under his desk. The grey-haired man she has seen in the idol room appears, giving him a pill and muttering some kind of spell.

A GESTURE HAS Preitty reaching for the laptop on the desk. She swivels it around so that Bibi can see. A page from a blue passport, elegant Devanagari and Roman script assembled against striated lines and inscrutable bar codes. Preitty taps delicately at the keyboard. The photograph on the upper left corner leaps and shudders, magnified into a pixellated cluster of cropped hair, chiselled jaw and the sparsest of Ho Chi Minh goatees. In keeping with the mysterious injunctions of the passport-issuing authorities, both ears are prominently visible.

'What do you say now?' the man asks.

Bibi is aware of a pounding in her heart, a dryness in her mouth. 'I knew him.' She has to swallow before she can speak again. 'But not well. We overlapped briefly at the paper when I had just moved to Delhi. But Sanjit was on the city desk, I was on national.'

'So you mean to say you did not stay in touch with Mr Sanjit or track his career when he moved on? Surely you couldn't have failed to keep up with his meticulous reconstruction of conspiracies? Mass murder, torture, financial fraud, India nothing but a Brahminical, Kautilyan, capitalist state swirling with inequity and violence. I'm sure you read those pieces, were probably inspired by them in your admittedly far more limited articles on detention centres and uranium plants and victims of pesticide factories.'

'My articles are from a long time ago, sir.' Bibi's voice is meek, deferential. 'As you well know, I am no longer a journalist. And Sanjit died in an accident some years ago.'

'We know the story,' the man says. 'What was it? That he was travelling in a Tata Sumo, a share taxi that fell down a ravine.'

'Spot dead,' Preitty adds. 'Seven passengers and the driver. Somewhere in Assam or Nagaland.'

'What a stupid way to go,' Bibi says with a flash of anger.

'But did he really go?' The man signals to Preitty and she closes the laptop. 'We sent people to check things out. The eyewitnesses turned out to be unreliable. The paperwork was a mess. How many bodies had been collected from the site? One set of documents said six, another said eight. There was nothing in the list of scrawled names to indicate that your former colleague was among those corpses, or that he had really boarded the Tata Sumo at Dimapur. An enterprising local website with an unpronounceable name ran a story that an army truck from the Rangapahar cantonment had deliberately rammed the Tata Sumo because a national journalist was on it, someone about to expose torture killings carried out by counter-insurgency units. In other words, a government cover-up. Of course! But we have our sources, and we know that no army truck was involved, and that the accident was a result of the usual drunkenness that plagues tribal people from the Northeast. Then, we made further inquiries that uncovered other reasons for thinking that Mr Sanjit is alive, although these details need not concern you. Not yet, at any rate. What we want you to do is to begin making some inquiries of your own.'

'What kind of inquiries? Why?' It is hard to hide the panic in her voice.

'You were good at finding people. Good at getting them to talk. Good at what you did. So what happened? Why did you stop? Why did you give it all up?'

'There will be an expense account,' Preitty says. 'A generous finder's fee.'

'It is not that others will not be looking for him at the same time. You are merely an extra dice being introduced into the game. A wild card, a free hit.'

'I can't do this,' Bibi says.

'What choice do you have?' he says. 'It's not like you are making anything of your life. How old are you? You stay in what is practically a slum. Your mother lives on her own in a rented house on the outskirts of Kolkata. You send your mother money every month, but you're not close, not to her or to anyone in your family. You're a disappointment to them, and you're an even bigger disappointment to yourself. You have no husband, no boyfriend, no children, no savings, no property. You're not even young any more. You have no mentor to promote your interests, no godfather to protect you. You have no close friends apart from the waitress you live with. Who remembers you? Who will forget you?'

Bibi can see the peacock below in the garden, its tail feathers spread out. It looks all wrong, enormously large, as it begins to whirl. Its dance makes her queasy. She is surely too far up to be able to make out such details, and yet she can see the mimic eyes in the peacock's tail feathers. They go in and out of focus, but then the yellow haze rises. It moves at the speed of an aircraft, blotting out peacock and pool with incredible swiftness until it hangs just outside the window, swirling mistily until something like the outline of a face, eyes wide in astonishment, forms behind the window pane. The wind shifts, the haze reappears, and everything is erased from her view.

Coughs possess the man's body so completely that Bibi is filled with a tenderness towards him in spite of his recent threats. Preitty speaks into her phone even as the man waves them away. 'Check the air filters,' she says.

The grey-haired priest shows up, unhurried, unflustered, scrutinising Bibi as she is led out by Preitty. Then the door shuts behind her, muffling the man's coughs and the priest's murmurs. The way back is shorter, more direct, without any of those levels, as if Bibi has imagined it all.

5

The day after the visit to the Chhattarpur farmhouse, Bibi calls in sick. Late into the morning she sleeps, sinking and swimming in dreams that are perplexing in their variety. Eyes on a peacock's tail morph into the cool, dispassionate gaze of cephalopods lurking in the ocean. Wingbeats of angels and hooves of the Buraq kicking over a jar filled with water. Vast alien presences whirling against stars embossed in a crystal sky.

SS calls to find out how long Bibi will be away from work, if everything went okay during her meeting. Bibi tries to hide the drowsiness in her voice. She is unwilling to reveal the truth, that she is out of sync with the world, many steps behind those fully awake. After she hangs up, she goes back to bed. All she wants is to return to her dreams, to the smell of cut grass and spring rain and the strange but vaguely familiar figures flashing past on the foggy highway of her mind. When she wakes up again, her pillow is damp, as though a window to her dream world had been briefly left open.

HER BACK AND legs ache as she steps out of bed and a new text dings its arrival. Her throat is hoarse with phlegm and there is some kind of fuzzy growth on the inside of her mouth. Standing unsteadily on the cold concrete floor, lit by the phone's lurid glow, Bibi checks her assortment of messages. Offers from health firms, clothing brands, recruiting companies. The only message not spam is from accounting, asking her to get an updated identity card right away, with an attested photocopy of her name exactly as it is recorded on the national register. Without these, they will be not be able to deposit her salary into her bank account.

Bibi goes into the kitchen, where Moi is making tea. She shows Moi the message. 'Is this requirement even legal?' she asks.

'Stop being such a diva,' Moi says. 'Just apply for a new-series Aadhaar card, like everyone else.'

They retreat to what passes for the living room, sitting cross-legged at opposite ends of a green reed mattress. On the coffee table, a circular sheet of glass resting on the burnished, splayed-out trunk of a tea plant, blonde women with hardened abs stare up from the covers of lifestyle magazines. Thick cotton curtains hang from the windows, the plump, round mynah birds printed against a background of bright orange and green evoking a children's room or a nursery school. None of this has been contributed by Bibi. Moi is the one who has handpicked every item in an attempt to hold at bay the gritty neighbourhood outside, one more Delhi village transformed into a slum by the surrounding urban sprawl.

In the tenements just across a low brick wall at the back of their building, migrant workers sleep in rotating shifts on bunk beds in squalid rooms. Sometimes, a drunken weekend erupts into a frenzy of shouts. Fists meet flesh. Sticks crack bone. Women scream and weep. If the brawl keeps going, it is called in to the neighbourhood police station by some angry local resident, someone who runs a business overcharging migrant workers but who hates their defiling presence in his village. The shouts and screams are then joined by the lazy, intermittent squeals of a Delhi Police van as it makes its unhurried way up the mud lane. A sudden silence descends on the scene with the arrival of the van, a moment, almost, of illusory peace, the red-and-blue flicker of the police lights no more alarming than the inviting glow of a dosa or kathi roll or dumpling cart open late into the night. Then the doors of the van slide open, walkie-talkies chattering into the dark as the policemen step out, cracking their knuckles and dangling their sticks. Once in a while, negotiations take place, but more often subdued wails and abruptly choked-off screams. Some evenings, more police vans come in, long, windowless vehicles meant for carrying prisoners that find it difficult to turn around in the narrow streets of the village and extract themselves in reverse gear.

Moi does not allow any of this to slow her down or distract her from her goal. She doesn't care about the policemen, about the slum dwellers, about the Dalits who clean Munirka. She chooses not to notice the shop that sells Patanjali yoga products, the most popular of them being large polypacks of Putrajeevak Beej, a product whose name Bibi waggishly translates as Divine Son Life Seed and which consists of blackened seeds guaranteeing its buyers the birth of male progeny. But Moi doesn't want to hear about the skewed sex ratio. She has no interest in climate collapse or capitalism or Hindutva. Moi, ten years younger than Bibi and these days her only friend, possesses not a grain of political idealism, no artistic or intellectual ambition and no interest in the larger context. That is what makes her a perfect friend, Moi whose life serves as an illustration of the ant from the ant-grasshopper fable, a pale, waif-like, always poised, sometimes glamorous ant who asks people other than Bibi to call her May and who works five days a week, twelve hours a day, at the upscale multi-cuisine restaurant Hex in the DLF Emporio mall, who works so hard that there are days when she makes Bibi feel quite ashamed of herself.

BUT IF MOI were all ant, she wouldn't be the perfect friend. Inside the ant, there happens to be a grasshopper, a creature given to fantasies, an insect with a self-destructive streak that mirrors what Bibi has come to understand as her own tendency towards self-ruination. The truth is that while Moi slaves away, eating frugally, saving all her share of the tips that come to her at Hex after she has patiently held out the grilled appetiser platter that weighs twenty pounds for the bejewelled ladies who lunch at Hex on weekdays, has smiled unwaveringly at the businessmen who play with their car keys and crotch while she waits for them to accept the perfectly folded cloth napkin she is offering them and has, without flinching, cleaned up the milkshake and beads of sweet corn spilt by the children brought in on weekends as accessories to family gatherings, large children given to flinging their food and their gadgets in the face of waitstaff and nannies, Moi constantly plots her escape, a quest that leads her into expenses she cannot afford and that mires her in mistakes that are borne out of anything but pragmatism.

Moi must leave India, and soon, before immigration laws make it utterly impossible for someone such as her to move to the West. To England, to America, to Canada, to Australia, to New Zealand—Moi's first choice is always an English-speaking country, although she will slum it, if necessary, in France or Belgium. Of how this will come about, and what it will lead to, Moi is equally certain. It is a process that will begin with her meeting a dull but considerate white man who will become her phareng husband and in whose wake will follow, as night follows day, a solitaire wedding ring on Moi's finger, two pale children and a passport that will pronounce her to be one of the world's elite, a winner in the lottery of life.

It is such a rubbish fantasy that it is almost liberating. Moi's scheme of self-improvement is reassuring in its tawdriness, showing up all schemes of self-improvement as inherently flawed, as false horizons of remaking. It makes Bibi's own fall, if that is what it is, appear much more acceptable, even inevitable. So Bibi listens, with a patience quite uncharacteristic of her, when Moi, while doing the Pilates moves demonstrated by one of those blonde models in the magazines or while painting her nails an eerily luminescent silver grey as recommended by Anastasia, a social media makeover star based in Sacramento, California, tells Bibi everything she has achieved in the thin slice of time she has off from work every week.

Bibi makes no acerbic comments as Moi describes the leadership and positivity seminars that she has dutifully attended, all held in slightly run-down, fading, five-star hotels in Nehru Place or Connaught Place. She listens patiently when Moi tells her about the sessions she has signed up for, offered by the Treta Yoga Foundation, or her subscription to the app-based meditation and mindfulness modules that will make her successful in achieving every single one of her life's goals. She lets Moi talk about the monthly advice she has received in the column of the world's most famous astrologer, the New York–based Susan Miller, and she pays attention when

Moi offers details about the parties she has managed to get herself invited to, where she is likely to meet a man who might actually be a possible candidate for the One.

And so it gets built, Moi's castle in the air. A management guru encountered at a 'Study and Work Abroad—Legally!' session has promised her a job when he opens his new office in Canary Wharf, London. A suave, startlingly young member of parliament with the right-wing Bharatiya Janata Party, a man who drives a BMW and wants Moi to join him at weekend farmhouse parties and at the annual Jaipur literary festival, has said that he will put in a word with His Excellency the Ambassador of desirable country number two, presumably between discussing a weapons deal and the latest leaks about offshore banking. Sometimes, Moi actually becomes friends with a phareng, although not yet, sadly, with a native English speaker. Still, Moi will tell Bibi, freshly dried luminescent nails taptapping furiously on her smartphone, that there is this tall French man, or this charming Italian, or this passionate Spaniard interested in her, all of them madly in love with Moi's porcelain complexion, her impeccable boarding school accent and her Victorian manners.

Bibi laughs at this, but gently. Moi will not listen to her when Bibi tells her that the men are impostors. She will not hear when Bibi says that Delhi is a shit city in a shit country in a shit world, where women are commodities, assemblages of body parts, repositories for centuries of wounded male pride and soak pits for capitalism, themselves filled with confused desires that often involve no more than becoming players in the worldwide game of pillage and despoliation. She will not hear Bibi when she says that it is too late for someone like Moi to make the leap across to the West, that the doors to the West, never fully open, slammed shut as soon as the bills run up over centuries of plunder began coming home.

Moi needs to discover the fraud for herself, and she does, usually while weeping over a trinket gifted her by a man before ghosting. Then it turns out that the businessman was married, that the youth politician does not exist because the name Moi has been given corresponds to no existing member of parliament, that the Frenchman is a Croat, the Italian actually a Slovenian and the Spaniard really from Colombia.

'EMBASSY PARTY,' MOI says on this dim November morning as she sits eating ramen and leafing through a glossy Indian magazine featuring an interview with a woman whose company organises what she describes as 'soulcentric' trips to Antarctica. 'French embassy. Met a really interesting man too.'

'And what might have been interesting about a man met at the French embassy?'

'Do you have to be cynical first thing in the day?'

'Did I say something wrong?' Bibi says, trying to look as virtuous as possible.

'Fuck off,' Moi says, disappearing into her room.

Bibi sips her ginger tea, knowing that Moi will be back. She takes her cup and goes to the window, trying not to think of the coughing man. There is a hint of sunlight in the air when she parts the curtains, the first in weeks. She walks to the other end of the room and unbolts the back door. It opens on to a sheer drop of three floors, seemingly offering a convenient option for an impulse murder or a planned suicide but in reality representing the future ambitions of their landlord Narender Tokas, BA, LLB, Advocate, Delhi Court, former member of the Youth Congress and now aspiring ward councillor for the BJP, a man who hopes to expand his rental properties farther, right up against the spread of tenements owned by his cousin Dhirender Tokas, with whom he has a long-standing feud.

Bibi sits at the back door with her tea, legs dangling in the cold, smoky air. She thinks of the farmhouse, of Preitty, of the man with the cough. She thinks of their belief that Sanjit is not dead, that she should try to find him, and of a USB drive filled with unreal items. As unreal as the sky above her, a vast, grey tank of industrial run-off in which a weak sun tries to drown its misery.

MOI IS WAITING for her in the living room, a hopeful expression on her face, holding out a card. Bibi takes the card. It says, in big bold letters: **THE WORLD**. Beneath that is a name, 'Vikrant Singhal'. There is no other information on the card.

'What's this?'

'A cruise ship,' Moi says. 'I was hanging out with some very exclusive people last night at the French embassy party. And this just happens to be the most exclusive cruise ship on the planet.'

Bibi touches the edges of the card. It is printed on thick ivory board paper. No address or website or email. On the back, a cellphone number has been written out with a fountain pen, presumably by the man whose name translates as victorious lion. 'Oh, Moi,' she says. 'Not again.'

6

The winter haze, having lifted ever so slightly for a few days, thickens again. It comes down on the city like a cover for Bibi as she returns to work, her morning commute now involving the company of coughing, masked strangers. A particularly malevolent respiratory virus is going around. The bulk of the Metro passengers—students and traders, labourers and provincials—have been transformed into figures wearing an odd assortment of face covers: blue surgical masks, handkerchiefs with elaborate borders, flower-patterned hand towels faded from repeated washing and tightly wrapped dupattas that, covering the head as well as the nose and mouth, have become makeshift, colourful balaclavas.

Sometimes, a carriage Bibi steps into is inexplicably empty. On such occasions, the stainless steel innards of the train compartment suggest to her an oversized, surrealist operating theatre, the seats elongated gurneys for an impossibly alien species. But when Bibi emerges from the underground station into Connaught Place, she is the one who is an alien, a mermaid tentatively exploring the upper reaches of an infinite but incredibly cluttered sea. The neon signs of the shops, lit even during the day, have a blurry, sunken glaze to them. Above them, the white buildings tower, like fragments of a ship glimpsed in a foggy ocean, adrift without functioning navigation instruments, endlessly circling the concentric rings of Connaught Place in the hope that its distress signals will be answered, its position traced.

BIBI TAKES MORE time than she needs to walk to work from the Metro station. She dawdles, peering into shop windows. She stares at the unaffordable, bright patterns of ethnic designer wear, the boutiques all owned by women whose names seem to be variations of Preitty's. Her own dark-skinned reflection floats on the display window like a gaunt, restless spirit.

Stopping at a café, she lingers over her coffee well past eleven, the bitter taste tingling on her tongue, the caffeine dose thumping through her blood. Around her, business types make implausible real estate deals and rich teenagers act out lackluster romances. Dangling from the ceiling, a television screen broadcasts the glossy-haired anchor's outrage over discarded condoms supposedly found on the site of a student rally protesting the closure of JNU.

Bibi sits, staring, dreaming, thinking of her past writing, of Sanjit. She surfs through social media sites, opening links to articles, reading a few lines before she zones out. The world did not stop when she stopped. There are new writers out there who have taken up the things she and Sanjit were once obsessed with. The articles are often uneven, amateur. Too many opinion pieces, and even the reported pieces are thin, veering into academic jargon or twee personal anecdotes. Yet, for all their failings, these writers are out there, peering through the haze, trying to construct patterns and meanings. She is not.

Bibi looks up some of the writers on her phone to see what else they have done. The search engine, sensing her affinity with these voices, directs her to a blog written by someone called Muktibodh. It is probably a pseudonym. The entries come thick and fast, then cease abruptly.

In the longest of the entries, Muktibodh ingeniously connects the Brahmastra superweapon being developed by the Indian conglomerate Ombani with a superbug resistant to every known antibiotic that has been classified as NaMo-03. 'Who knows what is being manufactured in the laboratories of the new private-public partnerships?' Muktibodh writes in a missive Bibi reads hunched over a second cup of coffee. He or she, but probably he, is a schoolteacher or minor government official, she thinks. Someone with time, an autodidact of the kind she met when she was a journalist, wearing the appearance of utter conventionality while nurturing a rebellious mind.

'Sometimes, it seems that India now is like the United States of a nineteen nineties television series called the X Files, with aliens and experiments and conspiracies of the deep state,' Muktibodh writes. 'Yet we are not quite the American national security state, that white supremacy determined to burn its toxic imprint upon the universe. If they are Rome to Britain's Greece, a mimic empire filled with a frenzy to outdo the original, we are a mimic of the mimic, a copy of a copy. Think of your dropped calls and ask yourself: is Ombani really capable of building a superweapon when it can't even run a mobile network? Are oily middlemen good at cutting deals, fixers of the soul who understand only the exact weight and distribution of human weakness, capable of building technologically advanced weapons? Who knows what the French, the Russians, the Americans, the Israelis are really building at these so-called sites of joint technology run by Ombani Labs? Who knows if the Indians will carry out anything more than screwdriver work, assembling superweapons like IKEA furniture and discovering, as they finish, that the instructions were confusing, that the assembly has been botched, that there are all these screws left over and that part Q has been attached to Z when it really should have been X connected to S?

'But, at the end of the day, I am not a nationalist. I feel no pride that the Indian-Russian joint venture BrahMos supplies its missiles as props for the American hit series *Patriot*. I care nothing for a world where India can develop and build its own superweapons, where it can gloat over Pakistan, or even over our overlords in the West. If another world is possible, I want it set to a purpose other than that of suffering and profit. What I can say for now is that things will inevitably go wrong with that so-called superweapon, and I only hope that they do not go so wrong that after the blinding light of such a device, there is only darkness.'

WHEN SHE FINALLY arrives at Amidala, late beyond all measure, Bibi is no longer capable of the mundane tasks that await her. Images of antibiotic-resistant superbugs and jerry-rigged, jugaad superweapons populate her brain as she logs on to her computer to read the accumulating messages. Underneath the unending banality surrounding her, she realises now, lurks the fantastic. Strange mutations break out in Calcutta slums, tulpa thought forms come off the internet into the streets of Gangtok and a border patrol in the mountains contracts a mysterious eye infection from Himalayan blue sheep. And yet, this is no more astonishing than the man who went to the Vimana office and metamorphosed into a monkey.

The stories she has read urge Bibi to wake up, to begin paying attention again, to realise that the haze around her obscures what otherwise should be quite obvious. A gradual dissolving of the boundary between the fantastic and the real is in progress.

LUNCHTIME COMES AROUND. Bibi's colleagues remain hunched over keyboards and phones, anxiously monitoring stock prices, the sinking rupee and the outcome of visa lotteries while watching clips of *The National Interest* on tiny, floating windows. Bibi, heedless of the fact that she has been in the office for barely an hour and has done no work, goes out. In the thick mustard air that surrounds her as she walks, she is no longer a woman, just an indistinct, bipedal shape. Yet even in the haze, where everything is a blur, Bibi gets the feeling that she is being watched.

She takes to mapping out Connaught Place by sound and smell and touch on these lunchtime excursions. The texture of the ground beneath her feet transitions from the smooth, new tiles of the underground passageway with ridged dividers at the edges to the cracked surface of walkways meandering under the wide colonnades of the Inner Circle. The sour tang of milk hits her when she passes the Wenger's counter, succeeded by the drift of incense, engine oil, and the stomach-churning smell of piss as she cuts through the back alleys.

Looping back one afternoon, she hears, somewhere between the small mosque at the end of B block and the crowded storefront for Lovely Visa Services, a one-sided phone conversation about overdue bank loans. Then, out of nowhere, comes the muffled tinkle of a bell, trailed by a lunch-delivery man bending gracefully into his turn, insulated tiffin carriers stacked high on the rear rack of his bicycle. Bibi stops, mid-stride, to let him pass. She thinks she can hear, just behind her, the dying echo of a single footfall.

SHE FINDS HERSELF thinking, again, about Sanjit. She had thought he would flourish after leaving *The Daily Telegram*. With the coming of the free market, a media boom was on. New magazines and websites everywhere, with bigger salaries and snappy editorial designations, money flowing in endlessly as India became, briefly, one of the great investment destinations of the world, as Indian businesses that had made vast profits in natural gas, mining and real estate began expanding into media.

She herself did well for a while in that milieu, poached by a monthly as a feature writer, and where, on her first day at the new job, her former boss from *The Daily Telegram* called to tell her that the American consulting firm McKinsey had been asking about her. He sounded half impressed, half envious, saying that he had managed to scare them off by telling them about her lefty credentials.

Yet Sanjit, during that boom time, moved uneasily from one job to another, on a trajectory that led ever downward. Fired from a weekly for being too critical of the Hindu right, resigning from another in solidarity with a junior staffer accusing the editor, a liberal icon and a great critic of the Hindu right, of sexual harassment. At drunken evenings in the Press Club or in dim bars smelling of cheap Australian lager, people complained to Bibi about his abrasive personality. He was too critical of India, of capitalism, people said. Embittered by failure, out of sync with the times. Others complained that he was shockingly unfriendly, so antisocial that even when he bothered to show up at a party at someone's house, he simply stuffed himself with the food on offer, drank copious amounts of other people's liquor and left without so much as cracking a smile.

For a while, he worked at an old, rationalist magazine, fusty, pre-liberalisation, a place where the office clerks took long, post-lunch naps at their desks and everything moved at a snail's pace but that was nevertheless a last refuge for people who still wanted to be anti-establishment reporters. When that shut down, sinking under the weight of civil and criminal defamation lawsuits filed at tiny provincial courts by men with small, modest businesses—men who nevertheless had unusually vast sums of money and swanky metropolitan lawyers at their disposal—Sanjit moved across the river, to Trans-Yamuna Delhi.

He became the sole employee of an internet site run out of a middle-class flat in a DDA housing complex, one of hundreds of thousands of such buildings erected by the Delhi Development Authority in the days of central planning. The site was funded by a retired civil servant with his savings. The man wrote what he himself admitted was a contradiction in terms, progressive Hindi fiction, his stories often involving gay characters who were, unusually, not portrayed as deviants.

Then, Sanjit published a piece on the suspicious suicide of an army officer in Assam. The young captain's conscience had been pricked after taking part in an operation involving seven undocumented Bangladeshi migrants, men led to believe by an Indian fixer that they had been hired as day labourers and that they were being driven to a field at three in the morning because they were expected to begin work very early. The captain and his men had been waiting for the migrants, confused, docile creatures who lined up as asked to and were quiet as a soldier stood behind each one. The gunshots were almost simultaneous. It took far longer to dress the corpses in camouflage and plant AK-47s on them. A dead undocumented was worth nothing, but a dead terrorist was worth five points. The unit had been short by thirty-five of the three hundred points they needed to claim a bonus and a lucrative posting with a United Nations peacekeeping mission in Haiti. Soon after, the captain gave an interview to the press with details of the execution. He was suffering moral pangs because the unit had trouble counting the bodies, there always appearing to be one more or one less than the seven undocumented they had killed, The executions had been all about numbers, nothing personal or ideological to it at all, and yet it was the numbers screwing them over. Even the photos they sent to HQ refused to be definitive, the bodies in the pictures never totalling up to seven. A day after the interview, the captain was hospitalised by the army for depression. He hung himself on the very first night of his stay in the military hospital. No one other than Sanjit believed that the suicide might have something to do with his statement about the fake counter-insurgency op. A week after the story was published, the retired civil servant was run down at a roadside crossing by a truck that came from nowhere.

After that, Sanjit lived a nomad's life, cobbling together assignments from India and abroad. He became like a ronin from the Japanese films he loved to watch, an unwashed, unshaven samurai with a bamboo sword in his scabbard, writing ever more complicated conspiracy stories that looped around the Gujarat mass murders of 2002 and the US global war on terror after 9/11. The pieces strung together surveillance, extra-judicial executions and witnesses turned rogue, his conclusions pointing ever upward, ever inward, to the seats of power, to the alliance between entrepreneurialism, electoral politics and militarism. Sometimes, as when he turned his sights on the past, digging up odd factoids about right-wing cult figures like Vinayak Savarkar and P.N. Oak, he sounded almost demented, unfazed by the torrents of abuse coming his way on social media and the periodic suspension of his accounts. Then, finally, silence while on a trip to the Northeast that involved looking into the deaths of four young Manipuri men who had iron nails hammered into their heads and hands before being executed at close range, their killers, a counter-insurgency unit consisting of seven men and a woman officer, recommended for Shaurya Chakra medals to be handed out at the Republic Day parade in Delhi, in front of the new parliamentary complex.

THERE ARE DAYS when Bibi lets her lunch hour bleed into the smoky afternoon, wandering knee-high pavements pointing towards the parliament. Monkeys with red scowls leap from the branches of jamun and neem trees, clustering on sienna sandstone ledges to jeer at passing human beings. She is eyed by helmeted men cramped inside security booths anchoring down the blast walls and angled yellow barricades encircling the prime minister's palace. Like a madwoman she weaves her way through traffic curdled outside the war memorial and the Supreme Court, making her way past Hotel Le Meridien, Hotel Shangri La and Hotel Imperial, until she is back at Regal Building, her work day nearly over.

At the office, people leave Bibi alone. Akanksha and Veer fall silent in the reception area when she walks in, staring separately at their phones. She gathers there is some tension in their romance. An old boyfriend has resurfaced, not long after Veer's wife obtained the services of a guru known for his prowess in black magic. Akanksha is now worried that the wifemade lunch contains poison that will target only her, Veer wounded that he has to contend with a younger rival.

The man from the accounts department, whose name is Goyal, is increasingly sick. A scaly, greenish outgrowth sits between his shirt collar and his round, fleshy chin, like a false beard gradually slipping off his face. He makes despairing gestures at Bibi as she passes, a movement something like a football referee's signal for a VAR replay. Having done nothing about getting a new identity card or finding out if her name is on the updated citizens' register, Bibi ignores him. She enjoys who she has become, heedless of consequences, strolling past colleagues bent deep over their computers. Apart from their characteristic Delhi coughs, they are silent as they map out complex travel arrangements for speakers who will arrive, in the span of a few weeks, at Davos, Aspen and Wuxi to discuss the future of the world.

SS says nothing to Bibi about the backlog piling up on her desk or how much time she spends chatting with the newcomer security guard slash peon Mohinder in the kitchen. Bibi helps Mohinder dry the tea mugs. Mohinder asks her about her mother. Sometimes, they talk about the clandestine Mars footage circulating in the back channels of social media. What the monkey did. What the monkey saw. Things that the government and the mainstream media are at pains to suppress. SS is increasingly distracted. Sometimes, as she passes his closed door, Bibi thinks she can hear what sounds like weeping.

ONE DECEMBER EVENING, a fog sweeps into the city. A sea of grey, risen from subterranean depths, part of some vast geological shift that has taken place, the oceans finally breaching the heart of the subcontinent to reclaim ancestral territory. The fog spreads over Delhi into the Gangetic plains. Flights are cancelled, trains stranded on tracks cutting through burnt, stubbled fields waiting anxiously for the winter crop. On highways where visibility is nearly zero, automobiles collide like dominoes, panicky shouts distorted in the foggy air as people extract themselves from their cars and run towards the shoulder of the highway. In the city, night-time traffic nearly ceases, solitary vehicles creeping forward in a jittery crawl, yellow headlamps and blinking hazard lights creeping in slow motion along empty avenues.

Bibi, making her way home in an autorickshaw because the magenta line is down once again, is brought to a halt by a military convoy. Black, enormously long trucks, completely covered, are at a standstill on the circle around the war memorial, bookended by smaller vehicles packed with tired soldier faces and oiled gun barrels. A uniformed figure looms in front of the auto, his torch stabbing at Bibi's face. It is an officer, young, nervous. 'Ma'am?' he asks Bibi. 'Which road should we exit through to get to Dhaula Kuan?' Bibi gives him the directions. The auto waits for the trucks to pull out, for their tail lights to dissolve in the thick white fog like memories fading in a river of amnesia.

THIS IS ONE of Delhi's famous winter fogs, different from the usual haze of pollution. The fog is moist, cold. It is alive, drifting and probing. Giant faces are visible in the fog, eyes wide open in surprise, tentacular limbs flailing in the air.

Unable to sleep, Bibi sits at the back door of her flat watching the fog, caught in a dreamlike trance because watching it is like watching something that is almost nothing.

The fog whispers to her, teases her. It asks her not to stand still.

The fog is a paintbrush, erasing the marks on an old, much-used canvas, erasing the streets, the cars, the malls, the hotels, the schools, the slums, the ministry buildings, the police cells, the army bases, the airport, the aircrafts, the malice of the glossy-haired anchor, the banal evil of the mask-like prime minister, erasing the ruins from the twentieth century, the ruins from the sixteenth century, the ruins from the eleventh century and the ruins from the third century BCE, erasing a countryside already erased and erasing a nation that has failed by every measure.

It erases Bibi too, bit by bit, so that when she finally locks the door and goes to bed, she is almost nothing. Then the fog enters her dreams, whispering, wandering, as Bibi waits forever for her papers in a government office where the walls are stacked high with metal filing cabinets, where her two dream children wait for her to be released by a series of faceless clerks as she is brought short, again and again, by forms that relentlessly demand the country of her birth and her father's name, details that Bibi cannot remember no matter how hard she tries.

Then, after days have passed, days that are like years, the fog lifts and is gone. Bibi wakes up and feels that she misses an old friend.

7

On a fogless but gloomy morning, Bibi discovers, via a text from Moi, that the money in her purse is no longer any good. All big denomination notes have been cancelled and must be exchanged for new currency. The transaction will require identity proof—an updated Aadhaar card and a copy of one's name as recorded on the revised citizens' register. Bibi wonders if she can use her debit card for the time being. Then she remembers the insistence of Goyal in accounts that she provide fresh documentation and pulls up her bank statement. Her last pay slip has not been deposited. Her balance is well below the minimum.

Bibi empties her purse out and puts away the discontinued notes. They have become play money. Like the postage stamps designed by the artist Donald Evans, they are banknotes for a country that does not exist. She uses her credit card wherever she can, for as long as she can, before it maxes out. Moi yells at her and loans her some cash and asks her to get off her ass and turn in her old notes and get the Mars ones. While she is at it, she can apply for the new-generation Aadhaar card and check if her name is on the updated register, Moi shouts.

Bibi does no such thing. Instead, she tells Moi, drawing on the depths of her useless past knowledge, that the ATM machine was invented by an Englishman born in Shillong in colonial times. She tells Moi that the two of them, like everyone born in Shillong, should get a tiny commission on every ATM transaction in the world. In lieu of that, a Universal Basic Income, not just for people born in Shillong, but for every human being, born anywhere, everywhere.

'You crazy Marxist bitch,' Moi shouts. 'No one gives a shit that you were born in Shillong. Everyone thinks you're from Bangladesh. We have to get out of this country. We have to figure out a way to leave.'

ONE SATURDAY, WHEN there is almost nothing left in the flat in the way of groceries, Bibi walks to the DLF mall. Moi is out for coffee with Vikrant Singhal, who has promised Moi that he will set up a video chat with the HR manager of *The World*. If Moi gets the job, she will start at the Asian cuisine restaurant, 'Orient', which can be found on the dining stretch of the cruise ship known as 'Global Village'.

All such details about *The World* have come to Bibi third-hand. She remembers Moi opening up Google maps to impress upon Bibi the current voyage of the ship, her fingers pinching and caressing, zooming far, far out to capture the planetary scale of the journey. Abandoning their usual, familiar Delhi boundaries and its unloved collection of sectors, blocks and pockets, the screen blossoms into the watercolour blue of the ocean and the cindery, sandy expanses of Asia and Africa. For New Year's Eve, Moi tells her, *The World* will stop at the Isla de Los Estados, the southernmost tip of inhabited land in the western hemisphere, at the edge of South America. Then, in the new year, it will make its way to Africa, Asia and, eventually, the Pacific Islands, before docking in New Zealand.

The walk to the DLF mall takes forever. Bibi makes her way through the knot of autos and share vans crowding the entrance to Munirka, crosses over to the edge of a slum and works her way through the crossroads. Then she proceeds along a pavement that, in spite of its recent provenance, has already collapsed into ruin. Ashy scrub and thorny kikar trees, invasive species introduced by the British, line the edges of the pavement, the surroundings laced with the faint but distinct smell of shit. On the other side of the road, through the haze, the craggy ridge and trees enclosing JNU suggest the possibility of a wilderness. But then, just as she is across from graffiti that says, in white, stencilled letters, *New Delhi Monkey Man,* she catches a whiff of tear gas and gunpowder burn.

Bibi is near a flight path, a landing route zeroing in on the runways of IGI airport. The planes look like they are in slow motion as they fly overhead, their navigation lights winking as they drift above the blue highway sign for Vasant Kunj. Bibi keeps going until she is directly under an aircraft, looking up at the pigeon-grey undercarriage of the domestic jet making its approach. For a second, she has the illusion that a giant figure is hanging from the belly of the aircraft, looking down at her with big manga eyes. Then the pavement collapses, and she steps onto the road. Over the trees, behind the angled latticework of the Ombani oil and gas building, the twin domes of the DLF shopping complex are visible.

She crosses a straggling row of coughing auto drivers. The underground parking garage displays a discreet sign for Moi's restaurant, housed in the more high-end of the two malls that make up the shopping complex. At the supermarket, the aisles are crowded with East Asian and white women, corporate wives trying to keep up first-world standards for expatriate families. A few Delhi rich are sprinkled among them, aspiring expatriates in their own homeland, hovering over imported strawberries and kale. Everyone around Bibi has face masks dangling from their necks, elaborate snout-like things with double filters angling away from the face, seemingly heading from their grocery shopping to some year-end, *Doctor Who*–themed, fancy dress party.

Bibi's credit card doesn't work on the first try. The cashier apologises. The networks have been troublesome all day, she says. She inserts Bibi's card again and the transaction goes through after a prolonged, heart-stopping pause. Bibi looks at the receipt printed out. The printout is more or less illegible, bank details and the amount charged blurred. She squints at what looks like a possible word: /^/^/^/^/^/^ *runpast* <@>>>>>>. As she leaves the mall, she can smell, throughout its walkways, the diffused tingle of perfume and air freshener. She tightens the straps of her pack, steps out and treks back through the brume and the broken pavements. As soon as she gets home, her mother calls from Calcutta.

AT FIRST, BIBI has trouble understanding her mother. But the details sink in soon enough. Bibi's mother is out of pills, and her neighbourhood pharmacy will not offer credit. The lines at the bank are too long for her to get the Mars notes any time soon and she does not know how to use a credit card or make mobile phone payments.

'My hands shake,' Bibi's mother says. 'My heart jumps around. I should not be alone in my old age.' Bibi's mother wants to know when Bibi can come with some of the new money. 'Come home,' she says, and a wave of anger flows over Bibi at that word *home*.

She wants to tell her mother that she has not had a home for a very long time, that she is neither the ideal, dutiful daughter her mother desires nor the feckless, irresponsible person her mother accuses her of being.

Bibi can sense the heightened pitch of her thoughts as she stands in the kitchen surrounded by food she cannot really afford. Yet on the phone, she is almost silent. Her responses are restricted to monosyllables. She wants to say that she is broken. That love, writing, friendship, everything has been soured. That she makes her way through her days like someone picking a path through ruins after a war. That for years now, her evenings have been hollowed out by loneliness, her only companion a derisive voice in her head, lacerating, embittered, a voice that doesn't want to shut up and that can only be silenced by Bibi's promises to quit, to give it all up, leading to long reveries of moving far away, to a place fantastically remote, as though only at the edge of the world, on a mountain that looks over shadowy, elongated valleys, or on an island where a single lighthouse peers over the edge of the continental shelf, can she reconstitute herself into a better, happier Bibi.

'If you had been married like your sister, I would not be in so much trouble. If I still had my son, if I had not lost him, I would not have such difficulties. If your father had made the right decisions, I would not be here, among people who hate Muslims and foreigners and cannot distinguish between the two,' Bibi's mother says. 'But you fritter away your life in Delhi, doing I don't know what, while things become harder for me than ever.' The money queues form at dawn, her mother says. The elderly men bring folding stools and umbrellas as they gather in front of the State Bank of India. The wives and widows come later, carrying their knitting and the vegetables they will prep for dinner as they wait. The rickshaw drivers of the neighbourhood stand perplexed around their vehicles, uncomprehending of the government fiat that has once again eliminated the cash economy they live in and trapped them in the trickledown of demonetisation. The vegetable vendors have been offering credit, Bibi's mother continues, but Anwar the fish seller has killed himself, caught between the unsold fish rotting in his baskets and the interest accumulating on the pages of the moneylender's ledger. 'When can you bring me my Calmpose sleeping pills?' Bibi's mother says. 'When will you come home to look after your aged mother?'

Bibi listens silently. Calmpose is an antidepressant, not a sleeping pill, Bibi wants to tell her mother. We are each on our own in these end times, she wants to say to her mother. As the waters rise, as the cities choke and as the fish seller hangs himself, every woman is an island.

8

A few days later, Anand calls. Four years have passed, but there is not a trace of self-consciousness in his voice as he makes plans to meet for lunch. Bibi takes the magenta line towards the airport, wondering why he has chosen a restaurant in the Priya cinema shopping complex, an area in decline ever since the construction of the DLF malls. Has he picked it for her convenience, because it is close to Munirka? Is he nostalgic? Or is he just showcasing his inside knowledge, demonstrating that he is still far more familiar with the ley lines running through Delhi than she will ever be?

The restaurant is at the back end of the square across from the Priya multiplex. Street children in rags and dogs with scabs attempt to intercept Bibi as she traverses the endless concrete. The assortment of businesses Bibi passes is odd: a scattering of banks, a Harley Davidson store and what is, from the designer-clad schoolchildren smoking outside an unmarked black door reverberating to house music, a sort of daytime nightclub. A fortune teller sits on the ground in front of an empty store front, hunched over his basket of wilting marigold flowers. His mobile phone number is written out in big, uneven numerals on a cardboard rectangle. Next to it, he has placed another cardboard, the phrases on it filling Bibi with a faint sense of foreboding as she walks by.

WHOSE IS THE EYE THAT FOLLOWS YOU?
WHAT IS THE KARMA OF OUR PAST LIVES?
HAVE YOU EVER SEEN THE FUTURE?

INSIDE THE RESTAURANT, there are long tables of unpainted wood and a bar gleaming with colourful bottles. The menu advertises craft beer, organic wine, terroir cheese. The owner, a man in his late twenties who has rushed out to greet Bibi, has tattoos spiralling off his forearms and a beard that on a different kind of face would mark him out for a maulvi or a sadhu. The bartender resembles a cut-price double of his boss, tattoos and beard included.

Anand sits at a table facing a window, papers strewn carelessly but artfully in front of him. At first glance, he looks like he hasn't changed at all. Bibi is ashamed, then angry, then ashamed again at the momentary leap in her heart as she sees the once very familiar face leaning towards her with that familiar inquiring look, hair and beard flaring like the halo around a Jesus or a Che. But then the angles of light shift, and she realises very clearly that he is no longer the same. He has crossed the seven seas and seen the world and in doing so he has become even more like a man who has never left Delhi and knows nothing other than an endless craving for power.

Lights are suspended from wooden cross beams in the ceilings. At the far end of the restaurant, there is a separate, open section for the smokers, solitaries scattered in front of their thin tablets with delicate cups of coffee, their thought plume exhalations curling into the cold air. Bibi wants to be out there in the smoking section, anywhere but with Anand.

As Anand speaks, Bibi thinks of how interiors bear no resemblance to exteriors in this city. The same could be said of people, except that the relationship is reversed: the exterior coiffed and polished, the interior in ruins. Inquiry has given way to self-satisfaction in Anand. He talks more loudly than he used to, cutting off her sentences and then interrupting himself to respond to incoming texts and calls, apologising for the disruptions without ever quite meaning it. He is still handsome but buffed over, glossy, smooth. From the tieless suit he is wearing to the designer labels prominent on his bag and the wallet left casually on the table, he is another iteration of the men who float through the ambit of Amidala, delivering their solutions to the world's problems at corporate retreats and leadership gatherings.

His teeth gleam, his skin shines and Bibi is relieved that she feels nothing for him, that she really is free after all these years. And yet she cannot help mourning that her leaping heart is gone forever, that all she has left in his presence is this watchful, melancholy, solitary stillness inside her.

'I follow you on social media,' Anand says. 'But you do not post a word. You haven't even changed your profile photo in all these years. Why such a closed book, dear?'

'I find social media difficult,' Bibi says, surprising herself with her abrupt honesty. 'All that self-expression, all that self-promotion, so many people and yet somehow everyone lonelier than ever.'

She realises what a cliché this is, and yet she wants to keep talking. She wants to say something about the sensation of being trapped in a ghost ship that, motionless in supernaturally becalmed waters, is being taken over by insanity. She wants to talk about the venality and superficiality around her, the endless selfies, the videos from drones, the infinite permutations of fake news offering variations on how to hate. She wants to voice her doubts that even the heartfelt posts, trailed by miniature Hokusai dots that means someone is busy adding one more comment to the discussion thread, those posts that talk of stalking, sexual harassment, heartbreak, failed careers, alienation, depression and anxiety, that even these seem to her to be fundamentally flawed manifestations of a fractured age, forestalling genuine solidarity for a quick dose of momentary, superficial comfort.

But he doesn't really want to hear any of that, and she doesn't really want to voice any of this. Instead, she lets him talk. He says he worries about her. He has thought about her all these years, about her talent, and he wants her to move on from Amidala. The world is a big place, he says, filled with two kinds of people. There are the passive many and the active few, the replaceable drones and the sovereign elites. New dynasties are being built in this constant cycle of change that the great Hindu sages predicted millennia ago. The names of foundations and think tanks fall from his lips like benediction as he talks, endlessly, of opportunities. He takes his smartphone out and shows her pictures: Anand delivering a TED Talk, Anand at a party posing for selfies with the Clintons and the Clooneys. He wants to collaborate with her, just as they used to in the old days. A photo of Bibi appears amid this overwhelming display of Anand. A photo of her asleep, almost naked, on a sofa at that flat he arranged for her during her last months at *The Daily Telegram*. The image blinks out. He puts his phone away and says that he wants to invite her to a conference in New York.

A business card is laid down at her side like a discreet tip. There is no physical address, just a phone number, an email address, an Instagram account. The coffee is served, along with snacks Anand has ordered, olives and cheese. The food tastes of ashes, the coffee smells of raw fish.

9

The new year arrives, but its smoky outline carries no promise for Bibi. One more digit being racked up in the account book of the century. Monday, January 1, 20—. Is it more ominous than the previous years, less fatal than those to come?

She stops looking up her old pieces, stops reading Muktibodh. When the search engine suggests that she might be interested in slum children going missing near JNU, she swipes the article away without looking. She recalls her dreams in brief, vivid bursts, new scenes inserting themselves into the kaleidoscope of government offices and wet streets: a flotilla of makeshift boats spreading right up to the horizon; refugee columns stumbling through a glittering salt plain; prisoners in flaming orange overalls, their feet manacled to a long, linked chain, clanking through a desert landscape like some obscurely mutated, many-legged beast.

Shadows linger behind her in the cold underground corridors of the Metro, yet the reflections in the shop windows suggest three-dimensional presences, tensely coiled, ready to reach for her. The glossy-haired news anchor is on every television set, at every hour, in malls and Metro stations and electronics showrooms and cafes because television in India, because life in India, is a never-ending loop of *The National Interest*. Yet the words he speaks seem to be directed at Bibi alone.

On Twitter, she has new followers. There are friend requests on Facebook from people she has nothing in common with. Spam inundates her inbox and she actually looks through it. Pursuing its own internal, secretive logic, it runs through distinct cycles: low down-payment options on new housing complexes, with round-the-clock power, swimming pools, gyms, central air-conditioning and security; these are succeeded by thousands of emails about job offers in the government, with possible careers in schools, railways, bauxite companies and the air force; then, suddenly, the potential jobs vanish and all she receives, day after day, are emails from internet-based astrological services promising to take care of the evil eye tracking her.

IT MUST BE the reappearance of Anand, his audacity in suggesting that she is wasting her life at Amidala. One late morning at work, Bibi holds herself back from her usual meaningless drift. Instead, she gives herself a point of focus, beginning with what she knows: Preitty. Once she settles into a rhythm, she finds herself progressing steadily, moving through gossip pieces and blog posts and stringed comments into the shimmering web that is Preitty's business. She scrolls through emails and documents uploaded on to WikiLeaks. She finds PDF files of wiretaps carried out by the income tax department, the text askew, the virtual pages perpetually bent.

This is a world within a world, and Bibi doodles diagrams on a sheet of printer paper to visualise the bewildering connections; that between Preitty, SS and Shekhar Gupta, between farmhouses in Delhi, her own apparently unremarkable office and the new detention centres coming up everywhere. Yet, there is something eluding her in these overlaps, something that has to do with Sanjit.

A series of links takes her to a grainy video posted by a foreign animal-rights group. Some kind of industrial space with bright lights, control panels, computers. Pools of reflection glare, voices raised against the sound of humming motors, a series of cages. Wires and electrodes, saline drips and pressure gauges. A monkey, a bear, a cow. Her heart begins to beat faster. What looks like an astronaut figure encased in a transparent cylinder, upright, small, almost child-sized. She forgets the time, forgets it is lunch hour. She has not been so absorbed in anything for years. Mohinder, of his own accord, brings her cups of tea as she works, his left hand steady as a hammer as he sets the mug down on her desk.

THAT AFTERNOON BIBI does not roam far, venturing instead into the warren of tailoring shops and travel agencies in the rundown shopping complex of Mohan Singh Place. Anxious men with bad haircuts and emaciated bodies crowd the counters of travel agencies, bony dark hands gripping bright new orange passports, slaves for a new century being prepared for dispatch to distant oil fields and construction sites. The alcoves in the tailoring shops are occupied by their left-behind craftsmen brothers, men snipping delicately at fabric, threaded needles held between pursed lips or between the big toe and pointer toe. Gleaming copper-toned scissors sail through seas of denim. In the reflection of the scissor blades, Bibi sees an eye examining her, an eye that reminds her of her dreams. When she turns around, she is unable to find its owner.

Deep into the innards of the building she wanders, climbing up to the India Coffee House of the coffee workers' cooperative. She sits there by herself over a cup of coffee and daydreams, wondering what to do next, ignoring the elderly, retired men casting curious glances her way.

But she has been careless, she realises, when she returns to work. It is foolish of her to use the office computer to do these searches, to leave her sheet of inelegant Venn diagrams beneath a folder of promotional material for Oculus Finial Solutions.

THAT NIGHT, A WhatsApp message from an unknown number appears on Bibi's phone.

Follow you on Instagram
Follow you on Twitter
Follow me as I follow you
Follow me sooner or later

Bibi deletes it.

10

It is a cold February morning as Bibi heads to work, a slow, steady drizzle leaking into the alleyways of Munirka. The shower is odd, unseasonal, unusual for this desert city where even the monsoons bring nothing more than scattered outbursts of gritty rain. The drizzle gleams like icicles from the signboards and the cars. It does not trickle away upon contact but glues on to the surface of objects.

The air is sharp and vinegary on Bibi's tongue. She clutches her favourite coat closer around her. It is her greatest indulgence, even though she bought it second hand from Chor Bazaar in Old Delhi, picking it out from a pile of bulky overcoats awkwardly folded in upon themselves, during that elongated, in-between time when she had left journalism for good but not yet drifted into the stasis of Amidala.

Moi took her in during that fugue state and looked after her, and it was Moi's idea to take Bibi wandering through Chandni Chowk, past the Red Fort and through the alleyways around Jama Masjid. The choice of neighbourhood was a selfless act on Moi's part, picked in accordance with her ideas about Bibi's tastes rather than her own. Nevertheless, Moi couldn't help but be alarmed by the squalor and chaos of the surroundings, by the indifferent quality and uncertain provenance of goods laid out on crumbling pavements skirting broken walls edged with rubbish. Half the objects were stolen, Moi was convinced, in keeping with the name of the market, while the other half consisted of indifferent knock-offs (Radidas sneakers, African Tourister backpacks, Bloody Mary handbags, Hamster tablets, GasBook laptops, Cortisone chocolates, Melanie Klein perfumes, Karlboro cigarettes) that evoked not so much a conscious desire to copy as a final, mad mutation of brand identities.

In that singular but honestly named market of thieves sat the overcoats Bibi had stopped to sift through, heavy woollen garments with unsubtle patches and mismatched buttons. Moi shuddered as Bibi unfolded one of the coats, black, not as wide at the shoulder as the others. Moi was convinced that the coats had been stripped off corpses, from the cold, clammy bodies of white men who had died in the hundreds somewhere in the vicinity of Old Delhi for reasons unknown. Any one of them could have become Moi's phareng husband, and yet they had chosen to expire unloved, far from their picket-fenced, two-car garage homes in the service of inexplicably secretive missions taken on behalf of their powerful, violent empires.

It was far more likely that the coats were the garbage of the west, Bibi told Moi, that they had been shipped in containers to a private port in Gujarat where they were sorted through by women and child workers before being sent on to Delhi, the one Indian metropolis cold enough for woollen coats to be worn in winter.

The coat Bibi had picked out was almost pristine. A faint line of stitching ran diagonally near the bottom hem, pinching the cloth together ever so gently, a scar from some skirmish Bibi would never know anything about. There was no label on the inside, either behind the collar or on the breast pocket lined with satin, although many days later, when she reached deep inside the pocket, Bibi found a tightly compressed wad of cloth that, when unfolded, revealed, in needlepoint writing, 'This belongs to Shmuel Lefkowitz, son of Miriam. Please help him home if you find him lost.'

When Bibi put the coat on that afternoon in Chor Bazaar, the weight that had burdened her for weeks seemed, oddly enough, to lift. She felt straighter, taller, lighter. The elderly man selling the overcoats, his beard hennaed a deep red, produced an old tin frame mirror. This he fussed over with a chequered rag before propping the mirror up against his neighbour's column of retreaded car tyres. It must have been a magic mirror. Bibi did not recognise the woman standing inside the looking-glass world, the coat falling perfectly down the length of her body, the afternoon sunbeams caressing a face a few shades lighter than the dark hair and dark coat. Even Moi was taken by surprise.

Years have passed since that moment, but the black coat is still like armour, like a magic coat. Bibi loves the way it adds to her inches, how she can thrust her hands deep into its pockets as she strides down the uneven pavements of the Inner Circle. It reminds her of her father, of his overcoat and his hat, which she'd borrowed for the school play where, with a pencil-thin moustache inked on to her face, she played the revolutionary Bhagat Singh. It makes her think of Satyajit Ray film adaptations of Tagore novels. It makes her remember Gogol stories. It is a coat to be lonely in when exiled to London and a coat with which to challenge arrogant Tsarist officers on Nevsky Prospect and a coat that will always take you home in Brooklyn, guided by the hand of a kindly stranger. It brings with it courage that she desperately needs if she is to match her mysterious opponents in the devious game they are playing.

AN AIR OF confusion reigns at the Amidala office when Bibi enters. SS has not come in to work, and an unannounced audit is being conducted, carried out by a firm no one has heard of before. Boxes of documents are piled up on Akanksha's reception desk. Two loutish men who resemble bouncers at a Delhi nightclub sit across from Akanksha, one of them rising to lock the front door behind Bibi after she has entered. Strangers sit at office computers picking through electronic folders. Others are silhouetted behind the glazed walls of the conference room, where staff members are being called in one by one.

Bibi avoids the people clotted into anxious little groups outside the bathrooms and the water cooler and makes for the kitchen. Mohinder is there by himself, calmly pouring tea into an array of mugs headed for the conference room. There is a rumour, Mohinder says, that SS has suffered a heart attack and is at an ICU in a hospital. He finds two empty mugs, takes a little from each of the mugs on the tray. When he has gathered his tithe, he gives Bibi one and takes another for himself. They clink mugs and say 'Cheers'. It is the kind of hospital, Mohinder continues, that has gift shops with teddy bears and flowers, not the kind they took him to after his arm got caught in a machine press at the Sri Ram auto-parts factory.

Bibi does not know what to make of the news. SS does not drink or smoke, and his ancestral, Brahminical vegetarianism is complemented by a contemporary obsession with fitness. He has subscriptions to American and Israeli workout programmes run by former special forces soldiers. He goes to the gym regularly. She has heard him talk of CrossFit, of his washboard abs, of the man boobs of the Jat and Punjabi men who crowd the weight room and carry out bicep curls in the squat rack.

Goyal from accounting is missing when Bibi goes to confront him about her salary. Someone she has never seen before, a young man with cropped hair, looks up from spreadsheets displayed on two monitors angled towards each other. Another man, older, heavyset, hovers nearby. The two eye her for a while, the older man coming right up to her. It feels like she is not standing in an open-plan office, in full view of other people, but in some enclosed room somewhere.

'Why are you not wearing your ID card?' the man with the spreadsheets asks. He fingers the card dangling from his own neck. He holds the card up to her. The firm is called Vistara Consulting Systems. Its logo is prominent on the white, shiny rectangle of plastic, the muscular, cartoon Hanuman dominating the man's blurry photograph. It looks very much like the Vimana logo, Bibi thinks, but then there are a lot of companies in India these days with such logos and names. Goyal is at home recovering from the Chinese flu going around, the older man says, dismissing her with a wave of his hand.

As soon as Bibi sits down, another man comes to her workstation. Also an unknown face, this time claiming to be an IT specialist, wearing pristine white clothes. There is a new security protocol for employee devices, he says, demanding her mobile phone. Bibi tells him that it is a personal mobile, not a company one. He is insistent. If the phone is brought in to work, it must have a security patch installed. Otherwise, it is very easy for hackers and terrorists to break into the office network. Is she not a patriot? he asks.

Bibi reaches into her overcoat and takes her phone out. When he brings it back to her half an hour later, there is a new app installed on it, a badly rendered Indian flag that sits askew on the home screen. Bibi taps it. A jagged, irregular wall of code covers the screen, a tiny cursor blinking at the far corner of an uneven wall of scrambled letters and numbers. Then the phone shuts itself off and begins to reboot very slowly.

FINALLY, AT THE close of day, there comes the interview in the conference room. Four men and one woman sit at the other end of the table, shuffling papers and affecting boredom. Their interest in her is excessively personal, the woman leading with questions about family and marital status. She lingers over Bibi's name, seemingly demonstrating prime evidence to her colleagues, and then asks Bibi if she is in the updated national register for citizens.

Her response to each of Bibi's answers is an exclamation of disbelief. The men join in slowly. They ask her about *The Daily Telegram*, what made her quit, and why a prominent businessman initiated defamation suits against her.

'Why always negative stories?' the woman demands. 'Why always India in a bad light?'

Something of Bibi's old spirit kicks in. 'Are you perhaps confusing journalism with public relations?'

'Another anti-national was there,' the woman says. 'The Chinese one writing Chinese nonsense. Was he the one who taught you to be like this?'

'Obviously,' Bibi says.

There is a slight intake of breath.

'What did he tell you?' the woman says.

'That there is more truth in good poetry than in bad journalism.'

'Haan?'

'That India is not a nation but a prisonhouse of possible nations.'

'. . .'

'And that the New Delhi Monkey Man was just one more provincial lost in the big city.'

The woman is so outraged that she cannot get a word out. The burly man, the one she saw earlier at Goyal's desk, gestures at his colleague. He holds Bibi's gaze for a while, his eyes small and hard, before he gives her the tiniest of nods. Her withheld pay cheques will be deposited, he says, but all her documentation is required within the month if she wishes to continue at this job.

11

The man is loitering on the pavement as Bibi exits Regal Building, tripping in her hurry to leave. His air of authority creates a barrier around him, the evening crowd working around him in spite of their rush. Bibi can sense his eyes on her. She turns right, opposite to the direction she usually takes. He is still watching her. She takes another right, hurrying into the alleyway behind Regal Building with palpable relief.

She pauses behind the building. When no one comes after her, she begins to make her way through the alleyway. It is windy and grey and street mutts with hideous burn scabs huddle together at the shuttered entrances of seedy-looking travel agencies. Discarded lottery tickets blow up against empty pint bottles of Director's Special whisky and Maa Ka Doodh vodka. The back wall of Regal Building is like a vast makeshift cage, padlocked rectangles of iron and wire stacked one upon the other. For a brief second, Bibi thinks she can see creatures imprisoned in that edifice. She blinks, furious at these meaningless apparitions and at the tears in her eyes. When she looks again, furred, dirt-encrusted air conditioners and air purifiers come into focus, protected by their cages and locks from potential resale at Chor Bazaar.

A chemical orange glow, sodium lamps reflected off the cloud cover of pollution, lights up the sky. The mutts raise their heads to look at Bibi as she approaches them, one by one, and let them drop as she passes, exhausted by the heavy burden of their trickledown lives. Just as she is approaching the government liquor vend, Bibi hears the distinct sound of footsteps behind. When she looks back, nothing can be seen through the yellow haze rolling down the alley.

The liquor vend, usually a reliable scene of ravaged-looking men jostling for bottles, is deserted, another victim of the cashless economy. Bibi pauses at the entrance and goes in. The floor is sticky under her boots. A bare light bulb hangs over the cashier, its glow fractured into jagged shadows by the iron bars enclosing the man. Behind him, coloured bottles and bright labels float towards the ceiling in a collage composed of shiny sports cars and semi-naked white women. The most prominent poster features what looks like a pale, stylised, single breast, an advertisement for the vodka brand Maa Ka Doodh. It is the best known product of a company whose owner is a billionaire, a former member of parliament, who, having defaulted on his loans and employee salaries, now lives in London, giving periodic, bullish interviews to Indian media from his Mayfair mansion about his plans to buy back Tipu Sultan's clockwork tiger from the Victoria and Albert Museum and make it the centrepiece of an exhibit commemorating the Sepoy Rebellion of 1857.

The cashier stares at Bibi in bewilderment. He reaches for his phone, fingers fumbling. Bibi turns around and exits just as the flash goes off. In front of her, a figure hurriedly steps back into the haze. A fuzzy face, simian, eyes wide open. Behind her, there are shouts from the liquor vend man.

BIBI PICKS UP her pace and puts the lane and office behind her. She exits near the Mohan Singh shopping complex and angles right. Rush hour traffic is at a crawl, duelling headlights attempting to pick out paths through the yellow vapour. Car horns and voices shriek out Delhi obscenities at the dreary streets and buildings and then subside again as she sinks into the creepy underground passage that will take her across to the Inner Circle.

Behind, there are footsteps again.

Up and out of the underground tunnel, Bibi hurries, alert as she turns into blind corners, listening for those footsteps that sound effortless as they keep up with her. Blood pulses through her body, directed by the control tower of her heart. The foggy colonnades of the Inner Circle swivel around her, Connaught Place a spinning wheel that drives faces in and out of focus, the movement of people around her fuelled by an urgency bordering on panic.

Bibi tries to make out if she is still being followed, if he is still out there, behind her, stalking her through a crowd that seems to be composed entirely of pursuers and the pursued.

English-speaking courses and computer-programming manuals with sharp edges are thrust at her midriff. She dodges them only to come across truncated limbs projecting out of malnourished bodies, crudely amputated torsos rattling dented tin cups with a desperation bordering on fury. Bibi pushes people aside, trips over barriers, forcing her way out of the covered arcades thick with people onto open ground where she hopes to find a little space.

She sees a courting couple, their involvement and completeness in each other a relief from the relentless attempts at commerce. When she comes closer, she sees that it is Akanksha and a thin young man, his clothes too baggy for his small, malnourished frame. A loose flagstone sends her stumbling. Teetering, tottering, she flings out her hands and slams into a wire fence encircling a sickly peepal tree. A knot of men eyeing Akanksha turn their gaze towards Bibi and break out in catcalls that provoke in her a sudden eruption of rage.

Spinning on her heels, she looks behind, no longer filled with a desire to lose her pursuer but to confront him. That same face again, taking hurried cover behind a pillar plastered with handbills. An electronic sign juts out to the side, the blinking words illegible from where she stands. Before she can change her mind, Bibi advances towards the pillar. The words on the sign become bigger as she closes in.

PILES
FISTULA
HYDROCELE
SEX WEAKNESS

JUST AS SHE reaches the pillar, her stalker breaks cover. A thick, frantic rush-hour match of commuters versus vendors cuts off his retreat. He changes direction abruptly, scampering to the other side of the road, towards the entrance to the Metro. Bibi has a glimpse of dark eyes. The rest of the face appears to be covered by a dun-coloured balaclava, the kind of thing called a monkey cap and worn by elderly Calcutta Bengalis visiting wintry hill towns like Shillong.

A wave of dizziness rolls over Bibi. Her credit card is almost maxed out and she has not eaten well for a while.

Someone takes her arm. Bibi jerks it away. Again, the person grabs her elbow. Bibi pushes, spins around. She sees a heavyset woman, pasty, eyelids drooping. She has some kind of symbol on her forehead. More people are approaching her, all women with smears on their foreheads that look like question marks.

Bibi panics, flailing, screaming, swivelling away, convinced that she is being kidnapped by a cult. The women stop, turn and slowly focus their gazes on another lone woman as she speeds towards the Metro gate, bag clutched across her chest.

With overwhelming relief, Bibi moves away, noticing now that the pedestrian-only stretch in front of her is dotted with groups that have set up booths all around the Metro overhang. The women are more aggressive, saffron-clad figures sallying out for sorties, pushing pamphlets into the hands of passers-by, while the men, thin and ravenous, watch from behind the stalls, flanked by bright posters of babas and matas. Familiar, celebrity faces are prominent in the airbrushed pictures of shining gold and glossy saffron, spiritual leaders who are regular guests on *The National Interest* and feature at the same thinkfests and cultural festivals that Bibi slots into the itinerary of Amidala's globe-trotting speakers. There are other booths that belong to unfamiliar, more obscure, groups—Guru 3.0, Divine Life, Hindu Sena. There is even an evangelical Christian one, The Prosperity Project, that has boldly set up shop in the area. Its displays feature dark-skinned Indians who provide a sharp contrast to the mostly pale, well-fed visages of the gurus being advertised around them.

Bibi is disoriented, dehydrated. Media images of cults come to her mind unbidden. Three generations of a trading family that hanged itself in a North Delhi haveli, fourteen bodies suspended in a row from the ceiling like carcasses at a butcher's shop, black tape in X patterns over their eyes, ears and mouths to prevent the entry of evil at the moment of death. A single suicide note found by the police, clustered with references to a manual detailing the steps to be taken that, through self-extinction, will allow one to reach an immortal, blissful stage of being.

The monkey cap is visible in the distance. Against her own wishes, Bibi starts towards it again.

YELLOW SMOKE BREAKS on building tops and glowing neon signboards as Bibi advances towards the Outer Circle. The sullen ruins of British architecture, she thinks, meant to be an imposing imitation of London, erected on parcels of real estate handed out to Indian collaborators as gifts in the aftermath of the 1857 rebellion. The compradors prospered even more after independence, pumping gridlock and fuel exhaust into the arterial roads, pouring concrete over earth and then earth over concrete before laying down bright green grass and naming it, in an updated act of collaborator's homage, Central Park. The giant Indian flag of the Jindal mining conglomerate hangs limply over this imitation Central Park, backlit by advertising: golden arches, a green mermaid, the diamond of Union Carbide Chemicals.

It is cold, the city a patchwork of congealed darkness and blazing lights as she steps on and off pavements, weaving her way through motorcycles and past cigarette kiosks. Screens flicker around her on Barakhamba Road. The glossy-haired anchor is everywhere, stalking people from giant, iridescent screens that hang from the sides of buildings, playing hide-and-seek with the prime minister, whose rictus mask stares back and down and across and over, in subliminal communication with his countless minions.

Near Mandi House, Bibi's quarry veers sharply left. The black coat is unbearably hot, sweat pooling around her neck. She opens the buttons and lets the coat flap open, taking ever longer strides as she tries to keep up with the man in the monkey cap. How does he move so fast? She is out of shape and her breathing is heavy, her legs tired. He is tireless, progressing without any change of rhythm. They pass by the boundary walls of mysterious government properties, entering an area of deserted pavements and roads strangely empty of traffic. In the distance, she can make out the ITO Metro station, the competing signs of media companies, and beyond them, the blazing, fiery arms of light looming over the Feroz Shah Kotla cricket stadium.

The sight of her old workplace, the drab building on the extreme left of the row of media offices, is perhaps what breaks her spell. What is she doing? Why is she following an unknown man along these empty streets? She is a fool if she thinks she is following him, when the truth is that he has been leading her away, to a deserted quarter, for his own purposes. Bibi stands in place frozen, overwhelmed by her own recklessness. Then she turns and runs.

THE METRO ENTRANCE at Barakhamba Road yawns before her, a mouth thrust out into the bricks and the dirt, carrying with it the usual overspill of male passengers. Bibi makes for the gateway. She is glad that the men in front of the metal detector are waiting in a long, zigzagging backwash that goes up the stairs and into the street. She heads for the shorter women's queue with a sense of relief.

The darkness is sudden, a vast eyelid closing on the city. There is a collective, infinitesimal hush, an extended moment of silence in which Bibi can see the silhouettes of trees and the blocky outline of the Metro canopy. The city, Connaught Place, the giant faces on the buildings, the buildings themselves, are all gone. Bibi feels she is both awake and asleep, that some other city is on the verge of revealing itself, that the shadows stirring around her inside the metro station belong not to passengers but to insomniac prisoners desperate to pass on a message. It doesn't last long, the blackout, the lights flickering back on even as the stuttering growls of portable generators begin to saw through the darkness. The crowds around

Bibi, jolted momentarily into inaction by the brief power cut, begin to flow once again.

LATE THAT NIGHT, Bibi finds what she is looking for. Familiar titles present themselves from the book—'The Dacca Gauzes', 'Homage to Faiz Ahmed Faiz', 'I Dream It Is Afternoon When I Return to Delhi'—but she ignores them. It is not an Agha Shahid Ali poem she wants right now but the yellowed, folded manuscript still tucked inside the pages. No title to the manuscript, just that abrupt opening. *'The first sighting of that astonishing, amazing, misunderstood creature that came to be known as the New Delhi Monkey Man occurred sometime in ...'*

Her phone beeps loudly, even though she is sure she has it on silent. A WhatsApp message from an unknown number.

Shall I tell you a story about following?

The profile picture is a mask, an image recycled from an old political campaign.

Bibi blocks the sender, turns off the lights and sits in the darkness. Five minutes later, another notification glows brightly. Different sender, same profile picture. Gucci glasses, trimmed white beard, holes for eyes.

I want to tell you a story about following.

She blocks the sender. A minute later, a third message arrives.

I will now tell you a story about following.

12

Cross-border raids on Pakistan have begun. In Kashmir, new crowd control devices are being used. Sonic bombs, pellet guns, numbing gas. The rupee is plunging further. A new strain of avian flu, suspected of originating across the border, is spreading through Assam and Manipur. The forced culling of poultry ensues, choppers and daos coming down on sinewy necks before the corpses are tossed into metal drums and set alight in a tangled mass of claws and feathers. A navy AN-32 carrying senior officers on their way to inspect a new base goes missing over the Bay of Bengal. Air traffic is troublesome everywhere, civilian and military flights often forced to abort landings at the last minute.

A test firing of the Brahmastra has not gone quite as planned, although a perfectly poised defence official describes it on *The National Interest* as a 'small hitch', the result of a problem in the software rather than the hardware. 'An absolutely normal performance until the very final phase, just before impact,' he says. 'I can assure patriots who were impressed by the targeting of a space satellite many years ago or by the recent piloted Mars landing that they will see India achieve something other nations have not even imagined.'

After the official has departed, there is a moment of respectful silence. Then the host and the sixteen assembled panellists who crowd even the largest of television screens express their belief that the rising frequency of bird hits over Delhi and Srinagar is being engineered by Pakistan in retaliation for the unquestionable superiority of India. There is a covert war being conducted against India, by Pakistan and China and unknown anti-national forces, the glossy-haired news anchor thunders, the guests shouting their agreement over each other as his fountain pen jabs at the map behind him, at these invisible, spectral enemies who are everywhere. The lone dissenter, a bearded Pakistani politician known for trying to enforce new blasphemy and heresy laws against Christians, Shias and Ahmadis, attempts unsuccessfully to get a word in.

BIBI WILLS HERSELF not to google her name or check social media. Her phone remains switched off. Yet she is sick in her guts. Up there in the cloud, on computers and phones thousands of miles apart, strangers are dismantling her life, insistently, deliberately and with great magnitude of error. Her name circulates on chat sites and social media, trailed everywhere by death and rape threats. Hindu men troll her endlessly on Twitter, and her name features on a right-wing list called Long Tongue Bitches. On a YouTube channel that goes by the name of Shastra Dharma, a balding Indian management consultant in a pink shirt describes with avuncular calm that Bibi is part of a centuries-old global conspiracy of Marxists, Muslims, Christians and a group he calls AfroDalits, whose ultimate objective is no less than the utter destruction of Hindu India and who must be systematically eliminated if India is to survive.

No one seems to be aware that Bibi's journalism is a thing of the past, that the article they are venting about, the one that was found on the USB drive at the Vimana office and is now being circulated on the web, is many years old and contains nothing of what she actually saw on that reporting trip. A photo from her college days in Calcutta and one from a long-ago office party in Delhi is being tagged and passed around, along with pictures of other women—a writer, an academic, a lawyer—being misidentified as her.

The defamation lawsuit, the one filed in an Assam court by the Delhi businessman, has come up like it is breaking news. There is an old clip of the man being interviewed by the glossy-haired news anchor, eyes glittering with intent as he says that he will have Bibi arrested for tarnishing his good name and bringing discredit to India. No one asks him what his connection is to the Hindu right wing, or to detention centres in faraway Assam, or if he is involved in trafficking children.

Everywhere, there are men, and some women, outing Bibi—as a Pakistani agent, as a prostitute, as a sex-crazed woman, as a lesbian, as the holder of fake university degrees, as a Naxal, as a plagiariser who stole her reporting from others. Sometimes she is a Muslim, sometimes a Christian, sometimes a Marxist, numerous versions of Bibi out there on the multiverse of the internet, living lives that are variations of the truncated one she has been caged in for all these years, blurry figures who have long since left this straitjacketed Bibi behind and gone dancing freely down a garden of infinitely forking paths.

SHE ENDS UP, inevitably, recalling her past, going back to the beginning of her time at *The Daily Telegram*. To that first lonely week in Delhi when she wondered if she had done the right thing in leaving her mother in Calcutta to chase after her own inchoate ambitions.

The flat harsh light of fluorescent tubes falls on her in merciless scrutiny as she shows up far too early for her shift. Computers stare, their blank faces glittering with thin layers of dust. In the glass-partitioned cubicle of the newsroom editor, a single terminal suspended from the ceiling cycles in manic fashion through green and red graphs of global stock prices. Under her feet, from subterranean layers deep beneath the newsroom, comes the heavy pounding of the printing press, worked by men whose union has just been broken and who have returned to their posts after a month-long strike that has not led to a single concession from the management.

She is about to sit down when the newsroom editor hands her an agency photo.

'Take this to Sanjit and fetch me a cup of tea,' he says.

'But sir, who is Sanjit? And where do I get tea?'

The editor returns to his cubicle without bothering to respond. Bibi sets off through a maze of narrow corridors and tiny, glass-partitioned cubicles, through rooms filled with massive filing cabinets, printers and ancient photocopying units that resemble nothing so much as time machines. She looks at the photo she is holding. The caption reads, 'A Sentinelese islander fires his primitive weapon at a coast guard helicopter conducting damage survey from the tsunami.'

A man trying to photocopy his palm on a Xerox machine gives Bibi rudimentary directions to the canteen. She enters a dim, low-ceilinged corridor that looks like the entrance to an underground interrogation chamber. She turns around, convinced she has lost her way. But at the other end, blocking the light, there is someone walking towards her very slowly.

There is something odd about this someone, backlit by flickering fluorescents. It is like the size isn't quite right, as if this person is a dwarf or a child, or perhaps there is something off about the gait, and Bibi has these impressions quickly, simultaneously, and then, as she and this someone come closer, she can smell the someone, a strong, gamey smell redolent of cages or workers' rooms in a factory barracks or inmate cells in a crowded prison, and the light in the corridor steadies, and she realises that this someone seems to be crawling, and she sees that this someone is a monkey on all fours, and not just any monkey, but a large male with a red face, an alpha of the pack, a monkey chieftain, what in the villages of the Northeast would be called a gaonburah and Bibi begins to back up, turning finally to run through the corridor and coming out into an extremely shabby canteen.

A Nepali boy is sitting at the counter. He is perhaps twelve years old, with a knife scar that runs diagonally across the left side of his face, from cheek to chin. The boy examines her with the practiced ease of an old lecher. The monkey chief snarls at the scarred boy. The boy retorts with a string of inventive, venomous curses about the monkey's mother's genitalia and pulls out a cleaver. From the far end of the canteen, a man steps forward and looks quizzically at the tableau. He claps his hands and points at an open window. The monkey lopes off towards the window and the boy puts his cleaver away.

'Is that for me?' the man says to Bibi, pointing at the agency photo.

'Are you Sanjit?'

He takes the photo, orders tea for both of them. He has a temporary little workspace set up in the canteen, the table strewn with papers and books. *The Half-Inch Himalayas*, by Agha Shahid Ali. They stand near the window drinking tea and talking. He wants to know where she worked before, how long she has been in Delhi. Outside, monkeys are frolicking, in utter command of the alleyway between *The Daily Telegram* and *The Times of India* building. She looks at her watch. Her shift has begun.

'Have you heard of the New Delhi Monkey Man?' he says, something like a smile momentarily crossing his face.

BIBI HAS TAKEN to listening to music on new, noise-cancelling headphones. The flick of a button and the external world is transformed into a featureless hum, her phone on airplane mode so that she will receive no messages. She immerses herself in music in the days to come, songs downloaded from Pakistani shows, mostly Abida Parveen and Quratulain Balouch and Saieen Zahoor, their voices operating from the edge of harshness, rising from a desert zone where it suddenly begins to rain and the drops turn into icicles, into freezing snow, as they hit the ground and Iqbal Bano sings, her voice momentarily drowned out by fifty thousand people rising in collective, defiant applause in Lahore, 'Hum Dekhenge'.

Careful to hide the screen from fellow passengers on the Metro, Bibi puts her playlist on repeat. Sometimes she listens to songs from the other border, her border, to songs composed by Lalon

Fakir and Abdul Karim, to Bhupen Hazarika's songs of melancholy boatmen and turbulent rivers that pay homage to a Paul Robeson whose passport was taken away from him, to songs about elephant mahouts and migrant tea workers sung by Pratima Barua and Ranen Roy Choudhury and Kali Dasgupta in dialects that possess no armies and no nations, the Koch and Goalpariya and Sylheti intonations looping through her head as she levitates up the stairs of the Metro to Connaught Place, nearly weightless, on the verge of floating to the sky like Remedios the Beauty.

She is almost grateful for the haze that obscures everything, hiding the tops of the buildings and the giant Indian flag. In spite of the canopy of funereal gloom stretched taut over the city, Bibi has taken to wearing huge sunglasses, knockoff Chinese Ray-Bans purchased from a Russian woman who sells her wares near the glass-fronted Life Insurance Building. With shiny wristwatches up to her elbows, she looks to Bibi like a cyborg, her flashing metallic arms and reflector shades warding off sexual innuendoes from men who come to scrutinise her along with her wares. A robot sister who these days recognises Bibi when she passes by, who seems always to be mysteriously pointing Bibi in a different direction, towards ITO.

Some days Bibi covers her hair with a scarf. On other days, she ties her hair into a bun and wears a hoodie, pulling its cowl well over her head. She does not know why she is trying to disguise herself, what she is trying to achieve. She keeps her headphones on at work, her head covered. SS, who has returned from his convalescence strangely diminished, looks at her with alarm if they run into each other in the reception or outside the kitchen but says nothing.

KRISHNA FROM SUNNYVALE, California, has commented at length on a mirror site posting the article on the detention centre. He has uploaded a shot of women at a Bodo village in Assam to illustrate his point about Malthusian demographic overload and the difference between indigenous people and illegal immigrants. 'Look at the Hindu women,' he has written, referring to the Bodos. 'See the grace of the sindoor on the forehead, the dignity of their clothing, how well cared for their children are. Look at the Muslim women next to them, with their heavy black middle-eastern clothing, how many more children they have in their effort to outbreed Hindus. Look at the poor hygiene and knowledge base implied in the stunted stature of the Muslim women and the bloated bellies of their children. Give me a good scientific reason why one should not give natural selection a helping hand and eliminate the unfit and the unworthy. In programming we call this process DEBUGGING.'

MESSAGES POUR IN on WhatsApp whenever Bibi turns off airplane mode, dispatched by different senders who repeat the same words, *libtard sickular pressitute urban naxal longtongue bitch how you dare* over and over again. Each time she blocks a number, the messages reappear from new numbers. All the senders have the same profile picture. Trimmed white beard, a smile that isn't a smile, holes for eyes.

Some send videos Bibi doesn't want to watch but that start playing automatically as soon as the message arrives, without her even touching the screen. There is footage of animals being slaughtered, of dishevelled men in dirty clothes getting pulled out from the back of trucks, being beaten to death with hockey sticks and iron rods as the cows look on in horror, of a man on fire, limbs flailing as he screams, of a demonstration demanding the release of a priest arrested for raping and murdering an eight-year-old girl belonging to a Muslim nomadic tribe, of a woman, obviously mentally disturbed, being hoisted on to some kind of makeshift stage by a group of men who snip off her hair in slow, deliberate fashion as the crowd assembled below roars in approval.

Then Bibi receives a series of stills, the light bleached out. The Hanuman temple at the mouth of Munirka Village; a tea stall at

Rama Market; the outside of Anupam restaurant. She blocks the sender. The images are soon being passed around on social media. Soon, another number with the mask profile messages her a picture that she has seen quite recently. It is the photo of her asleep in the Chanakyapuri flat, the one taken by Anand. Bibi deletes WhatsApp from her phone.

She powers the phone off, puts it away and picks up the manuscript she found inside the book of poems.

13

'The first sighting of that astonishing, amazing, misunderstood creature that came to be known as the New Delhi Monkey Man occurred sometime in the month of May, at the beginning of the new century. The name, in the way these things often tend to be in India, was a misnomer. For in spite of the use of 'New Delhi' to describe it, New Delhi Monkey Man made his presence felt mostly across the dying Yamuna River, in that Trans-Yamuna zone of housing society apartment blocks, slums and factories that New Delhi likes to pretend doesn't exist.

'Yet the name caught on, in Trans-Yamuna Delhi, in New Delhi, in the world at large. In Brooklyn, New York, cultural appropriation capital of the universe, a music band gave itself the name New Delhi Monkey Man. It's impossible that Trans-Yamuna Monkey Man or Noida Monkey Man or Uttar Pradesh Monkey Man would have worked quite so well.

'But what was New Delhi Monkey Man? Was he a monkey? Was he a man? Was he even a he? The Delhi Police, that selfless organisation whose reassuring slogan at the time read, "For You, With You, Always", at first said that New Delhi Monkey Man was nothing more than a man in a monkey mask going around frightening people. Concerned citizens were asked to call a special hotline if they saw New Delhi Monkey Man and wait for a van to be dispatched. Until said concerned citizens spotted said dispatched police van, easily identifiable by the large slogan on its side, "For You, With You, Always", they were asked to remain indoors and not attempt to apprehend New Delhi Monkey Man on their own.

'Still, what if New Delhi Monkey Man was not just a gangster with a monkey mask or a rowdy sheeter in a monkey costume? What if his tail was not made out of stuffed cloth like a Rajasthani puppet? What if it was a real tail, not something frozen in a stiff curve but a flexible thing, as alive with intent as the tail of Hanuman setting the island of Lanka on fire, a sinuous tail capable of grasping and snatching and allowing New Delhi Monkey Man to swing from balcony to balcony with the greatest of ease?

'Yes, what if New Delhi Monkey Man was Hanuman himself come to wreak havoc on a fallen, debased people who had deviated from the true faith of their forefathers? When Mrs Chawla, on observing New Delhi Monkey Man grinning at her with yellowed, third-world teeth from among the clothes strung out to dry in her balcony, recited loudly from the Hanuman Chalisa, "Jai Jai Guru Hanuman", did New Delhi Monkey Man smile and bless her, or did he become enraged and attack her? Neighbours of different political persuasions provided different endings to Mrs Chawla's story.

'And so, what if New Delhi Monkey Man was not Hanuman at all, but a kind of anti-Hanuman? What if he was a liberated Hanuman, a monkey tired of being a servant and operating as a prison for humans posing as gods, with a heart-shaped cell in his body that contained small versions of Ram and Sita, a monkey who no longer wanted to serve as a commando or an assassin in a genocidal war? What if New Delhi Monkey Man was a clone of some kind, a man-monkey hybrid escaped from a top-secret joint venture facility run by the Defence Research and Development Organisation and the Ombani Labs in some remote border area? What if New Delhi Monkey Man was a mutant creature produced by the toxic gas cloud of Bhopal in 1984? What if New Delhi Monkey Man was an extraterrestrial creature, an alien accidentally marooned on this planet? What if New Delhi Monkey Man was a strange new mutation, an outcome of Artificial Intelligence stirring into consciousness in the aftermath of Y2K? What if New Delhi Monkey Man had time-travelled from the past, coming at us from the Sepoy Rebellion of 1857 or from the killing fields of Partition in 1947? What if, while travelling through time, New Delhi Monkey

Man came to the new millennium not from the past but from our future?

'As observations of New Delhi Monkey Man proliferated, there were suggestions that he had clockwork springs in his shoes. These, operated by a row of glowing red buttons on his chest, allowed him to leap from rooftop to rooftop. We would also like to point out that "Monkey Man" was the westernised version of the name, a clever, polite, convenient media translation of the kind applied once to the words of a famous Indian leader when he described Muslims as "kutte ke bachche" and found it rendered as the Hallmark-sanitised "puppies". If one were to reverse the translation, and go from English to Hindi, New Delhi Monkey Man would, in the exquisitely racist, casteist and classist way of Indians, become Black Monkey or Kala Bandar.

'But what did Kala Bandar or New Delhi Monkey Man look like? More reports came in, saying that he was four feet tall, covered in thick black fur and wore a motorcycle helmet. Others said he had metal claws, glowing red eyes and three buttons on his chest that alternately flickered red and blue. There were accounts claiming that New Delhi Monkey Man was not four feet tall but double the height at eight feet and fantastically muscled. A sociologist at JNU suggested that New Delhi Monkey Man was a case of the return of the repressed, an eruption of the uncanny, an embodiment of all those marginalised people—Muslims, Dalits, tribals, Adivasis, feminists, leftists, environmentalists, Kashmiris, Maoist guerrillas, homosexuals, rationalists, poets, poor farmers, poet farmers, nomadic sheep herders, migrant workers, autorickshaw drivers, construction labourers, waitresses, maid servants, child servants, child beggars—feared by urban, upwardly mobile India.

'The news channels scoffed at this interpretation and ran clips of a man interviewed outside Hastinapur Moderne Apartments in Patparganj who, while declining to give his name to the reporter, said that New Delhi Monkey Man was neither a man nor a monkey but a robot assassin dispatched by an enemy foreign power on a secret, nefarious mission. The Delhi Police, responding to this last statement at a press conference, announced that New Delhi Monkey Man was not a robot assassin or a monkey but a man in a monkey mask who had been sent by the nefarious Inter-Services Intelligence agency of Pakistan to terrorise the peace-loving citizens of India and to test the resolve of the Delhi Police. It added that the Delhi Police had never failed a test of its resolve and that the proper response to bricks was stones.

'More appearances were reported, accompanied by accounts of attacks. The injuries were minor in nature, including scrapes, bruises and the occasional fracture, the majority of these occurring when victims fell down stairwells while trying to escape New Delhi Monkey Man. The socio-economic status of the victims was narrow in range. The rich and the very rich were excluded, by virtue of the high walls of their villas and their domicile in areas other than Trans-Yamuna Delhi. That left as potential victims only street dwellers sleeping in the open and conservative, middle-class, dues-paying members of housing societies.

'The Delhi Police suggested that New Delhi Monkey Man was not a man or a monkey but a kind of collective hallucination produced by the conjunction of a massive heat wave, frequent power outages and a well-known monkey infestation that for long had been affecting places as far apart as the laboratories of the Indian Institute of Technology in South Delhi, the offices of the Home Ministry in North Block, in the heart of the city, and the canteen of *The Daily Telegram* newspaper building, to the north. It asked people to refrain from sleeping in the open, although it did not have an answer to where street dwellers should sleep if not in the open.

'Perhaps in response to the Delhi Police statement, the zone of New Delhi Monkey Man's attacks expanded. He seemed to leap over the oxygen-depleted, effluent-laced, corpse-laden Yamuna River into the city proper, appearing at a concert of derivative rock music at the Indian Institute of Technology, where he attacked the drummer of a band playing a cover version of Bryan Adams's "Summer of '69". There was outrage in the media. Not even the city proper was safe, not even the flower of Indian youth. The Delhi Police responded that New Delhi Monkey Man had not been sighted at IIT Delhi and that the assault on the drummer was carried out by a thug hired by a fellow musician who was the drummer's rival in love.

'A month after this string of incidents, the monsoons arrived. The power outages reduced in frequency and the heat wave broke, giving way to a clammy, sticky season that promised to last into autumn. New Delhi Monkey Man disappeared as abruptly as he had emerged. Plastic bags choked the gutters of Delhi and drivers of two-wheelers massed under overbridges to protect themselves from the rain, but no New Delhi Monkey Man was seen leaping from rooftop to rooftop under skies grey with monsoon clouds and industrial pollution. Instead, he was reported leaving the city, seemingly exhausted by its ruthless ambition and its manufactured lies, as if, at the end of the day, New Delhi Monkey Man was just one more provincial who grew tired of attempting to make it in this heartless city.

'Conflicting versions of where he went and how were offered. In one account, he was seen on an Aeroflot flight going from Delhi to Moscow where he had to be restrained with adhesive tape after biting passengers and attacking members of the cabin crew. Another report put him, somewhat more modestly, in a second-class compartment on a train bound for Tinsukia in Assam.

'No sightings of New Delhi Monkey Man were reported from Moscow or from Assam, although shortly after, there were reports of a Bear Man rampaging through the villages of Assam. This creature made himself invisible right as he attacked, his viciously bearish features discernible momentarily, just prior to the assault. A spokesman from the Indian Army said that the Bear Man was a plot hatched by China, meant to distract focus from the systemic infiltration of India by Bangladeshi Muslims and intended to test the resolve and preparedness of Indian forces along the nation's northeastern frontier. The spokesman added that this was a test of the kind that the Indian Army had always passed with force and vigour and that the proper response to artillery fire was surface-to-air missiles.

'Of New Delhi Monkey Man himself, however, nothing more

was heard or seen. He had come out of nowhere, staring through the window of your flat high in the sky, and then he vanished into nowhere. His buttons, his wires, his motorcycle helmet and his thick black fur were no longer even details in a memory or a dream. Erased without a sign, forgotten without a trace, silenced without an echo. And that is where my part in his story, and your part in my story, begins.'

14

The phone has become increasingly erratic in its workings. At first, this is a relief. If Bibi tries, out of sheer, cussed reflex, to check social media, nothing happens. The apps and web browsers refuse to load. It is possible, Bibi thinks, that there is a problem with the network. She hears people in the office complaining about the servers, about the missing bars on their phones. On Metro platforms, commuters grumble about throttled data and frozen apps when they are not talking about Pakistan or China.

But it is not that Bibi's phone does not work at all. Sometimes, a silent war seems to be taking place inside that rectangle of polymer and glass, a schizoid personality lurking beneath the darkened, smudged screen and see-sawing from one extreme to another. So, often, nothing, just stalled apps and blank screens when she tries to use her phone. At other times, all her email is automatically downloaded even though she has this feature turned off. Most of it is spam that has evaded all filters to infiltrate her inbox.

These emails, which Bibi reads for no good reason, are strangely beguiling, more cipher than marketing. C.P. Cavafy, a man claiming to be a detective from the Continental Operative Agency, writes that he has concluded the initial stage of the missing-person investigation she hired him for. Further details are available by clicking on the link below. Other messages are more intimate: *Hello dear, Mrs Sufia Salwa is my name a childless widow suffering from a long-time cancer decease and from all indication my condition is really deteriorating and as a result of my present situation I have nothing in mind other than to help the lost. A great change is upon you and I will show you the way when you reply.*

WITHOUT WHATSAPP, BIBI tries to stay in touch with Moi through text messages. The ensuing conversations are surreal, like automatic poetry.

Hey M, you there?
Yesterday ended not quite right
What?
Dreams of impending dread ...
???
That she saw more than others yet another time always fulfills.

When Bibi talks to Moi in the morning, in that tiny window of time when Moi has just woken up and Bibi not yet left for the day, Moi denies receiving Bibi's texts or writing any poetry. She is listless and sullen, her eyes etched with black circles as she shows Bibi her phone.

It is true that none of the messages are on Moi's phone, just as surely as they are on Bibi's, the number on them indisputably Moi's.

BIBI'S PHONE RINGS at odd times, the screen displaying 'Unknown Caller'. In the beginning, she scrambles to press the cancel button, heart pounding, fingers jittery. But the phone always behaves like it has a mind of its own. It answers the call, turns the speaker on. Instead of the abuse or threats Bibi anticipates, or the heavy breathing succeeded by orgasmic sounds, the line buzzes with something like static. A hum of white noise, curiously calming. It slows Bibi's breath down, drops her pulse. She feels she is listening to the regular susurration of a tide on some distant, unpopulated shore. The patter of rain on a building, the sighing of the sea on a beach. If there is a voice at the other end, it is surely underwater.

Something, somewhere, is trying to pass her a message.

So, she listens to these phone calls that are not phone calls and thinks of water. She thinks of the ocean breathing to a geological rhythm, an ocean that still remembers the Ice Age, still remembers the things that came before this time they are calling the Anthropocene, its deep, cold recesses filled with monsters of incredibly alien splendour. She feels her mind clearing, feels a loosening of the pores in her body as she falls asleep clutching the phone like a child holding on to an object of great, if transient, magic. Often, she wakes up in the middle of the night to find the battery completely drained.

HER DREAMS TOO are infiltrated by these uncanny calls and messages. She sees detective Cavafy in a boxy, old-fashioned suit and a tiny Mrs Salwa, almost doll-like, walking along a rusting wharf, holding hands, their faces brightly painted. The sea lashes against a tangle of abandoned ships and fat raindrops bounce off blackened, heavy chains looped around massive bollards. In the distance, on top of a hill, the rain pours relentlessly on a building with gaping holes for windows.

Into her dreams other creatures then swim, ancient monsters that extend vast cephalopodic flippers, holding unending stares with giant, lazy eyes that are filled with compassion and mystery. Bibi feels herself unlock, unfold, phrases floating to the surface from the deep recesses of her mind. The fragments of books read and talked about long ago, sentences squirrelled away in notebooks whose pages are yellowed, written down unknowingly by Bibi's past self for a time like this everlasting winter of menace and brume.

In these dreams, her phone rings and answers itself.

But the sound of the static is also the sound of the rain.

And the sound of the rain is also the sound of the ocean.

15

Then, one morning, the phone refuses to power on. Bibi connects it to a point, waits for the battery to charge. The screen is almost black. If Bibi looks closely, she can make out dim, blurry characters floating on some ghostly layer beneath the actual screen. But even after she puts the phone under a lamp, the text, if that is what it is, remains indecipherable. She tries holding it at an angle, turning the phone this way and that way. She thinks she can make out the faintest sequence of letters. LINDED IN. URNED BY.

BIBI TAKES HER phone to a store at a mall in Saket. The place she bought the phone from, a glass-fronted outlet with pink and red swirls of branding, is gone. Instead, in that same location, a small, dim gadget store squats, looking like it has inexplicably shrunk its surroundings as well as itself.

The young proprietor's movements are languorous, his eyes bloodshot. He laughs when Bibi explains her problem and laughs again when she requests a cheap phone she can use while he fixes this one.

He turns the music up, the bass booming from portable speakers placed inside brown earthenware matkas resting on either corner of the back wall. It takes him a very long time to find what he wants among the overlapping nests of cables and chargers. Sometimes, an adapter blinks into electronic life in his hands, even though it is not connected to any visible source of power. Beeps, trills, vibrations punctuate the air. He beeps back.

The stoner brings a dented box to the counter, extracting a phone from it and checking the charge. With deft fingers, he inserts a SIM card and sets up a prepaid account with a new number. When he looks expectantly towards Bibi for her documentation, Bibi pretends that she cannot find her Aadhaar card in her bag and he laughs and waves her away.

THE PHONE IS a Nokia, small, bulging in the middle like a minor but self-important civil servant. It has no web browser, no apps. Bibi is astonished that it works at all. She tries texting on the tiny keyboard. The process is so laborious, her fingers constantly hitting the wrong buttons, that she gives up. Instead, she tries calling Moi while wandering through the mall. Moi's number rings on without a response.

Her throat is parched. Stopping to orient herself, she discovers she has entered a vast department store, the signage awry and the mannequins tilted towards each other in secret communion. Uniformed women with sunken eyes attempt to hand her flyers and coupons, dark, bony hands reaching for her like they are attempting to pass on mercy petitions.

Scarves and shoes stealthily close in on her as she progresses, a foliage of merchandise blooming in bright chemical colours. Distances are foreshortened, the reflections infinite. Behind her, a woman with a white dupatta covering her head moves from counter to counter, dusting listlessly, her feet skittering like an animal's on the tiled floor.

She finds herself among the perfumes and jewellery. It is odd, Bibi thinks, that there are so few shoppers in all these sections, and no staff either, no one apart from her and that woman. Bibi turns to look at her. The woman freezes, spins away. There is something strange in the way she moves, in the sound her feet make on the floor.

'Excuse me,' Bibi says, walking up to her. 'Which way is the exit?' The woman starts, looks down. Her image is reflected in the glass cabinet behind her. The dupatta is pulled far over her face but Bibi still has the fleeting vision of a bird beak in one of those reflections. The woman makes a strange, gurgling sound and begins to back away.

'Wait,' Bibi says.

With a sudden shuffling, the woman is off. Her running is ungainly, helter-skelter. She has almost made it out of the perfume section when she slams into a cabinet full of jewellery. There is barely any noise from the impact. Bibi thinks of a bird flying into a windowpane. The woman picks herself up and vanishes.

BIBI COMES HOME early that afternoon, not having bothered with going to work from the mall. She sits at the back door, watching the day as it slowly extinguishes itself. Her Nokia does not ring. There is a single number stored on it. It contains no text messages or emails and is as fresh as a new identity. There are birds in the sky and flowers on the plants in the rooftop of the slum across. Winter has gone, summer arrived, and Bibi hasn't even noticed.

Someone has just put up washing on the rooftop across from her. A row of children's knickers hang from the line, along with half a dozen stuffed toys, still dripping. The stuffies are small, misshapen, malnourished, like the children they belong to, emaciated, knockoff versions of the gargantuan toys sold at the malls. But, Bibi thinks, a mother's hands have carefully washed them and put them out to dry.

She decides to go and see her mother in Calcutta.

16

When Bibi is finally in Calcutta, humidity has replaced the desert heat of Delhi. Salty, dense droplets collect on her eyebrows and upper lip. Inside her mother's flat, the back half of the ground floor of a two-storey house hunched in defensive posture, it is pitch dark, the walls of the adjoining houses so close that none of the windows can be opened fully. The refrigerator is nearly empty and Bibi is unable to coax a single cup of drinking water from the gallon container that sits unsteadily on a plastic stool.

Her mother's bedside table is overrun by shiny strips of Calmpose pills. In a locker in a steel almirah, Bibi finds a manila envelope stuffed with crisp Mars notes. Her mother, more incoherent than usual, is unable to explain any of this in a plausible way. A woman called Mrs Chaudhuri has paid her, she says, for helping out with her NGO.

Bibi's mother believes that Mrs Chaudhuri is someone she knows from long ago. She says Mrs Chaudhuri was someone who helped Bibi's parents in those early years after they crossed the border and landed up in Shillong, that Mrs Chaudhuri's husband was a colleague of Bibi's father's and often visited them at home with his wife. An aristocratic couple capable of reading political shifts well in advance, Bibi's mother says. Unlike her hapless husband, they moved to Shillong only after they had arranged a smooth transfer of their assets across the border.

She pulls out old albums to prove her point, wrapped, like precious heirlooms, in colourful shawls. Bibi sighs as she looks at the pictures. Her mother is in one of her more manic phases now, which will give way at some point to a sullen withdrawal. Their past drifts by, simultaneously fragile and heavy, the black-and-whites sepia, the colour snapshots bleeding their synthetic, once-bright shades. But no matter how many times the thick black pages are turned, there are no photos of Mrs Chaudhuri and her husband to be found, as though they have carefully transferred their presences out of Bibi's mother's album into some other, more secure homeland.

BIBI CLEANS THE flat and orders supplies. Then she visits a neighbourhood agency to try and check the updated citizens' register and apply for a new series Aadhaar card. The man at the agency, whose name is Jishu, opens a browser window on his sluggish laptop and types in the serial numbers Bibi gives him. His first two attempts at the captcha test are a failure. Bibi tries the third one but has no better luck. 'Dolls', 'Prisoners', 'Headlines'—those are clearly not the right words.

'Maybe we're not human beings?' Bibi asks. 'The captcha tests can't tell the difference between us and computers.'

Jishu laughs in a demented way and punches the fourth captcha word in, one letter at a time. The word is MUSEUM. After a moment, the passcode appears on his smartphone.

THERE ARE COBWEBS in the corners of the unadorned room that serves as Jishu's office. Brown termite trails expand along the upper reaches of the walls, borders defining nascent nations. The remnants of a rice and fish curry meal sit on a military green filing cabinet where Jishu keeps his papers. His gadgets—laptop, desktop, printer, scanner, mini-ATM, smartphone, modem and a large, ostentatious calculator—are still encased in the plastic wraps they came in, and yet the battle to keep out dust has long since been lost. As for Jishu, thin, balding, with worry lines around his mouth and eyes, he looks old, almost grandfatherly. Bibi knows that he is more or less the same age as her, that when she first moved to the neighbourhood as a college student, he was one of the young men hanging out at the tea stalls, someone who described himself as an independent leftist. Now, it is obvious, from the ostentatious sacred rings adorning five out of his ten fingers to the screensaver of the prime minister that flickers on after every minute of inactivity, that he too is a devoted disciple of the new India.

An hour passes. Bibi examines the repaired smartphone she picked up before leaving Delhi. The young man in the Saket mall—like the younger version of Jishu, she thinks—has removed the app installed by her office. It was full of bugs, according to him, and he has done a complete wipe of the phone and installed a new system.

Bibi sends Moi a text. Moi's response is matter-of-fact, brief. She is fine, she writes. Singhal says her job interview is being delayed because there has been some kind of outbreak on *The World*. It has been quarantined and is sitting just off Robben Island, in South Africa.

JISHU WORKS LABORIOUSLY, slowly. He wipes his fingerprint scanner with a damp cloth, complaining that day labourers with dirty hands smudge the scanner when they come to get their Aadhaar cards updated. They are all illegals from Bangladesh, he says. Then he looks away from Bibi, embarrassed.

Bibi waits for the scanner to accept her fingerprints, for the network to move her data around, for the jumpy resolution of the laptop screen to settle down. Jishu hits the submit panel like it is the launch button for a new Mars mission. The screen shudders and a new window opens. A denial code. Bibi's new card has not been approved.

THE TWO OF them trawl through various fora to interpret this denial code. Finally, when they understand that it is asking for Bibi's record number on the updated citizens' register, they switch their attention to the register. The citizens' register has its own complex procedures, requiring a fresh set of fingerprints and another bruising session of captcha words and access codes. Moisture pools into Bibi's neck as she waits, and she can sense the summer leaving a thick, familiar layer of dirt on the inside collar of her shirt. Her skin is itchy, breaking out into rashes.

From the national site of the register, Jishu is sent to the Assam site. 'Complicated state,' he says tersely. Bibi wonders why her name is linked to Assam, where she has lived only for a brief period of her life, during the few years her parents were stranded there, trying to sell off the house her father had unwisely built in a town on the flood plains. Shillong, Calcutta, Delhi—these are the axis points of her existence, but they don't seem to count. Only Assam, only the border with Bangladesh, only the date when her family crossed this border. Did they come in the nineteenth century? In 1947? In 1971?

An answer of sorts is received from the Assam site. In spite of the garbled language and governmental acronyms, the contents are clear enough. For her name to be cleared and entered into the national register, Bibi will first have to contact the border police in Assam and then present herself before a tribunal. For now, she is on the D list, the so-called doubtful category of citizens.

Jishu prints out her receipts without any comment.

THERE IS WATER in the taps when she returns home, brownish liquid thick with minerals. The colonial-era reservoirs that supply this part of Calcutta are in ruins, the supply lines thrown into disarray by cyclones that originate in the Bay of Bengal and sweep into the city with increasing frequency. The minerals that give the water a brackish taste and brownish colour have, over the years, left a red coating on everything, the toilet bowl, the sink and the bucket in front of which Bibi kneels, trying to cool herself down with mugs of water, while in the house next door, new, unseen neighbours play Hindu rock that rattles the windows.

Bibi calls her sister, with whom she has not spoken for months. She tells her she will be putting her mother on a flight to Guwahati. Her sister protests. Things are difficult for her and her husband, she says. Their names are on the D list too. The troubles they knew in their childhood have returned. The graffiti is fresh, but the slogans are old: *Bangladeshis go home. Foreigners go home.* On the walls of the city, pictures of devouring crows and ravenous ants loop around the election slogans of the Hindu right, accompanied by stencils of a turbaned warrior wielding a hengdang, the local sword. There is no need for the slogans to spell out who the crows and ants are. The head of the BJP prefers to call them termites.

Bibi's sister and her husband are hoping that the children, with their tech jobs, will be able to immigrate to Canada, that they themselves will eventually be able to join their children there. 'Why can't you take her to Delhi?' her sister says. 'You have no children, no responsibilities.' Bibi understands her sister's resentment. It is true that Bibi has been free to make her own mistakes. Her sister, married young to a dull if entrepreneurial man found through the family network, has not. What remains unsaid is that Bibi has sent home money all these years, responded to every emergency, of which there have always been many. 'I'll do it,' her sister says. 'Maybe we should spend some time with her before we leave this awful country.'

ON THE LAST evening of Bibi's stay in Calcutta, Bibi's mother brings out an old iPad. Bibi's hope, when she gave her mother the iPad, was that they would use video chat, closing the distance between Calcutta and Delhi. But her mother found the technology too challenging and Bibi, after a few days of hopeless tutoring, lost patience.

Yet now her mother seems surprisingly capable as she opens a browser and pulls up an article on the BBC website. The article is about a distant cousin of Bibi's in Guwahati. Bibi does not remember this cousin. From what her mother says, he is a man who has done well in recent years, although he too is haunted by the possibility of his name featuring on the D list. He owns a car and a flat in a housing complex that has recently come up on the outskirts of the city. His children go to a private school and his wife runs a beauty parlour. Bibi nods as her mother offers these details and reads the article, which describes how one afternoon, just as her cousin was about to get into his new car in the ground-floor garage of his new flat, he was attacked by a leopard.

Disoriented, the leopard had fled through the streets of Guwahati, she reads. It ran into a politician's victory procession. Lotus flower banners waved in the breeze and men symbolically slashed the air with hengdang swords, chanting that they would send D citizens back to Bangladesh or to their graves. When the leopard manifested, pausing in its panicked but graceful run, the politician's bodyguards opened jittery fire with their short carbines. Bullets ricocheted off cars and embedded themselves in the plaster and concrete of new construction. Bullets missed the leopard, missed a D citizen foolhardy enough to come near this procession, missed those wanting to send D citizens back to Bangladesh or to their graves. The leopard ran for cover, seeking refuge in the dark, ground-floor garage of Bibi's cousin's building, flattening itself out under the chassis of his ocean-blue Honda Aspire.

THE BBC PAGE carries a photo of the encounter, taken from a security camera in the garage. Both leopard and man look equally terrified. The leopard is rising on its hind legs, its forepaws reaching out towards Bibi's cousin in a frantic sweep. Its jaws are wide open, its nostrils flaring. She can see the fear in her cousin's eyes as he tries to defend himself, his scalp already bleeding from the gash opened up by the leopard's right paw. His fists are up, his right leg raised in what looks like an effort to kick out at the leopard. There is a curious symmetry to their postures, a mirroring that transcends their species difference.

But there is a divide between them for all that, some tremendous abyss on whose opposite sides they stand even when in such apparently close proximity. Bibi's cousin has intruded into the leopard's world. Yet the surroundings, the unpainted concrete walls and floor, and the drab wheeled coffins of metal parked around them suggest that it is the leopard who is the trespasser, that it does not belong on this planet, that it is marooned here.

Bibi's mother talks about her cousin's injuries. Bibi keeps looking at the leopard. She feels its exhaustion and its rage, feels the smell of human blood in her nostrils, as if, like a character from one of those tales set in the Sundarbans, she herself is turning into a leopard.

THAT NIGHT, BIBI is unable to fall asleep. As small, emaciated Calcutta cats yowl plaintively into the night, she thinks of the leopard. What can it do where must it run how will it get away? How can it get back to the forest the dirt the leaves the rock, to the white disc of the night and to its own echoing barks chasing the dip of the valley and the rise of the hills?

Sleepless, she thinks of Anand, of seeing him after all these years. What could have been, what might have been, what has been, the frantic beat of these possibilities pounding in her heart. She thinks of Sanjit, of his love letter that had to come disguised as a story about the New Delhi Monkey Man. She wonders if he is truly alive, somewhere.

At four in the morning, she gives up on sleep. The cockroaches scuttle in collective panic from the rubbish bin under the sink as she enters the kitchen to make herself tea. Through the window furred with dust and grease come the soft noises of daybreak. The inquiring trill of a bicycle bell sounds sweet in its early morning solitariness, a lone rider wheeling across the housing estate that is for now mostly deserted and empty, its faded colours and mildew-streaked concrete possessing a melancholy beauty in the dawn light.

The arrival of the day will bring rubble and dust. It will bring giant Rorschach blots of cow shit and the sharp, ammonia-laced smell of the garbage dump behind the luxury housing complex built just a decade ago. It will insert the horns of cars and motorcycles, the sound of ring tones and loudspeakers, the thump of hammers and cement mixers as an old house is demolished, another pond filled in and a new block of flats put up by men who call themselves real estate promoters.

For now, though, there is still peace in the neighbourhood as

Bibi sits in the balcony with her tea. Another cycle bell rings and fades as more light filters through from the places she misses. In Meghalaya, in Assam, in Manipur, in the northeastern hills where India comes to an end, it is already morning.

She starts when she hears her mother's slippers striking the floor. But when she looks into the bedroom, her mother is still asleep, deep in Calmpose stupor, and in any case she hasn't walked so swiftly for many years now. That sound has been made by a ghost of her mother's, some what-could-have-been, counterfactual mother pacing the rooms, who knows that Bibi is trying to gather herself for what she must do when she returns to Delhi, who asks Bibi to find something, even if it is just a little patch of light, to illuminate her way through the heavy, gathering darkness.

Then other familiar Calcutta sounds flood in, the bass of the crows jamming with the shrill sparrows, a bird band performing just for Bibi, playing just outside the balcony. Then, because it is still dark in the balcony and no one can see her beyond her silhouette, Bibi weeps, the convulsion running all through her body even as the tears flow along her face.

17

The evening after her return from Calcutta, Bibi leaves work earlier than usual. The streets are crowded, a granular summer wind lashing at her face. Traffic is gridlocked along the radial and arterial roads of Connaught Place, the syncopated honks and Bollywood beats of stalled cars competing with dopplering police sirens and ambulances. The usual pedestrians are jammed into the pavements in front of her, maddened commuters desperate to make their complex connections jostling against the hustlers and loiterers, these latter mostly distraught, unshaven men clutching mobile phone chargers and packs of faded postcards who seem to be just one step away from a complete breakdown.

THE MARCHERS COMING down the street are different, stoic figures in dusty white clothes holding red banners that bring a sudden, playful touch to the grim, grey city. Stewards, running back and forth, use shouts and hand gestures to direct the turn of the marchers onto Sansad Marg. Bibi has the illusion she is looking at a large beast, its snout aimed towards the parliament. A ripple of motion flows backwards as the avant-garde of the marchers halts temporarily, somewhere just past Jantar Mantar, where they have encountered the first of the yellow metal barricades bristling with sticks, guns and water cannons.

Hammer and sickle, hammer and sickle, a last-gasp whisper from past centuries, a utopian dream that must own up to its dystopian terrors, the gulag and the cultural revolution and the surveillance and the bureaucratisation and the militarisation and the environmental despoliation, its futile attempts to mimic its enemy, but that, having carried out its long search of the soul, is here in another iteration in Delhi on this July evening in what is almost like a final attempt for humanity.

Bibi finds a doorway from where to stand and watch the marchers. There are some youngsters moving perfectly in step, the boys with red patkas tied in topknots, the girls with double plaits held together with red ribbons, tireless in spite of the miles they have trekked. The adults approach, wearing red turbans and dupattas to go with their white clothes, their banners and flags displaying a face that stares at Bibi with the same appearance she once adopted for her school play with the help of her father's hat and an inked-in moustache. It is the face of Bhagat Singh.

'This group's from Talwandi Salem,' Mohinder says, slipping into the doorway next to Bibi. The tea towel he normally uses to cover his amputation flutters from his shoulder. His stump, conical and smooth, peeps out from the short sleeve of his uniform tunic, gloriously visible to all. With his left hand, Mohinder strokes his moustache, as thin and precise as Bhagat Singh's. The column, standing in place for a while, begins to move again. There are roars, a joyous, chaotic chorus that the first set of barriers have been removed, that the masters have agreed, if reluctantly, for the people to approach them in their palace.

The red turbans give way to white ones and a scattering of green eye patches as a new group approaches. Not everyone is young, not everyone marches under the hammer and sickle, and not everyone can be said to be marching. A woman groans as she limps by, her gnarled feet scraping the ground, the stick taking her weight. Others shuffle past, faces and hands weather-beaten, skin cancer-ravaged. Even the young in this group look fast-tracked onto old age.

But for all that, they are not completely broken. They are not a mob or a rabble, even if saffron-clad kanwariyas have begun bubbling up at the edges of the column to jeer the marchers as they turn on to Parliament Street and constables of the Delhi Police are stepping out from lorries, tapping sticks on shields in their usual inviting, expectant way.

'Where are these farmers from?' Bibi asks as a new group approaches.

'From Mohammadpur,' Mohinder says.

They huddle in the doorway as the pavement is slowly overrun by men who look like plainclothes cops, who seem to have an understanding with the kanwariyas and the khaki uniforms across the metal fence that separates crowded pavement from crowded asphalt. Men with brush moustaches, cropped hair and comfortable sneakers, wearing shirts that are loose, the better to conceal the bulge of a nine millimetre pistol.

'From Nandigram, from Armoor, from Wahkaji,' Mohinder continues.

'You know every contingent, Mohinder? What would SS do if he heard you talking like this?'

'He would say, "Why do they hire a guy with one arm to do the security?"' Mohinder replies in perfectly American English, his voice all drawl. 'But he would not hear me. If he did, he would not understand me. You understand because you still hope that other worlds are possible.'

Startled, Bibi looks at him. But Mohinder has fallen silent, and the marchers demand her full attention. Emaciated sharecroppers walk past, but also men and women with flowers in their hair, anklets on their feet, bows and arrows slung on their backs along with large-eyed infants. A banjara caravan goes by, complete with a row of camels, sand-coloured, grumpy-looking creatures decked out in bridal finery, a baby camel suspended in a sling from its mother's furry, humped torso. People delineated by the British as criminal tribes and called savages by the Indian elites.

'From Shahipur, from Dhalaibil, from Bhalukbari,' Mohinder says to Bibi, rattling off names that sound like distant echoes from a long-forgotten world. 'From Charai Dang, from Bhatinda, from Idinthakarai and from Kumarettiyapuram,' he chants. His eyes are bloodshot, and he is in a trance. He looks like he is made of smoke. He sways on his feet, a man who has been sleepless for centuries.

In spite of the rising noise in the streets and the arguments beginning to break out as kanwariyas and plainclothes cops make experimental forays into the crowd, Mohinder seems to become ever more reflective, lost in his memories. 'I want to send you a video story,' he says to Bibi. 'A story about some of the worlds that are possible.'

IN FRONT OF them, the farmers have come to a complete halt. There are shouts, messages being passed down the line from the front of the column that has run into the police barricades. The drivers and bus passengers caught in the stalled traffic roll down their windows and lower the volume on their music so that they can photograph and film. Other vehicles are somehow working their way through the gridlock. Police trucks with wire netting on windscreens and camouflaged personnel carriers trailed by a row of OB vans, each with the logo of a different media conglomerate and a large Indian tricolour. A group of farmers waits, clutching Pepsi bottles in their hands. This is not a left group. Instead of hammer and sickle flags, they hold only these bottles, dented, much used, filled with translucent yellowish liquid.

'They are going to drink their own piss in protest,' Mohinder says. His voice is barely a whisper. It is not clear that he approves.

Bibi watches as, to the jeering of the onlookers and the frantic scurrying of competing television crews, the farmers open the bottles and hold them up. She does not know if what is on the faces of these people is abjection or agitprop, this contingent of men and women who came prepared to demonstrate their misery, who knew, unlike their hammer and sickle comrades, that they would never get any closer than this to power and its indifference.

They raise the plastic bottles of piss, letting the television cameras zoom in before they begin to drink. A series of pops rivets holes in the evening, followed by the tinkle of metal rain on stone. A canister bounces off the roof of a television van and a bottle goes flying out of a farmer's hand, its contents scattering on to the road in tiny, glittering, lemon-yellow fractals. A stun grenade slams into the fence separating pavement from street and explodes in a blinding flash of light. The ringing in Bibi's ears gives way to utter silence. Then, as she gasps for breath, the sounds flood back into her ears, the explosions and screams and shouts, even as another canister hits the pavement right in front of her.

Mohinder dances out, scarf wrapped around his face. He grabs the canister, swivelling his torso, and Bibi, astonished, looks as his right arm, not his left, takes the canister and arcs out for the throw. His hips pivot, and the right arm gets longer, ever longer, the arm that has been amputated all these years from an accident in a machine press, an arm that is now inhuman as it snakes out over the heads of the crowd and the police vans disgorging their masked, helmeted forces, an arm that tosses the tear gas grenade all the way back into the heart of a heartless parliament. Then Mohinder is just a small, disabled man, a security guard who sometimes doubles as the office peon, blinking as he pulls his scarf tighter around his face with his only hand, his left hand, as he and Bibi run, trying to make for the twisting, curling alleyway at the back of Regal Building.

Behind them, the screams and shouts are punctuated by the sound of metal downpour as more tear gas shells impact with the ground. People rush after Mohinder and Bibi into the alleyway, sometimes colliding with one another in panic, sometimes pausing to help a comrade. The overrun from the water cannons laps at the edges of the street, carrying broken twigs, dirt and solitary rubber sandals.

Bibi runs, pursued by the smell of burning chillies, eyes watering. She looks for Mohinder, but she cannot find him. Her clothes smell of piss and vinegar.

18

Mohinder's video is a dimly lit monochrome. Half-moons cupping his eyes, he shivers against a blank wall. Bibi can't see his arms. Another man comes and sits next to Mohinder, a man whose features she cannot make out because he is wearing a monkey cap. The man in the monkey cap looks at Mohinder and scratches himself in a manner fantastically simian. Mohinder begins to speak.

'I TOOK THE iron road out of my village in the spring of the millennium, the migrant train rocking its way over the mud-drenched plains. New century, same old world, millions of us riding the trains, millions doing ghost labour shifts at demonic mills, millions never in the records of companies that evaded medical costs and pensions by keeping us off their books.

'One bright morning in Himachal, a boy who roomed with us did not return from the spring where he had gone to fetch water. I found him lying next to the jerrycans, dead, but with not a scratch on him, suggesting almost that he had left his body temporarily and might return at any moment. None of us knew who he really was, where he had come from. We pooled together money to give him a cremation, divided his things among ourselves. Among his meagre belongings, we found prescriptions, receipts, X-rays from a hospital in Bhopal. Nasir, a cutter in a garment factory, and Dipak, who worked with me moving drums of fluorescent dye across a slimy floor, had some schooling and looked through these things together. They took a long time about it. Then they began to quarrel. Dipak said that the boy had some fatal sickness they had told him about in the Bhopal hospital, some fever of the lungs that eventually killed him. Nasir said we should take the papers to someone, maybe a reporter. They had been experimenting on him in the hospital, he said. In the X-rays, you could see something like lights inside his body. Like the New Delhi Monkey Man, he said, who, with his special helmet and special buttons and special shoes, was able to leap from building to building.

'We knew no reporters and let them squabble. Then everyone had to go to their shifts, and the papers were forgotten. Within three days, a supply order was cancelled, the lines closed down. We were all out of work and went our separate ways.

'No special powers came to me at the garment factory in Punjab where I went after that. I found no invention that could ease my burden at the steel factory in Goa where I worked next as a Tongsman, my face covered with a mask of rags, my hands encased in safety gloves I had to pay for out of my own wages. There, I shuffled to the beat of the production line with another Tongsman, the two of us using giant tongs to seize a red-hot rod as it shot out of the furnace, moving it to the cooling tank, stepping in and out like dancing bears on a chain, responding to the call of that factory fire vomiting out metal bones, in and out with body braced to take rods that weighed thirty kilos.

'In the dead of the night, when the liquor had been almost finished and the film on the television flickered with letters rather than pictures, we talked about rumours, of supervisors who came to a bad end, of spirits who haunted factory floors, of workers who acquired special powers. The right words, said at the right moment with the right ingredients, could give you the ability to leap through time so that you never felt the iron cage of work shifts. Some spells could turn you invisible when the ticket checker's eyes fell on you on the railway platform. Still others endowed you with the capacity to produce government papers—identity cards and legacy documents that would prove you had entered India before the cut-off date. Someone then inevitably talked of the New Delhi Monkey Man, whose buttons, flickering blue or red, had frozen his pursuers, neutralising the Delhi Police with their red-and-blue lights on vans that said, "For You, With You, Always".

'Then there was no more work as a Tongsman, no more money for buildings lying around like half-empty shells, the rods that we made at our factory sticking out of unfinished shopping mall floors like iron reeds in a concrete pond. I took the train again, going north and east. For a while, I worked on the trains themselves, a pani pare on the old Grand Chord line, where the train came to mysterious halts inside the ghost-ridden tunnels of Gujra Gujhandi, goat-skin bag swinging from my shoulder as I poured out water for passengers in the unreserved coaches, filling their empty plastic bottles again and again, while outside the compartment, it seemed to me, in the sliver of darkness between the train and the walls of the tunnel, thousands of nameless others waited for me to quench their thirst too, their eyes and mouths like desert wells dried up without centuries of rain.

'From there, I went to work at an incline mine shaft in Jharia, swinging my pick at rock with thick veins of black coal, sweat streaming under my helmet, the heavy battery pack cutting into my bare torso. My fellow miners told me about the ancient nameless things, child-sized guardians of underground treasures, who watched us from the darkness with their glowing eyes, creatures who had lived underground far longer than mining companies, who were older than the British, older than the Muslims, older than the Hindus. Sometimes, the creatures tried to trick us into going into an abandoned shaft. Their eyes glowed in the dark like headlamps to mislead a lone miner, send him astray. Sometimes, one would show up in uniform, like a fellow miner, and it would walk in our column to throw off the count. The supervisors would have trouble at shift end, cursing that the count was always one more or one less. But the creatures gave me no special power of theirs and I could not dissolve through the coal walls like them, sink into the pit in one place and come up in another far away.

'I got taken in on a road gang then, passing buckets of stones to feed a ravenous cement mixer shaking with malarial fever on a smoky, wet-pitched highway near Bilaspur. Paramilitary convoys with heavy machine guns mounted on their roofs passed by on their hunt for Maoist guerrillas hiding in the forests. Trucks with the logos of mining companies, Indian flags on their roofs and minerals in the back, went the other way. We on the road crew didn't look at them, didn't look up when a sanpharki snake bird flew above us, a creature that gave you bad luck if its shadow fell on you, although who could have more bad luck than us, we who never had any other kind of luck at all?

'I left the flat plains behind to work spreading out hundreds of kilos of army laundry on wintry, golden fields in the upper reaches of a misty town called Shillong. My dhobi companions and I called each other fond names and made bawdy comments about each other's asses while we sorted out the military green and camouflage fatigues. In spite of our vigorous washing on the banks of the Umshyrpi River, upstream from the tin and wood shacks occupied by migrants like us whose ramshackle communal toilets emptied straight into the river, we found bloodstains on the clothes. Sometimes, a smear of dried flesh, sometimes a fragment of tooth or bone. We cleaned the uniforms. Then we spread them out, detergent-scented, on the fields, arranging them like a message to gods or aliens in astonished orbit around Earth.

'Come liberate us from the inhumanity of our times, we signalled. The sky seemed to shimmer then, the cicadas fell silent and the clouds took on the shape of faces. But no response came back, and no alien power or invention was dropped amid the pine trees for us to use and so we sat like circles of shadows at night, those on the inner circle passing a burning joint, while others, on the outer circle, measured out their doses far more carefully than any army surgeon attempting to extract a confession with a truth serum, cooking one capsule powder of Spasmo Proxyvon with one millilitre of water in a Pepsi bottle cap before injecting it into a vein.

'Then, one day, when I was back here, in Delhi, working at a car parts factory in Manesar, a sudden, dizzy spell confused me and I forgot the difference between an auto part and a human part. The labour contractor cursed me and his own fate as he drove me to the civil hospital in Gurugram. He took me to the ICU, where they shouted that they had no staff and asked us to go to Safdarjung Hospital in Delhi. But the contractor had many other responsibilities, and so he left me there, bleeding on to the dirty, sticky floor, where I sat clutching my severed right arm with my left hand and looked at a smiling poster of a prime minister promising a clean India, a new India, until someone gave me an injection and I passed out. When I woke up, a man in the bed next to mine was holding out a plastic pouch of local hooch. It would help with the pain, he said.

'In the dark, his face was hard to see. But an arm was visible, unusually hairy. The fingernails on the hand offering me the pouch were long and sharp. An animal fug came from him, a sensation of vertigo and darkness. How do I open a pouch with one hand? I asked in desperation. Use your teeth, he said, scoffing. Where do you think you are? In a five-star hotel? In business class? My throat burnt as I emptied the pouch and drank the hooch. I passed out. In the middle of the night, I woke up, my right arm itching madly. Only when I tried to scratch it and touched the bandaged stump did I remember that I no longer had a right arm.'

'HOW MUCH TIME did I spend in that hospital ward in Gurugram? Other patients came and went, accompanied by weeping relatives whose fears and anxieties stank up the room. I saw dogs, street curs that looked unusually well fed, possibly because they had a working arrangement with the hospital staff about discarded body parts and stray babies. Impatient nurses jostled with loutish attendants while a doctor came by every now and then, shouting into his phone because the network was weak, the calls always being dropped. I was surely not allowed to occupy my hospital bed for long, not when there was no one to pay for it, and yet it felt to me that I spent months there, just as it seemed to me, lying awake in the night with a fierce itch in my right arm that could never be scratched, that it was only the two of us in that ward, perhaps even in the entire hospital, me and my neighbour with his mysteriously endless supply of local hooch that was better than any medicine.

'He told me of the strike at the Honda factory, of the bouncers brought in to beat up the workers, of the false cases and years of imprisonment the strikers spent as undertrials, of the wives who travelled for days, taking unpaid leave from their jobs, to see them in prison and were then denied permission to meet their prisoner husbands. There was no need for any of this information, I told him, although I added that I appreciated his generosity with the hooch. My bandaged stump was ample evidence that I knew the ways of the world, as was the fact that neither the labour contractor nor anyone from Sri Ram Auto had come to the hospital after I was deposited there. I liked my stories spicy with my hooch, I said, with a little chopped onion and some green chilli, or if available, with a dab of bhut jolokia, ghost pepper chutney, a taste for which I had picked up in the northeastern fringes of my wandering.

'So my neighbour told me tales of factory robots gleaming with lubricating oil conducting a go-slow on the assembly line, eyeless heads tilted together as they recited automatic poetry to each other. He told me about aliens walking on a red planet and sea monsters that lay submerged in water so deep that it was black not blue, each flicker of their lidless eye like a century in human time, and of djinns and angels and fairies that clung to the bottom of passenger aircraft when they got tired of flying. He talked of Artificial Intelligence becoming sentient, reaching out from computers to communicate with mutated creatures like him, part animal, part human, AI that struggled with guilt and shame and fear, that made mistakes, tried to correct their errors and reflected, in infinite strings of code shaped like helices, on right action and an end to suffering.

'He talked about a farmhouse where he was taken one night by a Delhi Police van with vomit stains on the floor, wired netting on the windows, and a slogan on its side that said, "For You, With You, Always", its red and blue lights switched off because they had figured out a thing or two by now about pursuing him. In the farmhouse, which had nothing to do with farming, they kept him in a single cell and fed him red and blue tablets. In his disturbed dreams, a news anchor shouted and a man with a trimmed white beard grinned at a man with a trimmed black beard. He heard the sound of people being moved around, other prisoners. Some were brought in for experiments, he believed. Others, Muslims, Kashmiris, were kept in reserve for the moment when the Special Cell of the Delhi Police needed a dead body or two for an encounter. It was exactly like the detention centre in Assam he had known, the one that had been both a kill farm supplying undocumented border crossers every time the army or police required terrorist corpses and a laboratory for experimental subjects like him and the one who became known as the Bear Man. His memory came back to him in bursts. He was sick all the time in that farmhouse, but paradoxically, he was also stronger than he had been ever before. His arms were thick and hairy. When he took off his shirt and looked at his chest, he could see lights glowing, first red and then blue, just under the surface of his hairy skin.

'There were times, of course, when I suspected that I was delusional, that I was imagining everything, hallucinating that my neighbour looked furry as he told me his stories late into the night, lights glowing in his chest, wearing a motorcycle helmet that had mysteriously appeared out of nowhere. How was it possible that two nearly illiterate patients at a municipal hospital could talk such high philosophy, in such complex language, when all those people educated in computers and English had not very much more to say than kill all Muslims?

'I thought then that he was the New Delhi Monkey Man only in the way I was a man with a right arm that still itched. Then it became clear to me that the stories I heard, or thought I heard, were all unreal, their teller as well as the tales; that the man on the bed next to mine was a dying alcoholic or addict; that this place was not some strange, otherworldly hospital where time and space worked differently but a place that did not exist at all and that everything was the fertile, fervent dream of a pauper asleep in some hole under a concrete flyover or a long, drawn-out moment in a life being extinguished in an accident that had involved far more than a right arm being sliced off by a machine press.'

An incredible static interrupts the voice. Bibi can't make out what is being said. Mohinder and the man next to him can no longer be spotted in the flickering of images. Jerky footage of wind blowing over reddish soil. A monkey face in a helmet reflecting off a metal panel. Another burst of static takes over. The pictures are now black-and-white. Iron bars and barbed wire and glass walls. Eyes and limbs in an uncanny valley where animals look human and humans mirror automata. Then, briefly, he is there, bearded and gaunt. Sanjit. Bibi rewinds, hitting pause, zooming in. She thinks she can make out a metal cot, a hospital bed on which he is lying. Eyes wide open. If he is saying anything, she can't hear it in the static.

Pausing the video, she calls Mohinder's number. No one picks up.

The static fades, Mohinder and his companion return to the frame. The voice continues.

'Yet if it was a dream, it did not stop. If it was a hallucination, it did not end. If it was an imagined story, it continued to unfold. Now, other details began to insert themselves into my consciousness. Despite the air of negligence and squalor, of a municipal hospital just barely kept functioning for the dregs of society, I felt that my neighbour and I were constantly monitored. At the dead of night, when the stories had been silenced in trails of drool and vomit, masked figures different from the usual assortment of hospital staff emerged from the surrounding darkness to cut and to stitch, to take samples and measurements, figures that included white people speaking English as well as Indians, people who faded in the hot air just as I woke up to scratch that right arm and found that it really wasn't there.

'Then, one night, my dazed sleep was interrupted by the sound of the New Delhi Monkey Man screaming. It was time, he shouted, and the boats of our ancestors were coming in from the oceans and from the skies. Our masters would try their best to stop them, seize their magic boats, chain their ghost spirits, steal everything and turn it into what they called holy profit. But it was time, he screamed, and not even the masters could fight them all—the ghosts of our ancestors, the robots rising in the factories and the AI coming awake inside computers. They would try, but they would not be able to crush them all, the angels and the monkey men, the sky and the water.

'I pushed myself up on my bed, swung my legs on to the ground. I forgot that I was unbalanced, with more weight on one side than the other. I toppled over to my left like a baby with a too-large head. I cursed and corrected myself, reached out towards New Delhi Monkey Man. Looking at me from under his motorcycle helmet, he told me that he had a gift for me, but a gift I would receive only in a time that was still to come and when I would not really be alive. He had leapt into the future, he said, to a building being constructed in front of the hospital to house people who worked for our masters. In that future building, he said, connected to a hospital across the oceans, connected to farmhouses and to prisons, to places with secrets and to secret places with prisoners, he had left things for those I would come to know, things that he hoped would give people the courage to break free of their shackles, things that would make life difficult for the masters as they played their games of world domination and holy profit, although neither he nor the boatmen were sure that they were going the right way about any of this. They still had so much to learn.

'He fell silent and looked down at the lights flashing on his chest. I had the impression that the hospital room we were lying in had become as big as a graveyard, that we were the only people in the graveyard and that, even as I reached out to comfort him, our beds were moving farther and farther away from each other like they were coffins afloat in a vast flood. Then he asked me to save him because the masters were sucking him into their laboratory with a generator, he said, they wanted to carry out more experiments, he said, they wanted him to pilot the Mars mission, he said, and they did not want him to get on to the magic boat of his ancestors, he cried.

'He seemed then to swirl and eddy in a vortex, as if he really were New Delhi Monkey Man really being pulled into some demonic laboratory. I found myself reaching for him with my right arm, forgetting that it did not exist. But as I did so, my stump became an arm, and then this arm became something else, became incredibly long, became an arm that went on and on, an arm infinitely elastic and incredibly pliable so that I could, if I wanted to, send it out of the hospital ward, around the corridor, down the stairs, past the holes where the elevators had not been put in, past the extended families of dogs looking for body parts and unattended babies to feed on, pausing to scratch the flea-ridden ear of one such dog before going out of the hospital, and still I could keep going with this arm that was like an unending string for a red paper kite, this arm that was like a schoolgirl's red hair ribbon unfurling forever, and I could keep going with it out of Gurgaon, which had been renamed Gurugram, to Delhi, which had not yet been renamed anything, reaching over security barricades and under sentry towers until I found myself flying over municipal parks overrun with weeds and ant hills, over rotting trees entangled around collapsed buildings, over automobiles rusted into mounds of blackish red speckled with the white of human bones while yellow-grey smoke rolled as far as I could see, through the ruins of the parliament and the presidential palace and the war memorial, while shadows that resembled monkeys but were kitted out in spring-heeled boots, motorcycle helmets and jumpsuits that displayed rows of pulsing buttons, frolicked on brown, desiccated lawns and in sludge-filled canals, while, in the ruins of markets and malls, kanwariyas with glazed eyes and question marks in their eyes instead of pupils queued with infinite patience in front of ATM machines whose screens were filled with unending loops of the prime minister until night fell in this strange place and two moons rose, one far bigger than the other, and in their joint yellow light, I saw a vast balloonship float by, a slow, ponderous creature on whose sides were painted sigils in red, blue and white and a circle of five blue eyes and I wanted to go farther and see what was outside this sinister Delhi and its surroundings, but then I remembered New Delhi Monkey Man and stopped, and I pulled my right arm back into the hospital and I used it to hold New Delhi Monkey Man, pulling him back from the generator sucking him in, holding firm with my long right arm, holding him to my chest like a father holding a baby until the generator pulling him faltered, holding strong with a right arm that really shouldn't be there this hairy man monkey who really shouldn't exist, holding, holding, as we seemed to be dissolving into each other, until, suddenly, we became separate beings again and his bed became a boat and his ghost ancestor sat in it, his man-monkey ancestor, a boatman who turned a face towards me that was no face at all, and then the boatman pulled at his oars and the boat was gone.'

THE SCREEN GOES black. Bibi texts Mohinder and watches the video again.

19

The summer heat is trapped between earth and grey haze. A still layer of moisture sits on Bibi's skin, present just at the pores, her body like parched soil being forced to relinquish every last drop of fluid. Sleepless, she sits at the back door of the flat with a pack of cigarettes, exhaling into the still air, tapping ash on to exposed rebar. Sanjit's face, shimmering in her mind and churning her restless sleep until she explodes into wakefulness at this witching hour.

In the morning, the sky presses down upon her. It attempts to iron out the kinks in her character, erase the questions she is trying to form as she pulls up his face on the screen, expanded and isolated into a still from Mohinder's video.

She can't find Mohinder. He doesn't respond to her calls and messages and he is not to be seen at Amidala. There is talk of Amidala being shut down and it is not clear whether Mohinder has been fired or if he has simply stopped coming to work.

Bibi asks Akanksha if she has Mohinder's address. The receptionist's nails are bitten to the roots and her eyes rimmed with sleeplessness. Her affair with Veer is quite over. In a sudden burst of confidence, she shows Bibi her drawings. Eyes, limbs, wings faintly discernible through swirling smoke and wired netting. She has been having visions in her dreams, she says.

BIBI GETS IN touch with people who knew Sanjit. They ask her where she has been all these years, tell her of the things she has missed. Has she been keeping track of the arrests? Does she know how many people have been lynched, how many other than Sanjit are dead? Her interviewees listen to her questions about Amidala, the farmhouse people, the video. Sometimes, they offer her an additional detail, a new name or two, tracing faint outlines around the man who is Preitty's business partner, who is both arms dealer and agent of the deep state, close to the government that wants a superweapon and to the companies building that weapon. Always, they ask her to be careful.

AKANKSHA GIVES BIBI a rudimentary address for Mohinder. Taking a day off work she rides the Metro away from the city. Patterns of dust carpet the gleaming interior of the carriages. Thin young men with veiny forearms, their clothes a step above rags, rock in restless sleep on the stainless steel benches, mouths open. Women with covered heads slump on the ladies seats. The dirt on the floor of the carriages a reminder of the collision between two worlds, the unequal city extending its steel spokes and the countryside that is being churned, the grime and the rural passengers like the clues to some immense, unsolvable crime.

From the metro, she rides a rickshaw along the fraying edge of the city. Multistorey buildings hover, like poorly constructed spaceships, at the end of twisting alleyways of lopsided shacks and open drains. The ruins of old brick houses sitting like rotting teeth in lots earmarked for new construction. A giant sign for Boeing Aerospace Corporation looming over a new city coming into being, its boundaries edged by corrugated tin walls and low plastic tents around which small, dark figures clear rubbish with primitive tools in the blistering heat. The rickshaw passes a building that has no front but where people can be seen working in their individual offices, talking on phones and sitting in front of desktop computers like actors on some elaborate stage set.

Villages are metamorphosing into slums where the rickshaw drops her off. The air smells of sewage, cooking oil and raw onions. But at the tenement that Mohinder has given as his address, rows of brick houses without windows, the woman who answers her knock does not know him. 'A man with one arm?' Bibi asks. The woman laughs, says there are many men with missing limbs in this neighbourhood. As Bibi leaves, she sees a pond completely yellow, on whose saffron edges women bent like crows wash clothes and utensils, while behind them a blocky building rises, clad entirely in black glass, like a face wearing a mask.

BIBI GIVES UP on Mohinder. The sun drifts through the pollution haze like a runaway inmate as she searches for answers. No one believes Sanjit is alive. Everyone agrees that he would be out of work and possibly in prison if he were not dead. Heat ricochets between earth and sky, magnified by the glass-fronted buildings and the curved metal shields of cars. The encounters dislodge old memories in Bibi's head, conversations with Sanjit at the tea stall on ITO, just outside the newspaper office, their shared fantasies of disappearing and going off the grid. The sun shimmers off twisting steel sculptures meant to represent the rising power of India, giant bulbs straining up from thin, twisted stalks like bereft, perpetually uncoupled spermatozoa. Somewhere in the mountains, he said. Somewhere on an island, she replied, although she has never been on an island.

SS sends Bibi a cursory text message one day saying that she should look for a new job, that Amidala will cease to exist by the end of the summer. He attaches a series of emojis to the message, sunglass-wearing smiley faces.

MANGOES FLOOD THE market. The fruit seller in Rama Market tries to convince Bibi to buy what he calls a Brahmango, engineered by Ombani Labs. Bibi refuses and gathers her usual varieties. She eats them over the kitchen sink, her knife slicing a Langra, Dasheri, or Kesar into three segments. Juice dribbles down her chin, and she devours the sweet flesh like someone starving. Phone in hand, like she is expecting a call any moment, she sits at the back door, smoking into the night. She thinks about how, while she is looking for answers, they are always looking at her.

They are everywhere, present in the very architecture of the city, in its stones and its cables, in its yellow haze and its grey, grief-stricken sky, in the eyes that follow from posters and screens and in the cameras that blink steadily from computers and phones. She can sense the faint outline of their vast, fine surveillance net strung out against the day as morning comes over Munirka Village, the field of their totalising perception shifting subtly as she walks through the twisting, narrowing alleyways, past jutting balconies and hanging electric wires.

No one else seems to be aware of these observing others. In the narrow buildings rising above her, women with bony elbows and saris pulled far over their foreheads negotiate pots and pans in smoky kitchens. On the streets, diminutive female figures in knock-off jeans and polyester tops are killing time in front of stores before heading out for their call centre and salesgirl shifts. The largest of this group is clustered in front of a shop selling shiny dress shoes. So many forsaken Cinderellas.

Then, through a house gate left open, she observes Dhirender Tokas, the rival landlord to her landlord, reclining on a string bed and pulling at a coal-scented hookah. Resplendent in his pristine white clothes, he is staring intently. But he is not looking at her, his attention entirely on the children of the migrant workers playing in front of his tenement.

AT WORK, THERE is talk about a dust storm that appeared above Regal Building after the latest powercut. Akanksha shows Bibi a video of the storm uploaded on to social media. A tower of dust spirals like a giant spinning top over the Connaught Place skyline. Akanksha enlarges the image. The dust looks animate as it hovers over Regal Building, searching, seeking, before it begins to move across Central Park, heading in the direction of ITO and the Yamuna. Bibi sees what looks like wings extending out from the central cone of dust and sand.

Akanksha shows Bibi her latest drawings. Charcoal sketches of a winged dust storm, but one that is trapped behind a chain link fence. Bibi can make out something like a face. Manga eyes full of dismay or surprise.

THAT NIGHT, BIBI watches another dust storm from the back door of her flat for hours, tracking the shape hovering above the slum tenements. It resembles Mikael, the angel of mercy in the bedtime stories once told by her mother. Whirling and swaying in the haze, it produces a humming noise as it searches for something. She does not wake up at three that night. She dreams of Sanjit, of their old workplace at ITO. A meteor crashes through the sky. At the edge of what looks like the city, a few lights glitter. The darkness is overwhelming and the lights are melancholy, but Bibi feels strangely happy.

20

There is a crowd at ITO the next morning as Bibi exits the metro station. People are heading for the Yamuna to photograph the snow covering the river. Bibi makes her way past them into the service lane that runs across the newspaper offices.

She stares at *The Daily Telegram* building, ugly and grey, air conditioners barnacled along a carapace coated in PPM and grime. Everything seems to lead back here, to that time when she and Sanjit worked briefly in the same office. A black SUV interrupts her thoughts, honking impatiently. She moves out of the way so that it can disgorge its passenger. The man stepping down in pink dress shirt, laceless shoes and military moustache is Jagmohan, the chief editor. He stares at Bibi, checking her out, but does not recognise her as a former employee.

Bibi keeps walking, past the crowded tenements of the Valmiki sweepers and resettled refugees from the Partition, crossing a ragged park whose red innards lie exposed in giant, undulating anthills. Beggars squat in front of the ruins of Feroz Shah Kotla, staring at her in hope and expectation as they display their mangled limbs. Biryani carts are lined up across from them, their giant handis redolent with the aroma of saffron-spiked rice and grilled meat.

Old memories are dislodged in her head by the smell, tales of djinns and angels, creatures who exist in the intersection between human and divine. There is something about the beggars, a suggestion of other bodily forms, that makes her recall her dreams, of the dust storms wheeling across the city and of the New Delhi Monkey Man trapped in a cage. Without thinking, she pulls her dupatta over her head. The beggars interpret this as a practised gesture on her part and shift their attention away, content to wait for her return. Behind their cubist bodies, there is a ticket booth, empty and abandoned. A pair of metal gates bristling with sharp spikes lies wide open in invitation.

The sun pulses like a fresh bruise on the battered sky as Bibi goes through the gates. In the distance, across a Yamuna filled with white industrial froth passing for snow, the smokestack of a power plant adds its secretions to the haze. Metallic arms of light float over the cricket stadium, yellow blurs in an unending grey sea.

Bibi is struck by the openness of the squares she is walking through, by the steps rising up to the dirty sky. The scale of the place is disproportionate, expanding the farther she goes in. She has the sensation of being lifted off her feet, like she is whirling through the air. Crumbling walls of red and grey stone rise around her, with arched entrances that tunnel into narrow, black passageways.

A MOBILE PHONE rings somewhere inside the twisting passageway Bibi has entered. Loud, insistent, before being silenced abruptly. There is then only the flickering light of candles, the smell of burning incense and the blackened, soothing heaviness of the stone walls. Men and women move past Bibi in dreamlike stop-motion through the pointed arches. The black hijabs on the women no longer seem coarse and heavy. They ripple in the darkness and the women float, like angels, like djinns, like souls travelling between worlds.

A slash of red in the dark: blood on stone? No, just rose petals. Something brushes her face. The wings of a bird? Not a bird. She is standing under a cupola. She can see the bats, hundreds of them, hanging upside down in some kind of contortionist meditation.

She walks on, past sheets of paper torn from school exercise books, attached to the walls and inserted into the nooks and crannies. These are supplicants' letters to the djinn spirits who dwell here, she recalls from that visit years ago with Sanjit. People asking for cures for addiction, for love that will not break your heart, for relief from the unbearable cruelty of masters. In the darkness, Bibi allows prayers of her own to take shape in her head. Freedom for Moi, answers for herself.

A man steps out of the darkness towards her. There is something not quite right about him, something that is not human, Bibi thinks. He brings to her mind illustrations from children's books, drawings of animals forced into anthropomorphic postures. Foxes in pinstripes, crocodiles wearing judges' wigs, monkeys wearing helmets and jumpsuits. She thinks of the birdlike woman who trailed her around the department store. The man shuffles awkwardly in front of her. He is wearing a long black overcoat. It is far too big for him and seems absurd in the summer heat.

'Is there something you need to say?' Bibi asks.

The man nods. But he does not open his mouth. Bibi waits for a long time, with patience she does not know she possessed. The man shifts one way, then another, like a bashful child. Beneath the long coat, there extends something that looks remarkably like a scaly tail. He lifts his hands, mimes with digits that are like claws. The gesture is that of fingers tapping out a message on a phone.

21

Bibi is short of sleep the next morning as she directs her taxi across the thin, dark trickle of the Yamuna. In the smoky dawn, street sleepers shift restlessly under flyovers, the ground around them littered with plastic bottles and empty sachets. The taxi slows down when they come across a truck that has smashed into the back of another truck, its cab twisted, the windscreen shattered. Corkscrew-ridged steel rods are strewn everywhere, and a ghostly group of labourers, grey in the grey dawn, struggle to clear them off the road. Husks of shredded tyres litter the two-lane highway like moulted skin, as though some hybrid creature being transported to a secret facility has seized the opportunity of the accident to make a frantic escape.

The concrete blocks of middle-class neighbourhoods, staid, stolid structures concealing boundless despair, give way to waterlogged, uncultivated land blackened with industrial effluent. This early in the morning, the sun is a dim, copper glow in the sky. The taxi twists and turns along alleyways until it can go no farther and Bibi proceeds on foot.

The woman she talked to earlier is sitting outside her tenement door, combing her hair in long, slow strokes. She watches calmly as Bibi shows her the video, frozen in a close-up of Mohinder's face. She frowns, calls someone. A man steps out, looks at Bibi in surprise, and scrutinises the picture.

He talks to the woman in a low voice. Bibi sees the motion the man is making, slashing down on his own right arm. 'Mohinder,' the woman says. 'He was in an accident some years ago. The machine press sliced his arm off. My man says he bled to death on the floor of a government hospital.'

Death? Dead? It is not possible. Another accident, another rumour of death. Bibi keeps asking questions. How does the man know Mohinder died in the hospital? Was it not just hearsay? Did Mohinder have friends, someone she can talk to? With great reluctance, the man produces a name. Saleem the butcher, who works at the slaughterhouse. They will call Saleem and tell him that she is coming.

CROWS AND KITES wheel like harpies above Bibi as she steps out of the taxi outside a bunker-like slaughterhouse. The young butcher waiting for her is very handsome and very shy. He listens to her and says he does not know where Mohinder is but that he will take her to the technician. If she is Mohinder's friend, she will need papers. 'Papers? What papers?' Bibi asks, but already he is walking on, gesturing at her to accompany him.

They enter a wholesale poultry market, an unending settlement of concrete shacks stinking of chicken shit, the gutters lining the paved path red with avian blood. Skirting blue plastic drums and white broiler chickens stuffed into wire cages, they ignore the thin, insistent young men who ask them how much meat they want to order for the Brahmastra celebrations. Some of the workers are clustered outside a tea stall, holding out tiny glasses for a teenage boy who serves out tea at high speed, the men wincing but uncomplaining as the scalding liquid splashes on to their fingers. A few older Bengali men, wiry, with scraggly beards, stretch in exhausted sleep on a platform next to the small whitewashed room that serves as a mosque.

Beyond the poultry market is the fish market, far smaller in scale. The ground here is covered with shiny, glittering scales, iridescent in the strange sunlight, the passageway between the stalls clogged with the briny smell of the sea. Auctions are on everywhere, with people clustered around fat-bellied rohus, antennaed lobsters and small sharks kept in ice-packed thermocole boxes. Two African women walk past, dressed prominently in orange, stopping every now and then to look at the fish on display. They are accompanied by lewd comments every step of the way.

Bibi sees a pair of ragpicker children. A girl of six or seven with her hair cut very short, a white plastic sack over her right shoulder. She is guiding a toddler with her left hand. A fish comes flying from a stall and lands in the gutter. The girl looks around, lets go of the toddler and picks up the rotting fish. Reflexive shouts break out from the stall owners. The girl stops. When no one approaches her, she experimentally walks a few more steps with the fish, stops again as a new series of shouts begin.

Saleem the butcher approaches her, putting his wide-shouldered body between her and the shouting fish sellers. A Mars note, folded into a tight little wad, passes from his hands into that of the girl's, who has to put her plastic sack down to take the money and tuck it away inside her rag-like frock. Then she walks on with the toddler, holding the discarded fish in one hand and her sack in the other, heading for the broken wall at the end of the market. She turns every now and then to see that Saleem is coming with her.

A row of bulbous gas tanks painted dirty beige and stencilled with the logo of the Ombani Oil and Gas Corporation gives way to open ground. Even this early in the morning, the heat is fierce, bouncing off the hard dirt. They stop when they reach a canal. Most of the water has evaporated, and what remains is something the colour and consistency of Turkish coffee. Packs of blackened, feral dogs paddle in the sludge, trying to keep themselves cool. Their neck fur is raised in permanent, dirt-encrusted hackles. White canines gleam in their masked mudpack faces.

Beyond them, on the horizon, looms a giant, grey hill, a foot track cut into its side and winding up to the peak. There are people crawling along this vast hill, tiny, hunched-over figures with rags around their faces and hands, gathering things with incredible, Sisyphean patience into white plastic sacks. Fires flicker on the hill as cable insulation is burnt off to extract copper wiring. An acrid smell, laced with ammonia and rotting garbage, permeates the air.

THE GIRL GUIDES them to the edge of the canal and steps in. She does not sink. There is a path of sorts, Bibi sees as she gets closer.

A patchwork of bricks, wood and plastic. The children go first, then Saleem. Bibi does not want to think about what it might be like to fall into this sludge. Memories burst into her consciousness as she advances, teetering: two bamboo trunks lashed together to form a bridge jigsawing across spirulina-green water at the back of a military camp, her unsteady approach towards a detention centre that officially does not exist.

The ground squelches under their feet when they finish their crossing. It is almost alive, this sodden, plastic-coated earth, registering haptic feedback as they tramp towards the hill of waste. The boy skips, happy to be home. The girl leads on, through paths cut into the garbage, past dented car doors and air conditioners and refrigerator shells. There are huts and tents at the base of this hill of waste, a corona of human habitation ringed around the vast, amorphous peak rearing its smoking head of rubbish towards the sky for a blessing.

They stop in front of a man sitting outside a makeshift plastic tent. He has giant white sneakers on his thin but muscular legs. On his head, he wears a motorcycle helmet, grey matted locks cascading from the edges of the helmet. In his hands, he has a massive earthen chillum, fuming and pungent, from which he takes ferociously long drags before blowing out smoke with benign indifference.

Saleem talks to him while Bibi waits, reeling from the heat and the fumes. She cannot understand what they are saying. Her mouth is dry and she wishes she has some water with her. A pushcart is parked outside the tent, piled high with computer monitors, motherboards, printers and copying machines, everything caught in a tangle of wires and cables. The slope closest to her is a mass of plastic, rubber and metal. Bibi blinks, wipes the moisture away from her forehead with her scarf. She sees tablets, palmers, phones, cash registers, the bright colours of electric cables, the green and gold of circuit boards. Next to them is a heap of rusting car shells stripped of doors, tyres, and engines. Among them, she sees, implausible though this seems, the dented body of what looks like a fighter jet, crumpled like a tube of toothpaste.

Everyone moves into the tent, which is crammed with more

electronic junk. The sides of the tent are plastered with a patchwork of handbills, newspapers and old, discontinued banknotes from serial waves of demonetisation. Amid the cast-off material, there is an armchair and a desk, monitors and cables. The helmeted man sits at the armchair, pivoting vigorously. Saleem crouches down next to him. Fingers click on a keyboard as the man types in Bibi's information, teeth bared, looking like he is recalibrating government systems with nothing more than ganja-inflected indifference. Bibi hands over her old Aadhaar card and the receipts testifying to her D status, even as she wonders how any of this is possible. How can a shack in a garbage landfill have electricity or access to the internet? Who is this man?

Web pages load and LED lights blink as the man inserts a blank plastic card into a box. Electronic voices, static and the hum of a modem pulse through the heat-soaked tent. Someone asks Bibi for her phone. She hands it over, thinking she will be sick any moment now. She takes the Nokia out and gives that as well. The tent smells of dirt and ganja, but both men wear expressions of great concentration on their faces. They look like surgeons involved in the most delicate of operations, doctors bringing an adult child into life in some strange, otherworldly, maternity ward. Just outside the tent opening, the ragpicker children squat on their ground, their large eyes fixed upon Bibi.

She goes out and sits next to them. They have got rid of their sack and the fish. Each holds, instead, a cheap plastic cricket bat. The ground sways around her and she shuts her eyes. She remembers her dreams, the endless waiting in the government office, the dream children clutching their cricket bats. But there is no baby fat on the faces of these real-life children, has never been. Only the signs of eczema and malnutrition, their small bodies worn down by the toxic surroundings of the garbage landfill, their cells devouring each other in order to keep going.

Saleem comes out of the tent and presses a new Aadhaar card into her hand. The plastic is still warm.

'How much shall I pay you?' Bibi asks the helmeted man.

His laughter is deafening, ringing and reverberating in the open air, piquing the curiosity of the ragpicker children and setting them off on an echoing path of giggles. In Bibi's heat-dazed state, his chest seems to pulse with a string of lights alternating red and blue. He looks eight feet tall. When he has finished laughing, he glares at her. 'Why do you people find it so hard to understand?' he says. 'You don't pay me, you pay the boatman.'

WHEN BIBI GETS back to Munirka with her new Aadhaar card, Moi is standing stock still in the living room. The curtains are drawn, and she is illuminated by a single beam of sunlight that has somehow worked its way through the bird-patterned curtains. Always pale, Moi now looks transparent. She has become like her own description of the ghost she saw every evening at the orphanage in Ahmedabad, a ghost less frightening to her than her loyalty to the Bodo children trafficked to the orphanage from villages in Assam, its eerie manifestation never as terrifying as the possibility that her employers would discover they had misread her application and that she was actually a Christian.

One of Moi's string of many jobs, from the northeast of India to the western quadrant of the country, from the southern cone of the subcontinent to the DLF shopping mall palace at the heart of the capital. Orphanage warden, kindergarten teacher, Christian charity worker, call centre worker, saleswoman and waitress, a mishmash of labour that makes it seem like Moi has been living partly in the nineteenth century and partly in the twenty-first.

'Why aren't you at work?' Bibi says. She draws the curtains back, opens the back door.

A knock-off Louis Vuitton bag sits at Moi's feet, zipped up and strapped. Her eyes are bloodshot, the only spots of colour left in her face. Wordlessly, she hands her phone over to Bibi. The ticket on the screen is one way, from Delhi to Goa with a stopover in Bombay. Moi doesn't have to tell Bibi anything. The man from *The World* has finally come through.

THE FLAT IS hollowed out with loneliness when Bibi comes back from the airport. The floor is grainy under her feet, and a fetid, foul smell permeates the living room. The boundary between inside and outside has been erased with Moi's departure, some final holding, protecting charm having left with her.

Bibi opens the back door to let out the smell. Through the thick, yellow haze and the roar of evening traffic, she can make out the sound of bulldozers, engines and shouting men. The haze clears slightly. Bibi gasps. The slum across is gone. There is rubble everywhere, rubbish strewn amid the demolished shacks of brick and tin. Thin, agitated figures crowd a police vehicle. More police vans are arriving, trailed by an ambulance.

Men wearing surgical masks step out of the ambulance. A few constables begin to set up a perimeter with yellow metal barricades even as an OB van pushes its way through the alleyway, the satellite dish on its roof like an open, ravenous mouth. A solitary figure ignores the arrivals. She sifts through the rubble on her knees, searching for something.

BIBI CLOSES THE door. She mechanically begins to tidy up Moi's belongings, which are scattered everywhere. When she has finished, she counts the money she has taken out from the bank, leaving her balance well below the minimum. She adds it to the new Aadhaar card. Then she finds her bag and packs, pausing only to open the front door to let in more air. The smell in the flat is stronger than ever, like a burst sewage pipe.

Finally, when she goes to the bathroom, she sees the source of the problem. The squat toilet has overflowed, and there are dark turds floating in the brown water that has flooded on to the bathroom floor.

Bibi retreats to the far corner of the living room. She feels like crying and sits, hunched over, wishing Moi were here, even if she would do no more than scream that they have to get out of this country. Her phone announces the arrival of another message. Still, she crouches, waiting for the tears to come. Then she begins to laugh. She laughs even when a thin trickle of brown-yellow water appears under the bathroom door, spreading single-mindedly into the living room as if it is the earth that is weeping, dissolving itself in sympathetic pain with the fecal sky.

Bibi grabs her bag, takes her phone. She doesn't bother to lock the door behind her as shit water streams into the living room and begins to drip through the back door into the yard below. As she walks past the demolished slum, she sees the men in surgical masks holding up what looks like a very small body. The policemen shout at her as she stares and a white shroud is hastily thrown over whatever they have uncovered.

At the edge of the village, Bibi checks her phone. An unknown number. But not an unknown message. A fragment from a poem she knows all too well. LINDED IN? URNED BY? She recites the lines to herself:

I run past the Doll Museum, past
headlines on the Times of India
building, PRISONERS BLINDED IN A BIHAR
JAIL, HARIJAN VILLAGES BURNED BY LANDLORDS.

22

At Central Secretariat, Bibi transfers from the yellow line to the violet. A short ride, and then she is emerging from the underground into the controlled fury of a midsummer afternoon. The subway overhang at ITO is decorated with strips of black marble and shiny aluminium, the main wall painted a bright yellow to highlight the automobile tyre company that has bought advertising rights to the site.

She is in the landscape of *The Half-Inch Himalayas*, the book that was a gift from Sanjit, along with his New Delhi Monkey Man manuscript. The poem she remembers so well is called 'I Dream It Is Afternoon When I Return to Delhi', a fever dream of verse in which Agha Shahid Ali, Kashmiri, gay and insomniac in every place that is not Kashmir, imagines himself back in a dreamscape version of ITO.

The Doll Museum sits behind the subway overhang, somehow managing to look smaller than the Metro entrance even though in actuality it is far bigger. Concrete blending into concrete, grey upon grey, easy to miss in spite of being in plain view. In her early, disorienting months in Delhi, as Sanjit and she shared the poet and his dream world, Sanjit had pointed out the Doll Museum to her. If he disappeared someday, she should come to the Doll Museum to find him, he had said jokingly. There would be at least a doll version of him in there.

A single row of colourful tiled panels mark the entrance to the Doll Museum. Dark-skinned women pounding rice and feeding animals, people from a mythical world that now does not exist even in the imagination. The ruins of the Third World.

The clerk at the tiny ticket window is slumped over in the late afternoon heat. His eyes are glazed as Bibi rouses him. He takes his time to turn his attention to her, first wiping his face with a damp handkerchief and then drinking water from a stainless steel tumbler with infinitesimal slowness. There is something satisfying about his slowness, his refusal to concede defeat to the new world of efficiency.

A small, dirty staircase takes her up to the first floor. She can hear the thump of printing presses from adjoining buildings, smell the cloying bite of industrial glue. There is a guard sitting outside the entrance on the first floor, a large man whose girth makes the low-ceilinged corridor even smaller. Bibi holds the ticket out, an old-school, cinema-style slip consisting of two thin, translucent strips of paper, the top yellow and the bottom pink.

'Passport?' the man says. His loathing for her is palpable.

'Passport?' Bibi replies. 'Why do you need my passport?'

'This ticket only for Indians. Go get a foreigner ticket.'

'No.' Bibi is aware of the shrillness of her voice, of the pounding of her heart and the fury in her veins.

'No? Then show me your Aadhaar card.'

'I'm not going to show you anything.'

'Okay, tell me,' the man says, his plastic chair creaking as he leans back, spreads his legs wide open and rubs his crotch. 'Who is the prime minister of India?'

An extended moment of silence ensues. Then Bibi says it, just so that she can go in.

The man's laughter is shockingly loud in that enclosed space. 'Are you sure?' he says, gesturing at her with an obscene movement of his large, fleshy hands. 'Which country are you coming from, woman? How long before all termites are washed into the sea?'

Blood rushes to Bibi's face as she pulls the door open and goes in. But inside too, there is no respite. To her right, lit up by fluorescent strips, stands a giant Hanuman bedecked with garlands of stitched-together Mars notes. His cheeks are pinkish, scrubbed raw, without a hint of facial hair. The woman who squats at his feet has a glazed look on her face and a question mark on her forehead.

'Wait,' the man behind Bibi says. He has followed her inside. He looms over her, boxing her in. Then he takes the ticket from her, keeping the yellow strip and handing the pink slip to the woman with the question mark.

The museum is utterly devoid of visitors. There is no discernible order to the arrangement of exhibits as short, sharp turns lead Bibi into cul-de-sacs lined with glass displays. The feeling Bibi has is of wandering inside a compact, compressed puzzle, one that unfolds to its own inner logic the deeper she goes.

Separate streams of time have collided in this museum. History has gathered in pools and eddies here and there; elsewhere, it is still travelling, in sudden spurts, along branch lines and forking paths. The Soviet Union has collapsed, and the dolls of that vast region in their white, embroidered tunics and immense furry boots represent an entity called the CIS states. Yet Yugoslavia is still there, with its own display cabinet, as is Kampuchea. Zaire exists, and its dolls include an action figure, fists raised, of the great Third World hero Muhammad Ali. There are NAM nations everywhere in this museum, and Bandung still survives, even if an oversized Hanuman and his strange human attendants have been inserted into the entrance in recent years.

Bibi imagines an old-fashioned Indian travelling the world and collecting dolls wherever he goes, his foreign hosts flooding him with artefacts once they discover his strange hobby, this weird, twentieth-century Noah building an ark in the ITO neighbourhood of Delhi, an ark not for animals but for humanity, so that when the world ends, when the slate is wiped clean, when the counter is reset to zero, this is all that will be left, these doll people, these miniatures in their ritual costumes dancing to doll harvests outside doll villages in doll regions in a doll world.

The Japan cabinet is especially elaborate, with a stern daimyo at the centre of his court, his two swords ceremonially by his side. She passes Indonesia and Thailand, both with elaborate Ramayana displays. She wonders if the collector deliberately left Islam out or if mosques were eliminated when Hanuman was brought in. But Palestine is there, she discovers, small but defiant, with a Yasser doll in keffiyeh and fatigues. Around him, a line of dolls are doing the dabke. Cuba and Vietnam go by, and then she is in the India section.

This is a vast hall, arranged in a confusing way, the taxonomy demented, gone utterly haywire. There are too many figurines, different and yet similar. Odd repetitions, confusing variations, with 'Men and Women of India' succeeded by 'Brides of India', suggesting that brides are perhaps neither men nor women, that men do not play a part in marriage. There is then an arrangement by regions and states, these dolls increasingly faded and melancholy, their existence meaningless and hollow under the glare of strip lights and the harsh smell of cleaning fluids.

The northeastern border states go by, predictably dominated by tribal exotica, all tea garden workers and jungle warriors. A window is outlined in the passageway ahead, a small square pane like a porthole in a ship. She peers out. It is the usual grey haze. She is facing the back of the building, looking in the direction of the slums and the Feroz Shah Kotla ground with its tunnels of djinns. If she listens very carefully, she will be able to hear the monkeys that lurk behind *The Daily Telegram*, who have created passageways that go everywhere, that connect it all. She waits, listens, but she cannot hear anything other than the roar of traffic.

And there is no Sanjit at this end point of the museum, this part of the display where India exhausts itself, running out of space just as it has, over many decades, been running out of time. Bibi has been seeing patterns that do not exist, finding clues even though there is no mystery, assuming mistakenly that lines from a poem read obsessively many years ago somehow means that a man has come back from the dead with answers for her.

Her last friend is gone from the city and she has no home worth returning to. If this is the edge and the freedom Bibi has been seeking much of her life, why is it so dull now in its terror?

Her phone chimes. She can't bear to look. She thinks of having to exit the museum past the drugged-looking woman attendant and the guard and wishes that she could stay here forever.

SHE HAS ALMOST turned away when she sees it, the slight shift in the lower corner in this final exhibit that consists of the furthest stretch of Indian territory. So far away that this string of islands is not even on the Indian landmass. There is a crocodile doll down there, on the left. Its big, primitive, open-jawed head is nodding. She thinks of the person or creature met in the tunnel of djinns. Next to the crocodile doll is a bird doll, and it is nodding. Next to that is a monkey doll, which is also nodding. Around them stand an assortment of hunter-gatherer dolls. The Jarawa, the Onge, the Sentinelese, they are all there, and even if they are imprisoned behind glass and artificial light, they are all nodding.

Her phone dings again

The same unknown number from earlier in the day. But this time there are no words, only a picture downloading very slowly on to her phone. Grey striated lines that look like static bloom on the screen, sepia tones inundating the frame, until it is clear to her, in a flash of understanding almost blinding in its intensity, where she must go.

CLAUSTROPOLIS: 1984

I say again
without dharma, there can be nothing –
but no one
listens to me
It isn't the custom to listen in Hastinapur –

SHRIKANT VARMA

1

In Bhopal, I could lie low. In Bhopal, there would be instructions for me.

Because they told me not to take the express, I travelled on a local, in an unreserved bogie. The whisky was Director's Special, a parting gift from Gupta's people. I didn't even wait till nightfall before pulling out the bottle. In Bhopal, in Bhopal, in Bhopal, the night train chattered. It rattled like an iron cage holding senile ogres left over from some forgotten campaign of extermination.

The bogie was dark, except for the passing glow of laltains from small stations. The faces of the cunts around me moved between darkness and light like ghosts. I squeezed the neck of the whisky bottle and wanted to caress the pistol in my bag. I mouthed shlokas in the darkness and thought of the Sikhs I had slaughtered for the motherland.

THE AIR WAS cleaner, cooler in Bhopal. Firecrackers lit up the night. I bathed using Ganges water I had bought off a priest in the Hanuman temple, questioning him long and hard on his genealogy. If the priest was curious about me, he kept his thoughts to himself. He rolled out his family tree for me, his fingers skimming across the centuries. I looked at the intricate network of lines, the proliferating branches, the occasional dead ends. I thought of lists, classification, taxonomy. Manu is full of it. Who, what, where, when, how. What is higher, what is lower. The Brahmin high, the shudra low. The lund high, the chut low. Who gets to eat whom. Who wins. Who loses. Who survives.

AFTER I HAD bathed in the hotel with Ganges water and scrubbed my teeth with Monkey Brand tooth powder, I visited the New Market in the New City. Wandering around the lanes, past the Top 'N Town ice cream shop and Jai Hind Proteins, I went to Alankar Dresses and bought a Wrangler jeans and a red T-shirt with a little green crocodile on it. A barber shaved off the moustache I had worn all the way from Delhi.

A new man, I stalked the quarters of the Old City, the Muslim city, making my way through neighbourhoods named after days and nights of the week. Jumerati, Itwara, Mangalwara, Budhwara, I went, laughing to myself, fingering the spot where my moustache had been. Fine people, these addebaaz Bhopalis, hanging around the squares at all hours. My sweet tooth liked the wares in their bazaars. I found the place soothing, the big lakes dividing the Old City from the New City, where my patron's intermediary had an office. The sun dazzled in the clear November sky. Delhi, that rotting capital, with its smouldering bodies, seemed very far away.

SLUMS SMELL OF shit. This Bhopal slum was no different. A dwarf of a man stopped me as I made my way through Chandbarh to the railway station. I swatted him away absent-mindedly, but he came at me again, unshaven, dishevelled, skeletal, hands pressed together in servile greeting. He asked me to step inside and bless his incense factory. 'Guruji,' he said, sensing my life force. 'Guruji,' he repeated, timidly gesturing at his factory.

The factory was a shack cut into the earth, one of a row of mud huts set around a yard. On the other side of the yard, from a building that looked like it was about to collapse, that had a roof and a floor but no walls, came the sound of schoolchildren singing their daily lessons. I had no interest in the singing children. I didn't care at all for the incense factory and its owner. But I liked his daughter, a firm young thing with ripe, wilful breasts. Her husband was dead.

The incense factory man whispered the details to me as she made tea for us in a far corner of the room, her bangles tinkling against the metal cups. The husband was a truck driver, a fool who abducted a local woman along National Highway 44 between Gauhati and Shillong, and who was captured, stripped and beaten to death with the very iron rods he had been transporting to a building site.

In the evening, after I had roamed around the Old City and eaten my fill of biryani, I went back to the slum in Chandbarh. I was wearing the T-shirt with the crocodile, the new Wrangler jeans and a military green jacket I had bought, not so long ago, in Paona Bazaar in Imphal after a particularly successful assignment. Brut aftershave caressed my face as I picked my way past sewage drains and black, hairy pigs.

The incense man did not wish to leave when he saw me. 'Guruji?' he said. His earlier tone of reverence was missing. He stared at me. I stared back. He fell silent and lowered his eyes. I assessed his daughter, taking her by the chin. I liked what I saw. The curves, the big eyes, the breasts with a mind of their own. I thought of Rekha, the Bombay actress. 'Go,' I said to the incense man.

The life force of those like me is not to be trifled with by such as these fallen. The incense man backed out of his hut slowly. The smell of incense blended with the smell of shit as the door opened and closed.

MY PATRON HAD sent me instructions through his intermediary and keys to a grey Bajaj scooter parked behind the hotel. His orders were for me to follow a man, an operator at a chemical factory.

I could almost hear my patron's whispers in my head. His precise directions, his complex understanding.

Follow. Do nothing else. Simply follow. Become his shadow. Understand your target better than he understands himself, until you are three steps ahead of him in the chess game of his life. Then the moment will come. He will be busy. You will not. He will be in a hurry. You will be still. You will simply be waiting for him, like his reflection in a bathroom mirror. He will walk towards you, offer you his throat. His throat will do its duty, your knife will do its. You will simply watch. You will only be a conduit for what is already written into the ledger of his fate. Do nothing else yet. Just follow.

2

Yes, I followed him, this man an operator at a chemical factory. I followed him so well in the days that came at me clamouring for attention that I barely had time for the incense man's daughter. Follow under the November sky. Follow across the blue lakes. Follow through the filthy, winding lanes of the JP Nagar slums.

Follow to trade union meetings near the Railway Coach factory. Follow to the park across from the Ladies' Hospital where the operator joined iron-ore and textile-mill workers from Chhattisgarh at union rallies.

Drifting in the operator's wake. Becoming his shadow. His double. His doosra. Sitting at a table across from him when he went to meet journalists at the India Coffee House run by the Indian Coffee Workers' Co-operative Society. The chatter of men, the clicking of cigarette lighters, the clatter of coffee cups. Around me revolved the cooperative coffee waiters in white, their turbans flashing red and gold, green and gold, like the plumes of well-fed roosters.

Sometimes, I thought I was back in Calcutta, at the India Coffee House on College Street. I almost expected to see the black, bearded faces of Naxals everywhere, expected to see the reed-thin bodies of women Naxals, all busy discussing their revolutions, not knowing that I had been tasked with following Naxals fomenting revolutions.

I became the silent other of this talkative, over-excited man, this man an operator at a chemical factory on the Kali Parade grounds. Follow in the evening this man an operator on his own at an ahata opposite the GTB complex in the New City. On the ground floor the Vilayati Madira ki Dukan from where he bought a half of Director's Special whisky and trudged upstairs to the ahata. On one side, a sitting charge of one rupee, on the other side, slightly cleaner, a sitting charge of two rupees. Lurking on the one-rupee side, I watched him, following with my eyes as he drank his Indian-Made Foreign Liquor whisky in the two-rupee section, chewing peanuts mixed with onions and green chillies brought in by young runners.

Follow on other days to the Savage Bar in the Old City, where this man an operator went when he didn't want to drink at the ahata. Follow with my ears, listening carefully. The clink of soda bottles, the sizzle of kebabs, the whoosh of matches being lit for cigarettes. I listened and followed as he sang, late into the night, in a warbling voice, 'Ae meri zohra jabeen'. Then I followed him through the winding streets of the Old City. I lurked outside his house in the night like a ghost, following the cries of his wife as he beat her.

IT IS NOT an easy thing, to dedicate your life to order, to give yourself to dharma. My patron understands this. There has never been a time when he has not shown concern for my well-being, a profound awareness of how deeply I have sacrificed myself for the cause. But he was unavailable when I happened to be in Delhi, just back from a job in Punjab, when I was sitting in Gupta's farmhouse, wondering how everyone could have failed so badly as to allow this assassination of the mother of our motherland.

Men coming and men going in Gupta's farmhouse.

Gupta himself wanting me to join in.

From the red telephone in Gupta's upstairs office, I called my patron. Never had I been asked to take part in mob work before. That was not my training. But the secretary who answered my call, a secretary I had never spoken to before, did not understand my urgency and did not seem to know the C code. My patron was unavailable, the secretary said. My patron was busy in meetings. My patron was making decisions on what to do as the country burnt. In such times of adversity, every one of us should help out if we are called upon to serve. At such moments, we should not stand on ceremony or pause to look at account books.

The arrogance of that voice startled me.

I put the phone down and stared out at the men clustered on the lawn. Beyond them, in the gardens to the side, I could see an empty swing suspended from the branch of an eucalyptus tree. Still beyond, the glitter of a private swimming pool where Bombay starlets were invited to display their soft flesh, so the rumours went.

The sword of the righteous, my patron called me. I came out of the office, walked down staircases lined with dark portraits and made my way to the lawn. Around me the vans were getting ready, the men primed on drugs and alcohol. The erect lund of Bharat, my patron had described me, ready to fuck every enemy on behalf of the nation. There were shouts around the vans, over the diesel exhaust, someone saying that the Delhi Police would look the other way, that they would help out when needed. Has there ever been a time in my life when I have not been serving?

I did not care that the Sikhs were being taught a lesson, but why should I have to take part in mob work? I thought of all the complex jobs I had carried out for my patron. The followings. The extraction of information. The outright assassinations. The ones that had to look like suicides, the noose tightened just so over the strangle marks, the wrist sliced with a razor blade as another man held the target down, waiting, it seemed like forever, for the blood to pool out, for the pulse to stop. The killings posing as accidents, the truck rammed into a jeep in a head-on collision. Those that had to resemble heart attacks, the injection needle inserted in the right place. A fine, subtle weapon, my patron had called me. And now an unknown secretary told me to be selfless and to serve.

Should one unsheathe a sword to butcher a goat? Does one shoot a bazaar whore with a Beretta Model 92?

'Go fuck them for us,' Gupta shouted at his men. Cigar fumes trailed from the pashmina shawl draped around him. He did not notice me as I walked past him and clambered into the last van. 'Go fuck them so they remember this for generations to come. Go answer the five shots from Beant Singh's revolver, the twenty-five from Satwant Singh's carbine.'

I went. I answered. I did what had to be done. I did it with sword and with pistol. I did it with hand and with prick. There was no subtlety involved. I did it with kerosene, with phosphorus, with car tyres. For days afterwards, I smelt of burnt meat.

FOLLOW AND PERFORM a parikrama around the factory grounds at Kali Parade. Round and round the walls on the Bajaj scooter that coughs like an old man when I start it. Factory grounds on left, slums on right. Factory grounds on left, farmland on right. Factory grounds on left, wasteland for slum dwellers to shit in on right. Factory grounds on left, railway line to Indore on right.

Reservoirs, wells, ponds and waterways should be constructed at the intersection of boundaries, Manu says, as should temples of gods. The factory watchtowers at the intersections like temples to the factory gods.

A full week has now passed since my arrival in Bhopal. Follow the men who come and go through the main gates. Follow their name tags. This one Pimpalkar. That one Sahasrabudhe. That one Thomas. That one Shakeel. This one Jadhav. That one Biswas. This one my target Kanwar the operator. Men in smart tunics. Time cards being punched in. The long blast of sirens. A factory run like a military machine. A factory owned by Americans, by white men from a faraway land across the black waters. What do they make in this factory? What do they make in their white factories that have crossed the black waters?

One morning, I slipped in through the gates behind this man an operator at an American chemical factory on the Kali Parade grounds. The towers pointed up like rockets. The chemical tanks looked like locomotive engines. The electric lines overhead sliced up the sky. I followed, through control room and compression chamber and loading dock and warehousing complex.

As I lurked outside the formulation shed, a Sikh in a pink turban came out of an open doorway and tried to drag me into the shadows. His beard streamed like fire, his fingers were like ice. But I am a ghost among ghosts. 'I am the erect lund of Bharat,' I said. 'I fuck your ghost sister,' I said. I shaped my right hand into a pistol and shot him. Dhishoom! Da Chau! Dow, Dow! Then I sat and looked at the flag fluttering on the observation tower, at the green Shyamla hills in the distance.

THE INCENSE MAN'S daughter wanted to see Bhopal. In her slum quarters, sitting amid incense and shit, she had heard rumours of a great city, of lakes and forts and hills. I will show it to you, I said. I will spread its legs for you, this city snatched from a rightful Hindu queen by a marauding Pathan invader. The lakes, the railway station, the hills, you can look at it all.

The driver of the autorickshaw I hired was sharp as a razor. He felt my mad, aashiqui spirit. He knew I wouldn't haggle over the fare and went wild in his freedom, taking us where he wanted. No sneaking along tight slum lanes, past shacks rubbing against each other like testicles swollen in the summer heat. We roared across the New City instead, along roads wide and open and inviting.

At the lake, I asked the boatman to remain on the shore. He was long and thin, this boatman, almost a man of two dimensions. I took off my military green jacket. My biceps rippled under my crocodile shirt. The boatman's face was so expressionless as to suggest that he had no face at all.

I sat and pulled at the oars. Out into the blue water, out under the blue November sky, out, out to the place where I let the boat drift and held her against my chest. The sun struck brightly on our faces, bounced off my gold-rimmed aviator sunglasses. I took them off and put them on her face. I thought of Rajesh Khanna, of Sharmila Tagore in a blue sari, of a boat rocking under the Howrah Bridge in Calcutta. I even heard the song, 'Chingari koi bhadke', in Kishore Kumar's voice as we sat up and looked into the water, clear in the November sun.

'I can't see the bottom,' she whispered.

'Woman,' I said, 'when you're with me, you don't worry about what's down there. You look up, you look at the sky.'

UP, UP, THE autorickshaw roared, up to the hills past the All India Radio station, up past the palatial bungalows of politicians and industrialists to where the hills thrust themselves into the sky. I stroked her curves, this incense maker's daughter, this one that I called Rekha and Zohra and now wanted to name Sharmila. Up, up, up, the autorickshaw ran, coming to a spluttering stop outside a ticket booth and a sign. It would be quiet inside, even in the middle of the day, the driver said.

'The National Collection of Man,' I read on the sign. I paid the man at the ticket booth who wore thick, dark, blind man's glasses. I didn't understand what that sign meant. Who was collecting Man? Why were they collecting Man? Around us, the hills rose, dirt paths twisting through trees and bushes. There were eyes among the trees. Statues of people and animals were scattered everywhere. Statues with faces and limbs and eyes. My hands itched. Tribal statues, I thought, remembering my trips to Manipur and to NEFA, among frontier people who did not belong to India in any way except in territory.

Sharmila stopped in front of a statue, bigger than any of the others, hard to understand what it was. If I looked at a part of it, the thing in its centre, that was recognisable enough. It was a snake, and not just any snake, but a sinuous, twisting king cobra, patterned ridges cut into its body. The whole was far more confusing. Wings sprouted from the side, chicken feet stuck out from the wings and the tail flowered in a tuft that could have belonged to a lion. The parts made sense, the whole did not. Not a bird-man but a snake-bird. A snake-chicken-lion-bird.

'A sanpharki,' Sharmila said. 'They say it's bad luck for its shadow to fall on you.'

'What happens? Does your lund wither away and fall off?' I said.

She began giggling.

'I have never heard of such a thing,' I said, putting an arm around her waist. 'Bird-men, snake-birds. What else can you expect jungle dwellers to come up with? Why do they need to bring this stuff here? How is this a collection of Man?'

She began to say something in response, but I covered her mouth with mine. I dragged her deeper into this National Collection of Man. Huts rose around us, with horns on their roofs and totems at their doors. Inside an empty hut of the savages, there were masks and drums and claws and feathers and unrecognisable things. There was a large object that I looked at for a long time before I realised that it was a single breast. That aroused me further and so I pulled Sharmila down to the floor and began tearing at her clothes. I ignored her cries of pain. 'I will show you Man,' I said. I paid no attention to the masks hanging from the walls, looking stonily at us. I thought I saw a shadow in the doorway, the flash of a pink turban, but when I looked up from my thrusts, it was gone.

3

Follow this man an operator at an American chemical factory on the Kali Parade grounds. His name is Kanwar, his home a nameless village on the banks of the Narmada River. His education tenth standard fail in school, diploma fail in a Bhopal polytechnic. His work, after receiving on-the-job training at the factory, is as an operator monitoring production.

Follow Kanwar past posters on the walls of the American factory. Posters that weren't there even a few days ago, when I last did my parikrama, but that look like they have been there for months. Colours faded in the sun, edges curled by heat, cold, rain. Follow and read the posters fading in the sun.

BEFORE THE RETURN OF RAMA'S KINGDOM, FIRST THE RAT KING! WILL YOU SURVIVE THE PLAGUE? CONTACT MAHARISHI AND MAHARAJ!

UPROOT THIS DEATH FACTORY NOW! MASSIVE DEMONSTRATION!

WHO IS IT WHOSE EVIL EYE FOLLOWS YOU EVERYWHERE? WHO IS THE MAN BEHIND THE MASK? ASK MAHARISHI AND MAHARAJ!

WE DEMAND THE RELEASE OF THE WEST VIRGINIA SAFETY INSPECTION REPORT! MASSIVE DEMONSTRATION!

WHAT IS THE KARMA OF YOUR PAST LIVES? WHAT DOES THE FUTURE HOLD FOR YOU? CONSULT MAHARISHI AND MAHARAJ!

WHY IS A CHEMICAL FACTORY LOCATED IN A CROWDED LOCALITY? DO THE LIVES OF THE POOR HAVE NO VALUE? MASSIVE DEMONSTRATION!

FOLLOWING WAS COMPLEX. Following was simple. With the help of my patron's clear instructions, I pursued this man an operator at a chemical factory around the city of Bhopal. No one other than me was involved. No one other than my patron issued me orders.

Delhi was an anomaly. There, I had no clear instructions, only Gupta and his men everywhere in a demon's festival of shouting and screaming. Unmanly, disorganised monkeys, I thought as I holed up with the red telephone inside Gupta's office and dialled the special number. I read out the C cipher. Still, my patron did not come to the line. He was in a meeting. He was busy. He could not be disturbed.

He was not available for me. Only Gupta and Gupta's men were available, crammed into vans that would take us to Trilokpuri, the streets already empty except for corpses and mobs. The crying of women and babies came from rooftops as men with guns and swords stalked the alleys and the Delhi Police kept the roads clear for us. The acrid smoke of burning car tyres. The smell of charred human flesh. The driver's joke. What do you call a sardar on fire? A Sikh kebab.

MY MOUTH TASTED of ashes as I got off the autorickshaw. I needed to buy toothpaste before I returned to my hotel room. Scraps of paper, burnt phosphorus, blackened wicks lay on the ground. Had the world been celebrating Diwali all night while I lay with the woman in the slum? What was her name? And what was all this around me? I looked at the remnants of firecrackers. Gupta's men had been out again, teaching the Sikhs a lesson. But was I still in Delhi? I thought I had been sent to???

I could not remember. My head hurt. My tongue was dry and heavy, lying in my mouth like a limp cock. In the alley to my left, I could make out a charred corpse, its burnt limbs something between flesh and coal. Blackened stumps. Pink, exposed flesh. I went the other way, coming out on to a small maidan. My body tensed. So early in the morning, and already a loose ring of men surrounding a victim! I thought of Delhi, of circles of men, of yellow wax and kerosene and burning car tyres. I thought of locks of hair chopped off, of heads severed from torsos, of women opened up any which way.

But these were not those men. These were simply the defeated.

Bad postures, broken faces, insect bodies. I shoved them aside to see what smooth-talking fortune-teller, what disperser of root-and-herb home remedies, what fly-by-night seller of aphrodisiacs with dried lizards in glass bottles had their attention.

The morning light reflected brightly off a large, white bull. Garlands and beads decorated his horns. A bell dangled from his soft white neck. His back was covered by a red cloth fringed with gold, the letter 'Om' picked out in gold. Incense sticks smouldered from a censer behind his hump. His eyes were dark, clear, luminous. I felt a touch of the sacred.

Then I saw the man accompanying the bull. Slight and bare-chested, he had long hair and a beard. His saffron dhoti was fading in colour. The rudraksha beads on his neck were cracked all over. He did not seem equal to the magnificence of the bull, merely an unfortunate taken under the creature's regal protection.

'Have you ever been aware of things in the future?' the man said. 'Are you aware of the significance of your past?'

There was a murmur. The insects were listening to him with rapt attention.

'Today, you can. Today, my companion, the one and only sacred bull in Bhopal, Maharaj, can look into your past and into your future. Today, he can tell you how to break out of the jail cell of your time.'

Maharaj the bull nodded his head. The bell on his bull neck jingled. The insects grew quiet, shuffling their feet like goats being prepared for mass slaughter. Bull People! Insect People! Goat People! My head throbbed with pain.

'Ours is an age of darkness,' the man said. 'A time when a king can be shaken off his throne by assassins.'

'Kill the Sikhs,' someone shouted from the back.

'Ours is a time of fear and impurity,' the man replied. 'Blood in the cities. Hunger in the villages. Who can say, at such a time, that he does not need the help of Maharaj?'

'Kill the Muslims,' another man shouted.

'Ours is a time of much suffering,' the man said. His voice had dropped low. When he addressed the bull, he sounded like he too were one of the crowd, just another tired supplicant, a beaten man desperate for hope. 'Tell us, Maharaj, please tell us, who here has suffered recently from much grief?'

'Kill ...' someone said and stopped abruptly.

The bull was walking. He moved like a dancer, his hooves graceful as they struck the concrete of the square. His neck bell jingled in the quiet of the early morning as he shook his head in time to the beat of his hooves. From the slums behind, smoke rose from morning fires like a hundred sacrificial havans being prepared in service to Maharaj. I felt transported out of time, to the glory of ancient Hastinapur.

The bull came to a sudden halt. In front of him stood a thin, shabby man with bloodshot eyes. He swayed on his feet and looked like he would fall. Around him, the swelling crowd chattered in approval. No one doubted the swaying man's grief.

'How long has he been suffering, Maharaj?' the man said.

A series of loud reports rang out. I started and reached for the pistol. It was only the bull stamping his foot.

'Five stamps for five days! For five days, our friend has been caught in unending misery and prayed for deliverance. Is this true, sir?'

The man with the bloodshot eyes nodded faintly. Then he began to crumple, but the Insect People held him up. He was part of the show now, whether he wanted to be or not.

'Who among us is so heartless as to not feel the sorrow of our brother? Who here can say he has not felt pain without end, days without hope?'

The Insect People listened in silence and thought of their endless pain. The Goat People contemplated their hopeless days and wondered when they would be slaughtered.

'But even pain has an end if you can see the future,' the man said. 'Maharaj, tell us how long will it take for the planets and stars to realign. How long will it be before the gentleman's unbearable grief disappears in the face of incredible fortune?'

The bull looked up slowly, gazing into the distance, away from the crowd and square. Was he calculating the distance from this square of hopelessness to the railway station of fortune? Or was it that in his mind, a pair of wings had sprouted from his side, and he was flying?

He was flying away from the city of Bhopal, from factories and operators and fortune-tellers and assassins. He was flying to Mount Kailash in the Himalayas, flying so high that he could be touched by nothing. No nine millimetre bullet could bring him down from up there, no AK-47 rifle find him as a target. He was flying away from our century, flying out of our time.

I felt a shiver of premonition, the bite of remembrance. There was a jingling of bells.

'Seventeen jingles, my friends,' the man shouted. 'An auspicious number. Seventeen jingles for seventeen days. Then the world will be turned upside down and this gentleman will receive his happiness. From all pain will he be released on the third of December.'

A vast sigh of relief ran through the Insect People like a cool breeze on a blazing afternoon. The man with the bloodshot eyes blinked again. He held out a scrap of paper, something that looked like a medical prescription, something with the name Ladies' Hospital written on it. 'Wife,' I think I heard him say. 'Baby,' I believe I heard him say. The Insect People dropped coins and crumpled rupee notes into a white bag held out by the man with the bull who could only be the Maharishi of the faded posters.

There were no babies or wives here. All men, young, middle-aged, elderly. A country of men, this, a country of defeated men. Clerks and servants, shopkeepers and labourers. Insect People filled with insect worries and insect grief. Insect People foolishly chasing after insect hope. Who was worried about not getting back money loaned to a friend? Who was leaving soon on an uncertain journey? Who had an employment letter in his pocket? Who here was haunted by ghosts?

The jingles became louder before they died away entirely. I felt a nudge. The scent of incense drifted into my nostrils. I looked into the bull's eyes. Was he embarrassed to be exposing me like this, in front of the gutter-rubbish, Insect People of Bhopal, or was he enjoying singling me out? I have served, I wanted to scream. Bull People, Goat People, Insect People, I wanted to shout, I have been serving forever! I am the sword of righteousness! I am the erect lund of Bharat!

My hands itched as the man approached.

'Tell us how many ghosts follow this gentleman, Maharaj,' he said. 'Then tell us how the gentleman may be delivered from his ghosts.'

I pushed my way past the Insect People staring at me. The stomp of the bull's foot went on and on as if a squad of Bull People were coming after me. I ran through the alleys and I ran through the chowks, pushing my way past the Goat People. I ran past the shops and I ran past the morning traffic, not looking at the Insect People. As I ran, I saw an albino man staring at me from behind a shop counter. I saw a dwarf Muslim woman, all in black, a beige folder in her hand, stopping to look at me. Then I spotted the Sikh in a pink turban waiting for me near the bridge. I turned and I turned and I turned again. Only when none of my enemies were visible and I had a clear field of fire, only then did I slow down and make my way back to my hotel room.

4

In one of the camps I attended as a young man, we were taught about compartmentalisation. The mind is a box with many smaller boxes inside, the organiser had said. Keep a small box here for work. Keep another for sex. Keep another for duty. Let not the contents of the boxes get mixed up. Let duty remain in the box for duty. Let sex remain in the box for sex. When you wake up, tell yourself which boxes you will open today, and in what order.

Ideally, we should all be brahmacharis, abstaining from the unclean. No sex, no meat, no alcohol. But in the Kali Yuga, in a time of tamas, such abstinence is impossible. Then one must eat heartily, in accordance with Manu's laws. Then what matters is that the immobile are food for the mobile. The fangless food for the fanged. The timid food for the brave.

Did I know which box to open on waking up today? The box of duty demanded I follow the operator. The box of sex asked me to find the incense maker's daughter. In between there were so many boxes, the box with the bottle of Director's Special whisky, with one last peg left in it, the box with my Italian pistol, the box with my book of Manu.

I moved the curtains in my room and looked out. My patron had put me up in a hotel on Hamidia Road, near the railway station, with a balcony jutting out towards the back. A scattering of two-wheelers sat below, my grey Bajaj among them. Men appeared at regular intervals, like foraging ants, to fill up jerricans with water from a creaking hand pump. Ant People! Pans of rice steamed like funeral pyres outside the hotel kitchen. The corpse of a dog lay at the very edge of the parking area, belly bloated, flies buzzing around its death rictus. Dog People! An absurd scenario this, the fanged being consumed by the fangless, the brave by the timid. No, Manu is always right. This is the immobile being eaten by the mobile. The dead by the living. How quickly one's position in a hierarchy changes.

I stood on the balcony and leant out. What did I smell in the breeze: rice, shit or dead meat?

CLARITY AND ORDER were required. I carried out my asanas, sat long in meditation. Through my eyelids, in the corners where light bled through, there were splotches of pink. I refused to be agitated.

Om, I chanted silently.

Leave my presence, you stubborn ghosts. Know that you do not frighten me.

Om!

I bathed using the remainder of the Ganges water and read my Manu. I cleaned my pistol and counted out my cartridges. I felt the weight of the bullets in my palm, running my finger over the smooth, lethal beauty of their tapering points.

Then, before I set out to follow, I paid a visit to the intermediary at his office in the New City. I sent a message, a question that had occurred to me in my clarity. When will I be done with this assignment, my patron? I asked. When will I be finished with following? When will I leave Bhopal, and where will I go next in the service of the cause?

The intermediary frowned as I handed him the coded message. His fat lips trembled. He was a bookkeeper, his forehead mapped out by white-striped caste marks. He looked unhealthy and overweight.

'… cakes,' he muttered.

'What?' I said.

'Eggless cakes,' he replied. 'They must be eggless.'

FOLLOW THIS MAN an operator at an American chemical factory on the Kali Parade grounds as he gives letters to journalists and petitions politicians. Follow the operator, tenth-standard fail, polytechnic fail, virtually illiterate but with opinions beyond his station about design flaws, safety features and storage facilities in a modern, up-to-date factory run by Americans.

Follow past a poster flapping in the wind that proclaims, 'Sex Weakness, Hydrocele, Piles, Fistula'. In the glass showcase of Omni Bakers, soft, pink cakes gleamed. Were they eggless? I wondered. A man with a distended face sat with a drum in the square near Omni Bakers. 'Hydrocele, Eggless, Piles, Eggless,' he beat out, heedless of the bloody, wet-looking sores around his mouth.

I rode back into the Old City, following the operator past carts selling sabudana khichri and cassette tapes, following through a shrieking puzzle of autos, tempos and buses, following past the flashing lights of stores displaying plywood finishings and bathroom fittings. The erect minaret of a mosque cast its shadow on the Hanuman temple on Chhola Road. The chemical factory on the Kali Parade grounds used its sophisticated devices to send precise signals into my head.

Follow the operator to rallies about East India Company and multinational corporations. Follow as he meets Muslims in skullcaps. Meets low-caste Hindus. Meets jholawallahs.

Follow as the protestors shout, 'Company Raj nahi chalega, nahi chalega. Goondabaazi nahi chalegi, nahi chalegi.' Follow as they chant, 'Naya zamana aayega, aayega.' Follow chanting, silently, my own mantras, chanting whatever comes to mind. Beretta, Beant Singh's revolver, Satwant Singh's carbine. Swords, prick, burning tyres. Immobile for the mobile, fangless for the fanged, timid for the brave. Follow and keep an eye out for pink turbans.

WITH A MENACING crocodile on my heart, I visited the incense maker's daughter. The incense maker was home, in agitated conversation with his daughter. Something was happening in the slum, something involving children going missing.

'Yesterday, a child from the school over there,' he said.

'Later,' I said. My head hurt.

The incense maker looked up at me. Children were going missing, and the police would do nothing. He wanted me to come with him to the police. My presence would make a difference.

'Later,' I said. I needed to rest.

This incense maker would not be silenced. He was querulous, less deferential than before.

'The neighbours ask me questions,' Insect Man shouted in my face. 'I have a reputation. I have a daughter who has a reputation, although I curse the fate that gave me a daughter.'

My head hurt from his nagging. I reached out for his right, hairy ear and twisted it down, bringing his head with it. He bawled like a child on the floor. His daughter pulled me away.

'Later,' I said. 'We'll take care of the missing children later.'

The door opened and shut. The smell of incense met the smell of shit as he departed. I tried to forget about the missing children. I plunged myself into her. My mouth sought the taste of Rekha's mouth. My hands roamed Zohra's curves. My erect lund explored Sharmila's chut. Afterwards, when it was all done, I lay back on the threadbare mattress on the floor like a king reclining on his royal bed. Rekha opened the door at the back. The schoolchildren, the ones still not missing, sang an evening song. 'Glory to the soldiers of the nation,' they sang. 'Glory to its farmers,' they sang. 'Glory to the goddess who is the nation,' they sang.

The sky filled with the noise of chattering birds. From the A.H. Wheeler at the railway station, I had bought a copy of *Jasoosi Duniya*. Now I lay on the bed and read stories of murders and missing people. No pink-turbaned ghosts interrupted my repose. The fortune-telling bull stayed far away. The operator at a chemical factory on Kali Parade grounds conducted his life without me as his following shadow. I dozed. I read a story, 'The Ghostly Fingerprints of Calcutta.'

FOLLOW THROUGH THE winding lanes of the Old City this man an operator at a chemical factory on the Kali Parade grounds. In the heartland of India, following a man involves no roadblocks, no military checkpoints, no men in camouflage with faces masked, the tails of their black bandanas blowing in the wind, their automatic rifles held just so, their ability to shoot and kill protected by the Armed Forces Special Powers Act. In the heartland of India, following means making one's way past civilians, past Insect People unknowing of the protective work done by those like me, creatures unheeding of the ceaseless vigil of great men like my patron.

How would they understand the necessity of keeping those like this operator in check? In the heartland of India, although far from the busy secessions of the Sikhs and the Nagas, these Communist trade union people try to upturn the social order. They work in tandem with the Sikhs, the Nagas, the Manipuris, the Kashmiris, the Muslims. They eat away at the nation. And so this man, tenth-standard fail, an operator at a chemical factory, driven by his drinking and his own restless ego, finds himself questioning complex safety procedures laid down by Americans whose factories march triumphant throughout the world.

Follow this man an operator at an American chemical factory as he crosses the bridge into the New City. Follow him as he takes the road winding up to Shyamla Hills. Boats rock on the lake below us. Electric lines sag above the trees. Minarets thrust themselves into the sky from the quarters of the Old City named after days of the week. We keep climbing. Above are the sprawling bungalows of politicians and industrialists, the signal tower and broadcasting complex of All India Radio. Up there is the National Collection of Man.

I did not understand why my patron had me still following. When in the past had I been made to wait so long when the kill itself was so straightforward? No bodyguards, no troublesome witnesses. I could do it right now on an empty road like this or even in the crowded marketplace we had left behind. I would have a scarf wrapped around the lower half of my face. A shove would send this man an operator sprawling to the ground, his motorcycle falling on to him, its engine running, its wheels still spinning, his leg trapped underneath. Three shots to the head would complete the task.

The killing would result in protests by his comrades and an item or two in the newspaper, but without this man an operator going ceaselessly from here to there, from there to here, talk about the factory would come to an end. No more pamphlets and letters. No more flyers. No more Massive Demonstration! The factory would hum on like a well-oiled machine. Those men in their smart tunics would punch in their time cards at regular hours and be paid well for it. Whatever they made at the factory, they would keep making. What did they make in there? They made chemicals that became other chemicals, with which they made even more chemicals. Work would go on, lives lived in the manner they are meant to. I, erect lund of Bharat, would move on, my following over.

There was no traffic on this road at all, no one other than the operator I followed and a lone rider behind me. I saw the man behind in my rear-view mirror, keeping a steady distance from me just as I kept an even length between me and the operator. Dusk was falling, and soon it would be dark. My grey Bajaj scooter laboured up the slopes. The operator took a curve, vanishing temporarily from sight. The Bajaj stuttered. I gave the engine a little more. It died. I cursed and let it roll, coasting to the side. Behind me, a motorcycle accelerated with a deep growl and shot past. The rider wore a helmet, a scarf wrapped around his lower face. I tried to see the licence plate number but it went by too fast. A black Bullet 350, powerful, the favoured bike of the police and the army.

I let the sound die, waited for the darkness to come. I was following the operator, of course. But who was following me?

5

In the office of my patron's intermediary, there was spittle on the intermediary's face and cash to cover fresh expenses. A reply from my patron awaited me. I felt a burning urgency, an eagerness for a taste of my patron's wisdom. But the message was the eleventh in a series, which meant a fresh cipher, and the key gave me trouble. My hands shook as I leafed through the book of Manu brought to me by the intermediary. I could hear my heart beating faster as I deciphered the message.

Think you too good for follow following? Barely begun your assignment and yet you to know when to finish off? Patience and subtlety have I not taught? You to know when leave Bhopal? How long in Bhopal? In Bhopal? In Bhopal?

My ears burnt. I could hear my patron in my head. I could sense his all-seeing eye, feel his great contempt as sweat dripped from my face on to the message. I breathed to calm myself, to let the words slow down.

If you can remember what you have been taught, if you can cultivate unquestioning adherence to dharma, if you can nurture patience, then take this opportunity to make a new move in the game. So far you have only followed. Now make the operator your friend. Make yourself, sword of righteousness, the friend of this man a chemical operator on the Kali Parade grounds. Find out if he has in his possession company documents. If you become his friend, the operator will tell you if he has papers belonging to the factory and where he keeps these papers. The papers wish to return to their rightful owners. They have their dharma. I hope you will remember that you have yours.

WERE THE SCHOOLCHILDREN asleep or dead? The building without walls looked like a haunted house. Yellow drops of light came from scattered kerosene lamps, but the rest evoked the darkness of this dark age. I was like a boat lost at sea, surrounded by ghostly sounds. The eruption of hacking, phlegmy coughs, the cries of a woman being beaten by her husband, the prim voice of an All India Radio newsreader saying, 'Greece ke prime minister Andreas Papandreou…'

I cursed Papandreou and thirty generations of his ancestors as I got dressed. Behind me, the woman whose name I could not remember asked me to stay. I was nauseated by how low I had fallen as I stumbled through the alleyway, trying to find my way out of this slum.

What is it that Manu says? It is through adultery among the classes, the marrying of forbidden women and the abandonment of activities proper to one's station that originates the intermixture and contamination of the classes. A man scurried in front of me like a giant cockroach, turned and fled from my life force. I, righteous sword of the nation, I, codename Hastinapur and Shravasti and Somnath, I, erect lund of the nation, have been coupling with one who cannot read or write her own name. How then would this weeping, snivelling woman know the name of the prime minister of Greece? I wanted to go back and dangle her by the throat. Her father, the incense maker, could have sent her to school in that haunted building. Instead, he made her work in his incense factory, started with compensation money he had received for an accident. He had some kind of injury from working at a chemical factory, had trouble breathing. Couldn't sleep at night, she said, not without his evening medicine of country liquor.

Insect People. Insect People coming in waves from the villages. Insect People coming in on trains and on buses, with single bags that carry all their possessions. If they find a roof over their heads, a room with walls, they are content. The only furniture they need are nails, hammering them into the wall. The richer Insect People get, the more nails they possess. One nail for their bag, one for their clothes, one for a mirror. Insect People working as loaders at factories and bazaars,

Insect People working as maid servants and construction workers, Insect People taking compensation money and setting up businesses that their pitiful ambition calls factories. Insect People being led astray by trouble-making union leaders. Insect People giving their illegal squatter colonies the names of politicians, using the names as magic charms that might protect their shacks from being demolished by bulldozers but that can't prevent their children from disappearing. Insect People stealing and quarrelling and fucking and reproducing and dying and living the lives of Insect People.

Follow follow to the Savage Bar then, where the operator was busy getting drunk. Eyes like coal pits. Face flushed like a monkey in heat. Smoking furiously. A Monkey Man this operator at an American chemical factory on the Kali Parade grounds. 'I am a disco dancer,' the speakers mounted in the ceiling sang. Monkey Man gulped his whisky.

The music was too loud and there were too many people and there was too much talk and too much laughter and too much shouting and there was a frenzy in the air and the place was too bright but still so full of shadows that my head hurt and men with gold watches and thick moustaches waved their hands in the air to order more of everything and I could not tell if someone with a pink turban was hiding anywhere in that crowd and the walls were painted with figures of savages who were women in short grass skirts against a jungle background and the shadows of the men with moustaches and gold watches fucked the savage women on the walls and so the Monkey Men mated with the Disco Dancers in the jungle.

Follow follow this man an operator at an American chemical factory on the Kali Parade grounds. Become his friend, my patron said. Finish him off, my instincts said. The noise grew louder, the cigarette smoke thicker. The bottles fucked the glasses, the ashtrays spilt their cremated remains to the floor. The waiters, Insect Men serving the Monkey Men, ran faster and faster to bring them spicy peanut mix and soda water and Gold Flake King Size cigarettes.

I looked at Monkey Man an operator at an American chemical factory on the Kali Parade grounds.

Why follow follow? I screamed.

No one heard me.

How long follow follow? I cried.

No one answered.

Why become friends now after all this follow follow?

I wanted to cross over to his corner. Smash this Haywards 5000 beer bottle on his head. Slice his throat open with the jagged edge. No longer was he my target, I his assassin. No, this Monkey Man an operator at an American chemical factory on the Kali Parade grounds was my jailer. I was his prisoner. This shit city all around me was a jail city. Savage Bar! Savage City!

I needed to breathe. I needed to leave before I killed this man an operator. No more follow following but took the grey scooter, fixed up by a garage on Hamidia Road and running good and true again. Sent it howling through the streets. Wished I had a black Bullet 350 between my legs. Left behind the American chemical factory, left behind the railway station, left behind the city squares named after days and nights of the week. Abandon this Old City. I crossed the lake of the thin, faceless boatman. My scooter climbed. Abandon this New City. The scooter kept climbing. Abandon this Savage City. The numbing haze of whisky counterpunched the cold wind coming at my face and hands. Abandon this Bhopal.

Who knows what lies outside the city? What if there's nothing at all? I rode the tunnel carved through the darkness by the headlight. The fuel gauge flickered. I stopped and pulled the scooter over. I looked down, back at the city I had left behind. It glimmered with lights, but then clouds rolled over it, obscuring everything. I looked up at the sky. It was as I had suspected. No stars in the sky, no lights in the city. No sky, no city, no nothing.

Set fire to the Sikh gurdwara on Block 36. Break the shutters of the shops on Block 29. Burn the scooters. Burn the buildings. Burn the people. Block 32. Block 30. Block by block. Body by body. Corpse by corpse piled up. Block 29. Block 28. Molotov cocktails. Phosphorus. Kerosene. Knife and Sword.

An old man cowering at the back of a shop. Old man with thick owl lenses. Old man whose hair turns out to be thin and pathetic when I rip his turban off. Old man who begs on his knees and calls me his son. But I am not his son. I am my patron's sword of righteousness. I am the erect lund of Bharat. I am the subtle weapon of my patron. I am the one who these days does mob work. I am the one who sees how the old man's scalp bleeds when I slash his hair off. I am the one who hears how the old man howls as he is dragged out by Gupta's men to be garlanded with a tyre set ablaze.

Block 26. Block 25. Block 24. Block by block.

6

That man an operator at a chemical factory was talking. My all-understanding patron, shawl draped over left shoulder, walked along a courtyard where the bricks were all uneven, weeds growing between them. Papers scattered on the lawns of Gupta's farmhouse and became kites flown from the rooftops of Trilokpuri by missing slum children. Two moons, slivers of white in the sky, tracked a woman as she stared at a blackened slick of land, oily and grimy, filled with the rotting carcasses of ships. Black, bearlike things roamed in packs and fished in a muddy river. Silent, drowned cities raised their buckled, mud-caked concrete shapes above raging, brown, flood waters. A faceless boatman poled his boat and the song Chingari played and got distorted by feedback that became a whisper and a lamentation and a howl. I woke with a start, crying followfollow, followfollow, my mouth parched. In the darkness of the hotel room, the radium glow of my watch said ten.

If it was ten, why so dark? I recalled returning to the hotel late at night, crawling into bed. I stumbled to the window. Outside, the buildings along Hamidia Road slumbered like ageing monsters, hunched together under a cold, dark night while dreaming their monster dreams. I poured water into my sticky mouth, down my burning throat, and pissed golden-yellow liquid. Had time gone back? Had I slept through morning and afternoon all the way to ten at night? Who had stolen my day from me?

To the Savage Bar in a rush then, the music low, the lights dim. The final phase of the bar before it closes. No escape from this man an operator at a chemical factory my jailer, no escape from instructions to become his friend. Caught in the grip of something like the first chill of a fever, pretending to be drunk, drifting towards this man an operator at an American chemical factory on the Kali Parade grounds.

'Cigarette?' I said.

He reached for the Gold Flake cigarettes in front of him. His reddened eyes glowered in their sockets. He shook the packet so that the sandy filter tip of one emerged by itself, like something alive. I took the cigarette and began coughing when he lit it for me. I recovered and sat down. The operator lit a cigarette of his own.

I ordered drinks for him, for me. I listened as he talked, even if I wasn't sure if he was talking to me, to someone else he had mistaken me for, or to himself. His entire life lay unfolded before me, his frustrated ambitions, his miserable marriage, his pride when he began working at the factory, his unease as he came to see that underneath the sophisticated production process and hard lines of industrial efficiency, there was a deep uncertainty. White men came and white men went, white men who fired off brief laughs and confident greetings that went 'Hi', white men flashing white shields of gleaming white teeth before they retreated into the inner precinct, although over the years, their explosive greetings gave way gradually to a remote, distracted approach, like that of astronauts on the moon dutifully collecting samples from an alien world, working briskly, eager to go home to their big cars and big wives and big children before the oxygen ran out.

The operator saw the factory, so new and so full of promise when it opened, begin to transform itself. He did not want to be part of that transformation.

'So I resigned, along with six others,' he said, looking up at me. 'We were like men in a fairytale, you understand? Like men in a story whose lives had taken a poor turn in our homeland, we went elsewhere to seek our fortunes. We took the train to Bombay, where we were recruited by a Middle East middleman for jobs at a chemical factory in Iraq. The factory was near Kirkuk, in the desert, not far from the border. On one side Turkey, on another side Iran, fighting a long, bloody war with Iraq. The money was good, the factory, run by Japanese supervisory staff, in spotless working condition. The security personnel were Iraqi, but all the other workers were foreign, men drawn from different countries to run different sections of the factory, like a kind of United Nations in the land of the Arabian Nights.

'No one team could talk to another. Not just because we didn't have much of a language in common beyond broken English. We were asked to keep within our specific sections, communicate only through our Japanese supervisors in rudimentary production speak. We didn't know how big the factory was. We didn't know how many personnel the factory had. We didn't know why everyone except the guards was foreign. We didn't know what the factory was making.

'After our shift was over, we'd be escorted back by guards to a bus with darkened windows. We'd be driven to our dormitory through smooth highways running across the desert, a ceaseless expanse of sand broken up only by oil wells and bare, brown hills on the distant horizon. At night, we heard the scream of fighter jets taking off from a nearby airbase. In the morning, before we piled back into our bus, we could occasionally see, in the far distance, across the horizon of desert sand, plumes of black smoke. Sometimes, the bus pulled over to let an army convoy pass, military truck after military truck heading for who knew where.

'In our dormitory, we watched endless videos of Hindi films with Arabic subtitles. We saw Amitabh Bachchan romance Parveen Babi and Mithun Chakraborty disco dance in flaring white pants and Rekha sing, her large eyes with a mind of their own, under the light of chandeliers soon to be extinguished by the East India Company. We listened, on cassette tapes brought from home, to Mukesh and Lata Mangeshkar and Asha Bhosle and Mohammed Rafi and Kishore Kumar and Manna Dey. Those sweet voices floated out over the grounds of the dormitory, disappearing into the desert sand and the desert sky. Maybe they would rise even higher and be carried back to India on the monsoon winds, the clouds carrying home our messages of longing, of homesickness.

'We liked the food they gave us at first, but gradually we began to miss what we were used to eating back home. People drank more, smoked more. Some began to get pills from the factory pharmacy to help them sleep. Jadhav took to standing at the window with the lights off, watching through the curtains. He thought our quarters, a building empty except for us and the cook and cleaning man who came in once a day, was guarded not just by soldiers in uniform but by secret police. Mukhabarat, he said. Secret police. We didn't know where Jadhav had learnt the word.

'Jadhav began to tell us stories we'd never heard, stories we did not know where he had picked up, Jadhav with his Hindi and his broken English. He talked about Harun al Rashid, the Caliph of Baghdad, walking alone in the night through his city, disguised as a commoner to find out how things really were in his kingdom. He told us, with the curtains drawn and the television on, the building occasionally shaken by the sonic booms of fighter planes flying overhead, of the Caliph one night seeing an imperial barge sailing down the Tigris, a barge just like his except that it was black in colour, on which, surrounded by guards dressed in black, with attendants and dancing girls dressed in black, resplendent on his throne sat a man dressed in black, a man who except for the colour of his garments looked exactly like Harun al Rashid, a Black Caliph who was a night-time version of Harun al Rashid the Caliph of Baghdad. Our factory in Kirkuk was like something set up by the Black Caliph, Jadhav said. It was not of the daylight world. Its intentions, its purpose, were hidden from us, and we had made a mistake, crossing over from our natural realm of the daylight into this nocturnal world. We had no business working there. All these chemical factories were opening up passages between places usually kept apart. If we entered the realm of the Black Caliph through these factories, other creatures could enter ours.

'We didn't understand any of this, but we didn't need to be told that we were in the wrong place at the wrong time. We had doubts enough of our own. Arguments broke out with the Japanese supervisors because we were given only selected flow charts, never enough to know more than the immediate process we were engaged in. It all began to feel so familiar. We had left our homes, put thousands of miles between us and that American chemical factory on the Kali Parade grounds, and yet here we were caught up once again in something whose purpose was kept secret from us. Once again, I, an operator, adjusted the dials and read the outputs of my own little section and was supposed to know no more. Once again, around me, a factory of unknowable dimensions, of unfathomable purpose, hummed on.

'Jadhav began to miss his shifts. In the dormitory he stayed, all by himself, while we went to the factory. He would be running a high temperature, soaking the bedsheets, when we left. When we came back, he would be sitting by the window, curtains drawn, the lights off. Sometimes, he appeared to be talking to himself. Sometimes, just before we opened the door to the dormitory, it seemed that there was another voice in there, talking back to him.

'More stories came out of Jadhav's mouth, things he couldn't possibly know. He spoke of the Buraq, a horse with the head of a man and the tail of a peacock that had carried the prophet Mohammed on its back to heaven. He talked about angels. Some were made of particles of light. Others, he said, took the shape of dust storms. He had even met a djinn and now the djinn came every day to talk to Jadhav. The djinn had asked him to leave, he said, and yet the djinn had also said that Jadhav would not be able to leave even when he went back to Al Hind. The djinn had taken him out of the dormitory, out of Iraq, had shown him the end of the world. Jadhav had flown over brooding, abandoned building towers in India, the windows all blown out, trees sprouting through their lower floors, with feral cattle-like creatures staring out from inside these buildings, eyes gleaming white in the darkness. He had seen trees shrivelled and withered, from the diseased branches of which hung, upside down, human-shaped things that tried to catch his attention. He saw children, or perhaps they were child-sized adults, fighting over scraps of spilt rice that were black in colour, the winners devouring the grains raw, and he saw birds resembling crows fighting creatures that looked like dogs over a dried-up human corpse. Everywhere, crops had rotted into blackened, burnt kelp and the earth was speckled with white salt that looked like blood under the light of two red moons.

'Shakeel, who was Muslim, swore that he had never mentioned the Buraq to Jadhav. Yet, Shakeel said, Jadhav seemed to have the essence of the stories right, even if some of the details were strange. What did this djinn look like, we asked him. Handsome, like a film star, Jadhav said, which we all agreed was a very strange answer.

'Again, I wanted to quit. All of us did. But first there were arguments with the Japanese supervisors, with the Iraqi officials. One morning, they sent a man to talk to us, a man who kept his sunglasses on even indoors, a very large man with a moustache who said something about bonuses for all of us at the end of the year if we kept working. His eyes were dark round discs. In his big, meaty left hand, he held our passports. He put them on the table and flicked through them one by one, pausing to look at the photos on each passport and checking them against our faces. Flick, pause. Flick, pause. Black discs on the face of the Black Caliph who had stepped out of the story of the Arabian Nights into our workaday world.

'A few days later, we were woken up from our sleep by a noise in the dormitory. Some kind of disturbance made by something large, man-sized, sitting at the window. We rushed to turn on the lights. In a state of panic and confusion, we checked the window, the room. There was no one there apart from us, but Jadhav's bed was empty. From far away, we heard what sounded like running water. We rushed to the bathroom at the end of the corridor. Jadhav, lying in the cubicle. He had sliced his wrist with a razor blade. In the white plastic shower cubicle, his blood ran dark red like river mud in the monsoons. We called for help. They took him away in a military ambulance, brought him back a week later, wrist bandaged, eyes glazed, heavily pumped up with pills. After that, they agreed to let us go.

'We reversed our journey. Back from Kirkuk to Baghdad, from Baghdad to Bombay, from Bombay to Bhopal, over yellow desert sand and deep blue sea and brown, blazing soil, flying in over ships and dhows with sails fluttering in the wind, riding on a train rattling its way to the heartland of India. I came home, where my wife was waiting for me. It was like I had never left. Again, my wife wanted a baby. Again, I tried. Again, nothing happened. No life grew out of my loins. My seed was as dead as before. Again, in my rage, in my frustration, I beat her.

'Still, it was all as before. I returned to the factory. They took me back without a word. I thought I would accept this life, this job, this factory. I didn't want to leave Bhopal again. My family was here, my friends here. Perhaps we could adopt a child.

'But one day, a journalist at the India Coffee House, a cheroot-smoking, anti-caste, atheist journalist, someone who had been transferred to Bhopal by his editor at *The Daily Telegram* in Delhi for refusing to change a report that attributed blame to Hindus rather than Muslims for a riot, this man showed me photographs from a foreign magazine. Iranian soldiers lying in rows inside a train, coughing blood and vomit, scarves stained red and green. Did I do that? I thought. Was that what I was a part of in that factory in Kirkuk? I began to lose the distinction between the Kirkuk factory and the Kali Parade factory. When I got drunk late at night, just like this, I began to think that those corpses were not in Iran but here, in Bhopal.

'I look around and see the agents of the Mukhabarat stalking people at night. I look and I see this city filled with people coughing blood, dying in the thousands. I look and see this American factory, the one I am in, making chemicals that will choke the blood out of living people. I look around and I smell phosgene. I smell mustard gas. I smell chlorine and Zyklon-B and methyl isocyanate.'

The operator put a cigarette in his mouth. His hands fumbled for a light. I reached for the matchbox to help him. Vimana brand. I'd never seen that before. The picture was of something that looked like a cross between a bird and an aircraft. Bird-plane. I thought of the snake-chicken-lion-bird at the National Collection of Man.

I struck a match for the operator. I was becoming his very good friend. My patron's approving smile washed over my head.

The flame cupped in my hands cast a glow on the operator's thick, black moustache as he dipped his cigarette into the light. He exhaled sharply and sat back.

'After my return from Iraq, I saw that the factory was more rundown, with far fewer technical staff. But there was something else, something I couldn't quite put my finger on.

'I was still dazed, imagining sometimes that I was not in Bhopal but in Kirkuk. I would turn a corner at the factory and start, thinking that the man in the black sunglasses was coming towards me. But it was always somebody else, somebody who turned out to be vaguely familiar when he drew close. I tried to suppress these feelings, as I did when I was startled by the sight of an Iraqi security guard appearing at the back of the formulation shed, by the contrail streaming behind a fighter aircraft above the flare tower. I reminded myself that there was no bus here to take me back to a desert dormitory, no Jadhav to slice his wrist, no big man in black sunglasses to examine my passport. This was the American chemical factory on the Kali Parade grounds in Bhopal. This was home.

'When I finally learnt the truth, though, it was so simple. Thomas told me, surprised that I hadn't realised this. The Kali Parade factory had stopped production.

'The market studies, optimistic about the future, had been wrong. The white men in America, at the main industrial plant in Institute, West Virginia, those sitting in the corporate office on Park Avenue, New York City, they had all miscalculated. There was little demand for products as advanced as theirs, meant for big people with big fields and big machines, in a primitive market made up of starving farmers and sharecroppers.'

'Zero demand for advanced things in the land of Insect People,' I said.

The operator shook his head. I couldn't tell if he agreed with me or not.

'By the time I got back from Iraq, they had suspended the production process. The chemicals already manufactured just sat in the storage tanks, too expensive when made into advanced pesticide and too hazardous to be gotten rid of cheaply.

'In the workers' canteen, Thomas and Biswas and Sahasrabudhe began to talk. Men whose names I did not know, men who had been hired while I was in Iraq, added fresh information. They spoke not about the new jobs we all needed to find but how the Kali Parade factory was designed differently from its original model in West Virginia. There was no emergency plan here. There was no computer monitoring. For cooling, unlike the American factory, we used brine, cheap but volatile.

'The chemicals kept sitting in the tanks, volatile, unpredictable, undisposable. I could hear the chemicals when I walked past the storage tanks. A kind of tingling, swishing sound, the buzz of electrolytes humming on the surface of the liquid, chemicals singing to themselves an atomic song, humming a lullaby of perfectly balanced equations.

'I began to hear rumours. In New York, after a meeting of the board, they would announce the closure of the factory. They would write it off in their books as a loss, take the tax break from the loss, strip the factory, ship parts of it off to some other country, to some other place with a more sophisticated market for pesticides. The chemicals in the tanks kept singing, of profit and of loss, of market share and of stock prices, of tax breaks and of sizeable assets.

'The scrubber unit isn't functioning. The flare tower has been dismantled for repairs. The cooling system, the one meant to prevent the stored chemicals from going into a runaway reaction, has been shut down. They need to cut costs. The chemicals in the tanks are singing.'

7

'At night,' the operator said, 'it can be hard to know whether you are in Bhopal or in Kirkuk. You stand there, in a square of concrete, silhouettes of tanks and towers rising all around you, trapped in an infinite geometry of right-angled pipes and spiral stairwells, dreaming an endless nightmare of valves and gauges, of pumps and flanges, the air laced with afterburn and sadness.

'Those on night shifts feel the buildings to be much larger. The grounds seem endless. Workers talk of seeing structures that have nothing to do with our production process, furnaces and incinerators and fractionation towers coded in unfamiliar alphanumerics, counters with readouts that are illegible. They speak of running into technicians and supervisory staff who know their way around and yet whom no one recalls having met before. There are beeps in the night, the hum of unfamiliar machines, the wailing sound of animals.

'At night,' the operator said, 'Kirkuk and Bhopal are one. At night, the Kali Parade grounds merge into the realm of the Black Caliph.'

Waves of nausea struck my body. The operator's eyes were like wells from which no light escaped. I could no longer hear what he was saying. He reached under the table and pulled out a cloth bag. I glimpsed the corner of a folder. In my head, my patron's instructions lined up in a perfect squad. They swung their metal-tipped sticks in unison, brought them down sharply on the ground with their left hands, clicked their boots and offered a salute, right arm swivelling across the chest, palm facing down. Then they swung their metal-tipped sticks into me. As my head exploded, a whore laughed a whore's laugh.

When my head cleared, the operator was gone. The Savage Bar was pitch dark. I made out a feeble glow in the distance, a last gasp of light from the stairway leading to the street. I tried to move. I couldn't.

Something pressed down on my left shoulder, on my arm. A heavy weight, the weight of corpses, of past misdeeds. Then I heard snoring and smelt a warm fug of booze, cigarettes and perfume. I tried to get my arm out, shift the weight off my shoulder.

'Darling, don't leave,' the whore said, clutching my arm possessively.

'Let me go, randi,' I snarled. When had she come into the bar? When did she settle down next to me? Where was the operator?

I pushed. It made no difference. She didn't move an inch. I twisted around and smacked her in the face with my free hand. It was like hitting a mound of dough. I hit her again. She groaned but refused to let go. I shoved outward, hard. Down she went to the floor, taking me with her. I rolled on a mass of female flesh, cloying and sticky and sucking me in like a toxic pit. I couldn't breathe. Her arms were stronger than mine. I sank ever deeper. Then, just like that, my panic was gone. In its place was something else. I was aroused as I began to spread myself. I began to swim in that stinking pit.

My patron's voice came to my head like an electric jolt. Where is your friend? Where is that man the operator at an American chemical factory on the Kali Parade grounds?

I climbed over the whore, ran down the stairs and came out on to the street. How could I have fallen asleep? Hamidia Road stared back at me glassily, emptily, without even the scattering of autorickshaws that waited for drunken, late-night fares. A moon drifted out from behind the clouds, sickly yellow in colour. I kicked the starter on my scooter. The engine coughed and died. Again and again I kicked, listening to its death rattle, tilting the scooter to the side to coax a last trickle of petrol into the chamber.

I left the scooter and began to run down Hamidia Road. I ran like a madman, like a bereaved father, like a broken-hearted husband, past shuttered shops, trailing electric wires and peeling posters. Sex Weakness! Hydrocele! Piles! A chilly wind pushed scraps of paper around. Massive Demonstration! The wind died down and I stopped. Far ahead of me, to my left, lit up in the yellow glow of a street lamp, a drunken figure danced down an empty side street. Had he forgotten his motorcycle? Or did the operator know he was in no state to drive? There was no time to think. Just follow follow.

Follow follow this drunken man a chemical operator on the Kali Parade grounds. Follow follow to catch up with him, hold him by his elbow, take him home, offer to carry his cloth bag for him. Follow follow so that this man an operator at the American chemical factory on Kali Parade becomes my friend, tells me what papers he has that must be returned to their rightful owners.

Through the quarters of the Old City I follow followed, trying to catch up. How does a drunken man walk so fast? Follow follow. How does this gap between us never close? Follow follow. He stumbled, he fell, he cursed. He leant against a wall and dozed for a while. Still, I remained behind him. The land stretched out before me like some vast, endless square in some city from another time. We passed the factory. Floodlights swept its perimeter. A siren wailed. Powerful engines burst into life and abruptly fell silent. 'Poison gas!' the operator screamed. A pack of barking dogs replied, but I couldn't understand the low-born language of the Dog People.

My heart beat like a piston. Sweat dripped from my pores. Through alleyways we went, past shops that had signboards saying they sold burqas. I cursed my patron's contradictory instructions and ran to catch up with the operator. He continued heedless of me, intent on a drunken dance through the chowks and the alleyways and the shut-up sabzi mandi where discarded vegetables rotted in corners next to giant garbage vats and Dog People stretched themselves, his drunkard's feet somehow always ahead of me.

He had reached his house. I was as far behind as ever. This man an operator at a chemical factory began shouting. He kicked at his front door, drunken kicks that missed as often as they hit. 'Mukhabarat,' he shouted. 'West Virginia,' he screamed. From the shadows, a man stepped out. The operator stopped shouting. A square of light spilt out as the front door opened. The stranger stepped back into the shadows.

'Tomorrow,' I heard the operator say to the stranger. 'Come tomorrow. Tomorrow, everything.' The man a chemical operator tried to grab his wife, missed and fell inside. The door closed. For a while, everything was silent. Then there was the sound of a crashing chair and a sharp cry. A male voice shouted its male rage into the night. The stranger remained in the shadows and listened for a while. Then he began walking.

I had sweated out the whisky. My throat was parched and I felt a great thirst. Still, follow follow this man a stranger as he makes his way out of the Old City. Follow follow for so long that time loses its shape, that limbs hurt, that I curse my patron for giving me an old scooter and confusing orders. Follow follow deep into the tunnel of the night. Follow follow this stranger this other man visiting that man an operator at an American chemical factory on the Kali Parade grounds. Follow follow the stranger as he walks up to Shyamla Hills, walks beyond the rich people's bungalows to the edge of a forest. Follow follow up high beyond the black lakes of this black city. Follow follow under a yellow moon and towards the grey forests of this black city.

The man plunged into the forest and was gone. It took me a while to see that there was a dirt track running through the forest. Follow follow along the dirt track, hardly able to see ahead. Follow follow over thorny scrub, past scurrying forest creatures, through trees with fingers that pull and that scratch, trees that are like the mimosa tree from which the vampire hangs in the story of Vikram the Conqueror. Follow follow past statues and totem poles that follow follow you in these endless grounds of the National Collection of Man. Follow follow past the huts of jungle dwellers and savage hunters. Follow follow past demon buffalo horns that rise to a yellow moon. Follow follow to a clearing and a forest shack. Follow follow and circle a shack at the back of which yellow-saffron clothes dry on a line under a yellow-saffron moon and a yellow-saffron bull snorts and chews cud. Follow follow cautiously towards the shack. Follow follow to the explosion at the back of your head, to the ghosts who await you in the darkness.

8

Sunlight bled through cracks. Bird noises created a din. I raised my head and looked around slowly. I lay in front of a shack, one of those fake jungle-dweller huts. I got to my feet slowly, rubbing the patch of dried blood at the back of my head. I checked out the back of the hut first. The bull was gone, as were the clothes that had been drying, although the bright yellow nylon line remained, trembling in the dawn breeze. I went back inside the hut. It had walls made from uneven wooden planks, a dirt floor and a low sloping roof woven from bamboo and thatch. There was a bunk halfway up the wall. I peered into it. Nothing.

I raised myself into the bunk and rolled in. A slight tinge of incense and sweat. I looked down into the hut from the bunk. At the back wall, facing the door, a long painted plank of wood showed the face of a tribal warrior with an elaborate headdress of black and white feathers. The man's eyes were fixed on a distant point, like he was staring into the far future. I made my way down. He looked straight out through the door, into the distance where a piece of paper soared amid the trees like a kite free of its string.

Past the totems and huts and trees I follow followed, keeping my eyes on the paper, watching as it got trapped in a branch and flapped madly before sinking down. The sun rose in the December sky as I bent to pick it up. A thin and flimsy sheet of paper, cheaply printed. A leaflet of the sort I had seen on the factory walls.

Before the return of Rama's Kingdom, first the Rat King!
What is the karma of your past lives?
What does the future hold for you?

The need-to-know rule, my patron called it. To know only what is sufficient for the task at hand. The target, the location, the support, the timeline. Beyond that, no need to know. It was that way in Amritsar, in Dhanbad and in Shillong. Cash and need-to-know instructions from an office. Nights above a rice hotel or in a rented room. For relaxation, a bottle, a blue film, a procured woman. Days waiting or following. Railway stations and bus terminuses. Heat, cold, rain. Mosquitoes, millions of mosquitoes. Listening to questions being asked in a police cell or army interrogation room, alert for the key piece of information, for what could be acted upon. The smell of piss and vomit and terror. The occasional visit to a house set back from all others, the beeps of its radio transmitter audible as one approached. The various tasks that I had to perform, knowing only what I needed to know, I, the unacknowledged, anonymous lund of Bharat.

In Imphal, they dropped me off in an army jeep with masked licence plates, the soldiers in mufti pointing out the house where the target was sleeping. In Punjab, I waited at a highway checkpoint, the informer sitting back in a car with tinted windows, his face covered in a cheap shawl, ready to identify the target. All that I knew of the target was what I needed to know to complete the job. All that the policemen, soldiers or intelligence officials knew of me was my code name, chosen specially for the occasion by my patron from the names of classical city states. Somnath, Shravasti, Hastinapur … Names uncontaminated by foreign invasion, names filled with the glory of Bharat.

Most of all, there was no need to know anything about my patron. Those glasses, that white dhoti, the smell of the cardamoms he chewed. There was his uncanny resemblance to a very well-known figure, a fact that struck everyone who saw him for the first time, but before anyone said anything, he smiled in that way of his, like he was saying, yes, of course I know about the resemblance, and I know I might almost be a double of the father of the nation, but of course a double, a doosra, an individual who has his own characteristics, not the non-violent, satyagraha, cleanliness-is-next-to-godliness, I-sleep-naked-next-to-my-nieces-to-test-my-will father of the nation, but the kind of father a new, uncertain nation with an old, glorious history needs, a menacing doosra version of the original father, who regretfully was killed, very sad, very sad, but we must all make sacrifices for the greater cause, and anyway, are you sure this resemblance between me and Gandhi actually exists, and is it not perhaps a trick of perspective, a matter of the angle, and if you came closer, would you still think I resembled somebody, anybody, or would you just see me as I really am, defender of the realm, protector of the faith, triumph of the will?

There were rumours of money made in colonial times, food hoarded during the famine, arms purchased from retreating, demobbed armies and stockpiled, but no need for me to know any of that. No need for me to know of the networks being established and that whoever took the throne in Delhi, this state within the state would always remain unchanged, sometimes working with it, sometimes working independently of it. Not that I was required to know any of this, not at all, but at times I suspected that my patron's vision went far beyond 'India Is Indira and Indira Is India', or even beyond 'We Hindus Are All One and a Nation', to something that was not so much a nation but a state of being, a stage of consciousness. To my patron all this must be merely the movement of ants, worms, atomic particles, to him it must be insignificant this one man the anonymous prick of India follow following another man an anonymous semi-literate operator at an advanced American chemical factory on the Kali Parade grounds in Bhopal in the winter of 1984.

Word came to the hotel. New instructions awaited me with the intermediary. In my heart, I desired the embrace of the incense maker's daughter. Instead, I hurried to the New City on the grey Bajaj scooter, its brakes fixed, its engine tuned, its tyres firm and its tank full, to receive my new orders.

I sensed an urgency as I read the instructions. I felt an impatience. There was cash for expenses in the envelope handed over by the intermediary. There was a train ticket for December 3, two days from now. A reservation for a second-class berth on the Gitanjali Express from Nagpur to Calcutta. I was expected to get to Nagpur on my own, on one of the many trains running there from Bhopal. But before that, I had a final task to carry out. I heard my patron's voice in my head. I could not tell if he was pleased or angry.

Tonight at ten, you are required to be at the formulation shed of the factory. The operator and his comrades will be conducting a secret meeting in the workers' canteen. The meeting is a conspiracy, but that is not your concern. What happens after the meeting is. The meeting will end, the workers will part with their conspiracy in mind, and the operator, the one who you have followed all these weeks, will go by himself to the formulation shed to hand over documents in his possession to an unknown third party. The transaction must not be completed. The unknown third party will not make it to the factory. You will be there instead to take possession of the papers. Dispose of the operator as you see fit once you have confiscated the papers. Here is an example of what you will find in the operator's possession.

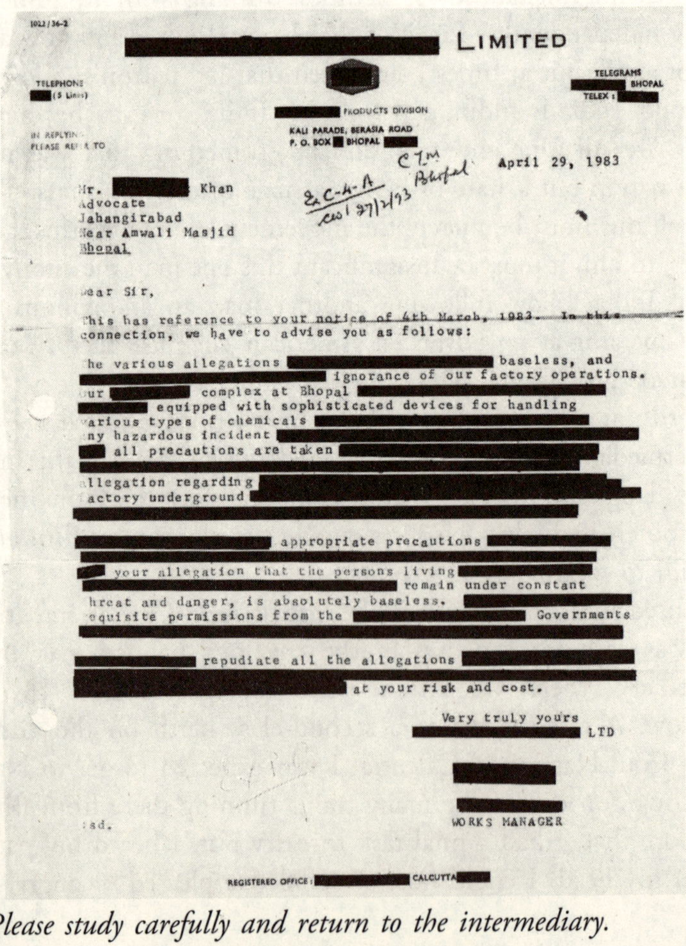

1022/36-2

LIMITED

TELEPHONE (5 Lines)

TELEGRAMS BHOPAL
TELEX :

PRODUCTS DIVISION
KALI PARADE, BERASIA ROAD
P. O. BOX BHOPAL

IN REPLYING PLEASE REFER TO

April 29, 1983

Mr. Khan
Advocate
Jahangirabad
Near Amwali Masjid
Bhopal

Dear Sir,

This has reference to your notice of 4th March, 1983. In this connection, we have to advise you as follows:

he various allegations baseless, and ignorance of our factory operations.
our complex at Bhopal equipped with sophisticated devices for handling various types of chemicals
ny hazardous incident
all precautions are taken

llegation regarding
actory underground

appropriate precautions

your allegation that the persons living remain under constant hreat and danger, is absolutely baseless.
equisite permissions from the Governments

repudiate all the allegations at your risk and cost.

Very truly yours
LTD

WORKS MANAGER

:sd.

REGISTERED OFFICE : CALCUTTA

Please study carefully and return to the intermediary.

9

Towards the slum in Chandbarh, I sped on the grey Bajaj scooter. In Bhopal, in Bhopal, in Bhopal, the engine coughed. Baseless allegations, appropriate precautions, it growled at the singing schoolchildren in the collapsing building. The incense maker's daughter was alone, tying up incense sticks and putting them into plastic packets. Thousands of incense sticks lay out in the back yard, drying in the sun. The mix sat in buckets, a glutinous black mass of chemicals like perfumed dung. I reached out my hand to shut the back door. One last time.

A string of jasmine flowers looped around her hair. Her eyes, lined with kajal, were dark pools of water. Bright green glass bangles were pushed up against her elbows. A fine dusting of incense powder covered her hands. She smiled at me. 'They found one of the children,' she said. 'She got lost inside the railway station. But there are others, still missing.' I changed my mind. I left the door open.

Squatting next to Rekha, I began counting out incense sticks. One, two, half a dozen, one dozen, twenty at a time to be tied up with red string. Put the bunch into a transparent plastic case and add it to the pile. Pick up incense sticks again. Count again. Tie again. Put into fresh plastic case again.

Rekha stopped to show me the colourful packets in which these sticks would be sold after they had been sent to a distributor. The pictures swirled around me, lotuses and vimanas and goddesses afloat on waves of sandalwood, nagchampa, jasmine and, faint but clear, the smell of this woman. The winter sunlight streamed in through the open door and the slowly collapsing school across the yard hummed with the voices of children reciting their daily lessons.

In the cold December evening, I left my scooter parked at the hotel and walked to clear my head. My last nights in Bhopal, in Bhopal, in Bhopal. The first day of December, of December, of December. Tonight, an interrupted transaction at the formulation shed of the American chemical factory on the Kali Parade grounds. Tomorrow, papers handed to the intermediary to find their way back to the rightful owners and a berth on the Gitanjali Express to Calcutta.

In Bhopal, in Bhopal, in Bhopal, having done with the incense maker's daughter, I walked. Towards Bharat Talkies, towards the lakes, back towards the railway station. I fingered the spot on my upper lip where I had worn a moustache from Delhi. I thought of the ghosts from Delhi, from everywhere I had been in the service of my patron. Wherever I walked, unanswered questions follow followed me like Sikhs in pink turbans. Was Maharishi the one who had ambushed me? Was he the man on the Bullet motorcycle? Who did Maharishi work for? Who was the unknown third party taking delivery of the papers tonight?

Outside the railway station, an Insect Man pushed a handcart filled with handkerchiefs, belts and purses under the neon glow of a Jain Bhojanalaya, a Brijwasi Bhojanalaya, a Krishna Bhojanalaya. Cripples and beggars and Muslim autorickshaw drivers filled the road, some of them bunched in suspicious knots at stalls selling cigarettes and cold drinks. A policeman stumbled as he stepped hurriedly out of a still moving autorickshaw. Three charsis sat at a cigarette stall, the owner and his friends passing around a chillum, heedless of customers. With red eyes, they laughed loudly at nothing, operating in a world other than this one. Time moved differently for them, space bent around them. But I was locked and loaded, ready to travel down my assigned path towards my target.

A long-distance train was pulling in at the station, covered in its own shit. Dim lights flickered around the platform and the overbridge. A whore cursed out two railway policemen, who listened attentively, like laggard students who knew that they deserved the tongue-lashing. Insect People bedded down on platforms on either side of a red maalgari loaded with coal, spreading out rags and blankets for the night. I walked past the deserted ticket counters and climbed up to the overbridge.

'The Gorakhpur–Bombay Express has arrived,' a shrill female voice announced on the PA system. 'The Gorakhpur–Bombay Express is seven hours late.' I watched the crowd swirl around the Gorakhpur–Bombay Express, the crush of red-shirted coolies with suitcases piled high on their turbaned heads, the wave of passengers getting off colliding with the wave getting on. A pink turban seemed to bob momentarily in that turbulent sea. I follow followed it immediately, but a crowd rolled through. When it cleared, there was no pink turban.

I thought of my Gitanjali Express ticket, of the assignment tonight. I was missing something. What conspiracy were the workers planning? What did they hope to gain by handing company documents over to a third party? I thought of what the operator had told me that night at the Savage Bar, of safety protocols deliberately allowed to run down because the factory had become a loss-making concern.

I gripped the railing hard. On Platform 3, the rush around the Gorakhpur–Bombay Express had died down, and the train sat there, grateful for the break, catching its breath. What kind of chemicals were in the factory? Were they like the poison gas chemicals the operator had worked on in Iraq? What kind of damage would happen if an accident were allowed to happen? Would hundreds of Insect People die?

Someone tugged at my jeans. A crawling man, an Insect Man. He held out a piece of paper. With his other hand, he rattled a tin cup with a few coins in it. There was something familiar about him, something very familiar about that piece of paper with 'Ladies' Hospital' written on it.

'Wife,' the Insect Man said.

'…'

'Baby,' the Insect Man said.

'…'

'Please,' the Insect Man said.

I turned around and looked back at the railway tracks, at the never-ending dance of iron on dirt. The tracks danced like swords aflame in the hands of a warrior monk, cutting through the gathering mass of darkness. They danced like rods in the hands of men primed to kill, retaliating against traitors and assassins. Blow by blow. Block by block. Block 25. Block 26. Block by block.

I took the unresolved questions—the operator, the Maharishi, the unknown third party—and flung them in the path of the advancing men killing with rods and swords, destroying with kerosene and chemicals. The Gorakhpur–Bombay Express, crowded with Insect People, began to pull out. Behind me, one Insect Man still chittered. 'Wife, please. Baby, please.' I thought momentarily of the incense maker's daughter and then flung my memory of her in the path of the speeding Gorakhpur–Bombay Express. I gave her to the mob advancing block by block to open up every hole of hers before they set her ablaze. The Insect Man I sent sprawling to the ground with one slap on his face. Then I zipped up my Paona Bazaar jacket, pulled up its collar, patted the Beretta pistol in its holster and walked towards the grey Bajaj scooter waiting for me.

Follow follow one final time that man an operator at a chemical factory on the Kali Parade grounds. Follow follow he who crossed the black waters to become an operator at an Iraqi chemical factory run by the Mukhabarat. Follow follow the man who my patron asked me to befriend, the man who possesses incriminating company documents that must be returned to their rightful owners.

Follow follow to the American chemical factory on the Kali Parade grounds against which people make baseless allegations. Follow follow to the American chemical factory on the Kali Parade grounds whose management has taken all appropriate precautions. Follow follow to the new American chemical factory through the winding lanes of an Old City where no industrial disaster is likely to happen.

Follow follow to the American chemical factory that looks desolate, whose gates are locked. A group of Dog People howled from the slums nearby. This time I understood their low-born ghoul tongue. They moaned in the Paisacha language, in Bhootbhasha.

'Have you ever? Have you ever?' they sang to me.

'What unknown third party is here today?' I sang back.

'Have you ever felt that you had become a person of the opposite sex?' the Dog People sang.

'What unknown patron is behind this unknown third party?' I retorted.

'Have you ever had the experience of leaving your body and of observing things from another place?' the Dog People sang.

'What does the operator hope to achieve by handing over the papers?' I replied.

'Have you ever been aware of things in the future that you could not have known about?' the Dog People sang.

'Yes, and so I know that no industrial disaster is likely to happen in this city.'

Searchlights blazed out from factory watchtowers that are like temples to the factory gods. The searchlights demanded that the Dog People maintain their distance. Painting white cones in the darkness, they ordered the Dog People to know their place.

Ghoulish howls rose from the Dog People. The searchlights retorted that they keep treacherous opinions and subversive ideas to themselves and not contaminate the holy American chemical factory with their barbarous Paisacha tongue.

Follow follow to the edge of the boundary wall where slumland gives way to farmland sloping upward. The scooter coughed and stalled, undone by the barbarous chants of the Dog People. I parked it against the factory wall. The posters on the wall warned me of the evil eye and asked me to contact Maharishi. The posters threatened to uproot this death factory and unleash Massive Demonstrations! The night air was filled with the smell of shit and garbage. Far away, lorries groaned in agony as they were dragged on to the Nagpur highway and beaten to death. The railway tracks screamed a long, piercing cry as they were raped by a train going to Indore.

I took my jacket off, bunched it up and waited. A searchlight swept the grounds, alert to keep the Dog People out. I waited till it had gone past me. Then I placed my jacket on the wall, over the shards of glass. Up and over I went, feet scrambling for purchase on the wall, hands on the jacket through which the glass stabbed, dropping to the ground and keeping low as the searchlight came back for its return sweep. Then I sprinted, releasing myself into the darkness this dark night this dark age this dark factory this dark Kali Parade.

10

Follow follow through jungle glass and shivering trees, scanning the grounds for lights and for activity. Follow follow through waterlogged grounds, trying to aim for the workers' canteen where a conspiracy is under way. Follow follow past rows of cement vats where chemicals sing their chemical song. Turning this way and that way, trying to find solid ground. Turning this way and that way, trying to find a brick to step on.

The searchlights swept the wall behind me, warning the Dog People to keep away. What did they know of chemicals? the searchlights said. What did they know of the complex operations of an American chemical factory where all appropriate precautions had been taken? Massive Demonstration! Massive Demonstration! The Dog People replied in volleys of barks. This death factory! This death factory! They howled in unison.

Ahead of me, shadows and shapes formed in the darkness. Clusters of trees, warehouse buildings, discarded objects on the ground, white plastic sacks that carried names I couldn't quite make out in the dark. -WIN? -VIN? Still, I advanced, follow following step by step, trying to make my way to the workers' conspiracy canteen. Still, I persisted, follow following on bricks placed like stepping stones in the waterlogged ground. The trees whispered to each other in the darkness. Then they thinned out, giving way to an open stretch of ground. I follow followed, walking with caution, walking with intent towards the administrative area of the factory.

My route twisted and turned along the vast factory grounds. The first of the MIC tanks appeared in front of me, and then, mysteriously, I found my access to it blocked by a group of trees. I changed direction and kept follow following, checking my watch to see that I had time enough before the conspiracy meeting ended. At last, I was close to the main building. I could find my way to the conspiracy canteen from there.

I follow followed in the direction of the main building. In the dark, I almost missed it, almost fell into the trench in front of me. Deep, with sloping walls, the trench sat between me and the main building like a moat protecting a fort from an invader. Liquid swished and swirled below, making my head swim. Thick, dark liquid, with streaks of yellow like fat veins in a meat curry. I looked for a way across, trying to ignore the burn of the chemicals around my nose. My eyes watered. The handkerchief I had clapped to my mouth was no use.

I retreated, looking for another route. But I could no longer see the main building. My head swirled from the chemicals. I was short of breath, an old man, a once-proud warrior bowed down by a heavy burden, carrying, like Vikram the Conqueror, a chattering vampire on my back, a Betaal who would never stop telling me his complicated conspiracy stories and who would never let me finish my task.

I caught my breath and began follow following again, trying urgently to locate the main building. Impossible! It was farther away than it had been before. Impossible for it to be so far away given how long I had been follow following through the factory grounds. I had made no progress at all, creeping step by step towards a blurred horizon of buildings and factory towers. My legs were moving in slow motion, my body jerking like that of an insect trapped in viscous fluid.

A series of beeps filled the air. I froze in my tracks. It was a familiar sound, a call sign being pumped out by a radio transmitter. I tried to read the code, but it evaporated into the air. I began to spot outlines of Nissen huts, isolated, semicircular sheds that were locked but looked like they had been abandoned decades ago. Graffiti scarred the walls of the sheds. SAGE OR FRAUD? asked big, furious letters painted below the graphic of a monkey in a helmet. I felt I was visiting not a factory as much as the ruins of a factory, a place where terrible things had happened and terrible things been forgotten.

I needed to rest. I needed water, air. I could follow follow no longer, no matter that time was running out. I slumped down against the wall of a building shaped differently from the Nissen huts, long and low and rectangular. I saw fresh lorry tracks, deep, heavy grooves cut into the mud in front of me. Accompanying them were the tyre treads of smaller vehicles, suggesting that a military convoy had passed this way not too long ago.

I checked my watch and follow followed the tracks to a set of giant metal doors. Unlocked and pitch dark inside, and yet radiating a kind of machine warmth from engines not yet cooled down. I took out the Vimana match box I had stolen from the operator. In the light of a match, I could make out, hidden in the shadows at the back, a lorry. It was long, almost too long, painted in a dark unreflecting colour. A stench of chemicals came from it. A slimy residue had pooled around it. I struck another match and looked at the plates on the lorry. They were blank.

I didn't understand why I was here. My task was simple, to follow follow my way to the formulation shed before ten p.m. Why was I here instead of there? The factory, the factory itself had stopped me. My route had been diverted, my path made labyrinthine. My will had met the will of this place. The match went out.

I lit another one. I looked for the metal doors I had come through. There was still time. I could not be that far away from the formulation shed. But where were the doors? The flickering light found only black walls. There were no doors. It was as if there had never been.

THE CLOCK WAS ticking and I was trapped. Time became distorted, decades and centuries bending around me. Other lives, other stories pressed their images upon me. Shapes scurried in the darkness and a bearded Chinese man stared at me from the hospital bed he was shackled to. When he saw me looking, he rattled his chains. I heard beeps again and the visions faded.

Far away in the distance, there was a prick of light. I began walking towards it. The shed went on for far longer than should have been possible, the ground sloping down. I was descending underground through a long passageway like an incline tunnel in a coal mine. I lit my last match. The walls of this tunnel were smooth, coated with the same black paint as that on the lorry.

The match went out and I lost my orientation. I did not know where was up or down, front or back. I was drowning in a dark, bottomless pool filled with a thick, burning liquid. A voice began to chant loudly. *Ulding bam isoner spram inded blam*, the voice shouted, louder and louder in my head until I thought I would pass out from the pain of the words booming inside my skull. I crashed against a wall so hard that my arm went numb.

When I had recovered, I realised that I could see something. Light came through a crack between a pair of metal doors set in the wall. I peered through the crack. I saw nothing. I pushed the doors. They were heavy. I pushed harder. The doors gave way suddenly and I fell into the room. It was filled with people. All squatting on the floor, looking at me in silence. A room full of Sikhs! Men in pink turbans, women with pink dupattas over their heads, children and babies, all staring at me. I blinked. I waited for my vision to clear. I tried to breathe but could feel a burning at the back of my throat. No, not Sikhs. A yellow glow lit up the room full of dark-skinned folk. Muslims. Bengalis. Staring at me like they expected me to start counting. I blinked again, looked again. The room was empty. There was a noise, the beeps of a transmitter, and a chemical stench, sharp and burning.

FOLLOW FOLLOW THE beeping noise. Follow follow the chemical stench. Follow follow to another crack in another wall that bleeds light, to a crack that weeps sounds, where engines growl and men murmur. Carefully, I planted my eye along the crack between the doors. A wave of chemicals hit me again and I grew dizzy. When my vision cleared, I saw men in green uniforms and others in white laboratory gowns, men with masked faces moving around a vast room filled with control panels. In the centre, in the cross-wire of all their activity and attention, placed inside a cylinder with glass walls, there was a thing.

I do not know how to describe this thing. An elephant trunk on a humanoid face. An oversized rat king. For a moment, it looked like the elephant god Ganesh. Impossible, I told myself. I was seeing things. The fumes had affected me. I blinked to clear my eyes. I opened them again.

It was still there, sitting on a chair in a glass cage at the centre of the cavernous room. Not a Ganesh, no. The trunk was a tube dangling from an oxygen mask, the creature a pilot or cosmonaut wearing helmet and goggles. Another wave of nausea hit me. I backed away from the crack and bent over, gagging but trying desperately not to make a noise. I breathed slowly, got myself in control, and returned to the crack.

It was neither a Ganesh nor a pilot. It was no thing of this earth. It was an alien creature, definitely trunk and not oxygen tube, definitely eyes not goggles, definitely giant rat monster not elephant god. Its eyes stared at me through the glass walls as they pumped the chamber with gas. Its eyes watered. The creature saw me looking at it through the crack. Its eyes were luminous, silent and pleading as they filled with tears.

I TURNED AROUND, barely knowing where I was going. I had breathed in too much of that gas in this death factory filled with monsters who wept slow, fat tears. Follow follow, away from that thing, follow follow and don't think about what you saw. I had been too long in this factory, too long in this city, too long on an assignment where the facts were all concealed, where everything was twisted, as in the realm of the Black Caliph. I was not so different from that man I follow followed, that man an operator at this American chemical factory on the Kali Parade ground.

Back through the tunnel, blundering in the darkness, trapped in a factory that is also a laboratory for experiments on weeping monsters that is a centre for conspiracy that is a clandestine meeting place for an exchange of papers that is a place against which baseless allegations have been made that is a place whose management has taken all appropriate precautions that is a place where no industrial disaster is likely to happen.

The ground sloped up, up, up. The factory was playing with me, all the buildings connected through secret underground tunnels that had minds of their own. My route led me out to a shed. I was standing inside the formulation shed, at the back, the very place where the Sikh with the pink turban had tried to drag me into the darkness.

I had been asked to wait for the operator in front of the shed, but it was not yet ten. There was still time. I had not yet failed my patron.

MY HEAD GREW clearer. I observed my surroundings. No Sikhs in pink turbans. My Beretta in its holster. My watch at twelve to ten. My breathing slowed, my pulse dropped down to resting rate. At five minutes to ten, a shape became visible at the front of the shed. Backlit by the floodlamps outside, the man an operator stood at the mouth of the shed.

That man an operator stood there on his own, looking at the folder in his hand, looking at his watch. He took a cigarette out, put it in his mouth without lighting it. He took the cigarette and put it back in the packet. I eased my Beretta out of its holster and moved forward. Then I stopped. Why was there another man lurking in the shadows? Why was another man, whom I had not seen until now, standing between me and the operator?

I waited as the dial of my watch crept past ten o'clock. My legs hurt from standing still, but I waited. The stranger waited. The operator waited, the most restless among us, and yet the most free, pacing back and forth against the mouth of the formulation shed. Perhaps twenty minutes went by. Howls of the Dog People sounded in the distance, moody warning songs sung under the purple moonlight. The operator began walking away. The stranger moved out of the shadows.

I tried to warn him, I swear, this man I had follow followed for so long, this man an operator at an American chemical factory on the Kali Parade grounds, this man who crossed the black waters to work in Kirkuk under the supervision of the Mukhabarat, this man that my patron wanted me to befriend, this man who beat his wife at night, this man whose seed was dead, this man with documents about an American chemical factory on the Kali Parade grounds against which people had been making baseless allegations and whose management had taken all the appropriate precautions, this man I had follow followed through a city where no industrial disaster is likely to happen, this man who had been my target, my double, my doosra, I tried to warn him.

A sliver of white space separated the operator from the stranger. I was shouting, taking my safety off, when I saw the muzzle flash. The shot thundered through the formulation shed and was still echoing as I came out of the darkness. The stranger turned, his eyes a flicker of surprise, the sound of the second gunshot dissolving into the echoes of the first one. He fell next to the operator. I reached for the folder that lay between them as blood pooled towards it.

I looked at Kanwar. He was lying face down, the exit wound at the back of what used to be his head. I had follow followed him for so long, but now he was gone to a place where even I could not follow follow him. The man who had shot the operator was staring up at the roof. There was enough of his face left to say that he wasn't anyone I knew.

11

I have feasted on death again. In Bhopal, I have feasted on the death of an unknown man the assassin of that man an operator at an American chemical factory on the Kali Parade grounds. This was not part of mob work as in Delhi. It was not the kind of killing carried out amid the mayhem and rape of Gupta's men. Say what you will, this death had definition. This death had meaning.

The faces of the dead call for attention. The bodies of the dead demand scrutiny. The face of the assassin I had killed called out to me, even if it was half a face, even if it was a half face I did not recognise. He was a warrior, one who had taken my prey. He was my rival and he had defeated me. His death would not alter the fact of that defeat. And yet, because he was a warrior, because he was not one of the Dog People, not one of the Insect People, because he was a killer, one of the fanged, one of the brave, in destroying him, I had become a killer of killers. I had acquired double merit, double credit. I had rendered the brave timid, the fanged fangless.

I brought the Beretta to my face and sniffed. The whiff of gunpowder, the memory of violence. I inserted a cartridge into the empty chamber. A worthy weapon this, made, my patron once told me, by an Italian company five hundred years old. From my bag, I drew out the bottle with the remainder of whisky in it. As I drank, I thought of the thing I had seen in the factory.

Was it because of the chemicals I had breathed? What could it be other than a hallucination? I drank whisky and thought of stories whispered in the backchannels of deep state work, tales murmured by intelligence men on long, lonely nights of vigilance, incidents buried in termite-infested case files.

Rumours of laboratories and classified projects and occult knowledge. Vimanas and robots and superweapons originating in mysterious frontier zones, on mountains and islands. My mind went back to the creature, the alien or the Ganesh, alive, trapped in a glass cylinder. I vaguely recalled stories of thought-form experiments carried out somewhere, even though I wasn't sure what thought forms were. Stuff from Tibetan Buddhism, tulpas, tulkus, something like that.

Fiction or truth? I wondered, lying on my bed. I caressed the pistol in my hand and thought of Rekha. Is the yearning of one human being for another fiction or truth? Am I, with all my code names, fiction or truth to those I work for? Was I fiction or truth to those I eliminated? I thought of my patron, who had always seemed to possess such a firm grip over everything. Where did he stand in this shifting world, with its chemical vats of truth in an endless factory of fiction?

Once one starts doubting truth as fiction and fiction as truth, there is little not polluted by the mingling of the two. Where did Manu place truth and fiction in his order of things? Is truth high and fiction low? Or is fiction high and truth low? Which of these was in play when the other assassin fell and I survived? In Delhi, when the secretary said my patron was unavailable on the phone, was that truth or fiction? Was the operator's fear of the factory and impending disaster truth or fiction? My patron had thought of it as fiction, as falsehood, as had whoever dispatched the other assassin, all of them convinced that the operator, the workers, were part of a Communist plot meant to discredit industry, creating a fiction intended to blacken the reputation of an American multinational company and the glory of the motherland.

The quiet of the early morning was gone. The shrieks of buses and autorickshaws filled the air as Insect People went about their daily work along Hamidia Road, unaware, unheeding of the events that had unfolded last night. I remained in bed, wondering about truth and fiction and toying with my pistol. I played with my lund and scratched it with my pistol. I drank whisky in the light of the morning and murmured shlokas to myself. I mixed it all up, the high and the low, the truth and the falsehood and remembered the Sikhs I had killed for Gupta. I wondered if I had actually killed them for someone else.

I sat up on the bed, trying to shake out the thought bothering me underneath everything swirling on the surface. I almost found it, but it skittered away at the last second, vanishing into the day.

ON THE WAY to the office of my patron's intermediary, I stopped and made a phone call. The man who picked up, the man in Calcutta, listened quietly. He gave me a name and address in the Old City. The money would be ready for me in two hours, he said.

Some kind of digging was going on near the office. Standing knee deep in muddy water, Insect Men in grimy clothes grunted as they swung their picks into the road. Rolls of cables towered above them. A Bull Man holding a clipboard watched the proceedings, standing in front of a billboard for some kind of new business called Diners Club Credit Card. I didn't understand what that meant, and the thought came to me that I was being left behind in this world being remade around me.

I parked my scooter and tried to find my way through the mess of mud and cables and grunting men. A good part of the pavement was gone. I had to descend into the pit the men were digging. I jumped over puddles and clambered over cables. I finally reached the intermediary's office. A metal grille was pulled across the front door, a chain with a heavy padlock looped around it.

I sat down at a nearby tea stall. The offices and shops around the intermediary's office were functioning, even if workers and customers had to scramble up and down the dug-up road. Only the intermediary's office remained without activity, so shut up and dark as to seem that it had not been open for decades. Dirt had blackened the window frames. The glass was layered in dust and cobwebs. It was as though I had imagined all the times I visited the intermediary there, that I had dreamt it all.

But the document folder I had recovered existed. It was next to me as I sat at the tea stall, flies sipping at my cup with the confidence of pimps taking their cut. I looked at the intermediary's office and tried to recall its interior details. Instead, images of all the offices I had visited climbed into my mind from some deep, dug-up pit.

Wherever I had travelled in his service, my patron had intermediaries with offices. Trucks in the back yard, with rainbow-smeared pools of diesel and engine oil on the ground. The grunts of workers loading sacks or gas cylinders from an adjacent godown. Narrow stairwells leading upstairs to dimly lit rooms where men sat behind giant ledgers. Paintings of Ganesh, Lakshmi, or of a sati woman on fire. The click click of a telephone dial from an inside chamber. An atmosphere of weighty business being conducted, the sort that greased the wheels of the nation. Sometimes, men with moustaches and authority, the occasional policeman in uniform. Once, a bearded young man in saffron garments, a holy wanderer of the sort who often sought my patron's favour and who, while waiting with me for the accountant to be free, told me of the cosmic conspiracy against India. One day, when he led the nation, every Muslim would know their place or be eliminated. Like the law of action and reaction, it would cause India to rise again, he said, his face like a mask. Envelopes and packages waited for me in these offices, with instructions passed on by intermediaries, men with small eyes and dead faces. But rarely my patron.

The lunch hour came and the tea stall grew more crowded. The office of my patron's intermediary remained closed. I looked at the fading signboard above the office that said Vimana Traders. I did not recall seeing that before.

I rode to the market near the GTB complex. From Omni Bakers, I made a phone call to a local number I had been given. The phone rang a dozen times. No one answered. I tried again. No one answered. I tried five times with breaks of three minutes in between. When I still hadn't reached anybody, I went back to the Old City. At the main post office on Sultania Road, I booked a trunk call to Delhi. Again, I used the C code, wishing to speak to my patron. Again, the Secretary answered, the same one who had talked to me when I called from Gupta's farmhouse, the one who had said my patron was busy then and who said my patron was busy now.

There had been problems, the Secretary said. Orders had been confused, directives countermanded. In the tense national situation in the aftermath of the assassination, so many things had gone out of control. A great tree had fallen. It was natural that the earth would shake. That small creatures would get injured, perhaps killed. That those who had the downfall of the nation in mind would seize the opportunity to make their moves. What was that? The specific situation in Bhopal? Well, what could he say? Other national agencies had become involved, other agencies who were in touch with the Americans. This had complicated matters. At a time of such adversity, loyal soldiers like me had to be more selfless than usual. I could not possibly understand the gravity of the situation, the Secretary said, but surely I could wait at the hotel until a vehicle came to take me to a different intermediary. Once I had handed over the folder, I could leave Bhopal right away. I had a ticket on the Gitanjali Express for Calcutta, did I not? In spite of the complications, my patron would be pleased if I could complete the task.

'May I speak with my patron?' I said. 'I have not received wisdom directly from him in a very long time.'

'He will speak with you in Calcutta,' the Secretary replied. 'In Calcutta, there will be fresh work for you. In Calcutta, in Cal … cutta, in … cutta …' The line crackled and echoed with the ghosts of words.

'Surely, my patron …' I was unable to finish the sentence. The line had gone dead. I wondered if the Secretary had hung up on me.

I DIDN'T HAVE very far to go to pick up the money sent by the man in Calcutta. Up Marwari Road, not far from where I had follow followed the operator home, to the chowk, to a jewellery store that did not look like a jewellery store. It had neighbours that flashed colourful signs and glass showcases that sparkled with bangles and necklaces and twenty-two-karat gold. The jewellery store I was visiting was a narrow room with a low platform bed upon which a man with small, suspicious eyes sprawled. In front of him, on a little table, there was a wooden cash box, a black telephone and a yellow register. An attendant, a man with equally suspicious eyes, stood next to him.

They occupied the store in silence, the owner lying on his bed, the attendant standing, neither exchanging a word with the other. They seemed to be engaged in some profound meditation, reflecting on the meaning of life while the lowly business of buying and selling and bargaining went on around them.

I went in and mentioned a name and a number. There was no change of expression on the face of either master or servant. But master nodded to servant. Servant led me through a door at the back. Inside the dim room, I could make out an iron Aligarh safe that looked like the entrance to a fortress, a place where contending empires fought their final, decisive battle. With a jangling of keys, chains and levers, the man opened the safe. It took him a while. He brought out a white cloth bandi, a waistcoat sort of thing to be worn over a shirt, with numerous pockets covered by flaps.

The Aligarh safe was locked up, and we returned to the front room. The master took the bandi and began to empty out the pockets. He took out fat bundles of rupees, moving them to one side in neat stacks as he counted off thousands. His fingers skimmed on the river of notes. Gandhi faces flew past. It felt like my patron was watching me. The master kept counting. There was the precision of years, of centuries, in his count, the confidence of all the men of his caste who had financed kings and warlords from shops that looked not too different from this one, and who, from their nondescript surroundings, had seen empires rise and fall with indifference, calculating only their percentages.

The count completed, the bandi was refilled and handed back to me. No identity proof was required, no signature, not even my name was asked for, and yet there was not a glimmer of doubt in the small, suspicious eyes of the master that he might have made a mistake or that I was an impostor, no hesitation arising from the possibility that I might claim later that the money had not been given to me.

I took my Paona Bazaar jacket off and put the bandi on. Then

I put the jacket back on. I couldn't zip it up all the way with the bandi underneath. In the chowk, I wandered for a while on foot. When I was sure no one was follow following me, I went into a poori shop with an Air India maharajah statue at the entrance. A young man sat at the cash register. The proprietor, much older, sat next to him on a raised platform set off by itself. At the very back, in the kitchen, steel plates and tumblers clattered and clashed in the hands of Insect Men.

It was dark and filthy, with food droppings congealed in layers on the floor, but I could watch the entrance and people out in the street without being seen. An Insect Boy in a grimy undershirt and shorts brought me my lunch. Pooris, sabzi and achaar. I ate like I was starving, getting him to refill my plate twice and finishing off with a bowl of sweet gulab jamuns. I did not know when I would eat next. As I ate, I remained alert. The proprietor remained perfectly still on his platform, eyes shut, blissful smile on his face.

I wore my life's savings on me, money that I had kept separately from the regular bank account I used. No one, not even my patron, knew about this money and the gold merchant in Calcutta who acted as my private banker. Now I was sweating even in December from the weight of my money. I wanted to take my jacket off, but I needed it to cover the white bandi. The bandi itched and chafed. Underneath it, the butt of my Beretta rubbed against my ribcage, impatient in its holster. I would never be able to draw it while wearing the bandi. I cursed the master and servant with their shifty eyes. Around me, the lunchtime crowd thinned out. The proprietor remained in asana.

I envied him his calm, the self-control that allowed him to meditate in the middle of such everyday activity. I couldn't help contrast him with my restlessness, unable to scratch the itch of my pistol, the money on my body as heavy as an iron vest. But when I got up to pay, something struck me as wrong about the man. I stopped and stared, drawing the attention of the boy taking payments at the register. It was not a man at all, just an extremely lifelike statue. The perfect meditation that I had been admiring was the repose not of flesh but of stone.

12

At seven that evening, a man asked for me at the hotel. Black beard, sunglasses on face even though the sun had long since fled this city. In his hand, a visiting card that said Shri Ram Traders, the name of my patron's agency in Imphal. Follow follow this bearded man this sunglassed man into a jeep with new red leather on the seat and steering wheel. Follow follow with your eyes as Black Beard drives carefully through the crowded streets of the Old City. Follow follow as he picks up speed in the New City, heads towards Shyamla Hills. The road is empty. Mist drifts over from the lake into the path of our headlights.

It was the second of December, and it was cold. The folder sat on my lap. I kept my hands in my jacket to keep them warm. On my left side, I felt the comforting thrust of the pistol butt. I had emptied the cash out into a bag in the hotel, discarding the empty bandi. The bag was with me; Black Beard would drive me to the railway station once the folder had been handed over.

The jeep slowed and turned into the grounds of the National Collection of Man. The ticket booth was shut, but the place had no gates and the jeep kept going, bumping along the uneven track, its bouncing headlights picking out statues and huts on the hillside.

The jeep came to an abrupt stop in front of a shed filled with totem poles. Animals and birds and warriors and women crowded together like city dwellers waiting for a long-delayed bus. Wordlessly, Black Beard gestured at me to step outside and wait. Wordlessly, I obeyed. Black Beard turned off his engine, killed the lights and sat in his jeep.

The hills were dark and there was something wrong in the sky.

I thought I saw a movement from the nearest hut, a creaking of its bamboo platform. Its demon buffalo horns criss-crossed the night. I let my eyes adjust to the light and looked at the jeep. It was empty. Black Beard was gone. I waited and looked at the totem poles. Some reached up to the bamboo roof, others were shorter, wood decorated with the figures of buffaloes and jungle warriors. A man grinned on the totem pole closest to me, holding a severed head in each hand.

I thought of the things my patron had called me. If there were time and opportunity, I would carve out my name with those accompanying phrases on that totem pole with the head hunter. *Sword of Righteousness*, I would carve. Then I would write, *Erect Lund of Bharat.* Finally, I would add, *Fool Who Understood Nothing Until Far Too Late.*

AT THE HOTEL room this morning, before the burn of whisky blurred fiction and truth in my mind, I went over the contents of the folder. The letter shown to me by the intermediary was in it, but not blacked out. There was also a five-page handwritten telex with the title 'Inspection Report', sent by Larry Mulder in Bhopal to W.J. Woomer and C.D. Miller in Charleston, West Virginia. 'Average life expectancy ...' Mulder had written. 'Solids in condenser. Two complete unit shutdowns. Water contamination and trimerization. (Exciting time!) Need reply as soon as practical.'

There had also been a small green notebook with a plastic cover and binder rings. Scribbled notes covered the first half of the notebook, feverish like the speech of that man an operator now deceased.

'A man flew in to meet management staff yesterday. Who is this man? Where is he from? I caught a glimpse of him as they escorted him through the control room. He was dressed like a Congress politician in white khadi, but he was gone before I could take a good look at his face. The mute they used to take shorthand notes at the meeting tried to remember as much as she could. But she didn't understand much. MILITARY AID. GRAND STRATEGIC ALLIANCE. SIKH SEPARATIST GROUP. WORKERS AND THEIR REFLEXIVE TENDENCY

TO LIE. IMPACT OF GAS ON HUMAN BODILY SYSTEMS. IMPACT OF GAS ON??? SYSTEMS??? TO BE REMOVED TO SECURE LOCATION.

'Sahasrabudhe, who was on duty, said there was a military convoy. Black cloth screens were set up around the central warehousing complex. Soldiers patrolled the perimeter to keep workers away. There was only a skeletal night crew in any case. At 0100 hours the operation began. By 0300 hours, it was complete. The screens were removed and the convoy of long black trucks pulled out. Sahasrabudhe, whose brother is in the army, tried to see if there were any identifying details. But the licence plates were blank. No regimental markings were visible on the trucks and the soldiers had no insignia on their uniforms. If it had not been for their guns, their discipline, they would not have appeared to be soldiers at all.'

There were a few other things in the notebook. 'Safety protocol running down, New York board meeting, tax break, sizeable assets.' Etc. etc. Things I had heard that night from the drunken man an operator at an American chemical factory on the Kali Parade grounds.

HE CAME OUT of the night like a ghost. His beard and hair had been trimmed and he was wearing trousers and a dark jacket. Without the disguise, his life force was clear. Without his bull, without his saffron garb, without his chatter about future and past, he was a man completely of the present. I held the folder out. Maharishi took it and skimmed its contents. He shut it and smiled. 'We should have …' he said.

I pulled him towards me in a tight embrace before he could finish the sentence. I was bigger, but he was thin and strong, a furious, sinuous snake striking at me. We tumbled to the ground. I let go, rolled, stood and sprinted away from the totem pole shed. I ran up the hill over slick, slippery grass. My foot caught on something and I fell. The blast over my head was very loud.

IN THE NATIONAL Collection of Man, savage spirits are gathered. Restless ghosts hover in the shadow of the horned huts. From far away, comes the sound of stomping feet and pounding drums. In the National Collection of Man tonight, there will be a reckoning. In the National Collection of Man, the ghosts of all my kills lurk in the shadows and watch, Manipuris and Naxals and Kashmiris and Sikhs.

I remain crouching in the darkness, follow following with ears, eyes, nose. I have my Beretta out. I just need a dose of courage. A headlight blasts its white beams into my face. An engine roars. I have the acid taste of fear in my throat as I crawl in the grass, roll and crawl. The jeep is nearly on me. A shadow of a man leans out from the left.

I fire once, twice. The shadow drops. The jeep begins to slow. I stand, aim for the man behind the wheel and fire. There is a shattering of glass and the groan of the engine as the jeep gets stuck in a rut.

I TOOK MY time approaching the jeep, circling around from behind. Maharishi was on the ground, still alive, his breaths rattling his chest. I took the pistol from his hands. A .38, by the weight and size. I put it in my pocket and went around to the other side.

In the driver's seat, Black Beard was slumped over the wheel, blood trickling out of his clenched teeth. I pushed him out, turned the engine off and took the keys. I went through Black Beard's pockets. He didn't have a gun, just cigarettes and a lighter. I took those and walked back towards Maharishi.

It took me a few tries to get a flame. In its tiny flicker, the size of a human soul, I could see Maharishi's face. 'Whatever a man wins in battle, Manu says—chariot, horse, elephant, parasol, money, grain, livestock, women, all goods and base metal—all that belongs to him,' I said. Maharishi gurgled, tried to raise his hand and failed. His eyes glittered. His beard looked sleek and glossy, the shine of blood and sweat on it.

Maharishi groaned as I reached under him with my right hand. I found his wallet in the inside pocket of his jacket. He spoke in short bursts as I opened the wallet.

'The scooter,' he said. 'Did you ever look at the plates, you village idiot? Did you look inside the dashboard compartment?'

In the flame of the cigarette lighter, I looked at the identity card of this fortune-telling holy man who was an inspector in the Punjab Police and I looked at his face.

'Too late,' he said. He mumbled. As I leant closer, he spat at me. 'Coming for you for all of you the factory the gas the gas the gas.'

13

My patron always said that I was the special one. Countless were the minions who did his bidding, many the soldiers enlisted in his battle of good against evil, and yet I was the one who stood out. The sword of righteousness. The erect lund of Bharat.

As part of our early training in the camps, we were presented with problems, with scenarios. Who would be so brave, we were asked, to infiltrate a camp of Muslim terrorists? Who would have the nerve to grow a beard and assume the deviousness of the enemy? Who could walk among them as one of their own? An eager hand was raised. It was Malhotra, anxious to please, obsessed with winning the favour of the camp counsellors. But what will you do, the counsellor asked, when, to test your identity, to make sure there are no spies, they make everyone present eat a ritual bowl of beef?

The bowl will sit steaming in front of you, filled with the flavours of murder and sacrilege. You will barely be able to look at it, that bowl, and the horror of it will be magnified by the fact that each bearded terrorist sitting to the right and left of you has a similar bowl before him, a bowl with flesh that might as well as be human flesh, its putrefying, repulsive odours assailing your nostrils. Around you, you will hear foreign murmurs and sounds and chewing, while at the edges of the square will be guards with guns and swords who might as well be Arabs, so alien do they seem. You will feel like you have been transported to a foreign nation in the Middle East. You will think you have died and gone to hell. What will you do then? Will you partake in this grisly consumption of the sacred cow and survive to report on their activities, or will you let them discover your true identity and butcher you as is their nature?

'I will die for the faith,' Malhotra shouted. 'But never will I allow myself to be polluted by forbidden flesh.'

The rest of the boys joined in, cheering. Only I remained silent. Fools, I thought, who for a moment of vainglory can sacrifice the greater cause. So it was that I came to the notice of my patron.

FOLLOW FOLLOW ONE last time to the railway station. Follow follow to take the first train out of Bhopal, no matter which way or where. Follow follow as a man on the run, as one whose only hope is to be forgotten by his patron. Follow follow on a grey Bajaj scooter that carries a licence plate from Punjab, land of the rebellious Sikhs, and in whose compartment are papers of a familiar kind.

Yes, follow follow on a grey Bajaj scooter that has Punjab licence plate PB 1859. Follow follow on a scooter in whose compartment is a driving licence, the property of one Amrik Singh of Patiala, Punjab, and that shows a blurry man with a blurry beard, a blurry picture of a blurry face that could belong to any man who once had a beard but who has now shaved it off.

Follow follow to the railway station on a grey Bajaj scooter as I recall the sort of papers that were placed on my kills, papers that said the man was from Pakistan, from Kashmir, from Punjab, from Manipur, from Nagaland, from West Bengal, from Andhra Pradesh. Remember the small amounts of foreign currency placed in their bags, the pamphlets and insurrectionary documents claiming allegiance to Azad Kashmir, to Khalistan, to independent Manipur, to Nagalim, to the Charu Mazumdar–Kanu Sanyal revolutionary line of the Maoist class struggle.

Some of them were all that, I have no doubt. Still, think of the letters placed on them, letters that spelt out, in every detail, a proposed attack on legislatures the pillars of the democratic government, on politicians the elected representatives of the Indian people, on businessmen the leaders of industry. Think of the visiting cards of civil liberties activists inserted into the belongings of these kills. Think of those confusing, dead creatures with their multiple, overlapping identities, those monsters of depravity who also had with them foreign weapons that they fired indiscriminately at our brave guardians of the law and who carried packets of condoms that showed the licentiousness and corruption they directed at the flower of Indian womanhood and who were found in possession of pills and white powder that proved their tendency towards foreign, corrupt, sybaritic behaviour.

What had been planned for me? They had wanted me dead at the formulation shed, one of a pair of corpses lying side by side on white sheets spread out by the police to be presented at a press conference.

I am a corpse.

I am a dead man.

I am a soul floating above the scene, seeing and hearing everything. The blinding flashes of press photographers, the swivelling television camera of the Doordarshan team, the questions from journalists with little notepads, the answers from medalled, paunchy police officials pushing each other to be in front of the lenses. Corpses on white sheets, corpses on a rough floor, me and my doosra, me the one who follow followed and him the one an operator at an American chemical factory on the Kali Parade grounds. In the police officer's hands, sealed in a plastic bag, the Punjab papers found on me. Reporters, are you listening? This man is Amrik Singh, a Khalistani terrorist trying to pass for a Hindu and trying to sabotage the American chemical factory with the help of one Kanwar an operator a disgruntled worker at the factory on the Kali Parade grounds.

But plans change. When the formulation shed encounter didn't work out, a second one was staged at the National Collection of Man. Same basic story. Here I am, dead man again, a single corpse lying on a white sheet, a second white sheet covering me head to toe. Reporters, are you taking notes? That man is one Amrik Singh, a Khalistani terrorist shot dead by our courageous policemen in a joint operation conducted by the Madhya Pradesh police and a special undercover task force of the Punjab police, shot dead in a fierce encounter where the accused fired indiscriminately at the policemen but hit not a single one, forcing the policemen to return fire, the accused dying instantly, on the spot. No, really, you Communist types must not get carried away with your conspiracy theories! It is a smear on our brave boys to suggest that this was a staged encounter, that this was an extra-judicial execution, that the terrorist was not a terrorist but a low-ranking informant or functionary of the deep state no longer useful to his patrons. No, this has nothing to do with the American factory, which is completely safe and does not store hazardous chemicals. No, yes, someone will remove the sheet so that his face can be photographed. This is the notorious terrorist Amrik Singh …

IN FRONT OF the railway station, the sounds of the press conference about my death fade. I wait on the scooter, engine running. What am I waiting for? The station is dark and quiet, but like all railway stations, it is not fully at rest. The tracks will start humming any moment now, a train will pull up and bleary-eyed passengers stumble off the bogies. I can push my way in easily, somewhere, anywhere, silencing with one look a passenger whose reserved side berth I have taken over, choking off his protest before it even emerges from his mouth. I am the sword of righteousness. I am the erect lund of Bharat. I have served.

Still, I wait on the scooter, engine running. Like the wind, I rode the jeep out of the National Collection of Man and back to Hamidia Road, leaving the jeep, key in engine and wiped of prints, near a shuttered auto repair shop. I could have walked to the station, but I went back to the hotel parking lot for the scooter, to check the papers in its compartment.

Twice they have tried. Twice they have failed. Now surely it is only a matter of time unless I leave Bhopal and get out of this life. Still, I sit on the marked grey Bajaj scooter, its engine running. Is it that I have nowhere to go? Where do you run to when your patron has decided you are expendable? Where do you go when you are a rusted sword, a flaccid lund? Where do you escape when the nation you have been protecting turns out to be enemy country?

The railway station, a tired assassin, settled into the arms of the night, its loyal whore. I wanted to rest too, ease my tired head, erase this life and start all over again. The overbridge where I had walked the night before cast its shadow over the tracks. A single stall remained open, its dim light making it seem farther away than it really was. I shut off the scooter and listened. Underneath the surface of silence, there was something, the deep noise of this city in the heartland of India. The stirring and squirming of Insect People. The stray barks of Dog People. The humming of tracks picking up the vibration of a train some distance away. The sound of the city telling me to get off the scooter, walk into the station and board that train coming in. Out of Bhopal, out of Bhopal, out of Bhopal. As if this is the last train out of this city. As if after this, there can only be corpses.

I kicked the starter and got the engine running. A train siren pierced the winter night. Movement broke out in the railway station. My last chance train rolled in and began to slow down. I sped towards the Chandbarh slums.

FOLLOW FOLLOW ONE last time to the slum of the Insect People on the grey Bajaj scooter with the Punjab plates. Still time, surely, to pick up the daughter of the Insect People. Still time to take a different train out of Bhopal. Time, surely, to disappear into this land before other men, with clear instructions from my patron, come looking for me.

A shadow darkened the dark sky. I looked up. It was right above me. What was it? Tail, feathers, tuft, mane. In the chemical factory of the Americans, they had worked hard to make one thing into another, to change things into powerful chemicals. The key to everything was transformation, the change from one being to another, from one state to another. This is why the snake-bird was so powerful, a thing in perpetual transformation, snake scales and bird feathers and all. I kept riding.

The grey scooter coughed, stalled. I waited a few beats, kicked the starter. One last ride is all I need from you, grey scooter with Punjab plates, I said. There is a train at one in the morning coming from Bombay. If Rekha and I can catch that, we will be out of Bhopal before the discovery of Maharishi and Black Beard sets off a hunt. I tried the scooter again. It refused my plea. I picked up my bag and began to run.

THE LONE BARBAROUS howl of a dog broke the stillness of the slum night. It stopped abruptly and picked up again, rising in pitch as other dogs in the neighbourhood joined in, one by one. I listened in confusion, listened in mid-run, to this infernal chorus of the Dog People. There was something about their singing that was different, something that felt familiar as I follow followed their song. Then I knew.

The Dog People were singing. That in itself was not surprising or new. That I could understand them was not either. But where they had been speaking in Paisacha, now they were singing in Urdu, language of an enemy nation, and singing a provocative, teasing, rebellious song that made the hair on my arms stand up.

They sang together, and they sang in tune, with a male and a female lead that alternated off each other and then harmonised together, their singing swelling and peaking and then trailing off until, just at the moment there appeared to be silence, a silence settling like a thick, heavy blanket over the claustrophobic, sleeping slum, the rest of the Dog People joined in, bursting out in a loud, tremendous chorus that met up with a joyous, thunderous beat that recalled the jungle drums of the savage hunter gatherers in the National Collection of Man and that was sung in a way that shook not just the slum but the walls of the houses in the Old City and the foundations of the buildings in the New City and that sent tremors through the bungalows of the rich on Shyamla Hills and reached out to shake the throne of Delhi and the control room in West Virginia and the board room in New York and seemed about to spin the earth into a different axis. The trees echoed their songs, the wind amplified it and the darkness of the winter night became the stage for this song about their uprising.

I recovered my senses. 'Silence, you low born!' I shouted. 'Cease your infernal howling, you debased foreign born! End this immediately, you jungle dwellers!'

They sang even louder. They sang with joy and they sang with passion, like they were looking at each other and laughing between each section of verse, winking with Dog winks and sticking out their Dog tongues, these Dog People singing about themselves in Urdu.

'Ye galiyoṅ ke āvāra be-kār kutte,' they sang. 'Kāle peele neele rangavār kutte,' they sang.

'Nonsense,' I said. 'Fuck you and your bitch mothers. Dogs don't come in colours of blue and yellow. Dogs don't come in rainbow hues.'

'Ye chāheṅ to duniyā ko apnā banā leṅ. Ye āqā'oṅ kī haddiyāṅ tak chabā leṅ,' they sang.

'Silence, silence,' I shouted, rushing headlong in their direction. 'Stop this call to insurrection,' I shouted. 'Stop this call to arms, stop asking dogs of all colours to unite.'

They paid me no heed and sang on.

'Dogs must remain dogs,' I said. 'It is the karma of your past lives. Serve your masters well in this life. Accept the cast-off bread thrown at you in this life and you may move up a station in your next one.'

'Ko'ī inko ehsās-e-zillat dilā de,' they sang. 'Ko'i inkī so'yī hū'i dum hilā de.'

I saw, suddenly, a massive silhouette blocking my way. It glowed white in the moon that had sailed out into the sky to battle these forces of darkness. Maharaj the bull stood in front of me, unadorned and unornamented except for the bell on his neck. He looked like an ascetic, one who had turned his back on the world of material illusion that is maya. But even without his garlands and his beads, without his red cloth and incense sticks, he still could not have passed for an ordinary bull. It was those eyes. Within them was wisdom, understanding and knowledge of the cycles of time. The bull had an aura I have encountered in only one other person my whole life, and that is my patron.

I went up to him. The singing of the dogs was so loud.

'Sacred Bull Person,' I said, bowing to him.

He nodded his head. The bell on his bull neck jingled. I wondered if this was meant to be a message. Was I running in the wrong direction? Had I been running in the wrong direction all my life? Maybe I was foolish to be thinking of rescuing Rekha, of taking revenge on my patron. Perhaps I needed to let go, turn around and enter into the vastness of the land, begin a parikrama not of the chemical factory but of the sacred Narmada River. In my wandering, dependent on the kindness of strangers for food, shorn of sexual desire, freed of my lethal Beretta pistol, in letting go of it all, perhaps I would come closer to banishing my many ghosts.

'Is that it?' I asked the bull. 'Is that my dharma? To become an ascetic?'

The bell on his bull neck jingled. He stomped his foot three times.

'I don't understand,' I said.

The singing of the Dog People was deafening.

'Silence, you beasts,' I shouted. 'I am discussing an important matter here.'

The Dog People sang louder.

'Maharaj, will you impart your wisdom to the Dog People? Ask them to accept their fate? Stop this absurd call to revolution?'

Maharaj the bull began to walk away from me.

'Wait,' I said. 'Fly away, Maharaj. Fly away from this city where no industrial disaster was likely to happen but is now about to happen. Fly away, fly high beyond the reach of the clouds of poison gas. Fly away from this city where corpses will be loaded on to trucks and driven out of the city and dumped into lakes to make them disappear. Fly away from here where the politicians will escape in private planes and helicopters, where the American company will say the gas can be washed off with cold water and that its chemical composition is proprietary information and cannot be released to

Indian doctors and that a dollar per dead person is plenty good for an Indian. Fly away from our century, Bull God, Bull Man, fly away from this one and the previous one and the next one, and come back only when you are sure that you will be safe. Fly away from this city where no industrial disaster is likely to happen but where three thousand will die in the next twenty-four hours, where twenty thousand will die over the next decade, where mangled, twisted girls will live out their youths knowing no one will ever love them, marry them, and where mangled, twisted boys will die, or will grow old and become mangled, twisted men, where coughing, wheezing survivors will limp their way over the coming decades to two ramshackle clinics operated by two activists who will not cooperate with each other while at the high-tech hospital on the outskirts set up for the survivors, the rich and the connected of Bhopal will go to have their diabetes checked, their hypertension looked at, and a beautiful public relations official will tell a visiting writer in the coming century that it is such a waste to have to use all this advanced equipment on the wheezing, coughing, low-born refuse of Bhopal who insist on showing up to get their gas-wracked bodies examined, where the factory will lie abandoned over the decades with not even ghosts for memories although one minister will propose that it be converted into an amusement park and Indian industrialists and luminaries of the Indo-American Chamber of Commerce will say that this disaster should be put behind in these new times when the free market brings trickle-down prosperity to all and Bhopal will be forgotten and Bhopal will become a heart-shaped void in the heart of India and the Sikhs who have been slaughtered in Delhi will be forgotten although their ghosts you will be able to see, as you will be able to see the ghosts of all massacres, all famines, all wars, you will be able to see them behind and between the procession of statues walking in victory around the Presidential Palace in New Delhi until a day will come when the ghosts will be silent no longer and will accept no longer the oppression of the masters and the complacence of the elites and the fear of the masses. Wait, what is all this I am saying?'

The Bull Man was no longer listening. He had walked away.

He was walking upright, on two feet. In front of him, the Dog People had massed. The Bull Man joined the ranks of the Dog People. Together, like some perverted version of a story from the *Panchatantra*, they sang into the night, 'Ye galiyoṅ ke āvāra be-kār kutte.'

IN THE NIGHT, the slum was quiet, the streets as empty as the hut that once had been an incense factory. Then I heard some coughing, heard some voices, heard Insect Mothers comforting Insect Children. The smell of shit and the smell of incense blended with the smell of sadness. It was a smell so strong that it made me choke, made my eyes water. I heard more voices from around me, more coughing from the children who sang their daily lessons in the daytime in that school building with no walls. I looked all around me at the empty hut that had once belonged to the Incense Man. Then I turned around to get away from the smell of sadness. I wept fat tears for what I had lost and what I had not known I possessed.

I collided with someone as I walked weeping tears, my bag of cash on one side, my Beretta on the other. There were people running. An acrid smell permeated the air. Chillies burnt to ward off ghosts, to drive away evil spirits. 'Run,' someone shouted. Run? I asked, weeping. 'Run to the station!' 'Run away from the factory!' Coughs and screams and shouts overlapped and I stumbled in the darkness, in the smoke, as someone barged into me, knocking the bag off my shoulder.

All around me, people were running. They were running the way Insect People in India run, with no purpose, with no coordination, running as only the weak run. They screamed as they ran, not just the women and children, the men screamed too, and they coughed as they ran. The midnight darkness was filled with noises, with screams and coughs and stampeding feet, with the occasional revving of a scooter or a motorcycle.

I had been trained. I knew better than to panic. I should turn back, ask the neighbours. I could find my way to Rekha and get out of the city with her. I bent in the smoky air and looked for the bag of cash. But my eyes were beginning to water! Those damned burning chillies. Tamasic this air! The incense maker's daughter? Burning incense sticks! Burning eyes! Burning black beards! Kali Parade! Black Parade! The parade of Kali, with a necklace of skulls, with dripping sword! Kali Parade! Black Parade! Where the Nawab had criminals executed, black cloth covering the faces of the condemned! Who would I see when I turn this corner? What would I see? The city was clogged with choking, coughing Insect People, Monkey People, Dog People, Bull People, Goat People. Where was I heading? Was this the way to Rekha's hut or the way to the railway station?

My assailant struck without warning. My breath was cut off. I reached for the hands around my neck, for the fingers that I could pry open. Fingers I would break apart like twigs before facing my assailant as a warrior, as a man who was the erect lund of India. Scrabble scrabble I went but found no fingers around my neck, found no hand on my neck, found just cloth, found cloth that flashed pink while I twisted and struggled and turned and retched. Then there were so many shapes blazing in front of my eyes, so many colours, and once more flashed that pink before the black cloth of the Kali Parade grounds came down over my head and I could see no colours other than black.

PARANOIR: 1947

The pilot is one who knows the secrets.

THE VYMANIKA SHASTRA

Sky-man in a man-hole
with astronomy for dream,
astrology for nightmare ...

A.K. RAMANUJAN

1

He must not falter when his turn comes. He has watched Walker demonstrate the stages involved. He has studied Captain Hayes's classic texts on horse management and riding. He has even seen himself execute the steps in his mind, beginning with the mount, easing into the trot, switching to the canter and finally moving into a gallop that takes the horse in a circuit around the field, back to the starting point. More than that Das is not required to do. The Bengal service may expect that its veterinary surgeons be able to ride, but it does not require pig-sticking, gymkhana-rousing skills of them.

Walker is a patient man. As he once again goes over how to adjust the reins, the stirrups and the saddle, Das thinks of the note that materialised this morning in his room. Is it a matter of the Committee finding out how steady his nerves are? Whether he can cope with vigorous motion? It could be anything, even a matter of how his aura responds to piloting of a primitive kind. He snatches a quick look at his surroundings. In his immediate environment, in this particular corner of the vast expanse of the Maidan, there is surely no one who should not be there, no one sent for the express purpose of observing his performance at the riding test.

A fresh evening breeze blows in from the Hooghly, carrying on its wings the sound of a regimental band from Fort William. Das and his fellow students are clustered nervously around Walker and his beloved horse, White Rose, which, in spite of its name, is a greyish mare of somewhat matronly appearance, whisking its tail at stray flies and thoroughly indifferent to the proceedings.

The leaves of the fossil-like banyan trees rustle. Invisible little ghosts scurry in the grass, stopping occasionally to tickle Das's ankles. Drums rise to a crescendo in the background, pausing for an elongated silence before the wailing notes of a bagpipe kick in. Das draws a sharp breath. He does not like regiments or military music, but he finds the sound of a bagpipe strangely moving, stirring in him, absurdly, some primal, melancholy response, something that lives beneath all the knowledge he has acquired these past few years of just how empires are run.

'Now listen here, gentlemen, it could not be simpler,' Walker shouts in his drill master's voice. 'This isn't quite like in the old days. If you had been studying before the war, you'd have been made to take a proper riding examination.'

'And proper riding lessons too,' a voice responds from the back.

'Hmm? Yes, well. All we ask today is that you complete one circuit, ek chukker, without falling off. Bas! Ghor sowaari khatam, certification complete.'

Walker waits for the students to laugh along with him, to show that they appreciate his throwing in a few Hindusthani words. It is his way of responding to the knowledge that the times are changing. Instead, what he gets is a babble of voices, a hubbub of questions and declarations, a small mutiny in the making.

'No!' Walker shouts. 'The creature will not throw you. It wishes to be ridden. Why does it wish to be ridden? Because that is its nature. Why is that its nature? Well, gentlemen, does the name Charles Darwin mean anything in this regard? A horse evolved to carry you, which is why it is a horse. A horse is not a giraffe. It is not a zebra. And yes, while it may be a Krishno'r jeeb, as Biswas there would like to remind us from the wings, sotto voce, that does not happen to be pertinent to the matter at hand. What d'you mean, the horse might bite you? What kind of surgeons are you lot going to be? Now Das, it's your turn to show everyone. Come on, then. Das?'

Das has been thinking of the letter, slipped into the pages of Hayes's *Veterinary Notes for Horse Owners* that morning by forces unseen, and of the uncanny echo between its message and Walker's harangue.

We are filled with joy that you take your riding examination today.

From such surmounting of physical boundaries do we prepare ourselves to traverse thresholds where matter dissolves into spirit, where time and space fall away, and where the glorious universe reveals itself to us in its infinite shades of compassion and love. A horse may be just a horse, but for you it is only the first of your many vahanas. You will not fail.

In substance, of course, there could not be greater difference between Walker's koi hai, boot-polish heartiness, and the sonorous poetry and complex metaphysics emanating from the Committee's letter, but he has not missed the way Walker's 'A horse … is a horse' mirrors, with subtle variation, 'A horse may be just a horse' in the letter. Such are the mysterious ways in which the Committee operates, Das thinks, quite forgetting that he has just been addressed by Walker and that the instructor, for some time now, has been holding out the stirrup with his riding crop.

Das stares, finally, at stirrup and at crop, at Walker's compact frame, aware that he is required to mount White Rose. As he stares, he feels himself receding, watching Walker from an ever greater distance as though the ex-army riding instructor, veteran of Gallipoli and, more recently, of the Burma campaign as one of Chindit's Bandits, is becoming part of some impossibly large tableau. Das squints to make sense of this, of how Walker stands there, one hand on reins now, the other waving the crop. He notices how smartly turned out Walker is in his khaki tunic and white jodhpurs, how supremely confident in his black riding boots.

He thinks of himself, wearing clothes a size too big for him, feet clad in strapped chappals bought from the cheapest of stalls in Shyambazar, and he begins to contemplate the absurdity of his riding a horse, and behind that, the even greater absurdity of carrying out the task assigned by the Committee. He is aware of his smallness, his inadequacy, and as he does so, he gets the impression that Walker is holding not just himself and the horse but holding together everything in the vicinity, Das and the other students and the old trees on the Maidan with their gnarled trunks and creepers and the fort piled up with red bricks, and that without Walker and his quiet confidence everything will fall apart, the ground tilting so that they all slide, one by one, horse and Das and others, into the opaque, milk-tea brown of the Hooghly River until, finally, the Maidan itself tips over completely and drops, trees, fort, river and all, into the sky.

THE INSTRUCTOR'S FACE appears against the sky, like a red signal balloon just launched. 'Must be the heat,' it says for some mysterious reason.

'Or panic,' says another voice that Das tries to track down but finds to be just beyond the edge of his familiarity.

'Did he shit in his pants?' a third voice says, and Das recognises the Bull's baritone and understands that he is lying on the ground.

Then water is splashed on his face, hands easing him into a sitting position while a canteen is thrust into his mouth to gurgle out warm, metallic-tasting liquid. The sun is low on the horizon, the horse still whisking its tail. The regimental band has begun 'Beating Retreat'.

'Might as well just put this off,' Walker says, his eyes not meeting Das's. The bagpipe swells again, as do drums and a myriad other instruments Das cannot identify. 'To begin tomorrow at the same time,' Walker shouts in a louder voice. 'Dismissed!'

AFTER WALKER LEAVES, there is a relaxing of postures and manners. There is a long discussion about hiring a gharry to take Das back to the hostel, on the northern fringe of the city, tinged with excitement about who will get to ride on the gharry and who will not. The Nose, by far the most senior among the students, wonders if it is possible to make a detour, a stopover in Sonagachi to be entertained by dancing girls, but his proposal is opposed, vehemently, by the Bull, who, devoted to physical culture, would like them all to go back to the hostel at a brisk pace and then spend an hour or two at the gymnasium.

Ahmed begins to take his pulse, but Das rejects his ministrations, telling his classmates brusquely that there is nothing wrong with him and that he has business of a personal nature to take care of in Chowringhee. Then, thrusting the canteen into Ahmed's hand, ignoring warnings from his fellow students about sectarian violence, he walks away from the group, stumbling, as he leaves, on a rhizome in a manner that sends a sharp pain stabbing through his right foot and robs him of the last vestige of any dignity. As he makes his way across the darkening expanse of the Maidan towards the bright lights of Chowringhee, he is aware of his classmates still standing there, their collective gaze lacerating him from the back, united, for all their differences, in their agreement about his cowardice.

He dives into the crowds with the relief of a pursued terrorist, but his emotions do not let up, not among the Europeans promenading around the shops and hotels of Chowringhee and not, as summer dusk shades into a black tropical night being diluted, here and there, with drops of electric lighting and kerosene lamps, among his own people thronging the streets of north Calcutta. He wishes the alleys and the crowds would swallow him up, and they do, but they vomit him out again outside a Kali temple into a thick haze of incense, sweat and crushed marigold flowers. He catches a glimpse of the mother, her ten arms holding an assortment of medieval weapons, her necklace a string of skulls, her right foot raised over the prone body of Shiva who, god of destruction himself, has laid himself down in his wife's path like some non-violent demonstrator before a mounted policeman, wanting to stop her apocalyptic dance. Between the foot and the body is the expectation of impact, the premonition of doom.

He stops when he reaches the squat outline of the McPherson Hostel, double-storeyed, red-bricked and green-doored. He hurries up the steps to the top floor, avoiding eye contact with the junior boarders, locking his door and collapsing on to his bed. Above him, the green ceiling fan revolves furiously on its long handle, heavy metallic blades whipping through the air like the propeller of some lunatic flying machine making a never-ending, headlong kamikaze descent towards him.

Only then, when he is completely alone with his shame, does Das think of the Committee. He sits upright in shock, his features contorted, knowing instinctively that his involvement with the

Committee has been terminated. A Vimana aircraft, its design taken from the pages of an ancient manual, is being painstakingly reconstructed in this war-torn city of the twentieth century. But he has thrown away his chance to pilot the craft by being afraid of riding a mere beast. He buries his head in his knees and weeps.

At exactly that moment, he hears the rustling outside the door. It seems that the Committee has been waiting for just such self-knowledge on his part before choosing to contact him. He watches, without surprise, as a note appears underneath the door, a rectangle of handmade paper folded in upon itself with an origami intricacy, apparently fragile and yet, Das suspects, intended to defeat the fingers of anyone other than the intended recipient. Das makes no effort to discover who might be on the other side, all his past experience with the Committee having demonstrated to him the uselessness of such attempts. Instead, he catches his breath, wipes his tears and begins the delicate process of disassembling the note.

2

It was not meant to have been this way. That he should have felt utterly lost all those years in the city, before he encountered the Committee, he understands. It was a process of initiation, a necessary confusion, although he had not known this at the time. By day, he had been a dutiful student of veterinary science, a village boy on a government scholarship; by night, he had drifted, sometimes in the company of a fellow student, sometimes alone.

When Das casts the net of his mind back, his years in the city flow through like water, years of war and famine through which he transforms himself from peasant to modern man, sure that there is no future left for peasants like his father in this world of blackouts, army convoys and watery gruel, but uncertain as to whether he likes modern man very much. On one side of the balance sheet, the losers, those skeletal people wandering into the city to die, on the other the Indian traders stockpiling rice and the Englishmen running their shilling-and-pence empire.

Fragments snag on the net of his mind: the sensualist Nose leading him through the alleyways of the red-light area where he gapes at the women on sale; the Bull introducing him to that secretive group of body sculptors devoted to becoming Super Men in service of the great Hindu race; Ahmed and him craning their necks to stare up at Gandhi spinning thread at one of his public meetings. He recalls the spiritual esoterica offered him by Biswas, the rants on weaponry delivered by Pagla Ghora, the Crazy Horse, before the man vanished and the clandestine Communist report on the famine, accompanied by sketches, passed around hand to hand at the hostel. He remembers so much and remembers feeling off-kilter through it all, unable to commit to any one thing, to body-sculpting or to sensualism, to Gandhi or to Communism, unable to choose, as if he were not himself but somebody else, living a life other than his own while his real life took place in another world, at another time.

The Committee rescued him from that.

He was given small tasks at first, an errand boy helping out while attending the general meetings, listening in somewhat bewildered fashion to the talks given every month by a different member of the Committee. He had books to study, *Isis Unveiled* by Madame Blavatsky and *The Lost Lemuria* by Scott-Eliot, left to make his way uneasily through these tomes in the reading room, its windows open to an abandoned garden with a dried-up fountain. There were even questionnaires to be filled out, asking him about exceptional, out-of-body and near-death experiences. He had struggled with these, his mind, always so good at examinations demanding the regurgitation of crammed facts, ill at ease when faced with questions that went:

Have you ever been aware of things in the future that you could not have known about?

Have you ever had the experience of leaving your body and of observing things from another place?

Have you ever felt that you had become a person of the opposite sex?

He had wanted to say no to all these questions, a modern man rejecting what was worse than peasant superstition, a student of science turning his back on magic, and yet he had scribbled on, with a shaking hand …

He became an assistant to Miss Srinivasan on her weekly rounds. Everything followed in order, his awareness of the compassion of the Committee, of its intention to end war, famine and riots in the city by building an ancient aircraft that would bring balance back to these savage modern times.

The Vimana! An *anti*-atom bomb aircraft! Completed and flown over Calcutta, it would create harmony and love, a manifestation of ancient wisdom quite different from those lines quoted by Oppenheimer. No, not 'I am become death, destroyer of worlds', but 'Shanti, Shanti, Shanti'.

The joy of knowing that would have been enough, of playing a small part in it, but there came a day when it was revealed, on a day he seemed at last to be living his own life, a man finally in his own place and time, that his aura had passed both overt and more subtle tests, a process that had resulted in his being chosen to fly the Vimana after its completion. His spiritual training had begun, and his ultimate goal was to take to the skies and bathe this damaged, crushed city in the universal harmony song of love. A copy of the manual, the *Vymanika Shastra*, or the ancient Sanskrit text, *The Science of Aeronautics*, by Maharshi Bharadwaaja, as revealed to Pandit Subbaraya Sastry, recorded by him and then translated into English in Calcutta by E.T. Edamaruku, MA, Hons, FRES, MRSI, Japanologist and Esoterist, was pressed into his hands. The pilot is one who knows the secrets, it said in the manual.

He had been given the secrets.

WE WERE MISTAKEN in our haste in urging you on. The failure is ours. Pls see Dr Bose.

The note, brief and to the point, lies unfolded in front of him, the writing in characteristic purple ink that was made, Miss Srinivasan once informed him, from the juice of the verbena plant, extracted with a syringe so as to make the process as painless to the plant as possible. He recognises her handwriting too, letters and words spaced out with mathematical precision, and yet the voice in the note is not that of Miss Srinivasan or any single individual but of the Committee. It is a collective voice, one filled with disgust at his failure, or if disgust is too strong an emotion to be associated with the Committee, with a sensation of pain. All he had to do was ride a horse, and he fainted. All he had to do was ride a horse, and his spiritual unfitness overwhelmed him at what was no more than an intermediate test.

Das opens the green shutters of his room. The veranda in front of him is empty of boarders, although their dried clothes stir lazily in the early dawn breeze like a series of disembodied men, torsos and legs hanging from the line, some upside down, some right side up. He has passed the entire night sleepless, caught up in his own private misery. In the semi-darkness, he can make out an electric lamp burning brightly at the tram depot across from the hostel. A man is standing just beyond its cone of light, completely still, so much so that it is easy to wonder whether it is a man at all or just a building fixture that appears, this far away, to resemble a man. From somewhere in the distance, the tinkle of a temple bell makes its way through the quiet of the dawn, growing distinctly louder until he realises it is the sound of a Number 1 tram beginning its run from the Belgachia depot to Esplanade. As the tram comes closer, its headlight illuminates the man standing near the lamp, its glare reflecting off the man's glasses. Das has the momentary impression of a predatory face, eyes covered by white-hot discs, before the tram sweeps forward.

He starts and steps back, as though the stranger is an emissary of the Committee on the verge of delivering a third, final note, one informing him that his association with the Committee has been terminated. He feels the hot flush of his shame as he recalls his fainting spell, and wonders, as he has all night long, why it happened.

He understands why the government has the requirement for surgeons. He has memorised the steps involved in riding. Unlike Biswas, he is not even scared of horses. He knows they are powerful animals, their hooves capable of crushing a man's chest or staving in his head. But then, a bull is powerful too, and Das does not remember being afraid of the humped, mountainous thing his father rented every year to plough the fields and to service the cows.

Since then, in the course of his veterinary degree requirements, Das has dealt with animals that might be considered far more dangerous. He has stared down the snarling mouths of police mastiffs, trained to spot bombs being carried around by native terrorists who probably do not smell too different from him. He has marvelled at the periodontal foundations of a Bengal tiger, admittedly one drugged rather heavily with opium. He has even put his hand up the vagina of an elephant, a creature superannuated from the stables of the Maharajah of Coochbehar and suspected to be suffering from a tumour. But last evening, when he had not much more to do than step forward, place his foot on the stirrup and sit on a horse, something stopped him from deep inside, something that will be understood by others—maybe even by the Committee? maybe even by Miss Srinivasan?—as cowardice.

He still cannot remember fainting, or what transpired between Walker holding out his crop and Walker looking down at him. It is like those few minutes of his life have been stolen, and he fears that the gap will always remain, an interruption that will render the before and the after as forever out of synchronicity and that his life will only proceed askew from this point on. But even though he does not know how he will repair this injury, he knows that if he faints again, he will fail his riding examination. If he fails his riding examination, he will not get his BVSc degree. If he fails his riding examination, he will not be allowed to fly the Vimana, and the Committee will turn him loose, rendering him outcaste. It is like that *damn* English rhyme, Das thinks, allowing himself an uncharacteristic curse word, that one about the nail and the shoe and the battle and the kingdom. There was a horse in there too.

3

At breakfast, he avoids the eyes of his classmates, sitting hunched over toast that Kaka, the mess cook, has brought him, thick slabs of double-roti with butter and coarse, granular sugar sprinkled on top. He cannot eat. He just sits there, pushing the toast around, wondering how he will see Dr Bose and appear for the rescheduled riding examination all on the same day. A boisterous cry from his classmates, a response to some filthy joke made by the Nose, interrupts his thoughts. Walker is suffering from too intimate a conjoining between himself and White Rose, the Nose says. This is why the riding examination has been cancelled, why a notice sits outside the registrar's office saying that Walker has been taken ill. White Rose the mare, the Nose continues, is a substitute for an original left behind in England, but before he can clarify to the assembly whether the original is a woman or a horse, Das excuses himself and returns to his room.

He takes his time getting himself ready, checking through the window for signs of the man he saw in the morning, looking around carefully on the off-chance that the Committee has really chosen to deliver another note. When he finally leaves, he does not take the usual route, climbing down instead along the winding spiral staircase at the back, landing lightly in the little yard where Kaka has his kitchen.

He looks around with curiosity at the things Kaka has gathered, reflecting on how little he really knows of him. He is a small man, Kaka, his arms and legs almost two-dimensional, his hair cut very short, dressed in a vest and dhoti that might once have been white. Kaka is not even the man's real name, just the polite generic term, meaning younger uncle, that everyone has settled on for him, and Das has no doubt that Kaka will remain younger uncle to a generation of boarders even half a century later, should he remain alive that long.

Every few weeks, Kaka falls into a depression, wondering why he has abandoned his home in an Orissa village to come work in this heartless city. He becomes slower in his movements, his eyes ringed by dark circles, his face covered in stubble. The toast often arrives burnt, flaky in texture and cindery in flavour, the tea is watery and cold, while the intervals between toast and tea grow as boundless as Kaka's silence. Somewhere around mid-month, he disappears, heartbroken about the children and wife he has left back home and whom he fails to send enough money. He goes to Jogubabu's Bazaar with the little money he has left, an amount so small that it is pointless to even try sending it home. It is better expended, instead, on ganja that makes him lose track of the hours and the days. While Kaka stays on in Jogubabu's Bazaar, the days running together, the mess kitchen remains closed. The boarders, although they should know better, congregate around the tables every morning, hoping against past precedence that Kaka has not gone off on his ganja binge but is merely suffering from some minor mishap. While they wait, the Nose wonders aloud whether Kaka has one wife back home in the village or two, one to lie on each side of him when he returns for his annual visit. From hope, the boarders move on to recriminations, to promises from the Bull to give Kaka a sound thrashing when he returns, but with a blanket wrapped around him so as not to leave any marks on the body. Eventually, like disciples on the karmic path to wisdom, they move on. The wealthy head for the market stalls of Shyambazar, while the not-so-wealthy retire to their rooms. The Nose asks the Bull to buy him breakfast in return for favourable introductions. The Bull informs the Nose that ejaculation, whether of an auto-erotic nature or involving intercourse with a woman, leads to a squandering of one's seed and a consequent weakening of the masculine life force and advises the Nose to be guided by the example of the great spiritual leader Vivekananda who retained all his seed and channelled it into his aura. Then, maybe the day after, Kaka shows up, unshaven, gaunt and speechless, like someone who has taken a Gandhian vow of absolute silence, and the cycle begins all over again.

Das recalls this routine as he looks at the chullah on which Kaka cooks his various meals. It is black with coal dust. Above it, suspended from the branch of a mango tree, hangs an earthen pot of yoghurt. There is a brown wooden cabinet under the tree that holds a special breakfast, a bowl with bean sprouts, another bowl with half a dozen hard-boiled eggs, both surveyed by a towering glass of milk. Das knows that this is being kept ready for the Bull. As for Kaka, he seems, given the impressively penis-shaped earthen chillum erect on the top shelf, to be switching entirely to ganja for sustenance.

He wonders what would happen if he were to turn up high at Dr Bose's. He chortles at the thought, stops self-consciously when he realises that he has never imbibed the substance and does not know what it is like to be intoxicated. He climbs over the back wall, which takes him into the living quarters of a colony of milkmen. He makes his way past the cows and buffaloes chewing the cud, all in violation of health department regulations, of course, but he cannot help nodding approvingly at the calm, placid movement of their jaws. How different from a horse, he thinks, these creatures with their legs tucked under them, and how vastly superior. The cow, the mother of the Hindus, and that mythical cow with its cornucopia of riches, Kamadhenu. As for the buffalo, he realises with dismay, leaping swiftly to avoid stepping into a large pat of dung, the undigested fibrous matter visible in the blackish green, the buffalo is not the mother or even the aunt of the Hindus. He sifts through his mind for non-scientific data about the buffalo, usually nominated by Western observers, quite confusingly, as the water buffalo. If the Asian buffalo is a water buffalo because of its habit of wallowing in mud and water, then why not call the Asian elephant, no less fond of water, a water elephant? But he also remembers that the buffalo, while not the aunt of the Hindus, is the vahana, the vehicle of choice, of Yama, god of death. In other words, it is the same kind of thing as his Vimana and his horse, something that ferries people from one world to another.

IT TAKES HIM a little less than an hour to reach the medical college where Dr Bose has his clinic. Dr Manobendro Bose is a psychoanalyst, someone once in direct correspondence with the founding father of psychoanalysis, Dr Sigmund Freud of Vienna (although Dr Freud of Vienna, the college librarian had tetchily informed Das on being asked for a book by Dr Freud of Vienna, had been forced, after the arrival of the Nazis, to become Dr Freud of London, where he died in exile). But Dr Bose, in spite of his eminent position, does not wear a Western suit. For psychoanalytic consultations, Dr Bose dresses like any Bengali bhadralok, in an immaculately starched white dhoti with curling folds like the fractal ruffs of a particularly vain cock. He wears thick bottle-top glasses that make his eyes appear distended and a ferocious moustache that should, but does not, muffle his crisp pronouncements.

Dr Bose is said to have arrived at Freudian psychoanalysis because of a long-standing interest in magic powers that included forays into mesmerism as well as yoga. Das finds that strange, but not as confusing as the association between Dr Bose and the Committee. From what he understands of Freud, having dipped into some of the Vienna-London sage's works at the veterinary college library, his notions of the unconscious have to do with an individual's childhood, as opposed to the Committee's far finer ideas of the unconscious collective childhood of entire civilisations. It is true, of course, that Dr Bose makes adjustments to Freudian ideas when dealing with the Indian mind. In his more jocular moments, He has even been known to call his clinic 'The Savage Freud Psychoanalytical Clinic'. He likes to play on this notion of Indians as savages, as primitive people, although sometimes he says that it is his patients who are the savages on whom he works Freud's enlightened method and sometimes that he himself is a savage savant, a savage Freud.

In spite of the play on words, Das still cannot see how

psychoanalysis and Dr Bose fit in with the Committee's plans. He realises, not without sadness, that his heart has sealed itself against the knowledge of the West. Once he had grudgingly accepted modern man and the West. Now, whether it is Hayes's *Training and Horse Management in India (With Hindustanee Vocabulary)* or Dr Freud's 'Psychoanalytic Notes Upon an Autobiographical Account of a Case of Paranoia (Dementia Paranoides)', he no longer believes entirely in their capacity to offer help, whether to repressed people who cannot speak their true selves or to those creatures who do not even possess speech: Krishno'r jeeb.

He is nearly at his destination, having crossed the YMCA swimming pool and waiting, in front of a row of stores devoted exclusively to orthopaedic appliances, for the red-turbaned policeman to allow him to cross over to the medical college entrance. Looking at the policeman, he knows that had he not encountered the Committee, he would have remained in that mode of rejection forever, obsessed with thinking of modern Western knowledge as committed not to life but to the extinction of life. It was the Committee that offered him the counter-knowledge to extinction and destruction, to the kind of learning capable of building a giant Vimana of compassion. Without it, he would not have discovered that even he has an active part to play in the turning of the gears of this compassionate machine.

With that thought in mind, he steels himself, crosses the street, and enters the dark, cool confines of the building. At the very end of those wandering corridors, with attendants on little stools parked outside forbidding doors, is the Savage Freud clinic.

4

His purpose in visiting Dr Bose is to talk about his fainting spell, he presumes. Perhaps the Committee thinks there is some hidden inner fear of horses that must be addressed by the Freudian psychoanalyst before he takes the riding examination again. But if that is the case, could the Committee have had a hand in Walker's illness? They would not harm a person, even temporarily, to achieve their ends, would they? These questions lead, inevitably, to a growing feeling of shame at his psychological unfitness, a condition so severe that it requires violent intervention by the Committee and immediate attention from a person as august as Dr Bose.

But Dr Bose, the man in possession of medicine for his unfitness, is nowhere to be seen. There is no attendant outside, just the door left slightly ajar to indicate that one might enter. Inside, the room is much the way he remembers it from prior visits, with a large mahogany table to his left as he walks in, its wood burnished to a fine dark sheen and covered with a baize green material soft to the touch. The table is empty, except for half a dozen coins scattered around its surface, an assortment of currency collected by Dr Bose, with odd shapes and in scripts that Das cannot decipher. The walls are bare, except for a calendar behind the table for Wachel Mollah's tailoring store in Chowringhee and the figurine of an owl. It stares down at the deck chair Dr Bose has his patients recline on, a contraption that, while quite comfortable once one gets used to it, never entirely loses its resemblance to a trap.

He walks to the window as much to avoid the deck chair as to see what might be outside. Although the day was bright and sunny when he set out from the hostel, it is now pitch dark on the other side of the green shutters. A summer storm is arriving, the clouds having overrun the skies while he was wandering the innards of the medical college building. The small courtyard below looks plunged deep in night.

Das finds the medical college a confusing place, and no part of it more so than this annex towards the back where Dr Bose has his Savage Freud clinic. He is always disoriented when he reaches the clinic, uncertain until the very last moment whether he will actually get there, the clinic seemingly changing location every time he visits. If he were to cast his mind back on the route he has taken inside the annex, for instance, he remembers going down a series of stairs to some kind of subterranean wing rather than climbing up, as must have been the case if he is looking down onto a courtyard.

The scene in front of him is so dark that he can barely make out anything. Gradually, he begins to see the buildings enclosing the courtyard, and across from him, a series of staircases and covered bridges connecting different wings of the building. As he watches the progress of a figure up the stairs, some of the staircases look impossibly steep. He begins to make out tiny details now, messengers holding files hurrying along passageways. Nurses appear, white skirts billowing out behind them, their hands perfectly steady as they carry trays with syringes and bowls of hot water along the stairs, greeting doctors who stroll through the bridges smoking pipes, all of them moving at far too slow a pace.

Sometimes, he sees people who can only be patients, including a ghostly figure whose entire head is covered in white bandages, leaving just a slit for the eyes, and who walks, one leg in a cast, with the aid of crutches. He waits as the figure vanishes around a corner at the end of a staircase and begins tracking it again when it reappears in the middle of a bridge, limping steadfastly on in a journey that seems to be unending, infinite. The little light available, yellow and in clearly demarcated patches, comes from open windows, and through them he can see messengers handing folders to clerks and nurses gathered in deliberation around doctors. He sees more bandaged patients, heads all swathed in white, sitting in chairs or lying on hospital beds or being wheeled out of rooms, and he almost believes that the sight in front of him consists of the same figure seen, somehow, at different stages of time.

A cough from behind makes him turn around. Dr Bose is even more daunting than usual, gazing severely at him from behind bottle-top glasses, a faint smell of antiseptic emanating from his hands as he points Das, wordlessly, to the deck chair.

'Sir, the Committee asked me to see you.'

He sinks into the chair. Behind him, somewhere to his left, the psychoanalyst's voice is flat and emotionless.

'Yes, the Committee asked. And you immediately came?'

'Immediately, sir. It was the fit I had yesterday, you see,' he says. 'I fainted, on the Maidan, just as I had to mount Mr Walker's horse. Then the Committee sent me a note, asking me to see you, so that you could get me ready for the horse-riding test.'

'The Committee told you I would help you ride a horse?'

'Not exactly, sir, no. I supposed that they wished you to remove the unconscious blockage that is preventing me from riding a horse by making me fall into a fit just as I am about to climb on to the horse.'

'You supposed all of this?'

'I assumed.'

'You assumed?'

'But sir, what other purpose could the Committee have in asking me to see you?'

'Yes, of course, I see. But first tell me, what is this Committee that you speak of? It is the Committee of what?'

At first, he is too shocked to respond. Then he feels a sharp flicker of rage. It is not like he has not encountered that flat, nasal tone or those probing questions before. But they are especially painful this morning, adding up to all the humiliation and worry he has been struggling with for the past twenty-four hours. Dr Bose, he had thought, would help him get better. Instead, he is being mocked. He is being treated as some kind of lunatic, a Monkey Man or Bear Man or Horse Man, someone to be scrutinised like a specimen as he lies on the deck chair with his mental belly sliced open while Dr Bose sifts through the viscera of his various neuroses, indifferent, uncaring.

'Sir,' he says.

He wants to say that Dr Bose not only knows the Committee, but that he himself is a member of the Committee. He remembers clearly now, that moment when Miss Srinivasan led him into the sanctum sanctorum, and where, seated at a long wooden table, he saw that gathering of enlightened men and women, some of whose names and faces he would come to know later, either from meeting them individually, like Dr Bose, or from their appearance in articles in newspapers and periodicals. Some would, of course, remain anonymous, shadowy figures.

He remembers that day as if it is the only day he has ever lived and how Dr Bose in his bottle-top glasses and immaculate dhoti was sitting next to the Parsi gentleman in a suit. He remembers Colonel Faiz in civil dress, the tall, striking Miss Gill, with her large eyes, alternately melancholy and joyful, the hamaal union sardar Kishen Lal with an amused smile lurking below his moustache, like he knows exactly how surprised Das is to find a porter, one of the great unwashed, sitting there at a table. And he remembers, of course, the Mother, who began life as Miss Thorne of Tower Hamlets, London, prime agitator in the matchgirls' strike, arriving at her place at that Calcutta table after a long, circuitous journey that had taken her to Manhattan, to Mexico City, to Istanbul, to Cairo, that had included countless years in the Himalayas deciphering old puthi texts wrapped in leaves. He had felt not lost but truly home for the first time since coming to Calcutta, knowing that Miss Srinivasan had led him into the secret centre of the world, to a place where an alternative version of official, officious history, something in direct opposition to all that business of Gandhi and the Congress, Jinnah and the Muslim League, Netaji and the Indian National Army, Linlithgow and Churchill and their empire of the jolly roast beef of England, was in motion, a gentler, kinder history in which he had been called in to play a central part.

'Sir, you know the Committee,' he says.

'I see. And you, do you know the Committee?' Dr Bose asks.

Das wonders if all this seeming unknowingness is a test. The Committee's rules are not always clear, especially when it comes to secrecy or recognition, and perhaps he was wrong to state so explicitly that Dr Bose knows the Committee. After all, his prior visits to the Savage Freud clinic, with the psychoanalytical sessions meant to determine his emotional fitness as a pilot for the Vimana, have all been under instructions from the Committee, yet never once has Dr Bose or he himself referred to the Committee on those occasions. Perhaps he would not have brought it up this time either, had he not been so disoriented by his failure to ride White Rose.

Still, even if Das cannot speak about the Committee, he can answer in the affirmative the question of whether he knows the Committee. He can say, definitively, that he has been engaged in its affairs on a regular basis since his first encounter with it. He can reply that he has been steadfastly preparing himself for the day when he will take charge of the Vimana, that mysterious flying machine he dreams of in his sleep.

Until then, every Tuesday, without fail, he completes his laboratory sessions at the college and rushes off to Sovabazaar to meet Miss Srinivasan. As he accompanies her around the city to conduct the various interviews, the drill is always the same. He walks slightly behind, and to her left. In his right hand, he holds a large black umbrella whose shade embraces them both in a welcoming dark circle. In his left hand, or in a bag slung over his left shoulder, he carries whatever Miss Srinivasan has entrusted to him that day. Sometimes, there are small bottles, plain glass containers with cork tops of the kind used by homeopathic practitioners; sometimes, delicate, toylike instruments made of bird feathers and dried twigs; sometimes a book bound tightly in thick cloth.

He knows little about Miss Srinivasan. Although she is possibly a year or two younger than him, she possesses a certainty that intimidates him. Small and precise, she is always dressed in a white sari and a white blouse with long sleeves and high collars. When his eyes fall on the back of her neck, a touch lighter than his own mahogany shade, he cannot see a single bead of sweat on it, even though he himself perspires profusely. But the thought of sweat on Miss Srinivasan's neck, non-existent though it is, makes him nervous. It makes him move away from her, shifting the circle of shadow, until Miss Srinivasan looks at him calmly, with eyes that are unfathomable, eyes that give him such a sensation of vertigo that he fears he is falling into them, at which moment she corrects the umbrella with a light touch, adjusting the circle of shade back to its proper proportions, and they walk on.

'You have worked together on some … Cases, did you call them? On *Cases* for the *Committee*?'

'We have worked together on some most unusual cases, sir.'

He remembers Miss Srinivasan and himself slipping on white gloves before entering the building in Park Circus. It is deserted and dark inside, the lift out of order, the staircase taking them to the top narrow and steep. When they reach the landing on the upper floor, he can see, through a French window left partially open, the criss-crossing wires of the tram route, lit up in a sudden lightning flash as a tram makes its appearance. A male servant lets them in, his hands encased in white gloves. The man they are to interview is slumped in an armchair in the drawing room, wearing a dressing gown, white gloves on his hands, and even though it is the middle of the day, the man is not so much a man as a void reeking of alcohol, tobacco and madness.

The files he consulted later told him that this was the legendary police detective Sleeman, the one who had taken the use of fingerprints in detection to the logical extreme in the very place, Bengal, where fingerprinting as a policing technique was invented in the nineteenth century. But Detective Sleeman had cracked up somewhere along the way, seeing fingerprints everywhere, fresh fingerprints in his own house that matched others on files kept carefully at the police headquarters in Lalbazaar in accordance with the Henry Classification System, fingerprints proliferating on cups and windows and screens and mirrors in spite of there being no fingers present that could deposit them. So Detective Sleeman became

Fingerprint Man, someone seeking the Committee's help to make the ghostly fingerprints go away, someone haunted by fingerprints without fingers, by traces without objects.

Das remembers Detective Sleeman well, just as he remembers many others: the judge, the explorer, the exiled prince. He remembers the inventor bewildered by equations that wrote themselves into formulae for poison gas; the polite young bell boy at the Great Eastern hotel who believes himself transformed, at night, into a giant monkey that can spring from rooftop to rooftop; the girl prodigy who is certain that she is the reincarnation of a famous singer, one whose face had been scarred by a demented admirer and who yet went on to lead a rebellion against the British; he remembers them all.

But he does not know if Dr Bose reads the reports compiled on these cases by him and Miss Srinivasan, if he is even required to, just as he does not know if there is a deeper rationale to Dr Bose behaving like he has no awareness of the Committee and that this is the first time the two of them have ever met. It makes him wonder if Dr Bose's intentions towards him are quite as therapeutic as he had initially supposed, a thought that makes him want to get up from the deck chair and run.

Yet he wonders if he would be able to and that doubt, accompanied by a creeping fear, keeps him supine. Dr Bose may call himself a psychoanalyst of the Freudian school, someone who, as a founder of the Indian Psychoanalytical Society, sent Freud a statue of Garuda on the sage's seventy-fifth birthday. Dr Bose may be a famous man, with many impressive degrees, a fluent essayist who discourses in Bengali journals on Freud and the *Upanishads*, someone who makes connections between the Sanskrit refrain 'Tat tvam asi'—'You are that'—and the TAT perception test. He is even a founding member of the Eccentric Club, and although Das does not have a very clear idea of its activities, the single report he has read about it in the *Amrita Bazar Patrika* left him thinking that the members of this private group, geniuses and stalwarts all, are a kind of crazy, comic version of the Committee, devoted to strange pranks, such as the occasion when they gathered, in formal dress, before an open sewer manhole, to sing 'God Save the King'.

With all his confusion about Dr Bose, he knows something about him beyond all this, something that has not been said or written about the psychoanalyst. He knows instinctively, from the core of his self with its village upbringing, that Dr Bose is really a wizard, a man with magic powers, and that he is uncertain of the kind of magic performed by Dr Bose. He knows he would not like to anger Dr Bose, and if he were to try to walk away, he wonders if the door would merge into the wall, or open on to a different floor, or into an empty void, or if the corridor through which he is running would twist into odd angles and send him into a dead end, or if the maze-like staircases in the courtyard would condemn him to endless cycles of wandering while Dr Bose watched coldly and impassively from his window. And which Dr Bose would be watching him then, the savage Freud or the savage shaman?

Then, it is not like he only wants to leave. There is another part of him that is becoming comfortable, his back resting on the thick canvas cloth that forms the seat, his hands placed on the wide arms of the chair. He can stay here for a while, he feels, shaking off everything that has taken over his life after he came to the city. Here he is safe, Dr Bose's voice sending soothing commands that wash over his body like waves of light until he is almost floating. He is being moved, weightless, onto a hospital stretcher, which is a flying carpet taking him somewhere. He can sense time pass, months and years. He is warm and cared for, in a place where no one can reach him and hurt him. On weekends, he is wheeled out into the garden, a blanket in a tartan pattern on his knee, looking at the rose bushes and the pomegranate and orange trees and the sky washed into a perfect blue that tells him how much the sky loves him until he bashfully drops his gaze and loves back, loving not just the sky and the trees and the blanket but the track curling away from the edge of the garden into the pine forest at the end. Beyond the forest rise the hills, smoke curling up from cottage chimneys, the voices of children singing evening songs in Khasi. But that, he knows, is only on the weekends. On other days, he remains on the hospital bed, growing used to the horizontal view, that ceiling with its lights shining and bright except when the duty nurse in her dark navy cardigan and with her pale, wrinkled hands turns them off at bedtime and who comes back to prop him up and draw the curtains back in the morning for when the doctor makes his rounds and leans towards him so that his bottle-top glasses reflect back to him his own face and Dr Bose asks, 'Perhaps then you should begin with how you first met the Committee?'

He comes to with a start, trying to retain the final images of the trance even as they dissolve and trickle through his mind.

'But to tell you how I came to the Committee,' he says, 'I have to first tell you of what came before.'

'Yes, then you must first tell me of what came before,' Dr Bose says.

He waits, wishing for someone else to take over this task assigned to him, but there is no one. He looks, with surprise, at the coin in his hand. He does not remember picking it up from Dr Bose's table, but now that he has it, he cannot help scrutinising it. How does he know that it is a coin from the ancient kingdom of Magadh? He has a sensation, almost, of levitating, feeling that he is not actually lying on Dr Bose's deck chair but is hovering in the air, suspended in some unknown medium. The person whose exploits he is describing, and who goes by the name of Das, is no longer him, just someone he once knew, someone trapped in the 1940s, while he is capable of ranging back and forth in time, a flying yogi, a soul in transit seeing the numbers rise and fall—1947, 185.., 198-, 2???

5

The first corpse was near Sealdah station. Sightless eyes aimed at the sun, skin stretched taut over bone, mouth an open hole.

Then the line between the dead and the dying began to blur. Emaciated groups, humanlike rather than human, wandering the streets of Calcutta. Bones wrapped in rags, festering sores cloaked in a foul smell, ulcers and decaying teeth. Peasant fathers led starving children by their hands to the church, begging for them to be accepted for conversion as rice Christians. Demented mothers who had killed their babies because they were unable to feed them sat howling in alleyways, bare stick-legs wide open. At the back of a hotel, a man on all fours lapped at a spill of gruel like a dog.

Skeletal figures huddled under a street lamp, shivering, while a few feet from them a row of vultures waited for the dogs to finish with a corpse whose guts were strewn all over the ground. The vultures grew impatient, swelled in number and began an assault on the dogs, which howled for their canine kind to come support them in combat. Air-raid trenches filled with decomposing bodies. Everywhere, mahajans bought up land deeds and brass utensils from destitutes. Pimps restocked their brothels with women and girls who had been purchased for a handful of rice.

The bodies began to rot. The smell of decaying flesh and shit filled the streets and doorways. The government rounded up those it chose to call 'vagrants' into lorries, drove them to the outskirts of the city and put them in warehouses that had been converted into detention centres. Under the new Armed Forces Special Powers Ordinance, the word *famine* was banned from appearing in newspapers.

Birla, Sarkar and Benthall, businessmen who in public supported

Gandhi, bought up remaining stocks of rice for the immense profit to be made from free trade. At the bottom of the caste ladder, so low that they might as well be living in an abyss, the sweepers responsible for cleaning the city and the doms who handled corpses struggled to keep up with disposal while they themselves crept ever closer to death. The word *starvation* was now censored and could no longer be printed in newspapers.

A relief group set out from the hostel towards the villages, hoping to help with the distribution of grains. We took the train to Midnapore. What could have been more hopeless? Middlemen on the train schemed how to drive the price of grain up even more. Destitute villagers sat along train tracks and underneath trees, eyes bloodshot, hands outspread in supplication, telling us that military trucks had forcibly collected all their harvest and that there was nothing to eat anywhere in the district. Our group dispersed, returned to the city.

Only Crazy Horse persisted, determined to penetrate farther into the countryside. I went with him, thinking of my family, wondering if famine stalked my own village. We took buses, walked, waited for ferries. We stopped at relief kitchens when we found any, helping with the unloading of grain, distributing infinitesimally tiny amounts of gruel to an endless horde of demented mouths, the earth itself having transformed into a gaping mouth and an empty stomach. We slept on the road, in party offices, with depressed strangers who had no food to share. We passed broken pitchers and torn mats and skulls where cremations had taken place, untidy mounds where people had been hastily buried. We came across an old man eating raw foodgrain scattered along the railway tracks. The railway police constables sat at their post and pelted him lazily with stones until he collapsed and never got up.

In the villages, clothes rotted in the blazing sun. They had been blown on to the fields by the cyclone that preceded the famine and that had been trailed by floods, because nature, as much as Winston Churchill and the free traders, had determined that my people were worthless and deserved to die in their millions, unknown and unremembered. Huts gaped at us with astonishment, their thatch roofs carried away. The lanes were covered with weeds and grass. The water in the ponds was bitter and turbid where it had not simply dried into thick mud.

As we went farther, we saw a rich winter crop ripening in the fields. There were no human beings left to harvest it. Utterly empty villages, howling jackal songs echoing deep into the night. A naked man fished in a canal. A shrunken old woman crouched under a banyan tree that itself had died, her bony hands resting on an empty pitcher. Over our heads, the burning sun. A woman scrabbled on her knees in the mud banks of a dried-up pond, breasts elongated and shrivelled, trying, but failing, to crack open a snail with a stone. I had arrived at the end of the world, and I was looking not just at the present but at the future.

I decided to turn back. Crazy Horse would not come with me. He could not go to London to assassinate Churchill just yet, he said, so this is what he would do, penetrating deeper and deeper into the desolation until he too had starved and become a vengeful ghost, spirit limbs contorted in unimaginable ways and reaching unbelievably far to haunt the masters in the intimacy of their London mansions.

When I returned to the city, I looked up the medical effects of starvation on the human body and mind. The shrinkage of vital organs and loss of functions, the breakdown of adipose tissue and muscle mass, chronic diarrhoea and anaemia, furred tongues and hallucinations. Postmortems tend to reveal the cloudy swelling of liver and kidneys, congestion in the lungs and intestinal mucosa featuring the denudation of epithelium.

I found myself unable to sleep, lying petrified in a state that was half wakefulness and half sleep. Sometimes I thought I was leaving my body behind in the hostel room while my spirit ranged far and wide, beyond famine-ravaged lands to cities and lands I had no knowledge of, to times beyond my reckoning but where humanity counted for nothing. No peace, no justice, only desolation. When I awoke from these nocturnal journeys, I felt that either I had been pursued in my dreams by terrible beings, by monsters, or worse, that I had been a monster myself, devouring all in my path.

Daylight brought no relief, only the sounds of the dead and the dying; it brought starvation and murder; it was impossible to avoid the idea, irrational though it might seem, that there was complete correspondence between my nightmares and my reality.

All I remember of my dreams are impressions. A factory tower that silently, eerily, filled the air with the smell of burning chillies; a face glowing like a mask on vertical buildings; a tiger with its jaws clenched around a wooden doll. There is, however, one episode I recall distinctly.

FIRST, I SAW a sign. *The Hero's Walk*. Then I saw an altar, a memorial, a monument, with steps cut into its side. But where was I? I wished to discover what was on top of the altar, which hero was consecrated there, but I turned around, I don't know why, and began moving away from the altar. I remember shades of grey, the fading daylight of dusk, paved ground stretching endlessly in front of me while I took one step and then another, step by stepstep, making no progress that I could sense towards a horizon marked by a blackened line of leafless trees, their branches like bones.

No progress, no movement in my movement, just step by stepstep and darkening skies, just branches like bones. I was afraid, like there was something I had to do before dark, such as find shelter, and yet I was walking along the open ground, towards those trees that looked like they might have corpses dangling from them, yet I was walking towards them step by step.

Corpses? Or monsters? The trees made me think of the vampire hanging from the mimosa tree, the Betaal that Vikram the Conqueror tries to carry away from the tree, the Betaal that insists on telling story after story to Vikram, trapping him in a prisonhouse of stories.

Still, I walked, step by step, step by stepstep, until there appeared in front of me a structure, a low wall, a circular wall, an enclosure. I peered over the wall and saw stone steps descending deep, stone steps plummeting hard, and at the very bottom, a pool of water. I felt a churning in my head, a number, ??, but it faded. A shape stirred in the water, sending out a series of ripples, and I was afraid. There was a face in the water. It was not my face. It was the face of someone under the water, looking at me, a face that was like the mask of a man, with holes for eyes.

I turned around. I ran. Behind me, I heard a voice. I looked behind. The mask face was now attached to a body. It loomed above me like a giant, and yet its proportions were all wrong, like that of a short man who had been stretched in a machine and made very long. Teeth fixed in a rictus smile, the creature floated behind me but without looking at me. Its gaze was focused on a distant horizon, and it waved its hands vigorously like it was addressing a crowd made up of thousands in some vast stadium. The ground reverberated beneath me with the voice of this thing, and then music began to play everywhere, a chanting and a singing as the creature waved endlessly at this huge crowd.

When I turned around, there was no crowd and no Hero's Walk. Instead, a building blazed with glass walls, and it was towards this that I ran. I don't remember a door or an entrance, I don't remember crossing a threshold, but I was inside the building. The dome of the ceiling rose high above me. A staircase looped around the building. It was like the lobby of a very grand hotel, or a palace, or a court. At one end of the lobby, there was a desk, from where a man scrutinised me with suspicious eyes. Behind him, the wall was filled with metal cabinets painted military green.

'You're late,' the man said. Then he turned and took a folder out from one of those cabinets. He opened the folder, pressing it down on his desk. 'Father's name, place of birth,' he said. I could not see his face clearly, but his voice was nasal. 'Now sign here, here and here,' he said, uncapping a pen and holding it out towards me.

I was dizzy. The cabinets were all gone. The floor underneath me swayed. I felt I was inside an aircraft, in a rocket taking off from earth. My vision cleared. I looked out through the glass walls. What I had taken to be dusk or twilight was nothing like that. It was morning, but morning that revealed an ashy grey expanse stretching as far as the eye could see. A blank stretch of grey, with streaks of yellow. Through this yellow-grey fog, an arch of some kind was faintly visible. Wind blew smoke, dust and fog around the arch. Hard to tell ground from sky, earth from space. A shape moved in the fog, that creature I had seen waving at its imaginary crowd. It flickered and then through it began to flow other figures that were humanoid but not human, so many of them, all swirling in the mist.

'How is it to be in the Palace, looking out at India Gate?' the man said.

Before I could answer, there was the sound of an alarm bell. A humanoid figure collided with the glass wall. The wall shook. Another hurled itself against the wall, and then another, both moving too quickly for me to make out what they were. Not monkeys. Not humans. But something like both. The man sighed and pressed a call button underneath his desk, his face transformed suddenly into a gas mask with angled double snouts.

The building shook. Many more of these creatures were coming out of the fog, slamming into the wall. I started running. Up the staircase I went. A crash was followed by the sound of breaking glass. I looked down and saw the monkey creatures pouring over the man in the gas mask, a sea of monkey fur that shimmered and shook and began to flow up the staircase behind me.

I ran. I hid. Someone was hunting for me. I was in the underground sewers of Calcutta. I was on the building rooftops. I was in the corridors and staircases of the McPherson Hostel, while behind me, something came relentlessly, some creature that seemed to belong to past, present, and future. I found myself in a crawl space, terrified, hearing things go by. When I emerged, I was out on the streets. I drifted past shuttered shops and parked lorries and found myself in the winding lanes of the area around Tiretta Bazaar. I heard someone behind me, whispering, searching, hunting.

The broad stretch of Central Avenue lay ahead, a sickle moon reflecting off its dark black pitch. I stumbled into a wall. When I looked up, there were two moons in the sky, of different sizes. There was a small gate behind me. I went in. I now know that I must have entered the medical college grounds somewhere close to where this clinic is located. But I was unaware of that in my dream, where I was not inside the medical college grounds but some place where ruin and labyrinth came together, as if I had travelled through time, through some dark, apocalyptic future of ours and then landed back in an equally dark present.

I walked across a courtyard overrun with trees and grass, weeds sprouting from the brickwork of buildings whose windows had been boarded up on the lower floors. But high up in the buildings, one could see dim yellow lights, casting shadows on parapets and balconies, staircases and bridges. There were people in those yellow rooms, carrying out experiments or torture, experiments that were torture, torture that was a part of their experiments, and under the shadow of yellow rooms filled with torture and experiments, I ran.

I stopped when I saw another creature standing on a bridge, looking down at me. It was not one of those monkey things but a human being. The moon glinted off the white-hot discs of his glasses. He saw me.

Again, I ran, away from those buildings and bridges. I was in the twisting alleyways, scurrying like a cornered rat, like a test creature in a labyrinth. I saw a green door in front of me, its paint chipped. I approached it in terror, aware of my pursuer behind. The door opened. I was inside. I saw the woman I would come to know as Miss Srinivasan. She was wearing a plain white sari with a crimson border. She looked like a schoolgirl, or like a very young school mistress, or like a child widow.

'You must come here when you are awake,' she said.

'But how will I find you?' I asked.

There was a kind of hammering sound, a pounding on the door.

'You have been finding us through your dreams, have you not?' she said.

I felt that stirring in my head again. The number three? No, the number thirty-three, and I began to recall similar moments in my other dreams that had included a street name as well as a number.

'Wait,' I shouted, as the hammering got louder. Miss Srinivasan became a crow. 'Thirty-three what?' I shouted. 'Thirty-three where?'

Behind me, the door burst open. Something slithered at my feet. I woke up with a scream.

The papers on my desk were soaked. The shutters banged violently against the window frame in the hostel room. The rope I had used to tie the shutters together was torn. The wind blew gusts of a dark, furious rain across the veranda into my open window. I limped across to the shutters. I saw a squat silhouette in the veranda and screamed again.

It was the Bull, sitting lotus position in the pouring rain. He did not open his eyes.

I locked the window and began to clean up, my mind numb, unheeding except in a mechanical way of the ruined state of my textbooks. I separated the books out in batches, opening the pages, placing weights on them and putting them under the ceiling fan. When my desk was almost clear, I saw it. It looked like a paper flower, so delicately was it folded. But my fingers knew what to do, and the flower opened to a pink rectangle of paper with clear purple writing on it. Thirty-three Beadon Square.

I walked to that address in the morning with a feeling of absolute certainty. The skies had cleared up as I walked through flood waters, umbrella in hand, trousers folded to just below the knees. I remember how self-conscious I was as I rolled my pants down before the door, patted my hair and knocked. Miss Srinivasan opened it. It was just as in my dream, I thought, although I was not being pursued by anything. She was there. It was the Committee. I was home.

6

Is that him talking? Is that him describing those events of long ago? Behind him, the psychoanalyst is silent. Das lies on the deck chair a while longer, eyes shut, and the sounds gradually flow back into the room, the susurration of his own breathing, the pagla ghonti of a fire engine making its way down Central Avenue, the dull scrape of the chair as Dr Bose gets up. He opens his eyes. Dr Bose walks across the room and stands at the window, his usual way of announcing that the session is over.

Dr Bose asks if he will come again the next day at the same time. Das agrees, but only out of politeness. He has no intention of returning unless the Committee explicitly directs him to do so, and he sees no reason for that to happen if he can pass the riding exam. He is determined that he will.

He is at the door when Dr Bose interrupts him.

'Before you go, may I see the note from the Committee? The one sending you to me for a consultation?'

He goes through his pockets for the note, where he remembers putting it. Then he searches in his purse, but it is not there either. He must have left it in his room. He cannot tell if Dr Bose is disappointed or satisfied as the door to the Savage Freud clinic closes behind him.

THE SUMMER STORM has passed, and the heat and humidity outside is fierce, the sun blazing down on buildings and traffic, beating pedestrians into the sparse shade offered by shop awnings. He is surprisingly calm, but he supposes that that was the point of the psychoanalytical exercise. In spite of the heat, he wants to walk somewhere, in a direction opposite to the hostel. He finds himself proceeding towards Chowringhee, towards the site of his shame from the previous evening, like a general returning to seize temporarily conceded terrain.

He advances slowly, mopping his face with his handkerchief every few minutes. His handkerchief is soon damp. He should have thought to bring his hat with him. At Curzon Park, he takes a break, easing himself onto a bench from where he can survey the tree tops of the Maidan. In the distance lie the shop fronts of Chowringhee, grand, forbidding, the stretch of the arcade along Esplanade cool and shady.

Is it true that the British will leave India any day now? He does not think that he can see any signs of that departure. There was a slight hesitation during the initial stages of the war, with the fall of Singapore and the retreat to Japanese forces, but equanimity has been restored with the dropping of the atom bombs and the production of mutant children around Hiroshima and Nagasaki. Bengal's own mutant children are dead and forgotten, and now the empire, like a giant ship listing initially because of strong winds, has righted itself and is sailing on. 'Let Curzon Holde What Curzon Helde'—was that not the grasping family motto of the man the park is named after?

In the distance, he sees the gleaming white uniform of a police sergeant convincing people to move along. The wheels of a tram click on the tracks as it curves gracefully on its way to the Maidan. Near him, something scurries on the ground. Das looks and sees three bandicoot rats, swollen with good health, black fur bristling, each the size of a small cat. Genus *Bandicota*, from the Telugu *pandi kokku*, or pig rat, he mutters to himself. Species *Bengalensis*. In other words, completely indigenous. They are triumphant, unafraid, utterly disdainful of his presence. Someone has left food for the rats, he realises, as he sees the small shrine set up in homage to the rats, with its offering of vermillion and flowers and sweet pedas and incense sticks. In the heart of the empire's possession, in Curzon Park, someone is worshipping bandicoot rats.

HE GETS UP and walks on, down the Chowringhee arcade, past general goods stores and a watch showroom and antique shops that he will never have the courage to enter. He pauses when he reaches the white facade of the Jadoo Ghar. He can hear the shouting of a crowd from somewhere behind the museum, the rhythmic pronouncements of a political leader punctuated by approving roars from his listeners. Something is happening in this city, something is happening in Delhi, Lahore and London. A new world stirring into being, its outlines still blurred.

He listens to the shouts carefully, but he cannot make out if they say 'Pakistan' or 'India.' He turns his attention back to the museum and, after deliberating briefly, goes in. He has never been inside the museum, and he does not see why this is not as good a moment as any. The Anglo-Indian ticket seller looks at him suspiciously, as though he is there to make a claim upon the museum's artefacts as a representative of India, Pakistan, or some as yet unknown third political entity, but he lets him through without a word.

Inside, the wide verandas of the museum are shady and cool, arranged in a rectangle around a large garden where a statue of the Buddha from the second century BC stands forlornly in the sun. There are Vishnus and Garudas around him, a Shiva with the cropped hair and chiselled face of a street goonda, multi-headed cobras spreading their hoods over reclining Vishnus and Buddhas. The past is not alive and present here, he realises. Instead, it is classified into the distant, the lost, the irredeemable, and no one around him, not the scattering of Indian visitors, not the British staff striding around purposefully and not the American sailors chewing gum, will be able to step across the line that separates them and their now from what has come before. They are all doomed to remain passengers on a train speeding away from the platform of history, on carriages clanking their way to extinction, towards the glory of the mushroom cloud.

The statue of an apsara stops him dead. Her generous hips and ample bosom were, a few minutes ago, attracting whistles and catcalls from the sailors, but the men have left now, tramping their way to the upper floors. He looks at her and wonders if he sees in the cast of her face a kinship. After all, are they not, him and her, present mortal and past immortal, part of the same civilisational fabric? But he cannot find familiarity in her face, only otherness. He has a vision, suddenly, of him walking here, along the corridors of the Jadoo Ghar with Miss Srinivasan, holding her hand, and it is such a powerful vision that it almost breaks through to become reality so that he can feel her hand in his, he can see the arch of her neck and the cast of her eyes, quizzical, as she looks at him looking at the apsara and squeezes his hand back with hers.

But then it is all gone. He is standing there alone. He walks away reluctantly, taking the stairs to the natural history section. In the rooms where the exhibits are kept, the high ceilings curve like the roofs of aircraft hangars. The sun is weak again, filtered by gathering monsoon clouds, and the streaks that make it in through the skylight windows create shadows everywhere. He walks through the invertebrate hall, specimens arranged in cabinets and in display cases distributed evenly through the room. In the vertebrate hall, the walls are bristling with antlers, heads mounted everywhere. Elephant tusks swoop up over the doorway, like the remnants of a species long vanished from earth.

He stops in the middle of the room, struck by a giant skeleton suspended from wires. It is about forty feet long, graceful in spite of its size, suggesting, even in its current state, nothing other than flight. He does not know what the creature is, but he can almost imagine it, the outlines filled in, flying, a human being astride on it as a mahout pilot.

'What is it?' he asks, speaking aloud. 'What kind of a bird is this?'

From the shadows at one end, a man emerges, a short, dark man like himself, wearing the tunic of a worker. Das squints to read the display card. It is not a flying creature at all, he realises with embarrassment. What had he thought it was? Some kind of extinct flying dinosaur? This is the skeleton of a whale, a specimen of the Lesser Rorqual. The attendant reaches out to remove the card.

'Wait, is that not a whale?' Das asks. 'Is that a bird? A flying dinosaur?'

The attendant glares at him. Then he puts up a new card that reads: THIS SECTION CLOSED FOR REPAIRS.

7

When the notice appears outside the registrar's office next morning, asking all fifth years to present themselves at the Maidan at 3 p.m. sharp, Das is not as perturbed by this as he expected to be. Perhaps as a result of Dr Bose's intervention, he is less panicked than many of his classmates. 'All absentees—and abscondees—will be considered to have failed the riding examination and will, consequently, be held back,' he reads aloud with equanimity, wondering if that 'abscondees', set off by prickly dashes on either side, is a jab at him. He certainly absconded in spirit, if not in body, on that previous occasion.

At breakfast, he watches the others, wondering how they will fare in the riding examination, noticing that the obscene jokes have dried out. Only the Bull looks calm, eating his special breakfast while intently reading an issue of *Super Man*, comparing its instructions on body sculpting with those in the booklet by Swami Shivanand Teerth of Pune on the Hindu way to muscle-building.

There is in such a Super Man approach, Das thinks, an absence of restraint, a materialist aggressiveness that he cannot sanction. He may have once fleetingly admired the Bull and his quest to restore race pride, especially during those days of the famine, but his own thinking has been refined through his involvement with the Committee. It may even have been this refined philosophy that made him hesitant when it came to riding the horse the first time. Whether considered a beast of burden or an instrument of war, both such approaches to the horse seem wrong, reductive towards what is a life form with its own validity. The horse has even been turned into a weapon of genocide, as when taken by the Spanish conquistadores to pillage the Indian peoples of the Americas. The horse, genocide,

SuperManism, he reflects. Sandow, the body-building guru of Bull's, was a Prussian, and it has been all too clear in the news emerging from Europe after the war exactly what Prussian SuperManism was capable of. And the same goes for the British, he reminds himself, morally superior though they might see themselves to the Prussians. Did they not, in their incessant lust for classification, think just a few decades ago that the Indian, an Indian of his kind, was inferior to the horse in the great chain of being?

It fills him with sorrow, these reflections of his, and he looks down at the pages of the book he has brought to breakfast with him. 'During the spring and summer months, the pilot's food should consist of buffalo milk among liquids, among grains aadhaka or tuvar dal, and among flesh, the flesh of sheep,' he reads. 'In the four months of rains and autumn, cow's milk among liquids, wheat and black gram among grains, and flesh of cocks and hens. In the four months of winter and snow, goat's milk, rava and black gram among grains, and flesh of sparrows.'

There was a time when he would have been filled with scepticism, if not outright hostility, for the passage he has just read. But these days he is a changed man, one who understands that not everything is what it might appear to be. And with that thought in mind, immensely comforting, he puts the manual away and returns to his room, hoping that he will be done with riding White Rose when he returns.

HE DECIDES TO travel to the Maidan on his own, waiting till his classmates have left. They are a strangely cowed group as they depart, calling out his name once or twice in a tentative manner. He keeps studying the manual of the *Vymanika Shastra*, allowing his mind to be filled with details of the clothing recommended for pilots. 'Silk, cotton, moss, hair, leather,' he reads, purified by twenty-five processes and washed with mica-saturated water before being spun into yarn. These will be interwoven with fibres from the ketaki flower, from palm, swallow wort, sunflower, coconut and jute, soaked with the oil of linseed, tulasi, gooseberry, bael and mustard. The finished clothing, as prescribed by the sage Agnimitra, will be handed to the pilot, along with benediction, a protective amulet and cheers. He can almost feel that collective goodwill as he reads on.

When the street is clear, he walks across to the tram depot and boards the second-class compartment of the Number 1. From his window seat, the city is unusually quiet. It is almost somnolent in the June afternoon, the cobblestones slick with rain, the buildings muted by the grey, overcast skies. A breeze trickles through the large windows into the car where it is spun, with giddy childishness, by the fans mounted on the ceilings as the tram trundles along, slowing down as it enters the crowded thoroughfares of Shyambazar. The car begins to fill up, its roominess squeezed out by the stark colour scheme of office babus, all shining white dhotis and spiky black umbrellas.

The tram gathers speed again, and it is when they are on College Street, right across from the Savage Freud clinic, that he thinks he is being watched. The car is emptier now, having deposited its load of babus near Sealdah, but although he surveys his surroundings carefully, he can find no source for the sensation. It is probably nothing, just a residue of his previous day's visit to Dr Bose, but the incident makes him uneasy. He gets off the tram and walks across the Maidan, snatching a glance behind him every now and then, unable to pick out a pursuer.

Most of the other fifth years are already there, gathered around Walker, who looks gaunt and withdrawn. It is almost the same arrangement as on the previous occasion, the Bull and the Nose in front, Ahmed and Biswas lurking at the back. What is different is that their group has today managed to collect a large number of bystanders. They consist mostly of shabbily dressed men, some in bare feet or threadbare sandals, people who look like they're out of work and who carry with them a sense of furtiveness. Many of them are unshaven, and some appear outright sickly, ribcage and collar bones on the verge of bursting out of their skin bags. It is astonishing that they are confident enough to crowd a gathering being directed by a white man.

Yes, the empire is collapsing, Das thinks. The British will leave the subcontinent on August 15, it has been announced. There will be two nations, a Hindu-majority one of India, and a Muslim-majority one of Pakistan, split into two parts, West Pakistan and East Pakistan. The latter is where his own village might end up. He does not know the exact details of what will go where. Nobody does. The maps are still being drawn to decide the boundaries of India and Pakistan, armies and bureaucracies and bank reserves are still being divided, but the killings have already begun.

Walker, remnant of the empire, is aware of the onlookers crowding his riding examination. Who are they? Indians or Pakistanis? If he looks at them, the men pretend that they're standing there by chance, at the same time beginning a slow drift away. As soon as he looks away, though, they drift back and begin staring again. Das is perplexed by this gathering that has, the more he looks at it, the lineament of a pulsating crowd, one on the verge of becoming a mob. For a moment, he can almost see the mob ransacking and pillaging, groups of men battering down a solitary and knifing him, men thrusting their way into houses looking for women to rape and kill, swords and axes shining in alleyways to chants in the name of Kali or Allah or the Guru. He comes out of his trance only when he hears Walker's voice calling out to him insistently.

He begins pushing his way through the mob, becoming aware that it is composed of more than out-of-work day labourers. There are some babus in there too, folded umbrellas held erect like they are presenting Das with a Bengali guard of honour. There are some scarred, brawny young men who look like ruffians, goondas. There is even a man who looks like a trader, elegant in his dhoti and pince-nez glasses, a man who has a faint, disturbing resemblance to Gandhi. But he is a menacing sort of Gandhi, a double, a doppelganger, a doosra of Gandhi's who has the effrontery to nod to Das in a familiar fashion. But Das has no time to dwell on any of this now, not if he is to correct his earlier error. He stands in front of Walker and the horse, and even though Walker is talking to him, it is the horse that transfixes him.

This is no bored-looking White Rose but a jet black mare.

'Take no notice of Nike,' Walker says. He sees the puzzled looks on the faces of his listeners. 'Winged goddess of victory. Greek. Otherwise, same drill as before. Das goes first, then the rest of you in the order handed out the last time.'

No one moves apart from the black horse, which seems far too frisky for a bunch of novices like Das and his classmates. Walker takes off his hat and mops his head with a large handkerchief. There is a rash that starts on his right cheek and goes all the way down to his neck, as if the boundaries of India and Pakistan are being messily determined on his face. He sighs audibly and puts his hat back on.

'Right, then. Just to show you how devilishly simple it all is, I'll ride one more time. Das, come and hold the reins so that you feel easy with her.'

Even though he is taken aback by how the composition of the scene has changed—the crowd, the horse, even Walker—to something far more ambiguous, he steps forward to take Nike's reins. Today, he is determined not to falter. Today, he will continue along the path chosen for him. Today, he will ride his Vahana on benediction and on cheers.

There is a white star at the centre of Nike's forehead, a little white raft in an ocean of blackness. Das swallows, even though there is no saliva to absorb in his dry mouth. The horse snorts and shakes her head, tugging at the reins. He tries to hold firm, taken aback by the power of the animal. Walker, short and slim, moves into his saddle like the Betaal returning to its mimosa tree hideout.

'I'll take it from here,' he says, gathering the reins.

Das steps back as Walker pushes his stirrups into Nike's sides.

The horse starts off in an easy trot, almost dainty in the way she sets her white-socked feet down on the grass. Some of the onlookers, the goondas and out-of-work labourers, clap, while the pince-nez gentleman, the menacing doosra of Gandhi's, catches Das's eye and grins conspiratorially. In the distance, a few Englishmen have stopped to look too. Walker guides Nike into a faster pace, moving like he is welded on to the horse, like a centaur out of

Greek mythology, man and beast in one, or taking a more familiar example, like a Gandharva, sometimes a human body with horse head and sometimes a horse body with man head. They hear now the clip clop of Nike's hooves, and Das can see dust rising where the hooves strike the ground.

Walker completes a circuit, and as he passes the onlookers, he stands in the saddle, taking his right hand off the rein. He sweeps his hat off and waves it dramatically in the air. Everyone, Das included, breaks into applause. As they do so, Nike swerves to the right, corrects her course, and swerves again. Walker slips in the saddle, and even as he is adjusting himself, Nike's forelegs come up, sending Walker sliding back. Then they come down, a horse playing rocking horse, and, with a weird keening cry that sends shivers down Das's spine, Nike raises her rear legs in the air, sending Walker shooting out of his saddle, over the horse's neck, like a stone from a catapult.

Walker is gliding over the Maidan like someone who is going to travel all the way to the Hooghly, sprout wings and coast over the Bay of Bengal; he will fly across the Indian Ocean and across the Arabian Sea; he will find a passage through the Gulf of Aden, the Red Sea and the Suez Canal; he will spread his wings over the Mediterranean, flapping them lazily, soaring over thermals until he is finally over the choppy grey waves of the English Channel, above the foaming caps that the English call white horses, home visible in the chalky cliffs of Dover.

When Walker comes down on the Maidan, it is with a shocking thud. He lies there more like a large doll than a man. The horse, her business still unfinished, goes up to the fallen rider and stomps the ground furiously next to Walker's unresponding body. The onlookers scatter with screams and shouts, while the aspiring veterinarians hesitate.

Das finds himself standing where he is, shouting at his classmates to fetch a policeman. He wonders if mad horses are treated like mad elephants, if they are shot dead for their madness. Menacing Gandhi is approaching him. In his hand, he has a cloth bag, the kind of thing Bengali family men take to the early morning market to put their fresh vegetables in. The man reaches into the bag. He presses something hard and heavy into Das's hand. 'I hope you will remember the favour,' he says. He smiles and moves away. Nike takes a few dancing steps towards Das.

The gun is heavy in his hand, but in an uneven way, weighted at the grip but light at the barrel, so light that the barrel seems to be floating up, like it is filled with helium and will carry him up to the sky, a man flying through the air while hanging on to a gun. Nike comes to a halt and looks at Das. She is perhaps the length of a cricket pitch away, her eyes locked directly on to his own. She takes a step, paws the ground, stops. There is something playful about her manner, puppylike, kittenish. Her nostrils flare, and from her jaws there dribble out lines of white foam.

Has he ever held a gun before? Then how is it that his right hand has curled itself around the grip, that his thumb has taken the safety off, that his left hand is cupping his right to make his aim steady? Who is sitting inside him making him do this? Who is the pilot inside the pilot?

THE ROTE SCHOLAR Das, shy and non-combative, can repeat verbatim from Hayes's manual on horse management that 'the most effective way to shoot a horse is to aim so that the bullet will go through the brain and enter the spinal cord'. It is best to shoot a horse in the middle line of the forehead, four or five inches above the level of the eyes. In the photograph Hayes uses to illustrate the ideal condition, a photo he took in South Africa in 1901, you can see a white man in a hat, his sleeves rolled up to above his elbows, pointing what looks like a toy gun at an old, sad horse.

In the distance, the band from Fort William kicks in with its drums and bagpipes, and a wind comes in swiftly from the Hooghly. This is the moment to fire, almost as in Hayes's textbook illustration, with Nike standing in front of him, looking vexed, like she has been interrupted while doing something of great import, and with Das aiming the barrel at the white star on her forehead. He is looking straight down what they call the line of faith; only when you believe you will hit the target will you squeeze the trigger.

He fires. The report comes to him from a great distance. Nothing happens. He has missed. The horse keeps looking at him, the star on her forehead unblemished. She takes a step forward. Takes another. Das wants to turn and run. Then Nike's left leg misses a step. He fires again. The horse stops. She coughs, and a reddish-black stream of blood billows out from her mouth, mixed with white flecks of foam. She gnashes her teeth and takes another step forward, thoughtfully, and this time he doesn't stop, firing round after round until the beast lurches and goes down on her side in the grass, her legs splayed in the air, dust billowing from the impact of the body, and Das steps forward, pointing the gun, hot in his hands, at the head of the beast, her eyes still open, still looking at him, her breath still coming, her chest spasmodic, a pool of urine forming near her hind quarters.

He looks on at the great beast he has killed. Someone takes the gun from his hand.

8

He has not quite turned the corner into the street leading to the hostel when he sees the car, sleek, black and shiny, waiting in front of the hostel gate. There is a push cart nearby, tilted at an angle, its bamboo handles pointing at the sky like some kind of indigenous, crafts-based, anti-aircraft gun meant to take down a Vimana. He ducks behind the cart, watching as the car sits incongruously in front of McPherson Hostel, in its back seat a sole passenger who, he sees, is the nameless Gandhi doosra who gave him the gun and then took it away from him at the end.

He does not have a clear recollection of what he did in the aftermath of the shooting. He thinks he fled the Maidan again, trailed by the cheers of his classmates. Later, he found himself stumbling blindly through the streets of north Calcutta, bumping into people and nearly getting run over in front of the medical college by a military jeep.

He stopped at the Hedua pond to sit and look at the water, wishing for it to pass on some of its tranquillity to him, its gentle ripple of currents and its oneness with the surroundings. He had failed, yet again, and this time through something worse than fear. Unless it was fear that made him shoot?

It no longer mattered. He had left behind village life to become modern man, turning away from the contained, miniature world of his illiterate father and mother. Dark interiors, open vistas of farmland and water, rules and rites and festivals, two or three pieces of cloth to be worn interchangeably, a brood of siblings growing behind and around him. But modern man turned out to be about extermination, while the peasants he left behind came into the city to die in their millions. Those that remained alive were channelled by their modern brethren to attack and pillage and rape. That too he abandoned, the brutish world of the modern man, for the realm of the Committee, old-new, new-old, for his assigned task as the soulful pilot of the mystical Vimana.

'There are thirty-two secrets the pilot should learn, and only such a person is fit to be entrusted with a Vimana, not others,' he chanted to the water. With death on his hands, he was no more a pilot, no longer a creature of compassion, and he would never see Miss Srinivasan again.

From water body to water body he wandered, ranging as far north as the Tala water tank before returning to the YMCA pool at College Square. He forced himself to eat at a rice hotel on Amherst Street, but he vomited everything out in an alley behind the hotel. Shivering, he sat through the night on a bench looking out at the YMCA pool, with a vague thought in his head of packing up his belongings and returning to his village. But that too was no longer an option. If the maps were being redrawn, it was likely that his village had become part of another country, part of Pakistan, and his family, even as he sat there in Calcutta, was joining a stream of refugees heading towards the city, their column meeting another stream of refugees, these latter ones Muslim, heading out from the India that had become a foreign country for them.

It was perhaps the awareness of no options left to him that finally brought him back to the hostel at dawn, hoping against hope that there might be a note there for him from the Committee.

But now that man, that menacing Gandhi, is there, lurking in his car, waiting for what purpose Das cannot fathom.

HE SEES A Number 1 tram emerge from the depot and takes advantage of the cover it provides him to scan the vicinity of the hostel in greater detail. He can see the usual morning rush building up, the milkman cycling away after his delivery to Kaka, the cleaner sweeping dead leaves and debris from the gate, while across from him, the Bull loiters on the street, along with three men Das has never seen before. The scars on one man's face, the one Das designates as the head goonda, tells him everything he needs to know. The other two are almost boys, skinny creatures with protruding cheekbones and prominent Adam's apples, there to provide numbers rather than weight. But it is the Bull who towers over them all, even over the brawny, scarred head goonda, the Bull whose forehead is smeared with a red tika dedicated to Kali.

Das hasn't been standing still as he figures all this out. Instead, he walks casually towards the tram, pretending he is just another early morning worker setting out for the office, hoping that no one will notice him if he acts in this manner. He slips onto the tram just as it picks up speed, pushing aside the thought that once again he does not know where to go and what to do, heaving a small sigh of relief that he has made a clean escape.

He has nearly made a clean escape.

The Bull turns his head, shouting something that Das cannot make out. The head goonda, released by the Bull's shout, begins sprinting. He is running like a football back desperate to cut off a marauding forward who has only the goalkeeper to beat, and although the tram is accelerating, the head goonda, it rapidly becomes clear to Das, is accelerating faster than the tram.

He sees the man's chest heaving, his legs a blur, his face streaming with exertion, and yet the man is steadily and surely approaching the open door of the second-class compartment. Das nods at the babu watching the proceedings with interest and snatches the umbrella out of the man's hand. The goonda leaps, landing gracefully on to the footboard of the car, his left hand grabbing a window frame. His right hand sweeps back. When it sweeps out again, it glints, parrying the sunlight with an open razor blade.

Das thrusts the umbrella through the door, and the umbrella, with a mind of its own, opens with a flourish, thick black cloth blotting out the shine of the goonda's razor. There is a shriek, then a thumping sound. Das closes the umbrella. The goonda is rolling away from the wheels of the tram. Das shakes the umbrella carefully, like he is fastidiously getting rid of a last few drops of water, and returns it to the mystified babu. He gets off the tram as soon as it reaches Shyambazar and starts walking towards Hatibagan.

The mansion is at the end of a long, winding lane leading off from behind Baghmari market. He does not know if this is the headquarters of the Committee, although it is the place where he underwent the viva voce that led to his selection as the pilot. He has been involved in the affairs of the Committee in other parts of the city, in the reading room on Beadon Street, where Miss Srinivasan and he compiled weekly reports on their interviews, in the function hall near Sanskrit College where the Committee members give their talks, in Ballygunje and Park Circus and Tollygunje. But this is where he has chosen to come in his desperation, to this North Calcutta mansion surrounded by high walls, located in the absurd nexus of the elephant garden that is *Hatibagan* and the tiger kill that is *Baghmari*, although the elephants and tigers are long gone.

He recalls a garden and a pond inside the grounds, a fountain with an apsara statue near the portico, more gardens and a small farm in the back. He recalls being asked to examine the farm's stock of milk cows and laying hens on one of those visits, the Committee as open to his accomplishments as an aspiring veterinarian as to his karmic piloting abilities. There was a library in there, too, and he recalls Miss Srinivasan showing him the room with its book-lined shelves, the two of them alone as she ran her delicate fingers over the spines of the volumes, talking to him of the poetry of Toru Dutt and Nazrul Islam and Rabindranath Tagore.

He had not remembered the wall surrounding the mansion to be quite so high, topped with shards of glass. He can see nothing beyond the wall, certainly not the two-storeyed mansion set far back inside the enclosed grounds. He makes his way to the gate. That he does not remember either, a gridwork of spiked black iron, its two halves shut with chain and padlock. There is a hut to the right, inside the gate, and he can make out a pair of feet, clad in old, battered hunting boots, sticking out from the hut.

Das tries to overcome his constitutional shyness, the introvert nature that has always prevented him from raising his voice, from standing out in any way, the deep fear that overtakes him when he is confronted by what is such an obvious symbol of power. These giant houses evoke for him guns, snarling dogs and humiliation. Nevertheless, he raises his voice.

'Bhai! Brother, please open the gate.'

The boots move slightly but there is no other response.

'Bhai,' he shouts a little more firmly, 'I am known to the Committee.'

'Go away. There is no committee here. This is a house.'

'Bhai, I have come here before.' He begins to stumble over his words. 'Vimana … Miss Srinivasan … Committee … horse.'

With a creaking and a cranking, the owner of the boots emerges from the hut. A man with a bandit moustache, its tips curling up ferociously. He is wearing an old army uniform, and on his shoulder rests a shotgun with a delicate string of amber beads wrapped around the barrel. The bandit stands inside the gate, staring at him fiercely, his eyes little pools of red.

'Go to the hospital,' he says. 'Go to the madhouse. Go to the zoo. Go anywhere, but go away from here.'

He is about to retort when he notices activity in the grounds. From the gate, he can see the path curling past the garden towards the mansion. There, underneath the portico, a car is disgorging a group of people. He catches a flash of elegant clothes, crisp white dhotis and English suits and expensive saris. Among them is Dr Bose, stepping out of the car in dignified fashion.

'Sir, sir, it is I …' he calls out, pushing his face against the bars so that Dr Bose can see him.

Dr Bose turns and looks, his face impassive behind the bottle-top glasses. A shiver runs down Das's spine. It is like the psychoanalyst has never seen him before.

'Sir, it is I the pilot. I am in dire need of help from the Committee. I have killed a horse, sir, although I did not mean to. I am being pursued by nameless, nefarious villains.'

With a slight tilt of his head, Dr Bose picks up the tail of his dhoti, turns and disappears inside. A hand comes out of the gate and plants itself against Das's face, and before he knows what it is doing, sends him sprawling to the ground.

THE FUNCTION HALL at College Street is locked, the reading room in the Beadon Street mansion closed and he cannot work up the energy to travel to Park Circus, Ballygunje and Tollygunje. It does not really make a difference. The Committee has vanished, and Das has nowhere to go. He is hungry, not having eaten since the day before. His shirt is covered with blood stains and vomit.

He wanders north again, towards Barrackpore, wanders back again, and when he is too tired to walk any farther, he instinctively makes his way towards the river. A ferry has just come in from Dalhousie, disgorging its passengers on to the bobbing jetty. He is filled with a longing to be part of this seething humanity, instead of being a fugitive, a man on the run by himself in a big city. He watches as the ferry empties out and refills itself. He finds himself staggering on to the jetty, ignoring the cry of the ticket seller in his booth.

There are three long bursts of the ferry's horn as the engine starts chugging and a man unties the rope. He jumps across the gap without knowing what he is doing. He has left it too late. Even though his feet touch the ferry, he is tipping backwards, falling into the water.

A hand comes out of nowhere and grabs his vomit-stained shirt. Then there is another hand. And another. Hands of all shapes and sizes grab him and pull him on to the ferry. Someone wipes his shirt for him. A woman, a cleaning maid by the look of it, offers him a paper bag of peanuts. He takes it and walks to the back, light-hearted all of a sudden, for he knows that no one on this ferry harbours any ill will towards him. He is mad, troubled, they have decided, and that makes him exalted, a holy fool.

He sits at the back of the ferry eating peanuts. Midstream on the Hooghly, the ferry settles into an easy pace. A group of boys comes swimming out towards it like dark, playful dolphins or rorquals, catching up with it in powerful strokes and boarding from the side, feet stepping lightly on the car tyres hung from the ferry as makeshift life jackets. They stand at the back of the ferry, their hair dripping, clad in nothing but underpants, with sinewy bodies that Mr Sandow,

Das thinks, would have been happy to begin sculpting into shape. They stand there by themselves, aware of the gaze of the passengers but not returning their stares, aloof kamikaze warriors intent on their mission. The youthful swimmers survey the city in front of them before, one by one, they dive back into the water. The leader waits till the very last before he makes his re-entry with a back flip.

The ferry slows down as it passes the crematorium, the river around it filled with mourners taking their ritual dips, the surface of the water a thick syrup of funeral ashes and marigold garlands. In the distance, the pyres flicker, while even farther on, he can see a procession arriving with a new corpse, 'Bolo Hori,' there is a shout from the procession. 'Hori Bol,' some of the passengers on the ferry respond. He nods his head like a wise lunatic and munches on his peanuts. A song comes to his mind, a song sung by fakirs at the dargah of Hazrat Shah Jalal, where his father had taken him for the urs festival celebrating the saint's death anniversary. It was a song that his father, a village singer, hummed happily all the way back home.

Das sings it now to himself:

কান্দিয়া আকুল হইলাম

ভবনদী পারে

মাঝি তোর নাম জানিনা

আমি ডাক দিমু কারে

মন তোরে কে বা পার করে

A fishing boat arrives out of nowhere. There is a corpse on the boat too, a shrouded figure on a cheap wooden cot. The boatman is standing as he rows, aiming for the crematorium. No one other than

Das appears to notice the boatman. He is tall, his arms immensely elongated as he pulls at the oar, with such power rippling through his strokes that he seems capable of pulling the ferry and all its passengers along with him and his little boat. Das tries to register the man's face, but it eludes him, this boatman without a name who has materialised out of the song.

THE FERRY BISECTS the river between the merchant mansions of Burra Bazaar and the smokestacks of Howrah. Ahead of them the new bridge gleams, clean and shiny in the morning light.

Das gets off with all the other passengers at Dalhousie Square, trusting in the crowd, letting it take him wherever it is going. Yet this crowd no longer possesses the goodwill of the rag-tag passengers on the ferry. There is a kind of pulsating in it, a geometry in its gathering, collecting in knots here but forming linear processions and ranked masses over there. Something of the twentieth century, something he has mostly missed out on in his life, is contained in these fluttering flags, the hammer and sickle, the saffron, the green. There are chants in the air, of Pakistan or Hindustan, he is not sure which, as he moves through the crowds like a ghost, past unsheathed swords.

What demonstration is he in now? Is he among the Muslim League supporters of Pakistan? Or are these the men of the Hindu Mahasabha who want sacred, undivided India? What distinguishes one group from the other? What distinguishes them both from the Communists? Is there a line that separates those propelled by hope and those driven by fear? Or is it all mixed up together? he thinks, passing the mounted policemen on their prancing horses.

He squeezes his way through the mob, the holy fool, drawing an occasional curse or a shove, but otherwise free to roam, free among the Muslims, among the Hindus and among the Sikhs. It is only as he making his way past a group of men who have no apparent affiliation that the trader with the pince-nez glasses, the Gandhi doosra, falls into stride with him, walking easily, like he has never left Das's side since the killing of the horse.

9

'Should you not try the Ballygunje location of the Committee?' the man says.

Das tries to hurry past without answering, but the man seizes him by the wrist. His grip is cold and astonishingly strong. There is a faint smell of cardamoms around him. Together they walk, side by side, almost like old friends were it not for the man's jailer hold upon his wrist.

'Perhaps the house in Park Circus? The one in Tollygunje?'

Das has been trying to formulate a question in his head, a question so complicated that he cannot find the words for it until it bursts out from his mouth.

'Who are you?'

'I am the future, Das. I am the free India you are all fighting for.'

'I have never been fighting for a free India. I sympathised, but it was too big an idea for me. I just wanted to be a modern man, get a job, look after my family, do my duty. Then even that became too big an idea for me, and I was lost, without ideas, without substance, until I chose the compassion of the Committee. That was an idea I could understand.'

'Are you sure you are compassionate? You took a life yesterday. Do you think the Committee will still think you compassionate after that?'

'They will understand. I was trying to save Walker.'

'The Committee has vanished. They will have nothing more to do with you. It was all a fantasy anyway, their compassion. Look around and tell me how much compassion you see.'

'I don't understand who you are, but I know the Committee

has a way to balance this madness. That it has chosen me to play a part in it. I am more than the killer of a mad horse.'

'Of course, you must not just depend on what I say. Why not read the note in your pocket?'

Das stares at the man. It is as though he expects the man to be transformed into a figure spinning thread on a charkha. But there is something hard and fierce about this man, a Gandhi made for a new age.

His hand has been released. He reaches into his trouser pocket, where all he has is a crumpled paper bag, empty except for peanut shells and a tightly folded cone of paper he had assumed to be a packet of salt for him to dip the peanuts in. His fingers tremble as he tries to pry open the cone. The writing is tiny but distinct.

Men of darkness eat food which is stale and tasteless, which is rotten and left overnight, impure, unfit for holy offerings.

When his vision clears, the man is speaking again.

'I want the Vimana. That is the only thing about the Committee that is not a fantasy. You will guide my men to the Vimana and they will take care of it. Then you will be given some money, which you will need to get your family out of their village. You have lost your home to Pakistan, Das, so be very thankful that you have me as the future of free India, as your patron in an independent country.'

He looks at the note again. The colour of the ink is indeed purple, but can he be sure that that is Miss Srinivasan's writing? Are her S's not more precise than that? And the way she writes T? Do they not lean the other way, to the left?

'There is really no need to think too much,' the man says. 'Your hunger for compassion and the burst of power you felt when you squeezed the trigger are ultimately not very different. You are merely evolving. Without the Committee, you would not have considered the horse or the Vimana. Without me, you would not have dared kill the horse or think of getting me the Vimana. How did it feel, when that powerful beast who had tossed the Englishman over like a doll went down to your bullets? The dhatura your friend the Bull mixed into its feed might have helped, even if he overdosed the first horse and killed it. How did that rush of power feel? Kill with the sword of wisdom the doubt born of ignorance, says the Gita. Be one in self-harmony, in yoga, and arise, great warrior, arise, says the Gita. And now, killer of horses and failed pilot, take my men to the Vimana.'

He thinks how he cannot give up so easily. Flying the Vimana is a matter of faith. It is why he was chosen, why he was selected so carefully by the Committee. Once he takes to the skies in the Vimana, this will cease, the Partition tearing people apart, the killings and the rapes and the starvation. All he has to do is hold firm, wait for the Committee to reappear and fly the craft.

The man gestures. From the mob swirling around them, the Bull emerges, accompanied by the thugs Das saw earlier in the morning. With them is the Nose, looking like he is setting out for an evening soirée rather than a raid or a riot. He stands aloof, dabbing a handkerchief soaked in cologne on his wrist even as the head goonda, the one who tried to jump on to the tram, grabs Das by the elbow.

'I don't know where the Vimana is. I don't know what it even looks like,' Das says.

The knee to his groin from the head goonda is swift, doubling him over. The razor blade flashes out again, and he flinches as it slices his right cheek.

When Das stands up again, they are all looking at him silently, strangers and former classmates, men transformed into instruments of confusion and rage. The red tikas smeared on their foreheads, the weapons in their hands, their need to clear the land, the city, of what they see as enemies, is the obverse of everything he has learnt from the Committee. After they take the Vimana, they will take the city. Today, they will kill the Muslims. Tomorrow, they will kill the Sikhs. The day after that they will kill the Communists. Then they will kill the women, after they have raped them first. Then they will kill the children, born and unborn, using hobnailed boots to stamp to death the foetuses in the wombs. Then they will kill a group that does not even exist. They will kill to restore race pride and they will kill to become Super Men. They will kill with the sword of ignorance the doubt born of ignorance and they will kill and kill and kill and kill and never cease. And some of them were once his friends.

THEY HAVE BEEN walking for a very long time through this labyrinthine city. A ragtag gang of men in what has become a city of men in a world of men, a place where there are no women, no children, where there is nothing but war in its various guises. Das senses the weight of the city around him, its dead hopes, its hopelessness, the famine that sent the starving into its streets not too long ago, the war with its raids and its blackouts, the public demonstrations and mass arrests and sectarian killings, and now this again, another set of killings to inaugurate what some are calling India and some Pakistan.

They proceed along narrow alleys, decrepit buildings towering over them. It has started raining, a steady downpour that turns the ground into mud, a rain that doubles and triples itself, falling not just from the sky but from the eaves of the roofs, from the walls and the windows, like the rain is trying, in one final effort, to put out the fires being lit all over the city. Walking along those alleys, surrounded by a band of men, Das is suddenly much older than his years, seeing not just what is past, but also what is passing and to come. He is filled with visions of future destruction, of a man with a face like a mask whose banal words and gestures produce fresh corpses and new ways of hating old enemies. He sees a cloud that smells of burning chillies spreading its deathly blanket over a provincial city and feral cattle, foaming at the mouth, as they overrun streets and squares quite empty of people. He sees babies ripped from wombs and masked men firing into bodies and an army of what looks like children encircling the land. Then he recalls, with an effort, the look on Miss Srinivasan's eyes as she adjusted the umbrella, the concentration in her face as she corrected his far too overzealous comments on a case. He wonders if he will ever see her again. He wonders if he will ever see his family in Sylhet again.

When he stumbles over the body, coming to an abrupt halt as

he trips over legs splayed out from a checked lungi, he thinks not of a man but of a horse. Then he looks at how small the body is, a shrunken adult, not unlike the corpses he came across in the thousands during the famine. He looks more carefully and sees that the body doesn't have a head. The Nose is the one who finds the head in the gutter, who looks at the anguish on the face and finds in it a familiarity and who calls out, 'Kaka?'

The Bull and his men crackle with anticipation at this signposting of territory. In the far distance, they see, there are men waiting in an alley, silently watching them. In the rain, it is hard to tell exactly how large the group on the other side is, and who they are. The Bull trembles with anticipation, certain that the enemy stands before him. Those are surely skullcaps and beards. Those must be flashes of green, a green to go with the green of the French shutters of the houses around them. Those are certainly the scouts and soldiers of an invading army. A shout breaks out from one of the men in Bull's group. He has found another head in the gutter. But this one confuses them, shatters the certainty of the interpretation that has been building. 'It's Ahmed,' Das whispers. 'Look at what you have done.'

The two groups, advancing cautiously towards each other, halt. If one corpse is a Hindu and one a Muslim, then who are the defenders and who the killers? The rain comes down with abandon as the columns stare at each other, trying to carry out a last, subtle act of interpretation, a final reading of colour, facial hair, headgear and the distribution of corpses before they decide whether to join forces or run towards each other and begin hacking.

Das has been forgotten. He stays low, pressed against the wall. Then he sprints, away from Kaka's corpse, away from Ahmed's head, away from the combatants and away from this city, away, if he can, out of the twentieth century.

10

He makes his way through streets and lanes that are eerily empty. The rain has let off, and in the gusts of wind that blow his way every now and then, he thinks he can hear the cry of some unfortunate victim, the shouts of distant raging killers. He even sees two men cutting down a third with axes, their silhouettes lit up by the afternoon sun that has crept out of the clouds.

He turns around and runs, towards Chowringhee, slowing down on Sudder Street when he comes across the first row of policemen and soldiers, on alert to protect European lives and European property.

It is sheer impulse that makes him open the small gate letting onto the grounds of the museum. The building is dark, all closed up, but he walks along its edges until he finds a door, a service entrance, not fully shut. He squeezes through it, walks through an empty office and comes out on to a corridor. The place is utterly empty. In the weak sunlight, he can see the Vishnus and Buddhas ranged around the inner courtyard looking at him, demanding from him, a representative not just of India or Pakistan or Britain but of modern man, an answer for the destruction he has unleashed upon this earth.

He stops in front of the apsara, looking intently at her face.

Behind her, there is another statue, tilted at an awkward angle. The statue shifts. It is wearing a hat.

'It's been a while, Mr Das,' it says.

The detective looks nothing like the way he did when Das last saw him. That air of being haunted by ghostly fingerprints, by crimes too horrible for a human being to witness, is gone. Instead, as the city erupts in murder around him, Detective Sleeman appears utterly composed, the brim of his hat pulled low over his eyes, hands cupped to light the cigarette dangling from his lips.

The detective exhales thoughtfully, his smoke rings sailing across the statues like a votive offering.

'I understand that the occult seances have been rather interrupted by the riots.'

'You have to help,' Das says. 'You must stop all this.'

'There is nothing I or anybody else can do when they are determined to murder each other. Two peoples fanatically at odds. Different diets, incompatible gods.'

'There's been far too much death. It is your job to stop murders.'

'To solve murders, not stop them. But that too was in a previous life. Now, I have only one concern. I want you to hand the Vimana over to us right away. I wish to secure it before the city goes up in flames.'

'But how do you know of it? Surely, the Committee …'

He has the wild hope that Sleeman too is a member of the Committee, sent to help him.

'The Committee? An international gang of master criminals on whom we've had our eyes for a very long time. The CID does not sleep, Mr Das, nor do the various wings of the state. And it is those other wings of the state, even, shall we say, other wings of other states, that have been responsible for setting me on your trail. Both MI6 and the OSS are rather upset that a craft of great interest to them should have gone missing from the port at Kidderpore when the ship carrying it stopped there to refuel. It was on its way West, to be dismantled and examined somewhere in the safe, underground desert reaches of Roswell, New Mexico. Something well worth our enquiries, given that the Nipponese, having stumbled upon a most interesting wreckage in the Sunda trench near the Andamans, went to such considerable lengths to salvage the craft and prepare it for dispatch home. Without, you will notice, sharing a word of this with their friend the Führer. Now, after all that trouble and elaborate plans, we surely would not want the Committee selling this object to our Soviet allies soon to become our Soviet enemies, would we?

And if there is one thing I can assure you, it is this. After all this hacking and chopping is over, neither your free Pakistani government nor your free Indian government will be kindly disposed towards the Committee. So, unless you wish to spend the rest of your life in the Cellular Jail in the Andaman Islands, it is better that you end your little game with me right now.'

In his mind's eye, the Vimana takes on bewildering, blurred shapes. An ancient craft of compassion? Or an alien mechanism? No, it is a rocket or aircraft of some kind, an advanced prototype built by humans, a thing shaped expressly for the purpose of death in the manner of the atom bomb. There is nothing of the past in it, nothing of compassion, and he has been such a fool all along.

Yet, just as this vision of the Vimana flickers in his mind and vanishes, another slips into place. He sees, now, something blurry, something that has come from another time, from another place, something whose purpose is unfathomable not just to him but even to Sleeman, even to the Committee, to all human beings trying to make use of it for their small, instrumental aims of power and profit.

'The pilot is the one who knows all the secrets,' he says out aloud.

'What's that?' Sleeman says, looking irritated. He drops his cigarette and crushes it under his heels.

'The darpana, like a magician, will change the appearance of your Vimana into such frightening shapes that the attacker will be dismayed or paralysed.'

'You call it the Vimana, Mr Das. But I call it by its rightful name, the MacGuffin.'

'Lalacharya says, "That which can fly in the sky with speed equal to that of birds is called Vimana." Acharya Narayana says, "That which can speed on earth, on water, through air, by its own power, like a bird, is a Vimana." Shankha says, "Experts in the science of aeronautics say, 'That which can fly through air from one place to another is a Vimana.'" And Viswambhara says, "Experts say that that which can fly through air from one country to another country, from one island to another island, and from one world to another world, is a Vimana."'

HE HAS BEEN walking with Sleeman along the deserted corridors of the museum for far too long. He has no idea where Sleeman is taking him and why everyone should think he has the answer to the object of their quest. He tries to recall, impelled by all those who believe he knows where the Vimana is, if he has ever seen it, if he does in fact know of its location, hapless Das who has been running around Calcutta for over a day now, battered and pursued, subject to the arbitrary kindness of strangers.

He tries to remember where it is, the Vimana, since everybody is convinced he knows its location. He attempts to recall what it looks like, whether it is a glorious Vedic craft of peace or if it is just another weapon of mass destruction, a more advanced V-2, a Fat Boy with greater destructive capability. He is dizzy and has to stop for a moment, reaching a hand out to the wall to steady himself.

When he closes his eyes, what is it that he can see? Is that what the Vimana is, a thing that reflects the innate quality of the seeker?

Someone is shaking him. It is Sleeman, his face contorted with urgency.

'We've got to get moving, Das.' His voice is interrupted by roars from the street. 'I've got a squad waiting at the back entrance. You just take us to the Vimana and then we'll take care of you. You'll have nothing to worry about. You'll be safe even amidst all the murder.'

There is an explosion outside, then the hysterical staccato of a Sten gun answered by the ponderous single shots of a .303 rifle. His ears are ringing. He can't hear what Sleeman is saying, although his mouth moves rapidly and Das thinks he can make out the words, '… your family.'

At the far end of the corridor, a door opens. Sleeman reaches into his jacket. Miss Srinivasan emerges, holding a notebook, looking like she is just about to teach a class. She appears as poised as always, her hair tied in two schoolgirl plaits, her face composed as she looks at the men. 'Is this the blueprint you've been seeking, sir?' she says. Sleeman relaxes, his hand coming off the weapon in his chest holster. A sheet of paper flutters from Miss Srinivasan's hand and falls to the floor.

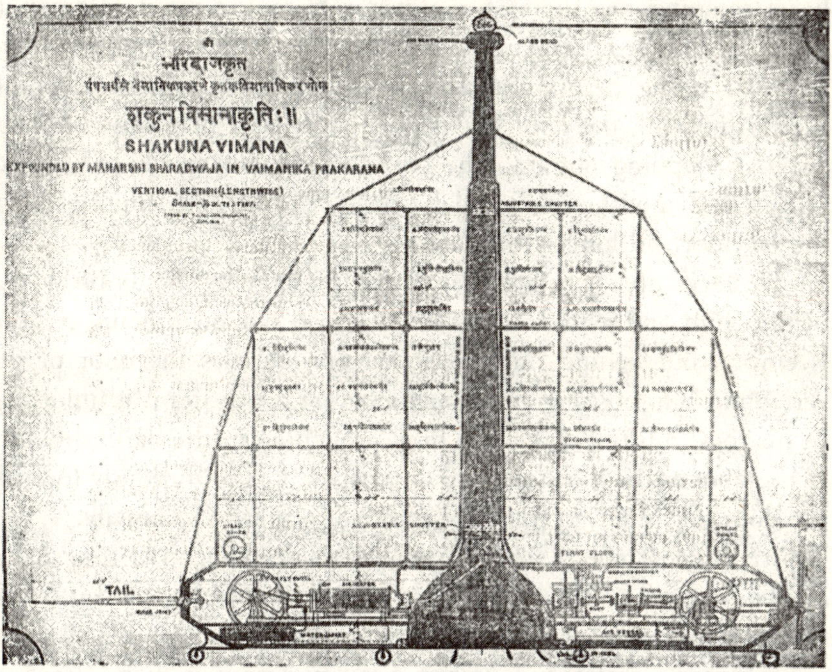

'He is unaware of the location of the Vimana, sir. But the rest of the papers are in there,' Miss Srinivasan says.

The detective scoops the sheet up from the floor and advances, his left hand flung out to indicate to Das that he should stay where he is. The detective steps inside the room. Miss Srinivasan closes the door behind him and shoots the bolt. Then she comes forward and takes Das's arm, leading him away even as a hammering begins on the door.

She does not say a word to him, but as they look at each other, he realises that she has known all along just how he feels. Love, that is the word, he thinks, such an embarrassing, awkward word, such a small word in this world of big weapons. There is a light in her face that he has never seen before, a light, he is certain, that has everything to do with him.

'Go now,' she says, releasing her hold. He wants to take her with him, but he cannot take her when he does not himself know where he is escaping to. There is a gunshot from the room Sleeman is locked in. At the far end of the passageway, a window shatters. There are men trying to make their way through that window. Behind Miss Srinivasan, the door bursts open. He has a final impression of Sleeman stepping out into the corridor and seizing her. She looks at him and mouths 'Go', and he does, turning and running down the corridor, no longer thinking.

He races up the wide stairs of the museum as shouts break out behind him and a man cries out. The corridor on this upper floor is empty, but behind him are footsteps. He tries the door of the vertebrate hall, pushing and shoving before he realises it is unlocked. In he goes, shutting it behind him, crouching in the dark, shoulder to the door as the footsteps in the passageway come furiously towards the door and then go past. He stands up, breathing heavily.

It takes his eyes a while to adjust to the light. The sun strikes off the antlers and tusks. It lights up the sign, THIS SECTION CLOSED FOR REPAIRS. In front of him, in the centre of the hall, the skeleton is no longer a skeleton. It is not, has never been, a flying dinosaur or a Lesser Rorqual. His heart sings as he steps towards it, making his way to the cockpit.

THE LINE OF FAITH: 1859

But the feeling soon wears off, and one moves among them with perfect indifference, treating them not as dogs ... but as machines with which one can have no communion or sympathy.

JAMES BRUCE,
EIGHTH EARL OF ELGIN

1

They had left the ruins of Paltangunj far behind and were looking for a place to make camp when they saw a procession whose contours astonished even Sykes. 'What in G-d's name,' he gasped, 'is that?' The rest of the company slowed down in response, reins jingling loosely on their mounts, their gaping mouths speaking for their sense of wonder. Only the Colonel remained impassive, like the observing machine whose prototype Sykes had once seen demonstrated by a Russian in Camden Town, a genius rather prone to gambling debts and requiring, just then, a temporary infusion of funds that had necessitated the demonstration.

The procession occasioning this range of responses was led by an armed escort, a detachment of a dozen ragged native soldiers in turbans and white leggings who nevertheless possessed remarkably new Enfield rifles for so bedraggled a troop. Behind them came three palanquins, each borne on the shoulders of four men, brocaded compartments that had some kind of coat of arms painted on their screens. These were followed by a row of bullock carts carrying supplies, the rearguard being completed by a seven-piece ensemble that was playing, even as it stumbled through the dreary stretches of Cooch Behar, a cacophonous rendition of 'For he's a jolly good fellow'.

Yet none of these things, wondrous strange though they might be, had made Sykes speak out aloud. The cause of that exclamation was the figure who occupied the very centre of the winding procession. Mounted on a grey horse, dressed native style in achkan, churidar and turban, with a sword on his belt and what looked like a cockatoo on his shoulder, his width threatening to spill off the back of the horse and pour into the ground, sat a vast, corpulent figure, head slumped down as if in sleep but in actuality positioned so because of its absence of neck, a figure that seemed to belong most naturally not even to the phantasmagoria that happened to be India but to some medieval allegorical woodcut, some representation of Sin or Death or Gluttony that had appeared on the outskirts of the barren lands around Paltangunj for the sole purpose of conveying to Colonel Sleeman and his hand-picked men the ultimate outcome of their special mission.

Sykes cleared his throat and called out for the column to halt. Bones and Tobin flanked him as he advanced. The coat of arms now stood out clearly, five balls—no, five *eyeballs*—staring out at him, blue orbs against a background of red and white, the whole surrounded by the flutter of a Latin motto that read: *Omnia Mei Sunt.*

Sykes, not knowing what the Latin meant and riding towards the heart of the column, stopped while still some distance from the figure on the grey horse. A flurry of activity resulted. The figure dismounted with some difficulty, helped down by two of the sturdiest members of the native soldiery. It was seated on a chair brought down from one of the carts, the canopy of a pink umbrella blossoming almost instantly above. Two more pehlwans met the first pair. Grunting with the strain, the quartet lifted the chair and advanced.

The Colonel had joined Sykes, and together they waited as this microcosm of the procession came towards them, stopping finally when they were all face to face, within speaking distance, the chair set down on the ground, the umbrella adjusted. The man, Sykes noted, was turbaned, bejewelled, and cockatooed, and yet for all that he was unmistakably a fellow countryman of theirs, if somewhat ripened by the tropical heat.

'What in G-d's name,' the Colonel said, stealing Sykes's phrasing, 'might you be, and what is your business here?'

The figure shuddered, movement breaking out in the folds of its flesh and the jowls of its face. It was moving its head in a bow, Sykes realised. The face, painted, and the eyes, lined with dark kohl, were crinkling into either a repulsive simper or a grimace. The mask shuddered with effort, and yet the blue eyes in it were still and unfathomable.

'I, sir, am the White Mughal,' it said. The voice, a falsetto, rang out sharply. 'I am the White Mughal, sir, and I have been most grievously harmed. I have been turned out of house and home by a band of native brigands, fanatical to the core. My palace has been seized, the gates of my kingdom barred to me and my loyal retinue left to wander these arid, parched lands. I crave restitution, sir, which it is in your power as an officer of her majesty to grant me.'

The White Mughal trembled in his seat, perhaps recalling all his loss in one wave of remembrance. However, he was merely perturbed by the activities of Bones and Tobin, who were examining the palanquins. Ignoring the protestations of the native guard, their shiny new repeaters notwithstanding, Bones had successfully convinced the occupants of the palanquins to temporarily vacate their premises by the simple expedient of thrusting the muzzle of his rifle through each screen. The former occupants now stood in two separate groups, discrete and distinct in the manner of everything in this astonishing, even abominable, land. The first consisted of three young females whose ages ranged from twelve to fifteen, slender for the most part. The second group consisted of three middle-aged matrons, chewing paan like a cow chews cud, all of them rather well provided for where it came to bulk.

'That there's the falana, lads,' the White Mughal said. 'I mean to say the zenana,' he corrected himself hastily. 'The harem, so to speak. Strictly no touching, although Bibi Chhappan Chhuri there, the Lady of the Fifty-Six Knives, might, if she were so inclined, offer you a singing performance the likes of which you will have never heard before in your lives.'

Sykes could not help starting. The lady in question was a member of the second group, and yet she was utterly unlike either them or the girls tittering and shying away from the ministrations of Bones and Tobin. Her two companions were bovine, uninterested in anything. But she, the Lady of the Fifty-Six Knives, looked at them as coldly and assessingly as the Colonel himself gazing at an enemy column through a Dollond telescope. As for her face, the container of her stone-like Gorgon eyes, it took him aback. The entire surface was criss-crossed with scars, short lines angled across her face in such close proximity to each other that they cast the dark features into an extra shadow of sorts. Sykes did not need to count the scars to know that there were fifty-six of them and that they had been etched onto her face with a knife.

THEIR ORDERS, OR that portion of it known to Sykes, had been to proceed north of Calcutta towards Darjeeling. While not strictly a slash-and-burn venture, rapine and booty were not prohibited at points in between. Once they had neared Darjeeling, however, they were to begin their search in earnest for the fugitive Magadh Rai, last seen only a few months ago in the general vicinity of that mountain town. He had been previously in the company of the Demon of Cawnpore himself, the man otherwise known as the Nana Sahib, one of the principal instigators of the Sepoy Mutiny. With them had been the ex-raja of Gonda and the Nana Sahib's brother. Harried by British troops, their hopes of ending English rule on their benighted country at an end, the Demon and his companions had vanished into the fastness of the Himalayas. They might have crossed over into Nepal, Tibet or Sikkim, or indeed be lying dead somewhere in the swampy lowlands of the terai. But Magadh Rai, that shadowy, febrile conspirator, had been seen again in the region. He, at least, according to recent intelligence received in Calcutta, was still alive and still active.

In Calcutta, that tropical city on the banks of the Hooghly River, much change had taken place since Sykes first became acquainted with it. He had played his part in stamping out the Mutiny, the rebellion that broke out just a year after his arrival in India. It started with a dispute over newly issued cartridges greased with pork and beef fat and became, somewhere along the line, a business of restoring the effeminate, verse-scribbling Mughal emperor in Delhi. Sykes had not comprehended what the trouble was about. He had chomped down on those cartridges himself, biting off the greased paper top to pour the powder into the barrel of his Enfield rifle, ramming the rest of the cartridge with the ball into the barrel before sighting his enemy along the line of faith. But still, Sykes had seen the joint-stock East India Company, whose writ had run freely over Bengal and a great swathe of India for nearly a century, being superseded by the government in the aftermath of the rebellion, the Company's Governor General replaced by a Viceroy.

Profit could no longer be the sole motive for running India, although it would always be paramount. It was also necessary, Sykes heard, to raise the natives from their superstitious mire, leading them up from those irrational faiths that plundered and rebelled over animal fat into the hallowed realm of civilisation.

But if the machine had been thus recalibrated, its parts oiled and changed, its output adjusted, there were things that remained the same. The European residents of the city, whom Sykes had seen hysterical in the heyday of the Mutiny—their throats would be cut by their n——r servants, their wives defiled, their children slaughtered—had recovered their swagger. The maidan was filled in the evening with strollers accompanied by those same servants, or their descendants, now quite docile. The gharries and landaus still went hither and thither along the quarters of the White Town spreading out from the star shape of Fort William, the walls angled to create criss-crossing enfilades.The Viceroy gave balls in his palatial residence just as he had when he was called Governor General of the Company, displaying to assembled grandees the singular marvel Jack the Andamanese, a swarthy dwarf acquired by the steamer *Pluto* while scouting distant islands in the Andaman Sea.

Only Sykes had been at a loose end in this aftermath, which was both the same and not the same as what had been there before. After the Mutiny was put down, his regiment returned to its barracks and the cannons washed free of blood and human fat, Sykes took to sitting by himself on the banks of the Hooghly while thinking about getting his discharge papers. It might have had something to do with memories of the engagements that floated back to him at night in the barracks: the gleaming faces of the natives as crops and huts were set on fire; the piling of rebel sepoys, dead and dying, into a dried-up well; the heads mounted on lances, at Captain Moffit's insistence, as war trophies; the forceful interrogations, carried out by officers apprised of the latest techniques; the hanged men swinging from a crude gallows, arms tied behind their back, their turbaned heads with the broken necks bent awkwardly; the mandatory Sunday morning service that preceded the court martial and the staccato music of the firing squad.

Sykes did not think it was just those memories, though. It was that and everything else, the voyage out from England, the years in America, first scrambling around San Francisco as a Forty-Niner and then, when California gold turned out to be as evanescent as yellow London fog, as one of Walker's Filibusters pillaging his way through Mexico, where he had done things that closely resembled the activities he had carried out in India under the enthusiastic command of Captain Moffit. It was hard to tell, too, in these melancholy moments, whether what he felt was sorrow about the deaths on his hands, or regret that, in spite of all the bloody work, he was still a miserable failure. He had no more to his name than his pay, from which was deducted room, board and equipment. He had taken to going to the native whorehouses in the black town to spend what little was left of his money, debauching himself in the arms of women whose whispers he could not comprehend, floating himself momentarily away from his sorrow—or was it regret?—on waves of Bengal opium come freshly off the factories at Patna, en route to China. It was after one of these debauches, on a morning when he had been uncertain whether he was in Calcutta or in California that he had been called in to meet the Colonel.

THEY WERE RANGED around a fire, five men hand-picked by the Colonel, Bones and Tobin and Yale and Ryeman and Sykes himself, ignoring the shrieks and disputations coming from the

White Mughal's people as they prepared their meals around a myriad small fires. The Colonel was deep in confabulation with the White Mughal in a gaudy muslin tent.

Sykes did not know up to what point their uneasy conjoining with the White Mughal would continue, although Bones believed that they would be going all the way to the White Mughal's fiefdom, where they would swiftly bring about a restitution of that Briton's rightful property through a series of manoeuvres that would allow them some plunder and restitution of their own before they proceeded up north.

'And Magadh Rai?' Tobin said.

'He must wait, that perfidious blackguard,' said Bones. 'But eventually we shall find him, strip him of his jewels, the Naulakha necklace and the diamond that rivals the Koh-i-noor, all of which we unfortunately must take back to Treasury, although we will be rewarded for our efforts, of course.'

Tobin, who had once had some scholarly pretensions, looked thoughtful.

'The matter is not about jewels but about intelligence,' he said. 'It is about choking off future rebellions, even though a jewel or two might be found among Magadh Rai's belongings.' He cleared his throat and settled into full-blown pulpit mode. 'The Nana, after all, is not the only leader of this Mutiny to have vanished in the regions to which we are proceeding. Nor, gentlemen, is he the most colourful. There was the Jat rebel Devi Singh, who, after taking the town of Raya, proceeded to form his own government in the schoolhouse constructed by those he had just evicted. He appointed a Board of Revenue, a Supreme Court, a Commissioner, a Magistrate and a Superintendent of Police. For this final office, considering his own people unqualified, he sent a letter to the Englishman who last held the post, and whom he had driven out of town, begging the gentleman to return and offering to double his salary.'

After the laughter had died down, Tobin continued in a more thoughtful vein. 'And then there was Danka Baba. I remember seeing him just before he was turned out of Lucknow for preaching jehad.

He returned later at the head of a mob that wounded Sir Lawrence. On the occasion I saw him, Danka Baba was seated in a palanquin preceded by a man beating a drum and a line of dervishes swallowing burning coals. A rain of fire would pour down on the oppressors, so Danka Baba said. He is said to have been well-travelled, having visited Persia and Arabia and England, where he promised to return, bringing his jehad all the way to the White Queen. When Lucknow was retaken, Danka Baba fled. A local chieftain later claimed the reward of fifty thousand rupees on his head.'

'No doubt the chieftain actually cut off the Baba's head and brought it in for the reward?' Bones asked.

'He did.'

'They are such literalists,' Bones said.

'But that is not the point,' Tobin said, annoyed at the interruption. 'The question is who knows whether the head really belonged to Danka Baba. There were rumours that he had escaped, either lifted to heaven by a host of dancing farishtas or on horseback towards the remoteness of Nepal.'

He paused and looked into the darkness, beyond which extended that fabled zone of escape into which every fugitive from the rebellion seemed to have vanished. First came the lowlands, then the forests, then the frozen wastes that were no more than deserts of ice. Beyond that, one faced the mountain range of the Himalayas. The roof of the world, the jagged horns that brushed the sky, the savage names that boomed and gonged. Cho-mo-lung-ma! Kan-chen-dzonga! Passes existed, true, but they were obscure and dangerous, open only during the summer months. Beyond those echoing peaks, there was whatever lay on the other side. Unknown kingdoms and people occupied those lands where India and China were only faint rumours. Tobin sighed. 'Who really knows where Danka Baba is now? Who knows where any of them are?' he said.

2

They continued their march in the morning, a slow affair since they had to stay with the White Mughal's ragged caravan. The Colonel, who had spent much of the night in discussion with the White Mughal, rode at a glacial pace next to his interlocutor, who had transferred from the grey horse to a palanquin. Its sliding doors had been contrived to remain open and thus allow the discourse between the two to continue. The other palanquins stayed close behind. Bones and Sykes and Ryeman rode in the front. Yale and Tobin brought up the rear.

There were frequent halts for refreshments, excruciatingly elaborate affairs that involved the setting up of table, chairs and canopy, and the laborious extraction of the White Mughal's quivering flesh from the palanquin and its rearrangement outside, between chair and umbrella. Iced sherbet was served often. An extremely ripe cheese was passed around during their afternoon meal. Sykes wondered about the source of such provisions. Roast quail, if that is what it was, made an appearance for supper. For tea, there had been cucumber sandwiches, which the White Mughal ate most daintily, dabbing at the expanse of his fleshy chin after each bite, pausing occasionally to offer the cockatoo on his shoulder a nibble.

Sykes and his fellows, unable to turn down the invitation to the high table, attended the proceedings glumly, if without any show of outward displeasure. Yet they took the opportunity to slip away as soon as the essential niceties had been observed. Only the Colonel was positively delighted by each such occasion, his small, hoof-like feet dangling from a canvas camp chair, his back boldly turned on the gurgling Torsha River below as he fired rapid questions at the White Mughal.

Glass, spies, the mutiny, small wars and gunboats were discussed at lunch. Tobacco, quinine, repeating rifles, finance capital and joint-stock companies formed the subject of discussion at tea. At supper, under the blaze of lanterns that attracted moths of such ferocious aspect as Sykes had never encountered before, the conversation took on a more speculative turn, entering into the realm of mechanical inventions and illegitimate daughters, eastern intrigues and the rise of the novel, the morality of prostitution and the abiding presence of the occult in modern life. The Bibi listened attentively and impassively throughout, her scarred face immobile except when she chewed or swallowed. A native who looked like neither servant nor soldier hovered near her. Dressed in a white dhoti, he was a lean, cadaverous figure to whom clung, for all his seeming propriety, a faint air of disreputability. Occasionally, a look passed between the Bibi and this man, but none other than Sykes paid them any attention.

ON THE DAY Sykes met the Colonel, he had been deep in a dream of the sort opium was wont to produce, all devil dolls and withered bodies and crumbling catacombs. Green lightning struck the steep walls of his nocturnal landscape. Men were violently wrenched from their souls and scattered across the barren landscape, watching their estranged spirits fly away.

His awakening from the dream was rude. Swaying on his feet, eyes closed, he was dragged out into the open. Buckets of ice-cold well water were poured over him, leaving him gagging and choking. Rough hands forced him into his dress uniform and poured the better part of a cup of scalding coffee down his throat. Yet only when he was standing at attention outside General Goodfellow's chambers did Sykes come to understand his situation, that his name had been recommended to the General by Captain Moffit, presumably just before the captain had been gutted from groin to throat by one last bhang-crazed sepoy who had forgotten that the Mutiny was already quashed.

The other men assembled next to him appeared to have been

similarly recommended, a scattering of loutish soldiers and subalterns sent by ambitious officers to the General for an expedition he had in mind. Yet the General himself was not to be seen. Stern portraits of regimental officers stared down at the gathered men from behind oil-painted facades, but there were no officers actually present in the room. An emaciated native pulled at the ropes of the giant punkah that waved ineffectually over their heads in an attempt to transform the treacle-like air into a cool breeze. On the window sill, an enormous crow flapped and cawed, glaring at Sykes with beady eyes. The men remained standing, all at attention, sword handles and pistols and boots gleaming, ignoring the sweat dripping from their foreheads and the rashes erupting underneath their stiff, starched collars. A band struck up far away, ceremonially bidding adieu to some dignitary visiting Fort William. The skirling bagpipes echoed in Sykes's head, evoking something, although what, he would not have been able to say for the life of him.

Half an hour after they had been standing there, the General entered. Busy debating the great chain of being with his companion, he paid no attention to the assembled men. With a tremendous scrambling and scratching at the windowsill, the crow flew away. Colonel Sleeman turned to inspect the men.

He was as squat and short as the General was narrow and long. In the Calcutta heat, his enormous bald head showed not a hint of perspiration. His feet were rather small, Sykes noticed, almost dainty in their patent leather boots, yet the effect produced was anything but ladylike. Looking at those small feet, Sykes expected to find not a man but an old, fighting goat rising on to its hind legs. It was quite a surprise to lift one's eyes from those feet and see Colonel Sleeman's smooth face, with not a strand of hair on it, a face that might have belonged to a baby that had lived and delighted in sin for a hundred years or more.

The Colonel began to walk up and down. His manner was languid, his inspection silent. His gaze was focused not on them but upon a point in some other universe visible only to the Colonel. 'I am looking for men who are not just strong outside, but who are strong within,' he said.

Sykes felt himself awakening from the effects of the previous night's debauch. He began to recall, in the recesses of his memory, something he had heard about this Colonel Sleeman, of the mark he had made in India soon after arriving from Canada at the height of the Mutiny. His reputation was like the long, trailing skirt of an elegant lady, bringing in its wake accounts of his deeds during the Crimean War and before that, his part in the suppression of the Chartist rebellion in Newport. There had been stories of his daring at Cawnpore during its retaking and, prior to that, of intricate, clandestine missions where he had introduced his companions to new techniques of persuasion in the art of gathering intelligence. There had even been a rumour that Colonel Sleeman had run a temporary jail all his own near Delhi, applying and improving upon principles of incarceration he had learnt from methods applied to recalcitrant Red Indians and runaway plantation slaves in America.

'I am looking for a band of brothers who will help me punish a sheep gone astray,' the Colonel said. In his hand, he held a rolled-up map. He tapped with his map ever so softly on the coat buttons of a large man with mutton-chop whiskers whom Sykes would later come to know as Ryeman. Then the Colonel placed his ear on Ryeman's barrel chest and listened, as if his taps had sent a signal deep into Ryeman's being and he was expecting a reply post haste. He stayed in that position for a while, this short, baby-faced, bald devil with tiny feet, as blissful as a child or a lover resting its head on the torso of a woman whose breasts it has suckled.

Slowly, Ryeman began to turn red. Sweat poured down his face but he did not move to wipe it off. His large right hand, resting next to the pommel of his sword, began to tremble. Still, the Colonel went on listening, careful as a pilot plumbing the depths of dark, unknown waters, someone hoping to find a safe spot where a ship might anchor, far from the probing arrows of savage islanders. When the silence in the room had become unbearable, when Sykes was certain that one of the men would break into a coughing fit or laughing hysterics and that the man being inspected would faint, the Colonel nodded like he had heard what he wanted to hear and straightened up.

He wandered aimlessly for a while, waving his rolled-up map. It descended on the head of one man, on the shoulders of a second. Another was smacked in his ear by the makeshift baton. He was a priest at one moment, handing out benediction, and a sergeant-at-arms the next instant. Ever closer he came towards Sykes. He seemed to float, those little feet barely touching the floor. Sykes felt that he had not awakened at all from his opium dreams. The Colonel's face danced, a white balloon with splotches of red, as he faced Sykes and tapped him on the buttons of his red coat.

'I am looking for a host of heavenly angels who will help me destroy a malfunctioning machine,' he whispered into Sykes's ears. He continued whispering, but the rest of his words were incomprehensible to Sykes. He felt the Colonel was putting a spell on him. Sykes became aware of his heart beginning to gallop. He wanted water most desperately and was struck by a painful movement in his guts. The Colonel leant his head on Sykes's chest, listening to the pounding of his heart. Sykes clenched his bowels with desperation, afraid that they would fail him. The room began to spin around him and Sykes knew he would fall. Then, from somewhere deep below the beat of his heart, below his conscious self trying not to faint, trying not to soil itself, something that did not fully belong to him answered the Colonel back. He heard it distinctly. Apparently, the Colonel heard it too. The gleaming bald head was lifted and detached from Sykes's body. The Colonel's eyes held his gaze for a moment. Then the Colonel floated off elsewhere.

Afterwards, when he was back in the barracks, Sykes retched his innards out over a bucket and shat out the rest into a pit. At night, shivering under a blanket in spite of the Calcutta heat, Sykes thought of the fact that he had encountered insanity many times before. He had done so under the tutelage of Captain Moffit and, before that, when accompanying the self-declared President Walker to Mexico. And still, he could not help being unusually impressed by Colonel Sleeman, who appeared to have expanded the frontiers of madness into new, unknown territory.

THEY CAMPED ON open ground not far from the river, Sleeman's rough riders holding themselves aloof from the White Mughal's bawling, shrieking retinue. Around them, the fields extended as far as one could see, their crushed, yellowed stalks signalling the wintry months to come. An occasional breeze swept through the camp, sending the flames of various fires leaping. The wind had a chill to it, a reminder that they were making their way up from the muddy, enervating, river plains towards the white teeth of the mountains.

Sykes, suffering because of his abrupt withdrawal from debauch, had spoken little. He watched, initially without much interest, the man he had earlier noticed exchanging glances with the Bibi. There was something in the way he stood at the entrance of the White Mughal's tent that made Sykes uneasy.

'Who is that?' he asked, more to himself than anyone else.

'It is the Bibi's Babu,' Bones answered with equanimity. He had managed to gather more information about the White Mughal's arrangements than the rest of them put together. 'The Lady of the Fifty-Six Knives goes nowhere without him, and the White Mughal, whose name is really Ponce du Maurier ...' He had to wait for the laughter to die down before he could continue. 'As I said, the White Mughal goes nowhere without her. The Bibi is a famous courtesan singer, the Babu her accompanist on the tabla—which are small Indian drums. The story is that she was assaulted by a rejected suitor, the one who made fifty-six cuts on her face so that she would have no other suitors after rejecting him and that the Babu was the only one of her companions who tried to come to her aid. He was ineffectual, of course, receiving a blow to his head for his pains, but it is said that on recovering he ran to find a hakim to minister to the lady's cuts.'

'How do you know all this?' Tobin asked.

Bones, smiling with self-satisfaction that for once he had more attention than Tobin, sat back. From the White Mughal's tent came the twang of a stringed instrument, joined gradually by a keening, high-pitched vocalist.

'Is that the Bibi?' Tobin said.

'It cannot be,' Bones replied. 'The Bibi does not sing at the drop of a hat. That must be one of the other women.'

The men shifted in their positions. It was unnerving, this singing, even though they all had some experience of the entertainment provided in India by singing nautch girls. What was the singer saying, if anything at all? The voice was harsh, lower in pitch than had initially seemed, with a somewhat incantatory quality to it. It rose above the music, and there were intervals at which it rang out unaccompanied, speaking rather than singing.

Sykes shivered as he saw, through words that he did not understand, a dark subcontinental river swollen and overflowing its banks. He saw the woman singing, half submerged in the black water, and the boat making its way towards her on the rising waters. Even though the river trembled with the force of currents running through it, the boat moved without hurry, slow as a leaf on still water. The boatman, standing and pulling at his single oar, was curiously elongated, his legs and torso and arms and head all straight lines and sharp angles. The strings had joined in again, their sound fuller. The boatman was nearly there, performing a final pull with his oar that sent the craft gliding towards Sykes, the water up to Sykes's breasts, for Sykes had become the woman in the water and had breasts and his flesh was brown and ripe and sweet. Resting the dripping oar in his boat, the man turned towards Sykes with his rectangular head and Sykes saw, even as a long arm reached out for him, that the boatman had no face at all.

Night had flung its blanket over the camp. The wind picked up, and the horses shifted restlessly. The moon rose over their heads. It was not the one they were used to in England, not a white man's moon at all, but a horribly garish oriental bauble, disfigured by bright purple streaks as though it were coming apart. Sykes, woken out of his reverie, his heart pounding, saw in that light that there was an additional figure, a sixth, in their circle. It was the Babu, squatting on his haunches and observing them all from not more than a foot away. The others saw him too at the same moment, the man having kept himself invisible until then with some strange occult power.

Ryeman stood up with a curse, stumbling on a root as he did so. Sykes saw the Babu's face, momentarily impassive before it registered the pistol in Ryeman's hand. A ball crashed into the ground at the Babu's feet. Laughter rang out around the fire as the thin man stood up and ran.

3

Sykes had a dream. The Babu, who had turned into something like a baboon, a hairy apelike thing in a white dhoti clutching a notebook, flitted around the camp. He moved strangely, floating one moment, vanishing the next and surfacing again at some other spot until Sykes got quite tired of his moving around. Then they had left the camp behind and were in the fields. Streams of mist floated above the ground, milky tentacles that somehow appeared to be alive. Sykes felt misty fingers reaching for him, pulling at him, cold and sad, as he kept behind the ape Babu. They whispered to him, 'Have you ever?' They asked him, insinuatingly, 'Have you ever?' The voices stopped when the Babu reached a raised platform. The height of an observation tower, it loomed far above Sykes.

Up to the platform the Babu climbed, chattering furiously along the way and becoming more of an ape with each rung he ascended. Sykes, observing from below, could somehow still see everything that passed up there on the platform. He could follow the Babu speaking his gibberish to a figure that sat cross-legged and tugged at its beard as it listened. When Sykes crept closer to hear what was being said—and he could not say how, because he was at the same time both above and below—the cross-legged figure looked at him, eyes glowering coal red, and Sykes, taken aback by the visage of Danka Baba glaring at him, fell backwards in panic, plummeting all the way into his waking in a cold sweat.

THEY TOOK THE course of the Torsha River, gradually leaving behind fields turning golden in the winter sun. They had to go up inclines now, through twists and turns in the trail that opened up flashing glimpses of the cold river tumbling playfully below, its white horses rearing their heads over rocky stretches. In the distance, Sykes could see forests, the trees tapering and tall and as much like cathedral towers as the drooping, squat trees of the plains had been like mosques and temples. He should have been comforted by these familiar seeming forests, but they evoked only unease. They did not remind him of England, or even of California, and he wondered if that was because the white man's dominion over these parts was still uncertain.

It made him consider exactly how the White Mughal had ended up here, and how long he had ruled before his kingdom was invaded by bow-and-arrow wielding tribesmen who proclaimed liberation of the territory. The territory would not remain liberated for long, of that Sykes was confident, his nightmares and shakes notwithstanding. He had no idea what kind of eastern-northern kingdom he expected to find when they finally reached the White Mughal's land, but he had built up a fantastical notion of it, with a wedding cake of a palace filled with columns and minarets and colourful flags, surrounded by camels and elephants, with dusky maidens in muslin to do their bidding. It had no basis in reality, he knew, but, achy and saddle-sore, he allowed himself to keep dreaming. He expected that when they got there, they would hear cries of torture and of rowdy carousing. He had images of the rabble occupying the White Mughal's palace, mostly just a mob with bows and arrows and machetes. Yet every now and then, those images were superseded by visions of a cold, fanatical army that carried out each manoeuvre with mathematical, mechanical precision.

But the first village they passed—'The beginning of my fiefdom,' the White Mughal gasped as they approached—seemed not to recognise its Occidental overlord. It consisted of a cluster of huts laid higgledy-piggledy next to the fields, and the emaciated inhabitants, a promiscuous mix of the dark Bengali species and the yellowish Mongoloid type, kept a sullen distance, averting their gaze as the column marched through. Only a toothless old man, twisted and wrinkled by age, came and stood in front of his hut. Apart from a cavalry hat, much too big for his head, that suggested he might once have served as a sowar for the Company, he was stark naked even in the cold, grinning with obvious delight at the appearance of the White Mughal and Colonel Sleeman, saluting smartly at the pair with his right hand while wagging his shrivelled penis at them with his left.

THEY WERE LOOKING for a camping ground, the day's march nearly at an end, when they came across the first of the corpses. It lay at the very edge of the forest. The figure was small enough to be mistaken for that of a child. His begrimed face was frozen in terror, his rags fouled and his body giving off a remarkable stench that forced the company to cover their noses.

Yale dismounted. He spent some time scrutinising the hole in the chest of the corpse. Then he scoured the surrounding area. 'A projectile wound,' he reported back, 'but not from any weapon I have seen. The flesh is cauterised around the wound. A tunnel has been carved through the man's body. I can find no ball in the vicinity of the body. What make of rifle or pistol could do this?'

The Colonel listened with interest, as did the White Mughal in his palanquin. Sykes and his companions found themselves assuming, without a word, the readiness of battle. Separating themselves from the rest of the procession, the White Mughal's soldiers and their new Enfields all tangled up in confusion and contradictory orders, they rode along the perimeter of the forest single file. Wary of an ambush, they skirted the edge of the forest. Little was visible amid the trees crowded together, the branches and leaves caught from time to time in great gusts of wind that made the men wonder if a storm was on its way. They found a second corpse with an identical wound in the chest. It was withered, the skin shrunken around its face, the creature having starved for a long time before it was hunted down. No projectiles were found, nor the footprints of any assailants.

Bones and Sykes were dispatched on a scouting venture into the forest. Leaving their horses behind, they walked silently through the profusion of trees, the bed of pine needles thick and soft underfoot. The little light left in the sky was curtained off by the trees. In the shadowy darkness, Sykes felt an unease stirring inside him. He heard whispers in the wind. The trees were calling out his name. 'Sykes,' they said. 'Sykes, have you ever?'

There were traces of the fugitives whose corpses had been encountered outside the forest, rudimentary things abandoned in terror. A basket of wild apricots, a red shirt of the Tibetan kind, an old matchlock. Of the assailants, however, there was no sign. Nor were there any corpses in the forest itself. The men had been killed only when they emerged from it.

It was a shock nevertheless to come upon the survivors. Huddled in a clearing in the forest sat some two dozen people, mostly elderly men, women and children. They were of the same dwarfish stature as the corpses. They appeared devoid of speech and Sykes had not the faintest idea what kind of tribe they were. Bones and he escorted them out of the forest, jabbing at them with their rifles to keep them from straying. When they emerged from the trees, night had arrived.

Camp had been struck nearby. Sykes and his fellows rode there with their strange captives, creating a great commotion among the White Mughal's people as they entered. When order had finally been restored, the Colonel asked the Babu to see if he could understand the captives.

The insidious Babu, who had revealed himself to be also a great polymathic interpreter in service to the White Mughal, pulled up his dhoti and squatted on his haunches. He chose to address an old matriarch, one encased in numerous nose rings and wrinkles, the most ancient of the tribe. She squatted on her haunches as well and they faced each other, rocking back and forth as they spoke. They spoke for what seemed like hours in what sounded like gibberish. Tongues were stuck out. Eyes were rolled. A gurgling hookah, its top glowing red with coal, went back and forth between the matriarch and the Babu as they drew long, satisfying drags. They took their time about it. Ryeman twisted the tips of his moustache into fine points and looked like he wanted to shoot the Babu.

It looked to Sykes that the Babu was courting the matriarch, asking her to marry him, while she, shy as any vestal virgin, rebuffed him coyly while at the same time subtly encouraging him on, giving him hope that should he only persist in his efforts, she would eventually succumb to his seduction. Occasionally, the rest of the group joined in, with hummings and sighings, and Sykes was convinced that it would all end with the ceremonial exchange of a goat and a jolly mountain-style wedding feast.

When the Babu had eventually finished, he wiped his forehead theatrically to indicate to everyone how hard he had worked. Then, turning to the Colonel, he reported that he had not been able to make much sense of the lady and her companions. The language they spoke, he discoursed in a professorial manner, was perhaps related to that of the Lepcha tribe. Their beliefs, however, he went on, were possibly an amalgamation of both Lepcha and Limbu practices, although there were elements that belonged to neither. As for the corpses, this is what the matriarch had to say.

A week ago, they had seen an army marching down from the mountains. It was a vast army. Dust from its feet clouded the sky. The ground shook and rumbled. There had been red coats of the English kind on some of the soldiers. Others were indeterminate in appearance, demonic even from a distance. Above the sound of their hoofbeats and the marching feet, a keening noise rose, unearthly, and a foul, pestilent smell, reminiscent of burning chillies, wafted in on the wind.

The tribe saw that this fearsome army was making for their village. Gathering their meagre belongings, they fled. They headed south but were ruthlessly pursued by a detachment even as the main army marched on in a different direction. Their pursuers had not been riding horses and yet they moved at an unbelievable pace. Across streams and into the forests they had come, but they had not captured the tribe, apparently intending only to drive them on farther.

The people of the tribe began to weaken. They had lost count of their days and nights. The matriarch insisted that she had been a young woman when she fled but grew old in the course of the escape. They had finally come to the Forest of Lost Spirits, where many of them, too weary to go on any farther, huddled together. The forest had protected them. Its magic was still strong enough to keep the mysterious pursuers outside. But some of the tribe continued fleeing, leaving the sanctuary of the forest. The matriarch had seen lightning bolts in the sky, smelt charred flesh. Then the pursuers had vanished, but it was, as she knew for certain, the end of the world she had known.

AT SUPPER, THE topic of discussion, naturally, was about the tribe and its mysterious pursuers. What was this strange, mongrel army, composed of British redcoats and Tibetan bandits? What weapons were they were using and from whence did they come? The White Mughal and his advisor, for the Babu was that in all but name, could provide no answers to any of these questions.

No, these mysterious soldiers were nothing like the tribesmen who had attacked the White Mughal and occupied his White Castle. Those interlopers, the White Mughal said, were quite familiar to him. They were his own unfaithful children, tenant farmers who had rebelled en masse. They had no reasons beyond their own perverse nature for the uprising, although they had been recalcitrant for a while, resisting his encouragement to cultivate indigo and opium.

'But surely the climate in these parts is not conducive to the raising of opium,' the Colonel said. 'Is the altitude not too high?'

'Not at all, sir. I hope to have the pleasure of showing you the wondrous red poppy flowers in my lands. As fine a source of Bengal opium as any.'

Sykes felt a painful jolt at the mention of the drug. His mind faltered and missed a step, plunging him momentarily into one of the Calcutta dens where he had found such relief. He stayed there for a while, smoking and dreaming. Strange sights swirled around him. In a barren, monstrous landscape, in a city of a kind he had never seen, one man astride a velocipede of a most astonishing design was pursuing another. Around them loomed the smokestacks and towers of some grim factory. In the distance, fantastic to behold, loomed the giant face of a man, his lips moving furiously. Sykes started and emerged into the cool evening air of the camp. In spite of the long detour in the chambers of his mind, the dinner conversation was continuing exactly from where he had left it. At the high table, time had not moved very much at all.

'The weaponry of my rebellious subjects,' the White Mughal said, his voice quavering, 'was most primitive. Bows and arrows and machetes, accompanied by insulting songs and gestures, the latter singularly inventive, was all they possessed. A single volley from my Enfield-wielding soldiery would have taken care of them.' He mopped his brow and helped himself to more sherbet. 'But I was loath to order bloodshed on my own subjects and since we would have been massacred had we stood our ground, there was no alternative but to retreat. I thought it best to quit the field peacefully, hoping to find someone capable of demonstrating a show of force of such obvious magnitude that my subjects would retire without resistance to their hamlets and accept the enlightened order of things, with a heightened, renewed understanding of the munificence of free trade and taxation.'

Having said all this, the White Mughal sat with head bowed over his plate. Sweat gathered on the folds of his flesh. His pallor was most unpleasant to behold and Sykes wondered, not for the first time, whether the exertion of the march might not prove too much for the corpulent man. But then he opened his eyes, and they were clear and piercing. Sykes had the impression of someone else sitting deep within the man, someone who had momentarily revealed the eyes underneath the eyes.

'I would not worry overmuch, if I were you,' the Colonel said. 'We shall be there soon enough.'

'Undoubtedly,' the White Mughal said, beaming at the company, 'I have in my good fortune found in Colonel Sleeman and his men just the power I sought.' He rubbed his large hands together. 'A toast, gentlemen. To your good health!'

Sykes was unconvinced that six men constituted a force of great magnitude, even if possessed of fighting calibre entirely different from that displayed so far by the native soldiers the White Mughal had tempted away from the personal bodyguard of some rajah of Assam. The mission they had left Calcutta for had become obscured by this business of escaping villagers, mysterious marauders, and the White Mughal and his unusual companions. He was ill at ease, querulous, and he wished the Colonel would assert himself, cease this endless chatter and expel the natives from the table.

The women of the zenana sat around without contributing much conversation beyond titters and picking at the food. The Babu remained on hand throughout, oily and ingratiating, ready to translate whenever the necessity arose, which was often. Nothing in his features or behaviour suggested that the violence with which he had been threatened the night before had left a dent in his confidence. Instead, he explained with certainty to the women, as and when asked to, snippets of the conversation between the Colonel and the White Mughal. He informed them that the berdache mentioned by Colonel Sleeman was similar to a hijrah, just as he told the Colonel and his men that the banshee referred to by the White Mughal was also known in these parts as a churail, a petni and a shakchunni. A jasoos was a spy, a murid a holy person of sorts, a bhokto a religious devotee. Sykes's head hurt from all the information. His eyelids seemed to be made of lead. He was grateful when he could finally retire to his tent.

EVEN IN HIS sleep, however, there was no rest. The conversation of the supper table went on in his mind as he stirred restlessly, part awake and part asleep. Two men sitting on opposite sides of what looked like a chessboard ventured their opinions on cannibals, bounty hunters, shamans, head hunters and lunatics. They talked about flying monks, necrophilia, Tantric Buddhism, reincarnation, cults, tulpas and tulkus. Finally, when he was so exhausted by such talk that he was on the verge of waking up, he fell into deeper sleep. He dreamt, naturally, of the White Castle.

It was nothing like the place of his Oriental fantasies. Something was being held inside it, something menacing beyond measure. He tried to warn the Colonel against entering the place. Terrible deeds and lies awaited them inside, he said to the Colonel, but the Colonel, his eyes like black discs, heard no word of his. Instead, he stood bent, his ear pressed to the wall, as if he had asked the White Castle a question and was now awaiting its answer.

It loomed above them, carved into the side of the mountain, a castle that had been bullied out of the rocks. Steep staircases ran everywhere. Covered bridges connected parts of the castle to one another. Everything moved, the staircases and bridges changing location. From the small windows cut into the castle came dim yellow squares of light. Sykes felt that the structure was watching, waiting, speaking. 'Have you ever?' it replied to Colonel Sleeman. 'Have you ever?' it said to Sykes in the howl of a native jackal. 'Have you ever? Have you ever?' the castle wailed at Sykes. He wanted to answer but could not think of what to say.

4

Every hamlet they passed was smaller than the previous one. As they pressed farther ahead, climbing single file up narrow mountain tracks with gorges plunging beneath, the habitations grew ever more scarce. The White Mughal had switched back to his grey horse, either because he thought its footing surer than that of his palanquin bearers or because he believed it incumbent upon his dignity to make his return in a suitably regal manner. It was harder to breathe and Yale complained of a gnawing pain in his head. The rest kept on, hands firmly on their reins, careful to forestall any skittishness on the part of their horses. At places, they dismounted and led their horses on foot, having blindfolded the beasts first so that they would not start at the sight of the drop. Pebbles and rocks skipped away from the slowly moving column before falling thousands of feet through the air. Fog and clouds drifted up from the mountain tops, obscuring the sky.

In spite of the precarious route, the march was monotonous to the utmost, as though they had been months on their passage rather than days. They bivouacked on a barren stretch of land where nothing grew save for a single stone chorten, rocks piled one upon another like the spine of some monstrous beast. Mountains loomed ahead, but they did not look like they were on earth. The formality of previous meals had been dispensed with. The Colonel still dined with the White Mughal, new topics of discussion flying fast and furious among the two savants. They discussed mechanical flight and the telegraph. They debated progress and the future and differed over the merits of Currer Bell's recent novel, *Jane Eyre*. The Colonel spoke, with increasing frequency, of a treatise that he wished to compose. It was to be called *Small Wars*. More than any novel, it held the key to the future.

The rest of the company, finding breathing to be an arduous task, ate in silence.

'DO YOU REALISE we are riding towards the Horse Latitudes?' Tobin said one day, breaking the quiet they had become used to.

He unrolled a survey map on the ground, using stones and his saddlebag to weigh it down. His motions were curious and jerky, rather like a man who had the palsy. His trembling, gloved hand pointed out where they were. All the others, barring Yale, who was suffering from the altitude, crowded around the map. It was true. They would begin descending soon, to the last stretch of green felt before the white glitter of the mountains. But they were moving north steadily. If they kept going, they would eventually be thirty degrees north of the equator. On the sea, that would indeed be the Horse Latitudes.

'It matters little,' Bones said, snatching up the map. 'We are not on ocean but on land. We may fall into a crevice or be swallowed up by a precipice. We may be buried by an avalanche or starve to death in a blizzard. But the one thing we need not fear is that we will be stilled by the deathly calm of the doldrums. We have no ship. We possess no sails. We may need to eat our horses, but there will be no occasion to toss them overboard.'

'You are remarkable, Bones,' Tobin said. 'You can demonstrate two shortcomings at the same time. Not only are you foolish, but you take pride in exhibiting your folly.'

Bones, stung to the quick, was about to retort, but he was interrupted by the sound of Yale vomiting down the nearby ravine. Then Yale's kneeling body pitched over and disappeared from sight.

Sykes was the first to reach the spot, the others close on his heels. It was not as they had feared. Yale had tumbled over, it was true, but this edge was not an actual edge. There was a shelf of sorts below it, and Yale was lodged on it, his face red with fury and exertion and agony, trying to push himself back up. Bones and Tobin climbed down to help him. Below the shelf was the actual drop. Down it went, an abyss that ended in a ghostly mist gliding along the precipice walls, occasionally unveiling what looked like a castle or a palace before the mist came back and covered everything in its milky haze.

They all stared at the mist like it was the becalmed sea.

'I can feel the ocean,' Tobin whispered. 'And although we are still moving, it will not be long before we cease to do so. Never say I did not warn you about the Horse Latitudes.'

THREE HOURS AFTER they had begun their descent through a narrow pass, they finally saw it, faintly visible through the mist, the White Mughal's White Castle, a Scottish baronial mansion squeezed into a quarter of the space required. It sat at the other end of a malodorous tarn, the surface of the lake almost entirely covered with thick green scum. A curious embankment, raised barely a foot above the scum, bisected the lake. This was the road they would take to the front door of the White Castle.

Sykes did not like the idea of using that path. Even the primitive weapons the White Mughal had mentioned would be sufficient to pick them off, one by one, as they approached along the narrow track, strung out like pieces of juicy meat on a long, sharp skewer.

He awaited orders to circumnavigate the tarn, tedious though such a task would be. He was surprised, then, when the Colonel ordered them to fall in behind the White Mughal's procession and march forward. They progressed single file along the embankment, their shadows grazing on the scum until they reached a stretch of dark, opaque water. No arrows or musket volleys greeted them as they proceeded. If there was a rebellious peasantry within, they were either especially terrified or remarkably well drilled.

On they went, across this mysterious tarn. The scum bubbled like potion in a witches' cauldron. Things moved underneath the surface of the water, sending out vast, slow ripples. The horses started frequently, perhaps sensing something wrong with the water. Sykes felt nauseous from the miasma of rotten eggs rising around him. His stomach turned, and he felt dizzy.

It was a relief to be across the lake and to be standing in front of the White Castle. It looked like a ruin going back to at least the Middle Ages, something that had experienced the Wars of the Roses and dreamt nightly of Roundheads and Cavaliers hacking at each other. Sykes failed to understand how that was possible given the part of the world they were in.

He tried to remember what the White Mughal had told the Colonel of how he had come by his kingdom. He recalled the phrase *terra nullius*, but that was of little help since he did not know what it meant. There had been something said about a local feudal lord, childless, to whom the White Mughal had played adviser, adjutant and architect. Opium contracts and troop levies had been mentioned, Sykes was sure, as well as perilous finances and copious amounts of debt incurred in the construction of a castle, Scottish baronial in inspiration, that had more or less handed the kingdom over to the East India Company, the entity that had advanced the monies required for the building. Also, had there not been another white man, one of two Englishmen trying to make their fortunes in these parts, of whom only the one had survived to become the White Mughal?

The answers to such questions had to be put aside. They were approaching a pair of wooden doors set in a rounded arch. Five blue eyeballs stared out at them from each door, along with by that mysterious motto: *Omnia Mei Sunt*! Yet for all that, it was hard not to think that the castle that had indebted this kingdom to the Company did not amount to much in its present state. Ivy crept up the stone walls. The small windows looked like holes hurriedly cut into a tomb. Birds flew in and out of the nests they had made in the chimneys. Apart from the birds, the White Castle appeared to be utterly empty. There were no overtaxed peasants running riot, waiting to greet their entry with songs of insult and volleys of arrows. There was no mysterious marauding army or, as Sykes had feared,

Danka Baba stroking his beard and threatening, in dulcet tones, to drive this red-faced army of English devils back to the sea from where they had risen.

Bones and Ryeman, their rifles at the ready, were aghast that there was to be no slaughter. Sykes wondered if the White Mughal had been parsimonious with the truth. Had this been merely a ploy to have a free, armed escort accompany him through troubled terrain? What exactly were they doing here if they were not to bring about the restitution of a Briton's seized property? Their quarry Magadh Rai might be in China for all that they had achieved in tracking him down.

The doors were pushed aside by the White Mughal's native guard. The rest of the retinue began to disperse itself swiftly. The company awaited instructions from the Colonel. He looked unperturbed. He dismounted and surveyed the facade of the White Castle with keen interest. Behind it rose slopes crowded with oaks, pine and bamboo. Bright bursts of colour came from magnolias and rhododendrons. Beyond that was a mountain, its snow-covered peak wreathed in clouds.

The Colonel turned and looked at his men while standing in the shadow of the White Castle. There was something in his face, half in shadow, that reminded Sykes of the Colonel's assessment of the muster that morning in Calcutta. Ryeman had not fainted but some of the others had; they had consequently been discarded as unfit, not strong within in the manner that the Colonel required. Now the Colonel stood encased in a coat of similar silence, assessing, listening.

Sykes felt a shiver down his spine. For a second, he thought that the convivial mask Colonel Sleeman had worn since that initial meeting with the White Mughal was about to be taken off. He expected a command of the kind President Walker might have given in Mexico, an order to open fire on the White Mughal and his retinue and to begin collecting the scalps, each scalp worth a dollar, the disposed of, weighted-down corpses vanishing into the bubbling tarn while the sun sank, blood red, on the distant horizon.

The Colonel's lips moved, but not to sound a command. He

seemed to be fashioning a silent spell. Sykes recalled his troubling dream, the one that had involved the Colonel listening to the White Castle. The White Mughal looked uneasy and patted the cockatoo on his shoulder.

'Xanadu,' the Colonel said. His shadowy face moved into the light. He smiled approvingly at the White Mughal and said, 'In Xanadu did Kubla Khan, a stately pleasure dome decree.'

The White Mughal's face shaped itself into an answering simper. Jowls trembling, he looked at the White Castle and recited, in his querulous, shrieky voice:

And all should cry, Beware! Beware!
His flashing eyes, his floating hair!
For he on honey-dew hath fed,
And drunk the milk of Paradise.

His hands were raised in the air. He could have been the Pope addressing a gathering of the faithful at the Vatican. 'Welcome to all,' he said. 'Welcome. My gratitude to Colonel Sleeman and his brave men that their very reputation was enough to scatter the ingrates who forcibly occupied my home.' Standing at the doorstep of his abode, he looked surprisingly spry. He bowed his giant head and looked at each of them in turn. Then he bid them enter into a long corridor. 'I thank you and welcome you,' he said. 'My kingdom lies at your disposal. I hope you will find yourselves comfortable bedded in the stables, close to your mounts. The Colonel, as an officer and a gentleman, will be housed in the special guest chamber.'

Sykes, looking around, could see no signs of a forced native occupation. No, there was none of that; just unlocked doors and echoing corridors with sagging floorboards and musty rooms with dusty carpets and a smell composed of native cooking and turpentine and sulphur and too many human bodies confined to an enclosed space. He felt a vibration of the floorboards and thought he heard a faint humming that was almost a song, but it ceased even as he stood there and listened.

'Before you partake of rest and refreshment,' the White Mughal said, clapping his hands, 'you must first examine the exhibits in my private museum. Come to my Ajaib Ghar, or shall we say, my wonder room. Come, gentlemen, the Wunderkammers in the Wonder Room await us.'

SYKES AND THE others trailed the Colonel through dim, echoing corridors. They walked for a long time, with many twists and turns along the way. Morbid faces stared at them from cloudy, greasy paintings. Antlers thrust themselves forcefully from gloomy heads mounted on walls. When they finally arrived at the Wonder Room, Sykes could not tell where it was in relation to the entrance. It was like they had tunnelled into the mountain, although that could not possibly be the case.

The general air of disarray in the White Castle did not extend to the Ajaib Ghar. Lanterns had been lit in anticipation of their inspection. Sykes was overwhelmed with an impression of disparate things, of a vast hall that would have been far too cramped with display cabinets and a curious assortment of objects were it not for the ceiling soaring high, with narrow rectangular skylights placed strategically along its surface. It made him think of the Russian who had told him about the Crystal Palace in London, of the wondrous exhibits that ran from entire trees indoors to the Koh-i-noor diamond, a collection that had caused the Russian to rail at the extinction of human sensibility implied by such ostentatious displays. Sykes had not seen the Great Exhibition himself. But it must have been something very like this, he thought, as he paused to examine a skull that was the size of an armchair, its bone yellowish white, each eyeball socket an enormous hole into which Sykes could have inserted his fist.

'It is merely the skull of an Indian elephant,' Tobin scoffed, noticing Sykes's surprise. But even the sceptical Tobin was impressed as they entered deeper. Butterflies of every hue were pinned inside glass cases hung from the walls. Snakes and snakelike things undulated in greenish fluids in long cylinders. Preserved sharks grinned from inside a tank. Good Lord, was that a human foetus in one of those jars? It was, a furry thing that looked asleep, the unborn member of some unknown native race. Further on, there posed a stuffed midget, an associate of some dwarf tribe taxidermised into stillness, comrade most likely to Jack the Andamanese. Bow and arrow poised in hand, the grimace on its apish face suggested that it was about to assault their party any moment now, that the arrow was being loosed from its string even as they watched. An alchemist or a sorcerer could not have done better than to claim the Ajaib Ghar as his den.

Subtle shifts took place as they progressed through the Ajaib Ghar and the objects of wonder changed from natural things to those made by man. Ingenious weaponry! Was that a cross-fertilisation between a pistol and a switchblade? Ryeman picked it up and began fiddling with it despite protestations from the White Mughal's servants. A concealed button released a blade from the butt of the pistol. One could shoot a bullet through one's enemy and finish him off with a stab through the heart. Or should it be the other way round? There was more advanced weaponry farther ahead. In a corner all its own, an observation balloon strained at its mooring. On a raised platform sat a howitzer that fired rockets, long menacing things with conical noses. Sykes was transfixed by the sight of a most curious mask, with little lenses for the eyes and a snout attached to a tube for the nose.

Further on, there were communication devices. They saw chapatis in a cabinet, hardened into brown discs.

'Excellent, most excellent,' the Colonel said, scrutinising these specimens, the likes of which had been used by the sepoy mutineers to conceal their messages of treachery as they were sent around, hand to hand. 'A simple method of clandestine communication. And most effective.'

'I intend to improve upon it,' the White Mughal said. 'By applying European rationality and order to native imagination.'

The Colonel paused to look at a most unusual device with a speaking tube and an earpiece, attached to a box with a crank and a roll of cable.

'A system of mobile telegraphy, sir, one that uses the horse itself to ground the electrical current,' the White Mughal said.

'Ingenious, undoubtedly so,' the Colonel replied.

'This here is a mirroring system,' the White Mughal said, placing in the Colonel's palm an object somewhat larger than a deck of cards. It shone in the Colonel's hands. 'One turns the disc here,' the White Mughal continued, his fingers wondrously dexterous for one so corpulent. 'That allows one to choose from a sequence of inscribed messages. *Enemy approaching on left flank. Enemy approaching on right flank. Abandon post. Reinforcements spotted. Remain at post. Prepare to advance.* And so on. The messages are visible, right side up, on a similar device in the hands of one's signalling partner.'

'Indeed,' the Colonel said.

Nevertheless, they fell silent as they approached what looked like the centrepiece item, placed in the middle of the hall and given its own display platform. It was a tiger, wooden, somewhat smaller than the real thing, perhaps, but still very large. Gaily painted, with fierce black stripes on a bright yellow coat, its jaws were closed around a life-size human figure. Ferocious eyes wide open, the tiger bent its head over the throat of the man, which was undoubtedly meant to represent an English soldier. It wore the distinctive red coat and a black hat, its arms extended stiffly to the sides as the tiger ripped its throat apart. The face had been given a ghastly white hue.

'One of a pair, sir,' the White Mughal said. 'The other belonged to that despot, Tipu Sultan of Mysore, and was seized after he had been vanquished at the Battle of Seringapatam. You will recall that the Oriental fanatic had the effrontery to name himself Citizen Sultan and professed to be moved by the egalitarian ideals of the French Revolution. When Tipu was finally defeated by Cornwallis, his tiger was discovered in the music room of his palace. It was taken to London as a spoil of war, to be exhibited in the Company's India House. No one could determine where the object had been made, but inside was an organ of European origin. When cranked up, the organ played the roar of a tiger, interspersed with the cries of a human being in distress. The hand of the victim moved up and down and his head started back in what everyone agreed was most lifelike in manner. Impressive, do you not agree?'

He pushed a button or a lever somewhere. A tiger's roar resounded through the room. The jaws of the beast opened and closed in clockwork fashion, as if it were devouring the English soldier. The soldier flapped his arms and shook his head.

'Few, however, know of this other tiger, made by the same, mysterious craftsman who fashioned Tipu's creature, although this other was not intended for Tipu but for a different, secretive client. Not only that, sir, mine has a few tricks not possessed by its counterpart. Tipu's tiger and victim may have looked lifelike to the observers in India House constantly cranking up its organ and creating a disturbance to those at work on the Company's affairs. But what, gentlemen, do you think of this?'

The White Mughal pressed a different button. The roars began again. The tiger's jaws moved as before, but this time, its eyes gleamed with what looked like life. The soldier shuddered, trying to escape the beast that had him by the throat, its arms attempting to fend off the tiger, screaming all along in a manner most convincing and turning, at the very end, to look at them.

'Help me, help me,' the astonished company heard it say, and it was all they could do to hold still and not fire a ball into the clockwork beast and relieve the agony of their clockwork brother.

5

In the weeks that passed, Sykes would come to wonder if the Ajaib Ghar was larger than the White Castle itself. Not that he was sure about the size of the White Castle. He and his fellows were housed in the stables in the adjoining grounds. Their entry to the White Castle was based on the Colonel's needs and their nightly attendance at supper. The conclusions that Sykes was left with were necessarily incoherent.

There were three floors and a basement. The rooms often felt especially small, although the poor light had something to do with that. Even in the daytime, the modestly sized windows, small, misty panes of glass set in wooden frames, let in scarce sunshine. Through those same windows he caught fleeting glimpses of the outside, of overgrown gardens where the statuary was always adrift and the yards stockpiled with lumber, fragments of a puzzle that he could not put together by circumnavigating the mansion from the outside. What he saw from the outside did not match what he saw from within, and vice versa.

They had come across no retainers other than the ones encountered on the road. If the White Mughal had subject cultivators, they certainly were nowhere in the immediate vicinity. As for the retainers, they were non-existent except at supper, which was taken at a table placed in the centre of the Ajaib Ghar, the White Mughal wishing them to wonder nightly at his acquisitions and what he claimed were his inventions. On the far side of the Ajaib Ghar, through a door neither Sykes nor his fellows had entered, lay the Library and the Laboratory. Being in the habit of affecting Oriental designations for what he considered the most important parts of his palace, the first the White Mughal called the Kitabkhana, or the Place of Books. The latter was designated the Tajurbagah, or the Site of Experiments.

It was in the Site of Experiments that Colonel Sleeman was sequestered for the greater part of the day, immersed in long disquisitions with the White Mughal. The rumours went that, inspired by the vast resources available at the White Castle, the Colonel had embarked on a long-desired project of his own.

Left, by and large to themselves, without any natives to suppress, and disconnected entirely from the pursuit of Magadh Rai, Sykes and his fellows found themselves at a loose end of the kind they could not have imagined when they set out from Calcutta. They were free to rot in the stables or to drown themselves in the malodorous tarn. Indeed, they could embark on whatever activity they wished to as long as it had nothing to do with finding that slippery fugitive from the Mutiny. He plotted on busily somewhere, advancing steadily on his plans of overthrowing the Crown, even as Sykes and the others went on with their enervating, dissipating existence.

When they entered the White Castle, either because the Colonel required something or to attend supper, they frequently got lost in the corridors and staircases. Rooms were often, infuriatingly, locked, the native attendants impossible to track down, the corners infested with insects and moths. The mansion seemed to change size, shape and orientation as if it were the interior of a particularly volatile mind. Sometimes, they had to creep along passageways so narrow that they were forced to march at attention, as it were. Yet the rooms could also become vast and cavernous, with glass cabinets that showed, among the usual crockery and knick-knacks, things like pendulums and test tubes, and with stuffed armchairs in distant corners where someone was always dozing. Bones came across a set of shrunken human heads in a cabinet, wrinkled and dried like oversized berries, but was unable to find his way back to it again. Ryeman claimed that he had been accosted by a native hag who demanded baksheesh, threatening to put the kala nazar on him when he offered to spank her instead. She mumbled things that left him dizzy and out of breath, he said, but he could not identify the creature from among the women assembled at the White Mughal's high table, native women looking so much alike. Yale said he often heard machinery of uncertain provenance thumping and beating within the mansion, while Tobin talked of screams and laughter that set the hair straight on the back of his neck.

Only the Ajaib Ghar remained unchanged, wondrously static and of fixed proportions throughout, pulsing steadily at the centre of the shifting, mesmerising White Castle and its world of fever dreams.

IT MIGHT HAVE been the weeks of prolonged inactivity at the White Mughal's mansion, but Sykes gradually began to find himself harbouring some rather mutinous thoughts of his own. It was one thing to sleep rough in the course of action, quite another to be housed with animals while doing nothing. With the Colonel shut up in the White Castle and the rest of the company busy playing interminable card games as they drank what appeared to be an unending supply of native rice liquor, with frequent curses at the n——s who had brewed it and the devil people populating this entire benighted landscape, the place began to grate on Sykes.

He wished to avoid the stables and the White Castle itself. So he took to exploring the surroundings. He walked through the forests that covered the slopes behind the mansion, climbing at a thoughtful pace over a carpet of golden needles, occasionally kicking a pine cone to watch it go arcing down a ravine. Chestnuts and geraniums and lilies flourished along his route. After an hour's climb, he reached an open spot, where, sitting on a rock covered with lichen, looking down, over the tree tops, at the crenellated folly of the towers of the White Castle, and still beyond, at plumes of smoke that suggested some vast army camped out in a distant valley, he thought rebellious thoughts that led him to wonder anew about the natives and if they might not have had good cause for their mutiny.

Such thoughts led him, naturally, to a consideration of Magadh Rai, in whose pursuit they had set out weeks ago. Nothing had been done about that, nothing achieved. There was something wrong about that man, the White Mughal, and the occult effect he had on the entire company, Sykes excepted. Even the Colonel, whose madness had seemed sharpened to a razor's edge in Calcutta, looked blunted, ensconced as he was in the Tajurbagah. When not in the Tajurbagaah, he was in the Ajaib Ghar. And when not in the Ajaib Ghar, the Colonel was in the Kitabkhana, engaged in penning *Small Wars*, a prose work on counter-insurgency that it had long been his ambition to write but that had overspilt the boundaries of his brain only now, in the fertilising presence of the White Mughal.

Neither Sykes nor any of his fellows had seen the Tajurbagah or the Kitabkhana. Sykes wished both to damnation regardless, together with the Ajaib Ghar and *Small Wars*. Then there was that pair, the Babu, always skulking around, and the Bibi, always stone cold, both of whom left him more disturbed than the White Mughal himself.

Lying on the rock, Sykes harboured fantasies of desertion. He could slip away and join the enemy, offering his services to Magadh Rai or to some brigand chief of these parts. Perhaps that explained the redcoats seen by the fleeing tribe, men much like Sykes who, tiring of God and Crown and John Company, had thrown their lot in with that which was not necessarily better but had the virtue of being unknown, joining armies that did not have leaders or, even, a purpose. Or he could disappear entirely into this alien zone in the shadow of the Himalayas, discarding uniform and weaponry to become a member of whatever tribe would take him in. Perhaps he would find a woman whose arms would offer him comfort, a woman on whose bosom he could rest his weary head. Perhaps from that woman would come children, and the children of those children, until generations into the future, blue eyes and a lighter shade of hair would mark the liberation of Sykes, soldier of convenience, in the Himalayas.

When Sykes had had enough of such thoughts, when he saw flashes from the towers of the White Castle, as if the White Mughal and the Colonel were signalling him with one of their ingenious contraptions to return immediately to his post, a post he had not known he was required to man, he got up and retraced his path, taking care to avoid the greenhouse that sat at the back of the White Castle. He had paused there frequently in the beginning, in what he assumed was a greenhouse, although he had not seen a single fruit or vegetable that could be consumed, nor a single plant that could be identified. Sitting on wooden steps arranged around a circle, the plants and shrubs mingled most promiscuously with one another in a tangle of leaves, fronds and branches. Sykes was particularly attracted to the most repulsive of the plants, trying his best to avoid looking at it and inevitably walking right up to it on every single occasion until he could either choose to look or to close his eyes and retrace his steps, in the process risking being impaled on one of the many ferocious thorny limbs that lay between him and his egress from the greenhouse. He chose to look, naturally.

It began innocently enough, in a sort of basket of fringed green leaves not unlike that of a banana plant. But that was only the penumbra, as it were. Pulsing in the centre sat what he supposed might be the fruit or the flower. There were more leaves here, but these were different, more tendril-like than the outer ring of green, more withered too, brownish, like the hair of a hag, within which sat another round of leaves, these latter, soft, white and fleshy, giving way finally to the sanctum sanctorum where red balls the size and shape of strawberries gaped like open wounds. It was like witnessing death, birth and copulation all at once. His mind boggled at it, his knees buckled, and his head spun in dizzy circles so that when he left, he often made straight for the stables to lie down on his bed of hay, staring at the rafters in a stupor, quite oblivious of the drunken gamblers at the other end.

These days he was wiser and avoided the greenhouse at all costs, although this involved circling around to the front of the White Castle where the lake bubbled and frothed. It came across like a carefully designed prison at times. The tarn, the castle, the greenhouse, the mountains. Beyond, where they could not see, strange armies with strange weapons circled and manoeuvred. Fugitive rebel leaders and peasant insurgents went about their jacqueries, dreaming of a world turned upside down. As for them, the special detachment chosen to hunt down Magadh Rai, they were no better than captives at the White Castle, although he could not say for what purpose. Sykes felt at a vast remove from his companions. He thought of Bones, who had revealed himself to be a most querulous gambler and was frequently losing to Tobin—they all were—and of Tobin, who had spoken, during their ride through the mountain pass, of the Horse Latitudes. They were there now, as becalmed as a ship in a windless sea. Their supplies were dwindling, their fresh water was running out, but their captain was locked away in his cabin carrying out experiments and working on esoterica.

PERHAPS IT WAS the seed of the idea he had planted in his own mind, of going native, but Sykes began to venture out even farther. He had known men in America who had done that, departing for the desert, for the border, looking for something that would save them from themselves. An Indian squaw, another language, a different belief, anything that would divest them of this heavy burden of civilisation: mission, quarry, line of faith.

He pushed deeper into the mountains. He discovered the traps and hideouts of local hunters. He came across antelope and wild goat and saw, from a distance, a bear grazing, drunkenly, on wild flowers. Eventually, he found a path that led to the nearest village.

It was not much more than a scattering of a dozen native huts, the larger ones made of loose stone slabs with pine planks for a roof, the others simply put together with mud. It served, apparently, as a kind of crossroads for passing caravans and sheep herders. On the day he visited it, a Tuesday, the weekly haat was going on, a trading of dried produce and grains, of salt and tea, an exchange of goods now given an air of urgency by the proximity of winter. At the very end of the road along which the stalls were arranged, there was a shack selling the liquor popular in these parts, the local brew known as chang. It was here that Sykes ran into the Babu and the Bibi.

They did not see him at first. They were sharing a smoke with a villainous-looking man of the type that Sykes had come to identify as a Tibetan. They laughed most uproariously among themselves, drinking chang and passing around a pipe that Sykes suspected was filled with something more than tobacco. He found it curious, even astonishing, that the cadaverous Babu and the scarred Bibi were capable of humour. That woman, especially. He had not seen the hint of an expression pass her stony, ravaged face in all their time on the march and at the White Castle. And yet here she was, making a joke with the Tibetan brigand, on whose back she laid a most affectionate hand.

Sykes's surveillance did not last long. It was hard for a white man to go unnoticed in these parts, and he had no doubt that it was his sudden arrival that was passed on by the chang seller whispering into the Bibi's ear. They all looked up at the same moment, staring at him in a manner that made Sykes wonder if he had not stumbled into some conspiracy. The Brigand, for that was how Sykes thought of the Tibetan, stood and glared at Sykes, but a word from the Bibi returned him to his seat. Instead, it was the Babu, completely restored to his oily, ingratiating norm, who came forward to greet him.

'Mr Sykes, what a jolly surprise this is. Will you not join us?' he said.

Sykes could not refuse. He entered the hut and sat down on the log of wood that served as a bench. He was handed a bamboo mug of chang, but the pipe was not shared with him. The Bibi whispered something to the Brigand, who laughed uproariously. The Babu managed, somehow, to look innocent and villainous simultaneously.

'Are you a most excellent hunter?' he asked Sykes abruptly.

'I am not—' Sykes began, before he was interrupted.

'Surely, you must be. All freeborn Englishmen are,' the Babu said.

The Brigand said something incomprehensible.

'You see, Mr Sykes, a terrible beast is said to have appeared here.'

'Is it a tiger?' Sykes said. 'One of those man-eating creatures?' He had never seen a tiger. In his mind flashed an image of the clockwork beast in the Ajaib Ghar.

'No one can say,' the Babu replied gravely. 'A woodcutter was found dead the other day, with most peculiar marks on his body.

Then a lady went missing while fetching water from the river. Her body was discovered in the forest, with the same peculiar marks.'

'Is that common behaviour for tigers? To drag their prey into the forest?' Sykes asked. He felt that he had been drinking and having this conversation for a long time. The beer was making him sleepy.

'It has been heard to happen. The thing is that no one is sure if it is a tiger that is responsible for the devastation, or—a monkey.'

'A monkey?'

'Well, Mr Sykes, you must have seen the small monkeys in these parts that are such a nuisance.'

'Yes, a bloody menace. But aren't they holy or something?'

'They are, but they are still a nuisance. A holy nuisance. Now, you do know that there is a larger species of monkey in these parts that is even more of a nuisance?'

'No,' Sykes replied shortly. He was beginning to suspect that he was being made fun of. He had half a mind to cuff the Babu behind the ear.

'They are a terror to lone travellers.' The Brigand whispered something to the Babu. 'My friend says that poisonous roots mixed with rice are used to kill this larger species.'

'Surely you could use such roots to poison the terrorising beast?'

'Ah, but we must know for sure if it is a marauding monkey or a marauding tiger,' the Babu said. 'A tiger, being carnivorous, would not eat rice mixed with roots.' He listened to the Brigand and translated. 'My friend says the creature could be something both or not quite either. Something, you might say, rather like a monkey tiger.'

'I have not heard of such a thing,' Sykes said as politely as he could.

'You will,' the Babu said with fervour. 'Now that you are in these parts, you will hear of things that are never quite one thing or the other but a mix of the many. Have you, while in Calcutta, heard of the goddess Kali?'

'I …' Sykes muttered. He remembered innumerable goddesses, their many hands and heads making it hard to tell one from another.

'She is most terrible, is she not, with her necklace of skulls, and blood dripping from her sword?'

Sykes looked, for reasons he could not fathom, at the Bibi, who, as far as he knew, was a Mohammedan, and therefore not part of the cult of goddesses.

'Here you will find that she is no longer only in human form. Instead, she is Tamdrin, and has a horse's head, and faces the Kanchendzonga mountain. Here you will find lakes that eat people and therefore go by the name of Maneaters. Here you will see that corpses with strange marks on them are most common, even if their killers remain invisible. You will find that there are things here that are perhaps monkey and perhaps tiger and perhaps man, perhaps even all at the same time.'

'I see. Thank you, but I must really get going,' Sykes said and stood up.

It had been bright and clear when he arrived here, but the sunlight was already weak and there was a chill in the air. The shadows were getting longer, and he was anxious to be on his way back through the mountain path back to the White Castle. Dust blew down the street as he left the village. A caravan was being readied at the edge of it, accompanied by a bleating chorus of sheep and goats. Half a dozen horsemen sat mounted, their faces covered with black scarves. Their eyes followed him in silence as he turned his back on the town and headed for the part where the barley fields gave way to the mountains.

6

The discussion at supper was livelier than usual. The Colonel announced that he was making considerable progress on his magnum opus. Weaponry, intelligence, tactics, all would require redefinition in the small wars of the future. The White Mughal, who had a piece of roast beef in his mouth, stared with intent at the Colonel. He was unable to speak and sat petrified, cheeks bulging, eyes gleaming with great meaning. His face was as red as the innards of the beef from the effort of chewing and swallowing. When he had finally finished and quaffed wine from his glass, he moved his massive head with some effort and addressed Colonel Sleeman.

'For some time now I have been meaning to ask the Colonel if he is connected to the illustrious Sleeman. The one who not so long ago destroyed that criminal tribe of assassins known as Thuggees, and who, having exterminated the brutes, penned some most curious works about them,' he said.

'You refer to *The Thugs or Phansigars of India: Comprising a History of the Rise and Progress of that Extraordinary Fraternity of Assassins; and a description of the system which it pursues; and of the measures which have been adopted by the supreme government of India for its suppression*,' the Colonel replied, dipping into his prodigious memory. 'No doubt, you also have in mind the companion work, *Ramaseeana, or a vocabulary of the peculiar language used by the Thugs, with an introduction and appendix*. Let us say that what you surmise to be a connection is not entirely unfounded. Such a connection cannot, however, be acknowledged in public.'

A clinking of crockery and the sound of chewing filled the silence provoked by this last comment. Sykes took this as an opportunity to surreptitiously examine Colonel Sleeman. He was in wondrously good humour, as he had been ever since meeting the White Mughal. His bald, smooth face gleamed like a moon descended upon the dining party. Sykes almost expected cherubs to be circling his pate, cornets at the ready. As for the White Mughal, pondering the unacknowledgeable connection most carefully over a slab of ripe cheese, he looked in far better health than during their journey. There was colour on the man's face. His cockatoo was missing, but he did not appear perturbed by this. Even his dimensions had changed subtly, shrinking to more manageable proportions.

'Yet if my understanding is correct,' the White Mughal said, his silent consideration over, 'the Colonel's treatise will not be concerned solely with the past, as *The Thuggees* and *Ramaseeana* were, fine works though they continue to be. The Colonel, if I understand correctly, is looking at the future.'

'Indeed,' the Colonel replied. 'Experience by itself is nothing. What one requires is a philosophy. My experience in the Americas, Britain, and India is, shall we say, considerable, as is my experience of the kind of war we are engaged in at this very moment. Wars comprised of jacqueries and of mutinies, of conspiracies and special missions meant to disrupt these conspiracies, of assassinations and massacres and insurgencies and counter-assassinations and counter-massacres and counter-insurgencies. Yet it takes a philosophy to understand that these small wars stitch together the fabric of the future. There may well be big wars for a while to come. Out of sheer habit, there will be wars between kingdoms, wars between nations and alliances that will involve great battle formations, complex logistical preparations and the most marvellous of weapons. Yet let me assure you that it is our understanding of small wars that will constitute the key that unlocks the future. I have embarked upon a book on war, but another way to understand it is to know that I have embarked upon a book on the future.'

'The future is a wondrous thing,' the White Mughal said. 'One senses it dancing close by. When I look at the inventions and curiosities in my Ajaib Ghar, I feel that the future is within reach.

That it is already here. That a bridge has opened up between a chosen few of us and the myriad marvels of the future.'

They spoke, then, the two savants, of steam-powered iron elephants pulling vast trains of cargoes through wide boulevards, of flying machines powered by clockwork and of cities suspended in the air from vast balloons. They did not stop at their castles in the air. Vast cities with gleaming towers were erected on the ground, errant rivers straightened and dammed. Factories burst out of farming soil, factories that were like military machines in their precision and order. The perfume of the progress of the factories filled the air and crowds cheered the captains of industry who strode about like colossi. Plants and fruits and animals, fantastically fertile and converted into nutrient solutions classified red, yellow and green, were piped into dispensaries.The Colonel did not hesitate to introduce, at opportune moments, graphic descriptions of future large wars, massive campaigns that reduced those gleaming cities to dark, ashy rubble, but that were succeeded eventually by the more frequent small wars, these latter fought on desolate landscapes by mutinous groups, by future Thuggees who thought nothing of beheading their captives and were countered by enlightened scholar soldiers who guided, with their minds, mechanised flying machines that devastated entire peninsulas. The White Mughal proposed that, in spite of such incidents as the Colonel described, the future would be one of prosperity and peace for all under the benevolent guidance of the white race, supreme. Factories would churn out luxuries like necessities, so efficient would they be in their futurism. Distant planets and stars would be colonised and alien species subjugated under the new imperium. This led to a discussion of whether the great chain of being would require further refinement and to the differences between man, woman, child, native, animal, automaton and alien, with particular attention drawn to the divide between man and automaton.

'Without a soul, an automaton, no matter how lifelike, can be nothing but the simulacrum of a man, a machine with which one can have no communion or sympathy,' the Colonel said, gesturing at the exhibit of the tiger devouring the soldier.

'Yet what are we but simulacra of the Supreme Being, poor copies we all? Who is to say that an automaton may not, eventually, come into the possession of a soul?' the White Mughal replied.

The argument raged on in good humour. The candles and lanterns around them flickered. The cabinets and displays of the Ajaib Ghar gleamed and the objects seemed pregnant with meaning. Tobin scratched at a rash that expanded along his neck as steadily as a particularly stubborn mutiny. Ryeman, a couple of stones heavier than when he had set out from Calcutta, sawed furiously at the roast beef on his plate. Bones sat attentive, while Yale simply looked dazed. Sykes, casting his eyes across at the Bibi's scarred face, thought there was something automaton-like about her, as there was about the Babu, his face frozen in the rictus of a smile. A howl pierced the night, rising octave by octave as more howls joined together in a ghastly chorus. Colonel Sleeman smiled, perhaps considering the chorus to be a special tribute to him. The White Mughal looked at him admiringly and promised to prove that the boundary between man and machine was temporary and could be dissolved.

MARCHING THROUGH THE maze of the White Castle, Sykes attempted to gain an audience with the Colonel the next morning. He wished to discuss his growing suspicion regarding the Babu and the Bibi, his fears that some kind of conspiracy was in motion around them. But it was a tedious process, as usual, to find his way through the confusing arrangement of rooms and corridors in order to reach the Ajaib Ghar. Staircases led him up to empty passageways and plunged him down again. Whispers tracked him as he made his way past closed doors. 'Have you ever?' they asked. Although his feet were heavy and his heart weary, Sykes ignored them. He paused only when he heard a woman's voice.

The door to the room was ajar, and through it he saw what looked like sky. There was no outer wall to this room; beyond, a constellation of buildings crouched. He had an impression of shadow and ruins, of windows boarded up and blown out. Yet there were isolated quarters that gleamed, cells of yellow light that made him think of the Colonel and the White Mughal's talks on the future and that mysterious room of theirs known as the Site of Experiments. The door shut in his face. When he wrestled it open again, there was no vista of distant buildings, simply an empty room, its walls very much intact, with cobwebs in the corners.

Eventually, he came to the Ajaib Ghar. He traversed it slowly, making his way towards the Kitabkhana where he hoped to find Colonel Sleeman. The Ajaib Ghar itself was bereft of human beings. The only illumination came through the skylight at the top, and Sykes had the feeling that the hall was less crowded than he remembered it. Watery sunshine bounced off the gleaming floor, which looked like it had been swept and polished recently, but some of the cabinets were empty. As he walked, he thought he heard the tread of stealthy feet behind him, a strange cough of sorts. When he turned around, there was nothing.

Shapes took on greater definition as he penetrated deeper into the Ajaib Ghar. He saw the observation balloon, a little deflated, no longer tugging quite so vigorously at its moorings. He passed the howitzer that fired the conical rockets, its shadow leaning drunkenly on the wall. Finally, he came to the platform that had held the twin of Tipu's clockwork, near whose grisly wooden maw they took their repast every night. It was dark in this part of the hall, and he saw the feet of the clockwork soldier first. There was something not quite right about it, Sykes felt, something wrong about that red-coated soldier doll lying supine on the platform. He took a step forward. There the soldier lay, his visage contorted in a permanent grimace. But the tiger? It wasn't there!

A ticktock skittering of feet, a clicking of claws on a polished wooden floor. Sykes swivelled around. There was nothing. Only a trace of movement left behind like a dying echo. Sykes reached for the pistol in his scabbard. The sound of it being cocked was loud. Among the cabinets to his right, in the space behind and between them, two spots of yellow glowed briefly and were gone. Sykes widened his stance, the better to stand for a while in the same position, if need be. Patiently, he listened. A faint noise reached him again, from behind the cabinet with framed chapatis displayed in it, a steady ticking and a tocking that calmly beat out the question, 'Have you ever? Have you ever?'

Behind him, a door opened. 'Put away your weapon, Sykes,' Colonel Sleeman said. 'It means no one harm. The creature is merely being playful.' Reluctantly, Sykes put his pistol back in its case and saluted. The Colonel's eyes glittered in the dark. In his right hand, he held a foul-smelling object. Sykes could not determine what it was. The Colonel advanced towards the cabinets. 'Come, kitty, kitty,' he said. 'Kitty, come.' A low growl emanated from behind the cabinets and became a purr. The ticktocking grew louder. But nothing appeared. 'You have rather unnerved it with your pistol, Sykes,' the Colonel said. 'They are intelligent, you know. I have finally been convinced on that point. Come, we will leave it at peace for now.'

The Colonel discarded the object in his hand and headed back in the direction he had come from. Reluctantly, Sykes trailed behind, keenly aware of a pair of golden eyes trained on him from behind. The hairs on the back of his neck rose from that fiery, feline gaze. Occasionally, he heard the stealthy clicking of claws on a floor, the ticktock of a clock. Colonel Sleeman opened the door at the end of the Ajaib Ghar and bade him enter.

THEY WALKED THROUGH the Kitabkhana towards a second set of doors. Sykes saw shelves rising steeply on either side of him in that vertical room, balconies running around the room giving access to the higher shelves. Yet the library was less impressive than he had expected it to be. The majority of the shelves were empty, both above and below. He observed one case filled with Indica, where he was not surprised to see *Ramaseeana* and *The Thugs or Phansigars of India*. He caught a glimpse, on an end table, of a few other volumes piled up in a disorderly fashion. There was an armchair next to it, a rumpled shawl with a tribal design of crossed spears flung across it.

The Colonel opened the doors to the Tajurbagah and shut them behind Sykes. It was so bright inside, in contrast to the gloomy, empty Kitabkhana, that Sykes had to cover his eyes. Opening them, he was unable to bring order to his chaotic observations. He might have been in a medieval sorcerer's den or in the quarters of a demented alchemist. Cables of various lengths trailed from floor to ceiling. A sulphurous, acrid smell permeated the room and a bubbling sound emanated from the floorboards beneath him. Strange objects were scattered haphazardly, objects whose geometry seemed all wrong to him. Their angles were in dispute, and so was their mass and volume. Two discs, each the size of a saucer, were bound together by some invisible force as they rolled in unison on the floor. Sykes looked for a connecting wire or lever but could see none. To his right, in what might have once been a fireplace, there flourished a shrunken twin of the greenhouse plant that had so grotesquely fascinated him, its red balls glowing and pulsing. In a glass cylinder, the taxidermised cousin of Jack the Andamanese snarled, dwarf bow and arrow pointed at Sykes. From the head of the dwarf, Sykes saw, cables ran out, passing through cleverly placed holes in the cylinder towards the wooden floor.

He stared when he saw on a shelf to his left, clouded by smoke, a mirror with images of the White Castle, as seen from outside. Sykes could read the lettering on the wooden doors, *Omnia Mei Sunt*, although he still did not know what that meant.

'Do you see, Sykes?' the Colonel said. 'You may rightfully wonder. Look around you at these marvels.'

'But, sir,' Sykes replied. 'Our mission. And sir, a conspiracy may be afoot.' He had imagined he would be more eloquent, but he supposed he had got the essence of his discontent across.

'That charlatan rebel leader, Magadh Rai? He is well within reach, even if it appears to not be so. Of conspiracies near and far, be not afraid.' The Colonel approached the desk in the far corner. Papers were strewn on the baize surface of the desk. A particularly thick sheaf of notes was held together by a curved khukri knife plunged through their centre. 'This magnum opus under way, these experiments, they are all ways of opening doors, Sykes, of reducing vast distances to trifles. If one can only turn the right page, one will be able to reach across and pluck Magadh Rai from his hiding spot. Manoeuvre our ideas well, and nothing and no one will be able to escape us for millennia to come. Time itself will be as nothing for us.'

'Are we not spending our days in vain, sir?' Sykes said. 'The mountain passes will close soon.'

'Not in vain at all,' the Colonel said. 'We cannot be stopped by snow in the mountains or by the absence of winds in the oceans. They have laid cables under the oceans and over mountains and deserts, Sykes. Texas can talk to Maine now, Calcutta to London. And what we are doing here is nothing less than setting up a telegraph line across time, into the future.'

'Sir, telegraph lines can communicate in two directions,' Sykes said. 'We may be able to send our messages into the future. It is unlikely that the future is able to signal us.'

'But it can! And it is!' the Colonel said. 'Look at everything around you, Sykes. What are they, if not messages from the future?'

REBUFFED BY THE Colonel, Sykes returned sullenly to his quarters. He felt a restlessness in himself, a desire for opium that would let him sink beneath the surface of recent events: the Babu and the Bibi at that nameless village, the ticktocking creature in the Ajaib Ghar, and the Colonel opening up telegraph lines to the future. But there was no opium, not even the Bengal poppy the White Mughal had spoken of cultivating. The chang, or the rice beer, the men had been drinking when they first arrived had been replaced by something else, some vile, sweetish, unnamed and unnameable liquor sitting in earthen jars in a corner of the stables and surrounded by the drunken bodies and drowned corpses of ants and insects.

Sykes debauched himself that night, drinking cupfuls of that sweet, milky concoction. It made him feel expansive, which in turn made him realise that he had been rather constricted of late. He laughed as he had not for some weeks and wrestled Bones to the ground, pushing his face into the straw until the back of his neck turned red and his legs drummed out a plea for mercy. He sang in nonsensical languages to the horses and then stumbled out into the open, pissing frothy, fuming piss under the moonlight.

7

Later, Sykes had a terrifying dream. He was back in the Ajaib Ghar, making his way through the long, deserted hall. A faceless, nameless creature stalked him as he tried to hurry towards the door that led to the Kitabkhana. On the other side of that door lay sanctuary. He reached for the door handle but there was none. Behind him, yellow eyes burnt. Claws clicked. Clocks ticked.

Then Sykes was somewhere else. It was surely the Tajurbagah, but so crowded with people as to resemble a lecture hall. Or was it the greenhouse? In the centre, surrounded by whispers and murmurs, captured in a cone of light, Colonel Sleeman held an object out towards the White Mughal. The two were talking, but Sykes could not understand what was being said. The Colonel put the object down on a table and picked up another. It was, Sykes saw, some kind of mask, one of a row laid out on the table. There was something familiar in its combination of ghastly colour and pained grimace, but only when the White Mughal took it from the Colonel, caressing it with his fleshy hands, did Sykes recognise its similarity to the face of the soldier doll being devoured by the tiger.

Through a parting in the crowd, a soldier. It was Yale. He marched down the steep steps and saluted Colonel Sleeman. There was an abiding look of curiosity on Yale's face, a look that imprinted itself on Sykes's brain even as the White Mughal, adjusting his bulk as deftly as a man-o'-war conducting an evasive manoeuvre, turned towards Yale and placed the mask on his face.

The sizzling sound, the smell of burning flesh, the strange rocking motion made by Yale! Sykes woke up violently, felt that he was still asleep and tried to rouse himself by slapping himself on the face. Men muttered in their sleep as he sat up. Sykes crawled out of his bed and opened the door to the stables. In the light of the moon, cold and bright, he looked around. Shadows passed over the restless faces of the sleeping men, while behind them, the horses, noses buried in their feed bags, looked at him with equine complacence. Sykes crept cautiously towards Yale. He was sitting up, gagging violently. 'Yale?' Sykes called, but Yale did not hear him. By the time Sykes reached him, he was lying down again, fast asleep. Sykes looked at where Yale had been retching. In the hay, something metallic glinted. Sykes reached for it. It was a clock spring, but not of a kind he had seen before. It behaved as though it were still wound. He could feel it moving on his palm, coiling and uncoiling.

Sykes did not know what happened to the spring as he made his way back to bed. Nor was he aware of falling back asleep. But there he was again in the Site of Experiments or in the greenhouse, watching with the Colonel and the White Mughal and a vast crowd—Who were these people? Who were they?—as Yale marched around, stiff as a tailor's dummy, wearing the mask that was mostly the face of a doll and yet retained a vestige of Yale's features. He marched stiffly, like a child's tin soldier, advancing towards a tall glass cylinder. There was a door in the cylinder. Yale stepped through it, turned around and stood at attention. The White Mughal walked over and closed the door, looming over Yale like some grotesque puppet master. Then he was gone, all of them, the White Mughal, the Colonel, the faceless murmuring audience. Only Sykes remained, creeping up to the cylinder. He tried the handle on the door, opening it gently. 'Yale,' he whispered, a madman talking to a marionette, wondering if he saw a responding flicker in the eyes. But no, it was a lifeless thing, painted up crudely to resemble a human being.

He had either opened the door to the cylinder or else the solid glass had vanished. He looked into the eyes but could not tell if they belonged to Yale or to the doll. The smell of paint was fresh, but when he touched it, the red-coated chest was dry and cold to the touch. Sykes found himself tapping on the chest of the doll, tapping as precisely as the Colonel sending a code deep into the recesses of a human being. The doll was hollow as a drum and boomed to his taps. Its eyes fixed upon Sykes. He tapped again. There were echoes but nothing that might be a reply. Yet, just before he awoke, he heard, from deep inside, a code that answered in questions, that seemed to go, 'Have you ever? Have you ever?'

WHEN SYKES AWOKE, he was cold and clammy. His mouth tasted foul as he stumbled out of the stables, his blanket wrapped around him. There was a horse tied up outside, a bay with white socks that he did not recognise. Sykes walked in the direction of the garden, towards the greenhouse he had been avoiding. He saw the Babu hurrying out from the White Castle. The cadaverous man made his way to the bay and rode out towards the tarn.

Clouds drifted through the sky, occasionally parting to reveal patches of brilliant sunshine. Sykes sat inside the greenhouse and looked up. At the very top of the mountains, a coat of white powder glittered. There had been snowfall in the night up there. Sykes remembered, with startling clarity, an expedition he had undertaken with the Russian in London, and of staring, at the end of a dim corridor, at a hatted figure in a glass case. This was Sykes back from America, Sykes back from the prospecting that had not turned up gold, Sykes back from filibusters in Nicaragua and Mexico that had produced only corpses that started out at a dollar a scalp and then, with inflation, ended up amounting to nothing. This was Sykes acting as a local guide for the Russian he had met at the rooming house in Lambeth, grateful for any odd shillings passed his way. On this day, they were visiting University College London at the Russian's insistence. The mummified man, the Russian explained, was the utilitarian philosopher Jeremy Bentham who had been employed at the India House, a man who after death had been made, in accordance with his wishes, an 'auto-icon'. There had been something like that about the Yale figure in the glass case of his dream, Sykes thought, something akin to the auto-iconised Jeremy Bentham, something that could be called humanoid but was nevertheless not human, something that was not quite inanimate and yet was undoubtedly not alive.

He looked, without intending to, for the repulsive plant. It had lost some of its leaves. The ones that remained were withered, and there was an odd sensation of absence about the flowers or fruits in the centre, like they were being remembered and did not actually exist. It was as if this were a memory of the plant that once was.

Sykes's mind skittered this way and that as he walked around the greenhouse. What eluded him, what was truly of import, was the White Mughal. Was the man truly a genius inventor, a philosopher shut away in this fastness? What was the source of the objects in his house? In contrast, why were the volumes in his library so scanty? Sykes had a sudden vision of an alien race of craftsmen labouring on the exhibits in some strange alien workshop, the subtle signature of their guild on each of the objects. The White Mughal became less benign, less foolish, as Sykes pondered, and his powdered, puffy face became the visage of a conjuror, a sorcerer with an unseemly appetite who had perhaps devoured his native subjects and, who, having done so, had found fresh prey in the Colonel and his men.

Sykes left the greenhouse. Circling around the front of the mansion, he approached the scum-covered tarn, across which Babu had ridden an hour ago. Its surface was calm, suggestive more of a field than a lake. Yet the feeling was of unknown depths hidden beneath that placid top, and of unknown things too. He began to walk along the embankment. The path was possibly much older than the mansion. As he neared the midway point, the water seethed and bubbled. There were breaks in the scum, patches of greenish liquid. He saw a long snakelike fish thing shoot under the surface. The odour of rotten eggs became more pervasive. He found what looked like an arm under the water, but on closer examination, this turned out to be a rotting branch, one blackened end splayed out like the fingers of a tortured corpse.

When Sykes had crossed the tarn fully, he stopped to survey the White Castle. Not a soul could be seen. Other than a thin wisp of smoke rising from the roof, there was no suggestion that the place had occupants. Sykes was about to turn and walk on when he noticed a slight movement to the left of the mansion, a brief flash of red.

Changing his mind about looking for the Babu, Sykes made his way back across the tarn. No further movement was apparent in the half an hour it took him to find the spot where he thought he might have seen something. In the hard, frozen ground, faint tracks were visible, the hooves of a single rider. The brush ahead showed signs of being forced. Sykes followed the trail all the way to the edge of the valley. He saw no one, and yet, he acknowledged to himself, the track was just wide enough for a skilled horseman heading for the village.

OVER THE COURSE of the coming days, Sykes attempted to transform his unease into the notation of specific details. He tried to be observant, recording what he saw in a notebook purchased, soon after his arrival in India, from a Jewish stationer in Chowringhee. He used a pencil, procured from the same source, aware that he was more or less mimicking the Colonel at work on his treatise on small wars and the future. To the uninformed, certainly, he would appear to have succumbed to the same disease, substituting cogitation and inscription for action.

Sykes did not wish to succumb to the speculative, fanciful turns common at supper in the White Castle. He attempted, instead, to be empirical, restricting himself only to the material facts. Yet when he read his pencilled observations back to himself, they came across as wildly impressionistic, things he had concocted out of opium dreams. The number of retainers were dwindling, he had scribbled. At supper, the men who served them looked different, even if he was not fully certain of this, natives looking so much alike. They carried themselves in a manner that struck him as surprisingly bold, their subservience a mere facade. The women of the harem were to be seen no longer, except for the Bibi. The Babu was often to be seen flitting in and out of the White Castle, sometimes on horseback and on other occasions on foot, gliding like some kind of eastern vampire along the path that crossed the tarn.

Even of his own company, Sykes could no longer be sure of the numbers. There was often a man extra or one man missing, he thought, and yet he could not be sure who the extra man was, who the missing one might be. He recalled dreaming of Yale being transformed into a clockwork doll, but he could not have sworn that it was Yale who was missing and not one of the others. There was a profusion of dolls now in the Ajaib Ghar, leaking in from somewhere and squeezing out all the other, disparate items that had been in the museum. Yet there were also times when the hall looked utterly empty, its cabinets vacant, although such an impression was likely to be succeeded by the discovery of a large doll just behind one. The tiger was no longer to be found paired with the prone soldier, who remained stranded alone on his display island, and Sykes often sensed the animal stalking him from behind the cabinets, its presence revealed only through the sound of its claws, its occasional cough and the yellow glow of its eyes. If the tiger's clockwork mechanism made a sound, it was no longer distinguishable from other such sounds. All through the Ajaib Ghar, one heard the noise of clockwork, magnified and resonant, echoing through the hall in a crescendo of ticks and tocks that for Sykes never failed to resolve into the question, 'Have you ever? Have you ever?'

He felt that the Ajaib Ghar had grown in size, and that there was no longer much more to the White Castle than the Ajaib Ghar itself, and yet in spite of its expanded dimensions, it was paradoxically crammed with the dolls. Most of all, he perceived a kind of troubling transformation in himself that he did not dare put down on paper.

SYKES DECIDED TO approach Colonel Sleeman again. He could not speak of vague suspicions of sorcery, of masks and missing men turned into dolls. He could, however, make a plea about a conspiracy afoot. To do that, he would require more intelligence. He decided to enlist Tobin, who had some acquaintance with native languages, in an effort to visit the village. They would ask there about the Babu, about strange horsemen and even about the White Mughal and his absent subjects.

Such was his intent when he returned to the stables that afternoon from his solitary post on the mountain. He was taken aback to find the Babu present. The man looked submissive enough, and yet there was far too much interest in his eyes, too much of a gleam in his thick black moustache, as he held out a note from the Colonel. Sykes read the note and passed it to Bones. 'All men are to remain within the grounds of the White Castle until further notice. I remain yours, &c.,' it said. To this, there was a curious comment appended, in the same handwriting, 'Tintinnabulum? Glottal stop. Exterminate the !Kung!'

There was little in the way of a response from his fellows to this order. Yale remained lying on his bed of straw, staring at the rafters. Bones looked uneasy but said nothing. The rest did not seem to care. Sykes escorted the Babu out of their quarters and waited till the cadaverous figure had been swallowed up by the front doors of the White Castle. Then he made his way back towards the mountain path. As he climbed, he recalled the conversation some weeks ago about the Horse Latitudes.

Had it been Yale who brought it up? Sykes looked up at the evening sky like someone trying to find his position at sea. The moon was visible, looming so red and so large that it could be mistaken for Mars. Yale had been right. They might as well be on a ship caught in a stretch of dead calm. They had been here for weeks, with neither forward movement nor backward. His shadow elongated by the moon, Sykes felt unease in the cries of a hooting owl and the eerie howls that sounded from somewhere near the tarn. Time was running out. Intelligence was out of date. Most important of all, intent was expiring.

Beyond all measure, he was surprised by Colonel Sleeman. He had expected their mission to be lit up by the fury of the Colonel's madness. Yet, the Colonel was the most becalmed of them all. Sykes stopped when he had reached his old observation post. Drums sounded from the valley on the other side. Somewhere, people were chasing away spirits. Sykes was determined that the horse ceremony would begin, the one that would release their ship and allow them to sail out of these enchanted waters.

8

It was not easy for Sykes to convey his desired course of action. Or, for that matter, the necessity of action. His fellows were gathered on the wooden steps of the greenhouse, watching him, the one who had called the assembly. He stood uncertain, facing the men, caught suddenly by a terrible doubt that he had misinterpreted the signs and quite misread the narrative. Who was he to attempt to seize the rein of events? Even more important, if he were successful in doing so, did he really know what his intentions were?

He looked at the ragtag band that stood before him, a far cry from the proud band of brothers who had set out from Fort William in Calcutta. Their smart uniforms had degenerated into the outfits of a retreating rabble. Bones was wearing a native dressing gown, with faded dragons brocaded on its sleeves. Tobin had on his head a conical bamboo hat, the kind worn by peasant cultivators, that cast his face in a cold, deep shadow. Bones appeared to have mislaid his riding boots and was shod in native sandals. Ryeman was squatting on his haunches, Indian style, having let his belt out a couple of notches to allow himself to breathe better. There were buttons missing on his coat and he had stopped shaving. Yale, who moved so stiffly as to suggest that his joints needed to be greased with oil, was in search of something infinitesimally small among the potted plants behind him. It was astonishing that they had agreed to listen to him at all, or that they had been willing to rouse themselves from their usual torpor and temporarily decamp their squalid quarters for a sudden confabulation in the greenhouse.

Clearing his throat, Sykes touched his pistol for comfort. Then he began his address.

The Colonel's steady withdrawal into his book demanded a response, he argued. They had set off from Calcutta to stamp out the last embers of an extinguished mutiny, not to indulge in theoretical speculations on what the Colonel called 'Small Wars'. They had made no progress towards their original goal. In its stead, surely they had all noticed, there had been a gradual, threatening transformation of men and material at the White Castle.

Sykes grew warm and passionate. Was it not possible, he declaimed now, that what they saw stirring around them was another mutiny, one far more uncanny, a rebellion that involved the sequestration of their Colonel and that would pit them perhaps not just against natives but against objects? At the Horse Latitudes, their quest for Magadh Rai had stalled, and yet it could not be said that things around them were at a standstill. Their sails had no wind, the ship itself did not move, but within that dead calm, one heard the creak of timber, as steady as some infernal ticking clock. One sensed the scurrying of vermin feet, heard the whisper of worms burrowing deep in the woodwork.

Light assaulted the greenhouse and was cut into shadows by the sharp blades of angular plants and elongated men. Sykes kept an eye out for the Babu or any other interloper. It was the reason he had chosen the greenhouse, it being relatively easy to remain hidden within the plants while making it impossible for anyone to approach without being seen through the glass walls. Yale had made his way to the grotesque plant that was the centrepiece of the greenhouse and was examining its fleshy, white bloom and withering red buds. Sykes heard his own voice and his doubts echo in the enclosed space and was seized by a feeling of being suspended in time. He could hear the others speaking. Having listened attentively to Sykes, the others were confessing to apprehensions similar to his own.

They agreed, although none could pinpoint the source, that they had heard rumours of a second Mutiny among the natives. Such a thing should not be possible, the first having been crushed so thoroughly. The Rani of Jhansi had been killed, the Mughal potentate Bahadur Shah Zafar, whom the sepoys had attempted to restore to the throne, exiled to Rangoon, his sons hanged by Lieutenant Hodson at the gates of Delhi, Bones muttered. But yes, and this spoke to the heart of their stalled mission, the Nana Sahib, the Demon of Cawnpore, had not been found. 'And where is Danka Baba?' Tobin asked plaintively. 'Who can say where Magadh Rai is?' There were other names being added to the rumour of rebellions. There was even talk of the Thuggees marching again, although that fraternity of brutes had long ago been exterminated by the Sleeman who was a predecessor to their Colonel. Here they were perhaps in the very vicinity of the White Castle, this criminal tribe of Hindus and Mohammedans on the move with the knotted handkerchiefs that were their most unusual weapons of war.

The plants in the greenhouse stirred restlessly, although there was no breeze. From far away, there came the sound of a horse neighing. Sykes heard his heart boom and recalled that long-ago morning inspection in Calcutta where Colonel Sleeman had picked them out. A circle of light appeared at his feet, bounced in rainbow colours and ricocheted off a nearby surface of long, serrated fronds. It originated in a glass device, a small ball, that Yale held up to scrutiny against the sun. Yale was speaking even as he looked at the object, his face expressionless.

Surely another uprising was not possible, he said. There could be no Thuggees operating around them, in an area traditionally not part of their sphere of influence, and in a time when they no longer existed. There could be no doubt, he said, about the great respect they all had for the Colonel, for his ferocity and madness. They were the chosen ones of the astonishing Colonel Sleeman, and it was their primary task to be loyal to orders. If Colonel Sleeman believed significant intelligence was to be garnered by their being billeted with the White Mughal, there was no question that this was the case and that they would ride out in pursuit of Magadh Rai when they were armed with perfect information.

Sykes was taken aback. All this was excellent, he retorted, but where was the action they had embarked upon? Where was Magadh Rai, chief conspirator to the Demon of Cawnpore, and why were they, weeks or months after they had set out from Calcutta, still lying about in the stables attached to this echoing castle? The Colonel, they must have heard, did not merely work on his opus. He conducted scientific tests with the White Mughal at the Site of Experiments. Flashes of light, tendrils of acrid smoke and abruptly subdued screams occasionally emerged from these quarters, sending those mysterious native servants scurrying hither and thither. Arrangements were being made too, it was reported, for a grand feast that would involve the singing of the Lady of the Fifty-Six Knives. There was more toing and froing from the White Castle than usual, strangers constantly arriving, some with what looked like supplies, others so unencumbered as to suggest that they were carrying messages. To Sykes, a number of the arrivals looked like Thuggees, and he was most gratified that the rest of the company too had heard something about a band of marauders in the vicinity. Magadh Rai was among them, Sykes had heard, but oddly enough the band was led not by Rai but by a woman of whom nothing was known.

Yale began to exhibit some signs of agitation as he discoursed. Men came and went from the White Castle at all hours of day and night, on foot and on horseback, it was true. Rumours echoed in the halls and passageways of the White Castle, no doubt. Whispers shifted in the branches of the trees. Somewhere in all that activity was information that would be acted upon. There was intelligence if only one had the philosophy.

Yale's face had a reddish tinge to it as he spoke. His left arm began jerking in a convulsive fashion. He looked like he had far more to say, but his speech gave way to a most unusual sound, something not unlike the buzzing of a hive of bees. Sykes wondered if Yale was having a seizure.

The sound in Yale's throat grew louder, making it impossible for conversation to continue. It was nothing like the buzzing of bees, Sykes realised. There was something alien in its provenance and the men grew uneasy as they observed Yale's antics. Tobin had covered his ears. Whatever it was, it passed. The red tinge faded. Yale slumped down, head between his knees. He seemed to have no further inclination to continue his objections. Sykes, concerned that the attention of the men would dissipate, hurried to bridge over the interruption.

'There is no help for it,' Sykes said. 'We have only one option before us. We must seize the Colonel and ride out from the White Castle.'

'Shock and awe,' Ryeman said, his whiskers quivering. 'Slash it and burn it.'

'We must proceed towards Paltanganj, the largest garrison town in these parts. There we can ask for further orders,' Bones said.

'But to seize Colonel Sleeman?' Tobin said. 'Let us be clear that what we propose is nothing less than a mutiny.'

Silence ensued from the use of this word, a familiar one that linked them rather uneasily to those others they sought to destroy. Sykes thought of the sepoy mutineers, incarcerated, executed, exterminated. The faces of corpses stuffed in wells grinned at him and his fellows, who were now proposing their own small mutiny, taking prisoner the man who had been destroyer and jailer extraordinaire while putting down the rebellious sepoys. He remembered hearing of the innovative use of water in Colonel Sleeman's interrogation of prisoners, of the prison he had designed according to the panopticon theory of the utilitarian thinker Jeremy Bentham.

'In Calcutta and London, they will certainly call this a mutiny,' Sykes said. 'A breach of orders.'

'We have no intention of turning the world upside down,' Bones replied. 'We are loyal soldiers. Our intention is to preserve order, to stay faithful to our duties.'

'Slash and burn. Shock 'em and awe 'em,' Ryeman said.

Tobin and Bones argued. Yale took once again to wandering the greenhouse. Ryeman laughed and played with a coiled spring in his hand.

The White Castle, Bones said, was being infiltrated by a secret society. Men who were Thuggees or Pindaris, mostly likely, and the White Mughal, for reasons of his own, was in league with them. They would not make it to Paltanganj after their mutiny, Tobin retorted, and if they did, they were sure to be clapped in irons.

They argued among themselves, bitterly, with fierce accusations. But at least they argued! In place of the lethargy that had settled upon them these past weeks. A show of hands was asked for. All raised their hands, even the eccentric Yale.

They would seize the Colonel and ride out. Making for the garrison town in Paltanganj, they would there seek further orders and fresh intelligence. Perhaps the Colonel himself, once removed from the malign influence of the White Mughal, would take charge. But what should be done with the White Mughal, the White Castle and its denizens? Ryeman was of the opinion that rapine and massacre were called for and that they should ride out with a flourish, the smoking ruins of the White Castle behind them, its gates flung open, its Ajaib Ghar erased from the face of the earth in explosion and fire and with the White Mughal's headless corpse propped up in front of the White Castle to greet any unlikely visitors. They would take his bloated head with them as a prize, bobbing on the end of a lance like a grotesque moon harvested from an alien sky.

THEY HAD PLANNED the sacrifice that would get them out of the Horse Latitudes. Now they scoured the White Castle for supplies and ammunition, keeping an eye out for the new Enfields they had seen in the hands of the White Mughal's bodyguard. But the soldiers were nowhere to be seen, and no guns or ammunition were found, although Tobin discovered in the Ajaib Ghar an eclectic collection of swords as well an assortment of metal stilts. They gathered dry food and warm clothing. At night, after they had returned from supper at the White Castle, they sat and discussed matters, bound together in a renewed brotherhood of conspiracy.

Having provoked a change in their affairs in such a pleasing manner, Sykes should have felt great satisfaction. Yet the word *mutiny* and its many namesakes tolled through his head when everyone was asleep. Coup, Mutiny, Strike, Rebellion, Jacquery, Revolution. The words boomed and gonged in the confined chambers of his mind. This disturbed him, but not as much as the words that came in other languages, languages that he had never learnt but that cared little for his lack of knowledge as a defensive picket for not understanding. These native words rattled in his head. Hool, Bidroho, Jumla, Sabha, Andolan.

Sykes thought, increasingly, of the men he had met in his lifetime. There had been those like President Walker, the White Mughal and the Colonel, certain of the forward march of progress, of the great chain of being and their part in it. Then, there were the others, like the Russian who had befriended Sykes and hired his services when he was floating around in London after his return from California. Even among the men he had fought with and sailed with, among the women he had whored with, there had been people like that, people who lived in a realm of whispers and murmurs that spoke of mutiny as a beautiful thing and that had planted in his mind names such as the Diggers, the Levellers, the Anabaptists and the Black Jacobins.

Were they embarking upon a sacrifice, a restoration or a mutiny? Which of these was the right course of action? Sykes did not know what he had set in motion.

THE EVENING OF the mutiny arrived. The five of them appeared at supper, restored to their uniforms, arms at the ready. The horses had been fed and saddled, their supplies packed. They were ready to ride at a moment's notice. Bones and Tobin had laid charges in the proper places.

Yet Sykes was ill at ease as they walked down a long, empty passageway towards the Ajaib Ghar. Glassy eyeballs surveyed them from the walls, trapped in the stuffed heads of tigers and yaks. There was evasion in those marble eyes, a refusal to reveal what they knew. The floor creaked, as if the White Castle were really a ship, and below the decks faceless enemies lurked in ambush. There were puddles all along their way, as though the castle had sprung leaks, and a faint sulphurous smell was discernible as they walked. When had they been press-ganged aboard this creaking, leaking ship? The walls around Sykes seemed to be hollow, the roof concealing secret chambers from which men would leap out to overpower them. The footsteps of his companions, walking behind him, sounded loud and silly.

They entered the Ajaib Ghar. The vast hall was shrouded in darkness except for a dim light far ahead. Sykes felt like he was underground. Shadows were arranged around him like pillars or totem poles, although they melted away when he drew near. They walked on, aware of something amiss. It became evident, eventually, that the Ajaib Ghar had been emptied of almost everything. No cabinets were to be seen, no dolls large or small. All that remained, under the single chandelier in the centre of the room, was the supper table where a group of figures awaited their arrival, lit up in a ghastly glow. Sykes momentarily forgot to breathe. He exhaled, and his breath boomed and echoed in the Ajaib Ghar, becoming the question, 'Have you ever?'

They closed in on the table. None of the native attendants were visible. The Babu, Sykes saw instantly, was missing. The Bibi sat demurely on one side of the table, while at the head of it was the White Mughal. In front of the White Mughal, laid out on the white tablecloth, like a corpse awaiting the ministrations of a vivisectionist, was the figure of Colonel Sleeman.

There was a gasp behind him. Sykes felt a breath of wind on his neck and then Tobin had rushed past, screaming obscenities. Sykes looked at the Colonel, at the Colonel's corpse placed on the table like some final, outrageous item procured by the White Mughal.

'G-d damn you, sir, what have you done to him?' Tobin cried.

Sykes heard pistols being cocked, swords coming unsheathed, loud imprecations.

'Let us not be hasty, gentlemen,' the White Mughal said.

They gathered around the table, looking down at Colonel Sleeman. He was not dead. Indeed, he was very much alive, even very much aware, lying on his back in regimental uniform, barrel chest rising and falling in a regular rhythm, bald pate shining in the twilight luminescence of the Ajaib Ghar, eyes focused upon something infinitesimally small in the air.

'The Colonel is merely undergoing a voluntary, necessary,

transformation. Do not be alarmed,' the White Mughal said. There was on his face not the slightest hint of concern. His cockatoo was nowhere to be seen, and Sykes recalled coming across some feathers and bones some days ago in the Ajaib Ghar.

'Very good, ha! One treats them as one does machines,' the Colonel said to the ceiling.

'Indeed,' the White Mughal replied. The sound of a sword leaving its scabbard briefly punctuated his voice. 'Have no concerns about your quarry. None shall escape. The colonel intends to …'

The White Mughal's speech ended as the point of Tobin's sword found a place of rest somewhere in the region below the man's many chins. The rest of the company advanced. Sykes was aware, uneasily, of shadows behind them, of whispers and murmurs, of a rather loud ticking coming from the table. He looked at Colonel Sleeman. The ticking emanated from a timepiece the Colonel held up to the light, examining it with profound concentration, quite unperturbed by Tobin's agitation or the perplexity of his hand-picked company.

'One minute,' the Colonel said.

'Unhand me, sir,' the White Mughal said.

'This is witchcraft,' Tobin said, his sword unyielding.

'Thirty seconds,' the Colonel said.

'The results, I assure you, will be magnificent,' the White Mughal said.

'I'll gut you like a sausage, you fat charlatan,' Tobin said.

'Time,' the Colonel said and returned the watch to his pocket.

Before the eyes of the astonished gathering, he rose to his feet and leapt off the table, landing lightly next to Tobin.

'You greatly dishonour our host, Tobin,' he said.

'Colonel, I intend no insubordination,' Tobin replied.

The Colonel's left arm shot out and grasped Tobin's sword-bearing hand. His right planted itself around Tobin's throat. Ryeman and Bones and Sykes leapt to part the Colonel from Tobin, Sykes looking for purchase on that hand on Tobin's throat. Around them, there was movement, chairs being pushed over, crockery crashing to the floor. They jostled and struggled with Colonel Sleeman, united against their demented superior, until Bones went skidding across the floor as the Colonel shook him off like a bear disposing of a fighting dog. Shorter than Tobin by at least a foot, the Colonel was somehow dangling him by his throat. Sykes tried, desperately, to pry that hand off Tobin's throat, but Tobin dropped his sword and the point struck Sykes's boot.

Ryeman tried to keep at it, struggling, panting, attempting a headlock on the Colonel. He was sent bowling backwards, crashing into the table. Sykes, kneeling, could see the light going out from Tobin's eyes. He took his pistol out and cocked it, aiming for the Colonel's thigh. Colonel Sleeman let go abruptly. Tobin dropped to his knees and gasped. Sykes rose to his feet. Returning his pistol to its scabbard, he attempted to seize his adversary. The Colonel drifted away from Sykes like someone on wheels. Ryeman tried to pin him against the wall. Colonel Sleeman headbutted him, striking his Adam's apple with such unerring accuracy that Ryeman dropped like a stone, gagging and clutching his throat.

There was a pause as the Colonel inspected them, hands behind his back. 'Tick tock goes the clock,' he said. He giggled and vanished into the gloom. Sykes ran after him, trying to make out the Colonel's form through the darkness. In the empty Ajaib Ghar, its weird collection scooped out so completely, it should not have been difficult to find the Colonel. Yet a fog obscured the hall. Sykes heard sounds, echoes, what for a moment he thought was the clicking of claws on the wooden floor. He could see nothing behind him. Then he heard, from some distance ahead, the Colonel singing in a jaunty manner. The words were indistinct. It was not a tune Sykes was familiar with. He saw the Colonel, opening the door to the Kitabkhana in a leisurely way. Sykes ran to catch him, but the Colonel waved at him cheerfully and stepped inside. By the time Sykes reached it, the door was locked. From the other side, he heard the Colonel singing. Sykes pressed his ear to the keyhole.

Tick tock goes the clock,
Summer's gone away.
Tick tock goes the clock,
Dark the angel's play.

There were footsteps and the noise of a door closing. Then he could hear no more.

Sykes returned to the table to consult. Tobin knelt on the floor, gasping and massaging his throat. The White Mughal remained seated, his face expressionless. The Bibi had vanished. Where was the rest of the company?

Sykes raced towards the entrance to the Ajaib Ghar. The hall seemed to expand around him as he ran. Moonlight glittered through the skylight above and whispers surrounded him, calling out his name. He felt he had been trapped here for an unconscionably long time, chasing shadows and pursuing echoes.

He saw them as he came to the entrance, arranged on both sides of the door, Ryeman on the left, Yale and Bones on the right, their backs to him. Sykes joined Ryeman and stared out with him, letting the shapes on the other side take on definition. He was not prepared for the sight that greeted his eyes.

9

Sykes supposed he could call them sepoys, those clockwork dolls ranged outside in the corridor. Facing him, bringing up the avant-garde, there was a squad composed of soldiers. He could not have imagined a more heterogeneous army, dressed in tunics of resplendent colour, a rainbow arrangement of dazzling shades, earthy hues of red, black and green in which sparkled the violet and green of dragonflies, the yellow and orange of fishes. Silent, unmoving, they held scimitars and talwars, pikes and daos. There were even figures wielding hammers and sickles.

Behind the soldiers, there was an even more variegated mass, a kind of doll kingdom that had in its ranks poets and cooks and priests and peasants. Yet it was the sepoys that occupied his attention. Red and blue buttons alternated down the front of their tunics. Some wore turbans, some did not. There were beards and curling moustaches. Not all were natives. A man on the left displayed a face that was of distinctly European cast, a grin curling up towards the red flashes of his cheeks, his eyes black slits under black eyebrows. It felt like the innards of the White Castle had finally burst, flooding its pathways with these creatures. He remembered the conversation between the Colonel and the White Mughal about the place of automatons in the chain of being.

As Sykes looked, it became clearer that some of the sepoys were women with their hair done up in double plaits. Sykes was confused. There were women dressed as men and back there, among the dancing girls, men dressed as women, but if they were all dolls, that did not make any sense at all since they were, of course, neither men nor women. He saw the dabs of colours on their faces, meant to give them a lifelike resemblance, splashes of pink and red and purple, some with marble eyes and others with eyes painted on, but these details only emphasised for him how alien they were. He could smell paint that had been freshly applied on the dolls and that was still drying as they stood in the confined space, motionless, to all appearances and purposes unseeing and unfeeling were it not for that infernal ticktock sound of clockwork echoing in his ears.

Sykes stepped out into the corridor. The figures remained motionless. He reached out tentatively with his left hand for the moustache of the sepoy in front. The surface was cool to the touch, Sykes's hand rough against the smooth sheen of paint. A faint memory came to him, from childhood, of the painted faces of Father Christmas and Sir Loin and Plum Pudding in a village lane with snow piled on the side, of magic and tricksters and carol singing. He pushed the sepoy's face. It was firm to the touch, stiff and wooden, although just as he withdrew his hand, he sensed an answering softness in the surface, just the merest suggestion of flesh.

He wondered if there was a way to get the clockwork dolls out of the way, to pile them into the Ajaib Ghar and clear a path of egress. He pushed against the sepoy's chest. It rocked on its base, firm but not heavy. Sykes turned to address his fellows. He wanted them to help him move the figures. There was a sound behind him. He swivelled. It vanished almost instantly, but he nevertheless saw it as it disappeared, the twitch around the lips of the sepoy he had touched. He stared. The sepoy was motionless, as were all the dolls, their figures receding down the corridor, all silent except for their ticking. Then there was another noise, a kind of stifled cough that came from somewhere in the middle and he caught a little of the expression on the face of a slender dancing girl before it dissolved into the contours of a mask. The dolls were laughing at him.

Sykes reddened. As he did so, he felt a rush of breeze behind him, and Yale was swiftly past, sabre drawn. A hand, mechanical, thrust Sykes to the floor and sent him tumbling backwards. He saw, with a smoothness of motion that was as striking in its beauty as it was chilling, the dolls rearrange themselves instantly so as to leave a space clear in front of Yale, into which stepped a sepoy with a beard. His turban was splendid, his eyes melancholic, his movements almost languorous as he parried the thrust Yale aimed at him.

TRUE-BORN ENGLISHMAN VERSUS native, Anglo-Saxon against foreigner, white man contra swarthy. The outcome was a foregone conclusion.

But could the sepoy be called a native? Was a native automaton more native or more automaton? Sykes would have expected a stiffness in its movements, a lack of limberness in the appendages, an approach mechanical that might bring great force to its blows but that would never be a match for a trained swordsman's skills. But the sepoy automaton belied his expectations. It used a curved, single-edged sword with a long handle of a type known as a hengdang, wielding it with precision and beauty, giving the impression somehow, even as his opponent was at his noisiest, huffing and puffing, with his forward foot coming down so hard on the floor that the White Castle shook, of being stilled at the very centre of its swift movements, almost motionless, almost silent. Was Yale's opponent a native or a thing?

For that matter, could Yale be considered English or Anglo-Saxon any longer? Sykes, watching him, thought of the dreams and the details and the White Mughal's announcement of a transformation. There was in Yale's cold fury something mechanical, doll-like, just as there was something angelic about the Sepoy automaton. That face of Yale's was like a mask carefully placed on what had once been a face. Sykes was certain he heard a ticktocking sound from Yale.

TO THE CLOCKWORK sound of their infernal mechanisms, the figures swooped and swung, wheeling and turning with a precision that left Sykes astonished. The swords clashed, the figures parted, and defence switched to attack. Brief flashing Xes were written in the air with swords before the letters were erased by the whirlwind of movement. Air and light parried shadow.

Sykes remembered tales of duels in the Calcutta maidan, under the shade of the peepul trees near the Alipore Bridge, of European gentlemen settling their disputes with swords and pistols, of Warren Hastings, Esq. versus Phillip Francis, Esq., men who had fallen out in their counting of the vast profits from the India trade. Yet the figures in front of Sykes did not move like human beings at all.

The pace had quickened, the fight went on, and no human being was capable of navigating space with such ferocity and speed. Impossible angle that, Sykes cried out in his mind. Yale had found an opening and gone in with his thrust, and yet the sepoy had somehow bent from his knees, stopping almost parallel to the floor before righting himself, and Yale had not managed so much as a scratch.

Perhaps Yale's transformation was incomplete, Sykes thought, in which case he would be at a disadvantage against this native machine. He saw signs of human distress in Yale. Flecks of foam were visible around Yale's mouth. The laboured sound of his breathing rose over the ticking of the clock. When the swords met, a wavering of Yale's weapon revealed that his hands were trembling. The sepoy, meanwhile, never changed. He could have been playing a chess match in the calmness of his intensity. The red tassel at the end of his sword's long handle was a brush over a canvas. His face no longer struck Sykes as expressionless but pensive in the manner of someone who had peered into the hidden meaning of things and found them to be complex beyond belief. His opponent, meanwhile, struggled. He had received a cut on his left, near the clavicle. A thin line of blood trickled out and became, as Sykes watched, a viscous black liquid. A burning smell permeated the air. Yale's eyeballs rotated furiously in their sockets and Sykes knew the fight could last no longer.

The blast took him by surprise, deafening him temporarily. When the smoke cleared, he saw Tobin to his left, pistol in hand. His ball had taken the sepoy's sword arm off, sending arm and sword clattering across the floor. A ringing sound echoing in his head, Sykes looked at the sepoy's wound, driven far more by curiosity than by horror. He was not sure what he had been expecting; perhaps something like the inner mechanism of a clock, with springs and flywheels in close proximity; perhaps criss-crossing telegraph wires that signalled commands; maybe, and he had no idea where this image came from, pouring out of the wound in an endless stream, an unending shower of tiny, glittering grains of sand.

Instead, he saw the gleam of what might have been bone and what was quite possibly raw flesh and what was almost certainly blood pouring out from the bearded sepoy's stub of arm, severed just above the elbow. It crossed his mind, for a moment, that the entire notion of clockwork dolls, of automatons, of Yale turning into one, had been imagined by him, and that, gripped by the hallucinatory atmosphere of the White Castle, he had lost his ability to distinguish between illusion and reality.

But he had no time to ponder this. The other sepoys crowded around their fallen, armless comrade. There was a blur of colours, a shivering motion in the crowd faster than the eye could blink. When he looked again, the fallen sepoy was gone and in his place, there stood a new rank of dolls, these ones armed with gleaming new Enfield rifles.

Behind him, there was a commotion. He saw Ryeman and Bones, faces flushed, with the White Mughal's bulk between them.

'Cease,' Ryeman shouted. 'Or I will gut your fat master like an overfed pig.' He held a knife behind the White Mughal's surprisingly small ear. Bones had his pistol pressed into the White Mughal's side.

The sepoys looked at Ryeman and the White Mughal. Silence flowed through the White Castle.

'HE IS NOT OUR MASTER,' the dolls chanted in unison. 'WE ARE NOT SLAVES.'

Bringing their Enfield rifles smartly to their sides, they came to attention. Their automaton feet stamped down. The building shuddered. Their brocaded, multicoloured coats shone in the dim corridor, illuminated from within by a mysterious source of light. Sykes fancied he saw glass valves and tubes in the chests of those in the front row, but then there was a rippling of shadows and they were simply brightly coloured coats, nothing more. The sepoys wheeled around and marched away and the corridor was empty and it was like they had never been there.

THEY RESTED IN the empty Ajaib Ghar, a grotesque company that had failed in its attempted coup. All they had achieved was the loss of their commanding officer, a vacancy that the White Mughal was keen to fill as he offered them endless advice on what to do. He spoke of negotiations that could still be carried out, of experiments unfinished and of dramatis personae yet to introduce themselves. He produced such a stream of contradictory information that Ryeman finally threatened to gag him, at which point the man sighed and sank his vast head on to his chest.

They were aware of the Colonel's presence, sequestered in the laboratory or the library, rebuffing all entreaties from his men to open the door. He could be heard singing from time to time, as cheerful as a butcher on a Sunday. Acrid smoke and sulphurous vapours drifted through cracks from his quarters into the Ajaib Ghar. There were shouts of tally ho, loud halloos, exclamations of surprise. On the other side, in the corridor where the duel had recently taken place, there was only silence. It looked deserted, yet should any of them but attempt to step into the corridor, they were persuaded back into the Ajaib Ghar by astonishingly accurate rifle fire. No other means of exit from the Ajaib Ghar existed.

They conferred briefly and agreed that their situation was dire. The Bibi had not been seen since the beginning of their mutiny. As for the Babu, no one could recall when he had last been seen, but the absence of both these figures suggested a plot of some kind afoot. Their supplies were in the stables and the ammunition they carried was limited. None had received lasting injuries, other than Yale. While his cut was not deep, his manner was curious, the things he said verging on the incoherent. He seemed to think he was in direct communication with the Colonel and sometimes affected the officer's tone and mannerisms. 'Indeed,' he said when asked if the cut was bothering him. 'A curious process, this transformation.' Then he gave Bones a tiny spring and laughed most hysterically.

They rotated sentry duties and dozed uncomfortably through the night. The clockwork sepoys showed no interest in coming into the Ajaib Ghar to administer the coup de grace. In the morning, they portioned out what food and drink could be salvaged from the wrecked supper table and pondered their situation again. They did not know what to do with the White Mughal. Tobin and Bones argued that since he had no value as a hostage and was straining their limited supplies, he should be turned loose to go and meet the sepoys. Ryeman offered to cut his throat instead, at which the White Mughal shuddered most theatrically.

A SECOND NIGHT passed with no change in the situation. The Ajaib Ghar, which was so vast, began to appear smaller, the corners where the men relieved themselves uncomfortably near. Sykes thought of the prisons the Colonel had pioneered and began to see faces in the darkness, these other, ghostly prisoners accompanying him in the Ajaib Ghar in one final, grand experiment being conducted by the invisible Colonel.

The men wondered what the automaton sepoys were doing and why they had confined them to this place. Bones subscribed to the theory that they were awaiting orders from someone. Who could that be? Tobin pondered over where they had originated, how they were animated, whether they could be said to have souls, at which point they all looked in the direction of the Kitabkhana.

The White Mughal, slumped against the wall, cleared his throat and held them with an expectant gaze. 'Gentlemen,' he said, haltingly. 'I may be able to provide some of the answers you seek.'

Ryeman rose, his intentions written plainly on his face.

'March in formation, men,' Yale said in the Colonel's voice. 'The enemy wavers. It is only a matter of time before we break through.'

'Oh, what does it matter?' Tobin said. 'We may as well let him speak.'

The White Mughal cleared his throat and began.

10

There were limits to human understanding, the White Mughal said. An umbrella implies the human form, a ship's sails the geometry of winds. The rational mind is evoked by a counting house, while there are those to whom idols suggest abomination. The most unusual inventions gathered in the Ajaib Ghar, however, represented something quite possibly beyond their comprehension. He himself had devoted his all to their pursuit and their understanding, and yet they eluded the grasp of his intelligence. Only Colonel Sleeman had come close to penetrating their mystery.

The White Mughal discoursed with eloquence while Sykes and his fellows sat around the table, restored to something like the suppers they had attended at the very beginning of their sojourn at the White Castle. The Colonel, of course, was not present, yet his absence took on significance in the light of the White Mughal's remarks. His personality impressed itself upon the men even if he remained silent behind his array of locked doors, with only the frequent emanation of sulphurous vapours suggesting that he might be busy experimenting in the Tajurbagah.

The inventions defied understanding and imagination, the White Mughal said. And this was because they were not his inventions, after all.

I am a polymath, the White Mughal had cried when they first met, a veritable genius. Really, Sykes understood now, he was nothing much more than an enterprising lout who had come to Calcutta from London to make his fortune and picked up a position at the Asiatic Society, where, in addition to obtaining a smidgen of expertise about the East, he had gained a great fondness for opium. It was this latter habit that led to a chance encounter in a den of inequity at Tiretta Bazaar, Calcutta's Chinatown. This, in turn, resulted in an invitation to dine at the Bengal Club until, through a series of not entirely implausible coincidences, he had become military and political adviser to the ruler of a kingdom neighbouring Bhutan.

He would modernise this little Himalayan Buddhist kingdom, the White Mughal decided on arriving there. Ensconced in the drafty palace, greeted with long, incomprehensible ceremonies, he picked up, to add to his other exotic habits, a taste for esoteric Buddhist manuscripts. He could not read them himself, but that was where the Babu, whom he met wandering in the bazaars of Darjeeling during a venture to purchase supplies, came in. The Babu claimed a familiarity with most languages of the East from Persian to Pali. The White Mughal was impressed enough to offer him a position on the spot. He wanted to establish a library in the palace, one arranged according to modern principles.

Yet the palace was far too antiquated a site for such ambitions, even if its ruler was well disposed towards futurism. Intrigues abounded, and gossip proliferated constantly. Of the White Mughal himself, some said he was a sorcerer, come to wreak great harm on the king, his people and the land. Others whispered, less fantastically but with no greater charity, that he was simply a European usurper, attempting to make his fortune in a realm where everything was allowed to the white man, and where all laws and customs were rewritten to satisfy the white man's ravenous, unquenchable appetite.

As much to get away from these rumours as to further his intentions of modernisation, the White Mughal suggested a new capital to the king. It was not an uncommon practice among great Oriental potentates. The construction of the White Castle duly took place in what until then had been a deserted valley, avoided by peasants and nomads alike for the vile reputation of the tarn located there. Then, as it would happen, the title to the kingdom fell to him.

Sykes was aware that certain relevant details were being passed over in this segment of the narrative. His fellows, however, did not seem to notice. Yale swayed back and forth, producing a most unpleasant creaking noise. Ryeman was attempting to collect the remaining dregs of wine into a single glass. Bones and Tobin had a glazed look in their eyes. Only the White Mughal appeared to be animated, growing into his story as he lulled them with his voice.

Shortly after his establishment as regent and headquartered at the White Castle, the White Mughal said, he acquired the first of his inventions. It was purchased from a nomad caravan passing through the vicinity, and whose chief haggler he paid the grand sum of three cowries and half a bag of rice. The object was not much to look at on first glance. It consisted of two metallic discs, each the size of a saucer. What distinguished it was that the discs were connected in some fashion, held together some eight inches apart by an unbreakable, invisible force. No wires or levers connected them. It was possible to pass one's hands between the discs. Yet they could not be pulled apart.

It was a most singular object, certainly, and he added it to his burgeoning collection. The other items were of a more conventional nature, gathered with single-minded determination from previous collections, objects purchased in Calcutta and Lucknow in auctions where he competed, through his agents, with merchant princes and nawabs and soldiers of sudden, great fortune. Yet the things thus acquired, among whom the White Mughal counted the Bibi, who appeared in the company of the Babu one monsoon evening with her most unusual story, could not be compared to that initial, single item picked up from a group of filthy, foul-smelling sheepherders.

HE MADE AN attempt at this stage to acquire the services of a scholar, someone who might be able to shed some light on the discs and also curate his growing collection. Word reached him of an inventor in Calcutta, a man of mixed race, very fond of drink, who might be persuaded to take on a salaried position at the White Castle. Negotiations were conducted via the offices of the Babu. A library and laboratory was set up adjoining the Ajaib Ghar in accordance with the inventor's instructions. Equipment was ordered, from London and Paris and Calcutta. Crates made tortuous journeys on ship and by land to deposit their lenses and weighing scales and sealed cylinders of chemical powders at his doorstep. Other things came from Calcutta, items that the White Mughal was not aware that he had ordered. On inquiring of the Babu, he was told that these were the man's personal inventions, not yet available to the world. Among them was the horse telegraph, the mirroring device and the observation balloon that had to be laboriously inflated in accordance with the inventor's instructions.

Then the inventor himself set out for the White Castle. The White Mughal sent an escort in recognition of his status. The party appeared after a long, arduous march. A guard of honour of native soldiers arranged themselves at the entrance. The musicians struck up 'For He's a Jolly Good Fellow', the only Western ditty they were capable of playing with any competence. The White Mughal watched as the palanquin doors were slid aside by servants who prepared to help the inventor down. There was nobody inside, or no human being. A goat-skin sack of water rested inside the palanquin, but it was hard to accept this object as the inventor to whom the White Mughal had paid such a handsome advance.

The palanquin bearers were questioned, as were the soldiers. All insisted that they had picked up, at Paltangunj, a very drunk man of Eurasian appearance. There had been routine halts, including one a few hours ago. He had been present on each of these occasions. Only magic of the darkest kind could explain his transformation into a sack of water.

There was much to the affair that did not quite meet the eye, the White Mughal thought, but nothing could be done about it. Under his directions, the Babu made inquiries all along the route, but without much success. There were rumours of an European expedition that had passed through the area, the possibility that palanquins had been mixed up. The White Mughal and the Babu spent some time looking over the copious notebooks the inventor had sent in one of his advance shipments. There were diagrams of other inventions that had been drawn from some realm of deep fantasy. An oculometer, a finial machine, even a boxlike contraption for dispensing coinage.

The White Mughal made attempts to find a second inventor. He had no luck. His collecting, however, went on, with other distinctive items making their way into the Ajaib Ghar. Word of his interest had spread in the realm, and items were often presented to him in spite of their having no collectability at all. His native soldiers brought him objects acquired through brigandage, hoping for baksheesh. Dishevelled nomads travelling in ragged caravans showed up to haggle over a two-headed lamb or a rotting fish with legs. A monstrous, diseased tooth in a jar was offered to him as the molar of a yeti, the so-called abominable snowman.

It was from such a group that he purchased, with some notions about beginning an animate collection, a most peculiar plant. Yet the plant, apart from being unidentifiable and most repulsive in presentation, had a tendency to produce headaches and hallucinations to those coming into contact with it. The White Mughal had it moved to a greenhouse and ceased his acquisition of animate matter for the time being.

Any regrets about collecting vanished when the Babu procured, through protracted negotiations with a gentleman in Mysore, an item that arrived packed in layers of burlap and straw. It was none other than the tiger-and-soldier mechanism. The Babu, wonderfully informed as always, said it was the secret twin to Tipu's tiger, possessing a few additional manoeuvres of its own. Yet even the Babu knew nothing of the craftsman who had made it.

The White Mughal found it gratifying to see these objects in the Ajaib Ghar. It was possible to civilise the world, to knit it together with vision. He served as a beacon of enlightenment and inquiry in the benighted mountains of Asia. Yet he was still intrigued by the discs purchased from the nomads, everything about which remained unfathomable.

SYKES OBSERVED THE White Mughal's words cast their spell on the faces of his fellow soldiers. Ryeman, if looked at suddenly, had the visage of an ape. Yale was a doll. Bones was scratching the supper table with unusually long nails. Tobin sat hunched over, shoulder blades jutting out and ready to burst through his uniform.

Would the White Mughal's tale cast any light on their present predicament? It was not like they could do anything but listen. They were spellbound, unable to stir themselves, unable to cease the White Mughal's ceaseless patter. Shadows had lengthened around them in the Ajaib Ghar. Sykes tried to recall if this were the second or the third evening of their confinement. He did not know for certain.

The White Mughal continued, heedless of the effect of his words on those around him, narrating his wonder about the origin of the discs and whether there were others like it. He began to pay careful attention to the accounts of his soldiers and the itinerant nomads, indulging them, in the hope of gathering useful information, by purchasing the increasingly useless, foul objects they kept bringing him.

He gradually heard of other mysterious objects. They were never in the possession of the raconteur in question, and none were discs like the one he possessed. What they shared with it was that they were incomprehensible, that they appeared to elude some fundamental principle of existence. He would explain what he meant by examples. Liquids that retained shape. Inanimate objects that propelled themselves.

The White Mughal became ever more certain that all these wonder objects, one of which sat in his Wonder Room, originated from a common source. He was convinced there was a lodestone up north somewhere, a seam so rich that could it only be discovered, it would yield miracles the likes of which had never been seen in any corner of the world, in any century. He imagined himself a Fellow of the Royal Society and a potentate to rival Solomon himself. He dispatched agents to make enquiries. They returned, starving, frostbitten, bedraggled, with not much more to show for their efforts than a handful of fresh rumours.

The White Mughal sifted carefully through these rumours, consulting the Babu every step of the way. He heard of a charismatic prince, schooled in London and Paris, who had transformed his backward kingdom through scientific inventions into a potent military power, one determined eventually to march south and claim the entire Indian subcontinent. He heard of a mountain republic governed by a council, some of whose members had travelled east from Europe in the aftermath of the 1848 revolution and who pinned their faith in a science that would bring about the triumph of the oppressed. There were accounts that made him think of the legend of Prester John and made him wonder if that fabled Christian kingdom in the east had finally been found.

Other tales attributed the inventions to neither kingdoms nor republics but to a monastery whose denizens aged very slowly and lived on to a couple of centuries. Among them could be found a disciple of Chopin's as well as an associate of the mathematician Giuseppe Lagrange. It was the latter who, in the fastness of his mountain laboratory in this monastery called Shangri La, had amused himself by producing trinkets like the connected discs and then moved on to increasingly complex inventions. Another report claimed, even more fancifully, that the objects originated in a place camped upon by an alien race, in resemblance nothing like Asiatics or Europeans. They were taller than seven feet, their skin shining green in the reflection of the snow. In other accounts, they were dwarfish, shaven-headed, with genders indistinguishable. They had journeyed from the stars in search of a companion who had gone missing in the Indian Ocean, using their mountain base to launch forays into a sea deeper than any other.

The final account the White Mughal received, from a spy who appeared to have penetrated farther than the rest, was simply of an immense zone of desolation.

There were no aliens there, no warriors or revolutionaries or monks. No trees could be seen, barely any light, simply the ashy residue and oil slick of a great devastation amid a dirty, greenish snow. In this Zone, of which the nomads most familiar with the region were unusually wary, lay traps the likes of which could not be described. Demons lurked there, the nomads said, as did portals to other worlds and other times. Sudden changes could be visited upon those unwary enough to come close to the Zone. A woman had been known to fly after going towards it. Another unfortunate had been rendered invisible. His wife and children heard him and felt him, distinctly. But he could not be seen. A third, a youth in his prime, vanished. He returned weeks later as an aged creature, toothless but insistent on recounting the horrors he had seen, with tales of a future when much of life had been exterminated. It was from this Zone that the discs had made their way to the White Mughal's Wonder Room.

NOT LONG AFTER the last spy presented his account, disturbances began to occur in areas where the Zone was said to be located. Reports came in of other spies making inquiries, agents dispatched by someone other than the White Mughal. Enterprising scavengers were spotted loitering around the edges of the Zone in the hope of salvaging something invaluable, perilous though all approaches to it were. Eventually, adventurers attempted to break into the Zone itself to capture some great prize. Nomads and villagers refused to act as guides, but they were press-ganged into service when the lure of money was not enough to convince them.

All efforts to enter the Zone failed, but there remained the mystery of the occasional eldritch object materialising in some village or in the possessions of a traveller. A link of chain that propelled itself was discovered on the corpse of a mendicant. A child who had wandered far from her village was found clutching a cylinder that perpetually refilled itself with a transparent liquid that could not be identified.

There was some way out for such things, which meant that there was some way in. A story began to take hold that the Zone allowed people in, but only those who stated their desires truthfully. It was like a wishing well in that regard. Yet no one was successful in gaining its permission to enter. A monk was said to have starved himself for forty days on its boundary, wishing only to gaze upon the face of the infinite and the formless inside the Zone, but without success.

Then the White Mughal heard a most disturbing account, of an emissary sent by the Nana Sahib, the Demon of Cawnpore, seeking an entry into the Zone in search of a super weapon that would expel the English. The emissary had failed, returning almost a lunatic, but the White Mughal was told of a second delegation being prepared. This one was made up of Danka Baba and Magadh Rai, conspirators who would not be deterred so easily. Finally, a curious incident occurred when the White Mughal sent some of his soldiers on a mission of pacification to a distant village that had rebelled against his efforts to collect revenues. His men returned terrified, with disjointed accounts of being greeted by precise rifle fire from an army of automatons. They had seen no tax-evading natives and, most terrifyingly, the village being defended shimmered, disappearing from time to time.

The White Mughal dallied no further. He understood that the gravity of the matter far exceeded questions of personal gain or glory. The fate of civilisation hung in the balance. A message was dispatched in haste to Fort William in Calcutta. Word came back to him of an expedition setting out immediately for the Zone, led by a certain Colonel Sleeman.

THE EXPEDITION'S MAPS had been imprecise, its intelligence scattered, its journey arduous to the extreme. Yet, the White Mughal understood, the expedition had succeeded in finding its way to the Zone. Many were the conversations he had had in the Kitabkhana, after supper, discussing with Colonel Sleeman over amontillado and cigars how he had found his way to that fabled realm, the details of the journey and what he and his men had seen as they stood, finally, on the edge of the Zone.

Sykes was perturbed by a subtle change in their surroundings. They were not in the Ajaib Ghar, starving and hunted, but somewhere else. Snatches of song drifted through his consciousness, tunes rendered by the voices of women, and sometimes he smelt, bubbling in a vast pot somewhere, the most delicious of curries. There was a confusion to the senses and he wondered if the other men registered these changes too. He looked at their faces. They were still and silent, like automatons capable of ceasing motion with the flick of an internal lever.

The Colonel described the march to the White Mughal. Information was picked up from the natives, often through new modes of persuasion he had schooled himself in while in the Americas. Some of the spies and adventurers spoken of in the White Mughal's report were tracked down and questioned vigorously. Entire villages or caravans had on occasion to be subjected to the scrutiny of the Colonel's intelligence. Sometimes, special attention needed to be paid to the children, who possessed raw, unfiltered information, more useful to the expedition than the garbled, tongue-twisting tales terrified adults were prone to blurt out. During all sessions of interrogation, however, it was important to be aware of the method underlying the process, the philosophy holding it all together. It was a question of the rational mind meeting the primitive. Man was encountering his distant childhood in these engagements. He had to adjust himself accordingly.

Colonel Sleeman therefore wrote out his questions with the aid of natural elements. The answers he sifted through with science. Fire was useful in provoking truthful responses, water even more so. Air could be withheld, the earth emphasised. Sensory faculties had to be paid attention to, especially the stimuli one could impart through sight and sound, through touch, taste and smell. Cold could provide a gradual change in the person being questioned but demanded patience, needing time to work its power. Sharp tactile influences, on the other hand, were swift in provoking a flood of information but often brought in their wake much that was unreliable and irrelevant.

The White Mughal felt an awe for the Colonel as he listened to his account, and how the expedition, carefully asking questions and as carefully considering the answers, had drawn ever closer to the source, relentless in its quest in spite of the Zone's efforts to protect itself with misinformation.

Sykes was aware of a stirring around him. His companions had given the impression of being lulled by the White Mughal's words. Now something was beginning to penetrate their trance state. Sykes found himself in the grip of most peculiar images, of village barns stuffed with limbs and of naked creatures cowering in freshly dug graves. A monotonous sensation took hold of him as he saw vast expanses of dirty, blackened snow and knife-sharp precipices. Prayer flags, their colours faded, stood out against the backdrop of a sky dappled with clouds. He heard men shouting, gesticulating fiercely.

Then he had a sensation of swimming, of floating in the air, of being uncertain which way was up and which down. Cries arose around him and he felt in himself the most curious of transformations, of pores opening up, of liquid running down his legs, of a different distribution of weight in his torso and along his hips. He was not displeased with his transformation, not at all, nor with the startlingly different tinge that his skin had taken on. A pipe sounded, dreamy and mad, rising sharply before it faded. Then he heard voices raised in confusion around him.

'Do you mean to say the Colonel led an expedition to the Zone?' Bones asked. 'An expedition prior to ours?'

'Not prior to yours, gentlemen,' the White Mughal replied. 'I understand that memory, as well as other facets of intelligence, were affected by the encounter with the Zone. You will therefore forgive me for stating the obvious. YOU were the expedition to the Zone.'

11

A wine glass coursed through the air and shattered behind the White Mughal. Shards of glass sparkled on the floor, dark spots blossoming on the White Mughal's jacket. The White Mughal dabbed at the spots with a soiled napkin. When he was satisfied, he addressed the men again, his voice steady and his manner unhurried.

'I mean to say that you are the remnants of the expedition to the Zone,' he said.

Voices rose and fell around Sykes but he could not interpret them. There was a scraping of chair legs, confused sounds. Beneath what he had thought of as his memory, what he had thought of as himself, he seemed to possess another memory, another self. In this new, subterranean memory, he recalled an expedition that had set out from Calcutta, swallowing village after village, encampment after encampment, a python with boundless appetite, until they had reached the edge of … He was unable to complete the thought. In fact, who was the 'he' who thought? Did he know who he was? Was he who he had thought himself to be? Had he ever?

SYKES CAME TO as if from a daze. Rain pattered on the skylights. A weak, insipid light filtered into the room. It was almost morning. Was it possible that an entire night had passed listening to the White Mughal's account?

The White Mughal was speaking of transformations. He mentioned Ovid, metamorphosis, changelings, fairies, transmogrification and the alchemist's stone. He named famous vivisectionists in Europe and the United States and Mary Shelley's novel *Frankenstein*. He spoke of Tibetan thought forms and ancient Oriental manuscripts. Every single surviving member of Colonel Sleeman's expedition had been affected by the encounter with the Zone, he said, but what had made it so hard to comprehend was that each had been affected in a distinct, individual manner, often most subtle to begin with.

Yale had been subject to the most obvious of the changes. He exhibited some curious tendencies, first noticed by the Colonel, including a stiffness in his movements, a lack of limberness to his joints. Yet, the Colonel had observed, it was not that Yale was truly lacking in dexterity. In errands given to him by the Colonel, he demonstrated speed, strength and a range of motion exceeding what the human body was capable of. The stiffness or ungainliness in him was simply the result of a dissonance between what one expected from the human form and what Yale was capable of. The Colonel took note of this matter and of mannerisms no less fascinating. Yale did not partake of any nourishment, whether solid or liquid, although he was once found by the Babu drinking oil from the lamps in the White Castle. He was often spotted in the Ajaib Ghar, petting the clockwork tiger, with which he had a particular affinity. He was also given to attempting to enter the Tajurbagah. In this, he had succeeded on a couple of occasions, where he showed a distinct partialness for the two discs, while on another instance, the Colonel discovered him attempting to purloin an assortment of chemicals and a Faraday cage.

The Colonel discussed his findings in tête-à-têtes with the White Mughal. He began to point out, and the White Mughal himself saw, the subtly changed characteristics of all the men who had returned from the Zone. Ryeman had grown hirsute, his posture more apelike with each passing day. Bones, with his prominent canines, wrinkles in his face and prehensile claws, resembled nothing known to man, while Tobin had acquired a pair of shoulder blades that pushed out as to suggest a pair of growing wings. In Sykes, one saw womanly traits and an almost native hue. 'Automaton, Ape, Monster, Angel and Native Woman,' the Colonel ticked off, bemused that only he appeared to have changed not at all.

On some nights, when the men, with the exception of Yale, were sound asleep, helped by the sleeping draughts administered with their food, the Colonel slipped into their quarters to take relevant measurements. He felt the sharpness of Bones's canines and ascertained the changing shape of Ryeman's skull. He calculated the length of what were undoubtedly wings emerging from Tobin's back and prodded Sykes's mammaries, perhaps lingering over this latter task longer than was strictly necessary for scientific purposes.

But Colonel Sleeman had not merely collected data. He had philosophised, with the able assistance of the White Mughal, on what was happening to the men in the aftermath of their attempt to enter the Zone. He speculated that the transformation in each individual was in some way a manifestation of already existing preferences. A lesser man would have been perturbed by such findings. The Colonel, however, had reconstructed the events as accurately as possible from their discovery of the Zone all the way to their pell-mell retreat.

There had been a blinding green light, he had narrated to the White Mughal, and glowing yellow slicks of snow. He remembered a kind of *splitting*, he called it, shadowy versions of some of his men walking vertically up cliff faces, while their originals stared bewildered at their doubles. The farther the doubles went, the fainter the originals became, until with a shimmer of rainbows, originals and doubles both vanished. The majority of the men had so disappeared, Yale among them.

Those few left unmolested found themselves unable to advance farther. Some felt they were impeded by an invisible wall. Others were incapable of motion. The Colonel, after attempting in vain to prod them on, advanced by himself. He suffered no difficulty in movement. On Colonel Sleeman marched, impelled by a power within that was equal to what he faced in this abominable Zone. The shrieks of his men sounded behind him. Before him, there lay a vast, unending city square over which tower-like buildings loomed and an unending corrosive rain poured from a gunmetal sky. He gradually became conscious that he was making no progress at all. The distance between him and the remnants of his expedition was exactly what it had been. On this unending square, he was an insect. On this unending square, he was kin to Achilles' tortoise. He looked up. The towering buildings were lit up in a green glow under the rainy, grey sky. Harpies shrieked in the air. It was a world abandoned by G-d.

He turned around, with regret. He was allowed to do so, to make his way back to his impeded men, to lead the survivors away from that place. They staggered, like men blinded and deafened by artillery batteries thundering in a field of war, away from the Zone. They spoke to each other not at all. Visions of what he had seen danced in the Colonel's mind. After three days of descent, shortly before they rejoined their mounts, the Colonel and his men came across Yale sitting naked, cross-legged, Buddha fashion, in the middle of a narrow pass. He was bereft of both speech and memory, although it turned out that both would return over the course of the next few weeks, if in a somewhat erratic manner.

WITHIN THE SANCTUARY of the White Castle, the Colonel had hypothesised on the nexus between Yale's disappearance and his changed behaviour. Had something been done to him in that absence? Had he come into contact with an object in the Zone, something like those discs but perhaps even more powerful? Perhaps, the Colonel had pondered, an object from the Zone was a sufficient but not necessary condition for transformation. Perhaps the Zone itself held the power of transformation, one it imbued the objects with. Who, after all, could say what the Zone is or does?

If it was the Zone that initiated the changes, this would explain the transformations in the other men. They were affected to a lesser degree by virtue of their reduced contact, while Yale had spent something like three days within the Zone. Yet there was one anomaly, as always, the Colonel noted. That was himself, unchanged in the slightest fashion. He scrutinised himself keenly, stripping down and asking the White Mughal and the Babu to examine him for anything that might strike them as out of the ordinary.

The Babu, gifted in many ways, was useless when it came to this.

He discovered something shockingly new every other moment about the Colonel's feet, the Colonel's head, the Colonel's member. The White Mughal was forced to bring a halt to his feverish speculations. The Colonel was very much the man he had been prior to the expedition. The Colonel decided to put aside the question of his bewildering stability and turned his attention back to his men.

He studied Yale's fascination with the Tajurbagah and the tiger. He saw that, after two weeks of proximity between Yale and the tiger, it appeared that a second transformation was taking place, akin to but also a reversal of the process Yale was undergoing. The tiger was changing too. But if Yale demonstrated attributes that could only be described as mechanical, the clockwork tiger was beginning to exhibit traits that were indisputably animate. Its range of motion grew more subtle day by day, its sounds becoming ever more graduated on the scale of realism until, one day, it simply stepped off the pedestal, entered the Tajurbagah and made the acquaintance of the Colonel. The Colonel wondered if there was a transformation contagion, passed on from the Zone to Yale. From Yale, it had been communicated to the clockwork tiger. Whence would it go from the tiger?

Certainly, the White Mughal continued, there was a new dynamism to the process of transformation brought about by the tiger. An energy pulsed through the Ajaib Ghar, affecting objects and native servants. It radiated ever outward, to the White Castle, the greenhouse and the surrounding realms, while undoubtedly changing Yale into an automaton. It sped up the process of metamorphosis in the other men of Colonel Sleeman's company. Only the Colonel remained unaffected.

In that absence of change in the Colonel, the White Mughal believed, arose perhaps the only act he could fault the Colonel with. He decided that he needed to transform himself, by any and all means necessary. He had a theory, where Yale, the tiger and the discs were the most powerful agents of transformation, so that were he only to place himself at the centre of their triangulation, he would be changed too. The White Mughal paused for breath. That was the origin of the misunderstanding he had been attempting to correct with the company, and he believed that things would not have taken such a drastic turn had those gathered listened to him instead of attempting their ill-fated mutiny.

SYKES DID NOT believe a word that the White Mughal had said. His tale rendered him a bystander, an innocent, the injured party. Having finished his tale, the man had left his seat at the table. Now he strolled with his hands behind his back, so much at ease that he could have been taken for a jailer with them as his prisoners. A damp smell came to Sykes's nostrils, a smell of mud and rot and old age mingling with their own bodily odours and that pervasive smell of sulphur. A pale morning light edged in through the skylight, as if uncertain of the scene it illuminated.

'I believe I may still be of assistance,' the White Mughal said. He had stopped pacing and stood at the door to the Tajurbagah. Sykes could hear a most curious noise behind him, like that of castanets. He looked at the source. It was Yale, clicking his teeth. Sykes thought of a tale the Russian had told him in London, of the Nutcracker and the seven-headed Mouse King.

'You lie,' Sykes said with effort. 'No such expedition took place. Explain, if you will, the corpses encountered near the forest on our way here. Who were those natives fleeing from?'

The White Mughal looked chastened, saddened. 'I hesitate to remind you, gentlemen, but it seems you have forgotten. You interrogated with vigour on your way to the Zone. On the way back, you pillaged with even greater force. Those who were forewarned and were able to, fled. Others were cut down where they stood.'

'That cannot be,' Sykes said.

'You did not leave me a single native cultivator, gentlemen. You were the ones who killed every able-bodied man in that column of escaping villagers. I rode out to meet you and beg you to desist. But you made me proceed on a forced march that challenged my faculties to the extreme. Then, you commandeered my abode as your headquarters, even while, in front of the greenhouse, you set up a firing squad. Every day, you demanded a new subject for your shooting until there were no servants left, none who had not been transformed into an automaton. The Colonel humoured you throughout, and asked me to do the same, so as not to interfere with his study of the transformation.'

'Slash and burn, kill and plunder,' Ryeman said, scratching himself most vigorously.

Sykes examined his memories. Nothing. No recollection at all of the massacres the White Mughal spoke about. He looked at his companions. They too had no idea what the man spoke of.

'How long have we been here?' Sykes asked. 'Three weeks, by my estimation.' He looked at his companions. They nodded in agreement.

'You encountered me in August, gentlemen,' the White Mughal said. 'Shortly after you had sacked and plundered Paltanganj, driven, I understand from the Colonel, by a demonic force that appeared to multiply your numbers and reduced the far more numerous soldiers at that garrison into gibberish terror and lunacy. If we could look out, you would see the snow thick and cold on the mountains. It is February. What have you done to my retainers, to my native bodyguard, to the prisoners from Paltanganj you forced on a march through the mountains? Do you not remember your martial law courts? If you choose to look in the lake, the bones of your justice are still visible.'

With trembling hands, Sykes reached for his pistol. Faint memories were stirring in his head, but they were not exactly as the White Mughal had described them. Even the expedition to the Zone held other mysteries, ones not illuminated by the White Mughal. Otherwise, why did Sykes recall a man who looked like a younger, slender brother to the White Mughal at the edge of the Zone? That man was not corpulent but lean and browned as a native. Perhaps the transformation wrought upon the White Mughal at the Zone had been to make him fifteen years older and a hundred stones heavier! He looked at the White Mughal again, at that face as false as a mask. Underneath those blue eyes, some other creature lurked, delighting in Sykes's confusion.

WHAT WAS THAT horrible smell? Why was there water underneath his feet? Sykes was aware of a transformation in the Ajaib Ghar itself, but before he could comprehend this change, the door to the Tajurbagah opened. The Colonel stood before them with a sheepish smile on his face like a baby awaking from a blissful nap. Drool trickled down his chin. He was wearing his red coat and boots but nothing else. 'Kitty,' he said with delight. 'Here, kitty.' In his hands were the discs from the Zone.

Sykes followed the Colonel's gaze, past the White Mughal, past the men gathered around the table, to the vastness of the Ajaib Ghar. It was lit up brilliantly by a sun that had broken through the clouds and was probing the hall with its rays. The tiger stood at the other end of the hall. Even at such a vast distance, its disdain for him, for everyone in the Ajaib Ghar, was palpable. It had grown larger and its proportions were more subtle, the bulges far less automaton and much more like the real thing. Yes, its colour was that of paint, the texture of its body that of highly polished wood as it padded forward with an easy, swinging grace. But its eyes were alive, assessing, intelligent.

Midway through the Ajaib Ghar, the tiger stopped. Behind him, the door shimmered with rainbow colours. The clockwork sepoys were arranged there. The Colonel giggled. 'Kitty,' he said. 'Pretty kitty.'

At his feet, Sykes felt the distinct lapping of water. From somewhere far away, there came the smell of something burning. The tiger had drawn closer. The sepoys remained at the door. Ryeman's hand began reaching, stealthily, for the pistol. The beast stopped and looked at him in a manner that was almost human. A blush spread across Ryeman's face as he withdrew his hand. The creature resumed its approach. It did not intend to harm them, Sykes thought. There was some other matter on its mind as it passed the supper table, ignored the Colonel sitting on the floor calling out to it and peered through the door to the Tajurbagah. Yale rose from his seat. Sykes could not withhold a gasp. He was completely transformed.

The tiger and Yale looked at each other. There was in their gaze what Sykes could only describe as a communion. Yale's arms and legs rose mechanically as he began marching in the direction of the sepoy dolls. The tiger walked next to him. On Yale marched, without a glance at his former comrades, becoming more mechanical with each receding, echoing step. The sepoys rearranged themselves as Yale reached them. There was an explosion of colours, a tinkle of mechanical sounds, and then Yale had vanished, just one more automaton among other automatons.

A manic laughter broke out behind them, accompanied by an unearthly scream. Sykes, turning around, was confronted with an astonishing sight. The Colonel had somehow manoeuvred the White Mughal's massive head between the discs in his hands. Even as they watched, the Colonel let go of the discs. The White Mughal rose violently into the air, impelled up towards the roof by the discs. His vast bulk obscured the skylight above them as his body met the ceiling. 'Help me, help me,' he cried, kicking furiously even as the Colonel, cheering wildly, aimed a pistol at him and sent a ball crashing into the ceiling.

Bones and Tobin approached the Colonel and were forced to take evasive action as the Colonel fired at them. Something exploded behind Sykes, filling the Ajaib Ghar with a thick yellow smoke and the smell of sulphur. Ryeman brought the Colonel down. The floor beneath them shook from an explosion. Sykes watched a line of liquid creep through the floorboards. Then, with a tremendous sound, a fountain of yellowish water burst from below, drenching people in foul, astringent liquid. 'This way,' Bones cried, gesturing Sykes towards the Site of Experiments. Ryeman and Tobin were already through, taking the Colonel with them.

'Help me,' the White Mughal cried as Sykes ran. He could not help looking up. The White Mughal had expanded even more in volume. The ceiling strained from the force of that massive body pushing upward. The skylight shattered violently and the White

Mughal burst out of the Ajaib Ghar, glass raining down. Sykes saw no more as he rushed into the Tajurbagah.

MORE EXPLOSIONS SHOOK the building as they made their way through the Tajurbagah, through a final set of doors that sent them hurtling out towards the back of the White Castle. They ran to their saddled horses, the Colonel offering no resistance as he was lifted on to his mount. His eyes were glazed, but someone had found breeches for him and managed to dress him.

They rode hard towards the front of the White Castle, wheeling to their left in unison as they galloped up the embankment. The lake bubbled around them. Sykes, bringing up the rear, sat loosely in his saddle, his gaze turned backwards, his eyes on the castle. They were halfway along the embankment when the clockwork sepoys appeared, pouring out of the front door of the White Castle, with no great show of hurry. The tiger was with them.

More explosions sounded behind, sending ripples through the lake. Flames licked at the windows of the White Castle. Smoke poured out of nooks and crannies. The sepoys took up formation in front of the castle. They were getting ready to shoot, Sykes realised, and he let off a round from his pistol. The distance was too great. The sepoys did not shoot back. Was their geometry at fault, their guiding mechanisms awry? No, they did not intend to fire. Rifles on their shoulders, they watched Sykes and his fellow riders calmly, dispassionately, while behind them the White Castle, with what sounded like an immense, world-weary sigh, sank slowly into the ground.

12

They rode hard but purposeless, with only a faint notion of where they were. The White Castle, while vanishing, had taken the known world with it. Darjeeling, their original destination, was now a name of legend, Calcutta and London cities sunken in the rising tides of restless, raging seas. They hoped to find a way south, but as they rode on, the mountains hemmed them in, looming over them like the sinister elders of an unknown race, sending them in directions that seemed all wrong.

Steep climbs that appeared initially to lead them towards a promising pass instead meandered on inconclusively, the trail twisting and turning and doubling back on itself. Sometimes, the trees closed in on them like an army preparing for an assault. At other moments, along open stretches of broken, rocky ground, the sun beat mercilessly on their heads.

Bones muttered about the Horse Latitudes as they stopped to consult their ever more speculative maps, but his words were nearly incomprehensible. His prominent canines, extending out of his mouth, chafed most uneasily against his reddened, raw skin. The rest of the company was not faring much better. Whether they were transforming or not, whether there was any truth to be ascribed to the White Mughal's account or not, something had happened to them all during their sojourn at the White Castle.

Sykes led the company, Bones and Tobin flanking him. Colonel Sleeman, who had proved to be most troublesome, with a tendency to veer off course whenever they were not paying attention to him, had been entrusted to the hirsute Ryeman. On they kept, picking their way through narrow passes, dismounting to lead their horses along rocky, treacherous pathways. Above them, silhouetted against a perfectly cloudless sky, floated the White Mughal, his faint cries more or less indecipherable. Occasionally, a wind magnified his words. Then they all heard, most distinctly, 'Help me! Help me!'

He maintained the same, steady altitude, rising no higher or lower, a fat blot in the sky. As the day grew on, the sun beating strong on the back of their necks, his cries of help gave way to a chanting and a singing and finally a murmured monologue, giving the impression that, up in those lofty, rarefied realms, the White Mughal had encountered a final, spectral gathering to listen to his unceasing lies.

In the evening, they found themselves on a plateau. The White Mughal was very close now, his blue eyeballs staring at them. He had become lean, almost as cadaverous as the Babu. 'Omnia Mei Sunt,' he cried. Sykes thought it nonsense until he recalled it as the motto he had seen on the White Mughal's coat of arms on the march from Paltangunj, and whose meaning Tobin had translated to him as 'Everything belongs to me.'

Did everything still belong to him? The White Mughal's proportions began to expand like he were filling up with vapours. He bulged and seemed on the verge of exploding, yet none other than Sykes paid him any attention. Sykes took the chance to survey his companions, at the transformations they were undergoing. He did not know what to make of the canines, the apelike chatter, the appendages. On a blanket spread on the ground, the Colonel sat cross-legged, a drooling idiot Buddha. What had he done to himself in the laboratory?

When all but Tobin, on sentry duty, were asleep, Sykes checked himself under the blanket. There was a full moon in the sky which revealed the White Mughal. He no longer made any sounds at all, but he had become so vast as to resemble a monstrous, elongated airship, swaying gently in the night breeze and connected to the company by an invisible string.

SYKES WAS TROUBLED that night by the kind of opium dreams he had not had for a while. The White Mughal floated like a vast balloon at the end of a string. He was wearing an Oriental dress of some kind, and it billowed around him like the sails of a flying ship. Colonel Sleeman held the other end of the string in his right hand. With his left hand, he waved a Union Jack, drawing circles in the air like someone carrying out a particularly intricate signalling manoeuvre. Artillery fire blossomed in the sky around the White Mughal. More balloon-like humans appeared around the White Mughal, like supporting warships. The sky was riven with lightning and thunder, and Sykes, deep in a hole in the ground, cowered.

When the sun rose in the morning, the White Mughal was gone. No one other than Sykes seemed to take note of his absence or remember him.

TIME PASSED IN fits and starts. Sykes often could not tell what season it was. There were long stretches when he thought they were in the heart of an endless winter, their extremities frost-bitten, their mounts steaming as they heaved their way up narrow, frozen tracks. On other occasions that did not last quite as long, they wandered in a vernal dream, the valleys filled with game, the streams running with ice-cold, fresh water.

Something had happened to the seasons in the parts where they travelled, a confusion of the right order of things. Spring and winter, summer and monsoon existed simultaneously in adjoining territories. There were weeks, months, years when the heat came off the ground in rippling waves, a desert wind scorching their face as dust storms loomed in suggestive shapes on the horizon. Then, it was always raining, the gullies flooded as thunder echoed and lightning flashed and they cowered under an outcrop.

Still, they wandered. There were nights when the skies were awash with stars as they slept in their rough blankets, the horses huddled together. Drifting off to sleep, Sykes heard the sky sighing like the tide coming in off the California coast. He felt himself free of all his agitation as he fell asleep.

They encountered villagers and nomads, but without exception they were hospitably greeted. It was a good thing. They were not capable of commencing hostilities of any sort. Bones and Tobin had stopped riding and taken to loping alongside the horses, while an increasingly apelike Ryeman maintained erratic charge of an increasingly erratic Colonel.

The Colonel had wanted a fierce band of brothers to hunt down a sheep gone astray; he had wished for a host of avenging angels that would destroy a malfunctioning machine. Now they themselves were astray, malfunctioning. Vengeance and destruction were no longer theirs. Sykes was grateful that their astonishing features led not to outright assault but to respectful tributes from the superstitious denizens of the realms they passed through, their eccentric appearance being taken as a touch of the divine.

Their maps were useless, their compasses prone to erratic behaviour. Sykes attempted to navigate with the help of the stars, but his knowledge of the skies was limited, patchy. The world above was as unfamiliar to him to as the world around him. They did not starve or freeze to death, but his sense of time unravelled even further. It became as unreal as the land and the skies around him. News filtered to him, fantastic things recounted to the strange band of misfits by the tribesmen they met. The rebellion had started again, Sykes heard, but the protagonists were more colourful than before.

From itinerant travellers and shamans, Sykes heard accounts that had in them something of the future visions the Colonel and the White Mughal had once sketched at supper. He listened to tales of wheeled carriages that took soldiers into forests and mountain valleys to rape and pillage. Enormous blockhouses had been erected everywhere around India, with fortified posts between the blockhouses dividing the land into stockades. Armoured trains patrolled the boundaries along railway tracks. Masked faces cast demonic spells across vast distances. Mobs gathered to kill and rape as giant, talking heads urged them on from the skies. Airborne, infernal engines doused entire villages in burning water. He heard of a peasant rebellion led by a flying monk. And the turmoil was not just in the lands below. Ahead of them, up above in the shadows of the mountains, equally fantastic things had come into being—the kingdom of G-d on earth, a republic without fear, or the beginning of the end of the world.

SYKES KNEW NO longer why he rode on in charge of his motley crew. It had been a long time since they had come across any settlements, and the company was utterly dependent on what Bones and Tobin scavenged from their surroundings. The weather was cold once again. He was relieved to see a village on a ridge ahead of them, perhaps half a day's ride away.

They came on to it just as the sun dipped behind a neighbouring peak. Sykes's relief gave way to surprise. The inhabitants were scurrying away rapidly as the company drew near. When they entered the village, there was nothing to be seen except a deserted street winding past silent, shut-up huts. It reminded Sykes, in a flash, of the abandoned prospecting camps he had seen during his time in California. Put in some forgotten utensils and discarded boots, and it would be perfect.

It might have been this old memory, surfacing from a past that was no longer his, that made him so careless. The first volley took him utterly by surprise. If there was no massacre, it was only because they had fired too early. Sykes did not have a clear idea of where the shots had come from, but the huts ahead were the most likely source. The street was too long and too winding for them to charge through the field of fire, and they began a hasty retreat in a mess of equine haunches and hooves and rearing heads and ungainly limbs, trying to turn in what had become a narrow causeway. Only the Colonel, drooling down his splendid red coat, cantered down the street. 'Tally ho,' he cried. 'The fox at last.' Sykes galloped ahead and seized the reins of the Colonel's horse, guiding it back and turning it around.

They had not fired too early, he discovered when they finally made it out of the village, to the mouth of a narrow pass. Beyond were wider, forested tracts where they might hope to conceal themselves. But tree trunks closed off the trail they had ridden down not a few hours ago. Behind the shrubbery, the glint of muskets and swords was unmistakable.

The company halted while still out of firing range. Sykes saw a rider come out from behind the stockade. Even from this distance, he could make out the scars on the Bibi's gorgon-like face. He did not need to think twice before wheeling his horse away, leading the company off the track, riding hard down the slope and plunging into the icy-cold stream, making for that one stretch of land available to them between the press of enemy muzzles, even though he knew in his heart of hearts that they were riding into what was called the Zone.

SYKES WAS NOT sure when the tracts of the Zone began to display the characteristics that moved them into the realm of the uncanny. It probably started with what at first was a pleasant change in that the land was flat. The mountains, a series of white fangs, loomed in the far horizon, in something like the shape of a semicircle. Sometimes, they leant over the travellers, like a coven of witches peering into a cauldron. Behind Sykes, it was all fog, mist and haze, with nothing to be seen of where they had parted ways with the Bibi's ambushing marauders.

At first, the flat land was easy going, an almost featureless stretch where the ground was sometimes snow, sometimes salt and often sand. They saw no animals and no sign of water. Only the occasional shrub or rock brought variety to the landscape. In the evening, the land seemed to have elevated itself through their day's journey. The sky brushed their heads. The moon was a red disc in that low, unstable ceiling.

On their second morning, they picked up tracks going north. Sykes estimated three riders. He thought the tracks were fresh, not more than a day old. He wondered why they appeared out of nowhere, in the middle of the desert, like riders dropped from the sky by airship. It made him suspicious and he looked all around. Behind him, the fog had rolled away. In the sharp morning light, he saw with a shock the place where they had entered the Zone. He could even make out the glimmer of the river in the distance, where they had crossed pell-mell, Ryeman struggling with the Colonel's mount. After all of the past day's riding, they had made a circle back to their starting place. Or it was as if they had not moved at all.

He examined the tracks again. One set of humanish footprints was visible alongside that of the riders, and another that could without too much invention be called lupine. He did not dare look at his companions, or indeed, at himself. He did not remember giving the orders to march on, and yet march on they did.

THE FLAT LAND was suddenly populated. Ruins built by some giant race, vacant structures whose roofs had fallen in, loomed in their path. Sykes and his companions soon learnt to avoid these buildings, which did not remain in place and could not be used for orientation.

There were trees that reached towards them, totem poles that leant into their path. Pools like mirrors reflected the sky before they inexplicably extinguished themselves. Vast rocks hunched in upon themselves like philosophers, the wind keening into their ears. Cyclopean arches dreamt of long-vanished palaces, and domes and flying buttresses materialised out of a sudden yellow mist even as the ground at their feet oozed slime and turds.

There was a constant olfactory assault visited upon the sojourners. They found themselves skirting a swamp that brought tears to their eyes with its smell of burning chillies. When they had left the swamp behind, they found themselves in an immense, dusty plain over which sat a yellow haze, equally noxious, acidic and redolent of used gunpowder and spent fireworks.

More than appearance was at stake. There were magnetic forces that twisted and tugged at them from the rocks and buildings should they not maintain safe distance. Tobin was once flung into the air, and only because of his monstrous wings was he able to right himself, swimming back through the most powerful of air currents until the crew were able to throw him a line and haul him back to safety. Sometimes, they saw ghostly airships sailing silently through the skies above, escorted by elongated white clouds. Towers loomed in the distance, giant paintings flickering on their surface, while the bells and howls and shrieks of an immense bacchanalia echoed from within and booming, echoing voices repeated words that they could not finish.

On they went still, on and on into a place that had no beginning and no end. Sykes felt his hair grow long even as the Colonel shrank, his head retaining its proportions and his body growing ever smaller until he had to be carried on Ryeman's back in a sling, a monstrous baby with a wicked adult face that crooned what sounded like passages from *Small Wars*. When they slept, Sykes was often woken by Bones howling plaintively into the night. Was that Tobin in the air, wings extended behind him, lit up by the moon?

13

Once again, the land before them changed. It was a vast, boundless tract, utterly featureless, through which they plodded at unvarying pace. Sykes had no idea how long they had been going when he saw, through the yellow haze, twinkling lights of some kind. Some instinct made him adjust their route, away from the lights. It was no use. The haze cleared in an instant. They were afloat in a dark, black ocean, the sky above bursting with stars, while in front of them, in the distance, there floated a fantastic island city bristling with lights. No matter which way they went, they were always approaching the lights, which grew ever brighter and now came accompanied by the sound of chimes striking clearly in the cold, bare night.

It was a massive tent erected in the desert, the lights around it dimming as they rode up to it. Sykes was jolted by a wave of tiredness as he dismounted. His companions fell in step behind without a word, ready to take part in some final parade. He blinked when he pushed aside the folding door and stepped inside.

BRIGHT LANTERNS WERE scattered everywhere, amid piles of soft carpeting. On and on the interior of the tent went, bigger by far than what had been suggested by its outside. Within that, an immense crowd had gathered, silent and expectant. Above, Tibetan prayer flags fluttered in a non-existent wind. Sykes rubbed his face to dispel this vision being thrown up by the Zone. He did not know how such a tent could be set up amid such a waste.

He coughed as he was enveloped by the cloying fume of some kind of native tobacco. For a moment, he thought he might actually fall to the floor. The wave of dizziness passed, and when he surveyed his surroundings, his eyes had adjusted to the eldritch brightness. There were people everywhere, in small clusters, a collection that outrivalled even the Viceroy's balls—or was it the Governor General?—in Alipore in Calcutta. There were the usual native grandees, the maharajahs and nawabs, but they had been pushed to the back, precedence granted to those who would not have made it past the guards at the gate in Alipore: a company of clerical babus, black umbrellas tightly folded; a group of what he assumed were Tibetan brigands, in the most immense furry boots; a sisterhood of singing and dancing women, vigorously chewing paan. They all sat in a circle, the space in the middle unoccupied except by a turbaned gentleman with hoop earrings and a ferocious moustache who sat cradling a giant lute-like instrument held erect, which he strummed in the most monotonous, droning manner. The fumes and the drones began to get to Sykes's head again, but he was now feeling sleepy.

He came awake with a start. In the stage before him, the ferocious gentleman with the vertical lute had been joined by a man with kohl-rimmed eyes and lips painted red, who held what looked like a giant, misshapen guitar across his body, his slender legs crossed elegantly, displaying the most attractive pair of feet Sykes had seen on any human being. The painted man adjusted the knobs of his instrument, plucking at the strings in a somewhat absent-minded fashion. The drone of the bandit accompanying him on the lute receded into the background. From some distant memory of a lecture by the Colonel, Sykes understood the instrument being played by the painted man to be called a sitar.

Sykes looked around. He was not surprised to see, on his left, Yale sitting cross-legged amid an immense company of clockwork dolls. Before them, its tail and paws regally placed on the floor, lounged the tiger in a languid manner.

The sitar jangled and vibrated under the contorted fingers of the painted man. The sound was sweet but with an undertone of sharpness, as though sizzling beneath the syrup there was something spicy. Then the music changed. The notes expanded in volume, bubbles of sound floating across the tent and cascading down over the listeners, making the agglomeration of babus, nautch girls and bandits shimmer in the haze even as his own skin erupted in sweat.

The music stopped and the tent was plunged in darkness. Then, in the new light that crept back, he saw, sitting between the two musicians, the still figure of the Bibi. Next to her sat a man. His face was cast in shadow, but Sykes could tell that he was a large man with long locks of hair cascading down his back and a resplendent beard. Sykes started awake as the light shifted. The man's eyes burnt like coals in the darkness. On the other side of the Bibi sat the Babu, tapping in experimental fashion on his tablas. The Bibi opened her mouth and began to sing.

Sykes did not understand what she was singing, but words and phrases whirled in his mind before they were swept away by a sudden climax of strings and drums, scraps of meaning flung across a tattered, threadbare sky. He thought of the Nana Sahib, disappeared into the vastness, and of Magadh Rai, in whose pursuit he thought they had set out. They had not found Magadh Rai or even been close on his trail. There had never been any Magadh Rai. Instead, here, at this *finis terre* that was the Zone, he was listening to a musical performance given by a trio who sounded like something out of an Oriental children's rhyme. The Bibi, the Babu and the Baba. That was all the Magadh Rai there was, there had ever been and there ever would be.

THERE WAS A pittering and pattering on the high roof of the tent, like thousands of little rodent feet scrambling for purchase above their heads. To the staccato of the tablas, raindrops slammed onto the tent ceiling and the Bibi's voice reached a high note and remained there, transcendent. It was raining in the desert. Skyes saw all his choices, his past and present and future, laid out before him. He observed the strangely peaceable Yale and the clockwork dolls and the clockwork tiger. He surveyed his companions, Tobin and Bones and Ryeman, no longer human and yet infinitely at rest.

Wars small and big, Sykes thought, and his part in them, had been rendered meaningless in the Zone, which might indeed be a realm of judgement and of release.

Sykes looked at herself and prepared to let it all go even as the song ended and applause echoed from one end of the tent to the other, picked up again like waves returning to the shore, echoed and murmured and reverberated as the performers nodded and curtsied, and Sykes felt, for the first time since setting foot in India, quite free.

TWO SHOTS RANG out in quick succession and the moment was gone. The Colonel, returned to something like his original form, stood in front of the performers, a pistol smoking in his hand. He had fired at the Bibi first, and then at the Babu, the blasts blowing them back to the floor. He aimed his third, final shot at the Baba but could not get it off. A paw yellow and black, the size of a dinner plate, swiped the pistol away even as the clockwork sepoys closed in. Colonel Sleeman was flung on to his back as the tiger straddled him, his arms thrown to the sides as the jaws of the beast fastened around his throat. The Colonel's face was a ghastly white hue as his hands attempted to fend off the tiger. 'Help me, help me,' Sykes heard him cry and it was all he could do to not fire a ball into the brains of the man who had ruined it all.

THE RAIN TURNED to snow, a million fish hooks flying across the desert, covering everything in blinding white, Sykes's quarry just barely visible. Still, they thundered on, hooves beating gallantly on the drum of the hard, frozen ground. Sykes tugged at his sword to keep it loose, afraid that it would freeze to the scabbard and be stuck just when he needed to draw. 'Have you ever? Have you ever?' the wind keened.

Under his ragged coat, Sykes cradled the pistol with its single bullet. His adversary rode on, the pace of his horse adjusted finely to Sykes's tired mount, keeping the exact same distance between them.

Sykes had stopped thinking and did not know how much farther his horse would run. The wind dropped off, and the snow turned to thick, fluffy flakes, falling gently, in a hush. The adversaries rode on, Sykes proceeding like someone in a dream, powerless to change the course of events. He felt he had been on this pursuit for days, for centuries, with only the foggiest notion of who his enemy was. The enemy was no longer a man, a human being. It rode on, just ahead of him, an indistinct shape on a horse. The moon came out above him and the first stars appeared. In the dark, he would lose his quarry.

Once, early in the chase, Sykes thought he had glimpsed the Baba's face as he turned and looked at him. His fanatic eyes gave him away. Sykes had come close enough on that occasion to reach for the pistol, intending to put a bullet between those blazing eyes before he fell behind, inexplicably, well beyond shooting range.

That was a long time ago. Since then, he had glimpsed nothing more of the rider's face, although visions danced in his tired brain where his quarry was sometimes the Baba, sometimes the Babu and sometimes the Bibi, the latter two restored to life in the Zone.

It seemed to Sykes that the horse before him was beginning to falter. He dug his heels in to try and extract a little more speed out of his mount, closing in infinitesimally. He reached for his pistol but was unable to find it. He tried for his sword and could not free it. But he no longer cared. He was rising on his stirrups now as his horse began to pull abreast. Sykes let go of the reins and prepared to launch himself. His feet left the stirrups and he was on his adversary, knocking him off the horse. He could feel his hands closing in on the throat as they came down, squeezing even as the Baba choked him in return and stars swam before his eyes. On they struggled, the blood pounding in his head. 'Have you ever?' the Zone asked. 'Will you never?' the Zone asked even as the hoofbeats of the runaway horses grew ever more faint in the boundless mystery of the Zone.

[illegible] had [illegible] thinking [illegible] much farther [illegible] would [illegible] and the snow [illegible] to their [illegible] miles [illegible] like someone in a dream, powerless to [illegible] the course of events [illegible] had been [illegible] for days [illegible] with only the [illegible] was [illegible] was no longer a [illegible] above [illegible] and the [illegible] would [illegible]

Once [illegible] in the [illegible] when [illegible] had [illegible] the [illegible] he turned and looked [illegible] him [illegible] to reach for the [illegible] hand [illegible] well beyond [illegible]

[illegible] a long time [illegible] nothing [illegible] of the [illegible] although [illegible] Baby [illegible] life in the [illegible] before him was [illegible] and [illegible] a little more [illegible] but [illegible] to find [illegible] his sword and [illegible] on his [illegible] to pull [illegible] of the [illegible] on the [illegible] he could feel his hands [illegible] again [illegible] before his eyes [illegible] the same [illegible] the [illegible]

THE LIGHT AT THE END OF THE WORLD

What may not be expected in a country of eternal light?

***FRANKENSTEIN*, MARY SHELLEY**

1

The stopover in Calcutta is brief, just long enough for Bibi to think of her mother and feel the enormous weight of her accumulated guilt. Then she joins the straggling line of passengers boarding the flight to Port Blair, afternoon heat hammering on the painted fuselage, sunlight skittering off the whirling blades of the small aircraft.

Bibi finds her window seat. The rest of her row remains vacant. Behind her, two young men play with their phones, comparing their Brahmastra ringtones until the plane begins to taxi down the tarmac, and the city, with the sudden jolt of a restless dreamer, falls far away below.

The provinciality of the passengers—traders, minor bureaucrats and a few off-season tourists—is similar to the make-up of flights going to northeast India. So is the kind of devastation Bibi can see as they head for the coast. The flight from Delhi to Calcutta had offered her an overview of a parched heartland; the Ganges and its tributaries reduced to runny trickles of brown surrounded by vast, undulating sandbanks; villages and towns abandoned except for the elderly and the dying; the arid land scattered with animal corpses; all remaining water sources guarded by caste Hindus determined not to share them with Muslims or Dalits. Now, on the eastern flank, Bibi looks down at a different kind of disaster.

The propellers beat steadily over the floodwaters. Huts and trees, ripped up by cyclones, drift in the rippling green, and people are crowded onto concrete rooftops and railway embankments. Country boats heaped with coal slash rippling tracks across the water, heading for brick kilns stocking up on fuel for the post-monsoon construction boom. Then the floodwaters run out of subcontinent and they are flying over the Bay of Bengal.

Bibi falls asleep, wakes up, dozes again, feeling that her sleep world is impossibly crowded. Who are all these people in the aisles with their vast wings, their simian features, their beautifully coloured doll faces? When she wakes up, the plane is preparing to touch down.

THE HOTEL THE taxi driver takes her to is called the Lighthouse. Hidden from the road by high walls and dense foliage, it is an old complex of sloping roofs and a new, unfinished wing jutting into the garden. Beyond the reception desk and the bar, a massive veranda looks out at the astonishing blue of the Andaman Sea, speckled with wooden fishing boats. In the far distance, at the end of a curving arm of land dipping into North Bay, stands the distant lighthouse that gives the hotel its name and that is memorialised on a twenty-rupee note kept framed behind the reception desk.

The manager of the hotel is from northeast India. So are most members of the staff, he says, including Luni, who sings every evening at the bar. There are no other guests, and the hotel workers crowd around Bibi like she is a distant, glamorous cousin come to visit after a long period of separation. They urge the manager to upgrade her into the best possible room. The manager, laughingly, complies.

BIBI TRIES THE number that has brought her to the Andamans. The call will not go through. She wanders along empty corridors in the residential levels, built along the downslope of the hill on which the hotel sits. Floorboards creak as she passes closed-off rooms in dark, musty wings. No matter which way Bibi goes, she cannot find a signal. Bibi makes her way out into the garden. A faint signal appears, but it vanishes as soon as she touches the screen.

Near the wall that faces the bay, where the ground slopes up sharply, there is the outline of a cave. Bibi pushes away the vines and leaves covering the entrance. It is not a natural cave, or if it is, the walls have been reinforced with brick. The moss-streaked interior is cool and damp, the roof so low that she has to stoop to enter. She peers into the darkness, moving the beam of her phone around. It does not run deep, only about ten feet. A bunker from the war, or perhaps the mouth of a tunnel that has been walled off. Faint drawings are sketched on the wall, figures with giant eyes and bulbous heads on stick limbs.

She returns to her room, extracts her Nokia and goes up to the reception area with both her phones. The smartphone connects to the hotel Wi-Fi but cannot find a mobile network. The Nokia has a faint signal, just a couple of bars. Bibi tries texting from both phones. The messages are not delivered.

Tashi, the manager, studies the number when Bibi brings it to him. The area code is local, he says. The problem is probably the network in the islands. The telecom is rudimentary here, sporadic 2G, he says, but with static from the advanced network of the military. Electronic voice phenomenon, interference, unpredictable lags are common, as is echo syndrome, the sudden, repeated appearance of old messages. It is not unusual to open one's laptop in the morning and see that emails from years ago have downloaded onto one's inbox.

He tries sending a WhatsApp from his own phone but receives no response. It is unclear if the text has gone through at all. Finally, Bibi calls from the hotel landline. The automated voice of the telephone exchange tells her that the number she is calling does not exist.

2

Along the bay beneath the hotel, where Bibi goes for a walk that evening, carcasses of old steamers rot into slimy soil. Thin young men are drinking in busy groups along the waterfront, emptied pint bottles of Maa Ka Doodh and Director's Special littering the ground as they hold their phones up in frantic efforts to find a signal. Behind them, military officials jog in tracksuits and white sneakers, trim, moustached men staying in shape as they maintain their unsinkable aircraft carrier.

The road climbs, away from Hotel Lighthouse, an unbroken stretch of wall on her left marking military property. On her right, the land plummets. It resembles the hills around Shillong descending towards the flood plains of Bangladesh, rushing towards the haor wetland that is Bibi's ancestral home. But that is not Bangladesh down there, only the boundless expanse of a rain-dark sea that cradles India and Bangladesh, that, expanding into a watery realm holding the world, is indeed the world.

A sudden shower sweeps in, forcing Bibi to look for shelter. Ahead, she can see a couple walking on through the rain. They look small, almost the size of children, holding hands in the drizzle. The man seems to be wearing a suit, the woman is clad in a baggy dress. The rain begins to taper off and Bibi follows the pair. She reaches the horizon where she last saw them, silhouettes blurred by the staticky rain. There is no one visible.

In front of her, the road plunges sharply past a crumbling wall topped with rusting barbed wire and broken glass. The ruins of a vast government building squat behind the wall, deserted except for some emaciated cows grazing listlessly on uneven ground.

The wind picks up. In the blur of the rain, the tropical trees around her look like conifers, and the wall ahead appears dense with moss. The air smells of tea and kerosene, heavy with sentiments, tingling with possibilities just beyond her reach.

AT DINNER THAT night, Bibi is the only guest. She feels she is in a small, underground club. The lights have been dimmed, and Luni is singing just to her. She leans back into the music, asks Tashi if she can bum a cigarette. Tashi brings her a drink and an ashtray and sits with her. Bibi finds that she is slowly but surely getting drunk. Luni joins them and Bibi realises that she is spilling her guts out, telling them everything. But they do not laugh at her as she recounts her story, at the whimsical pattern-making that has led her to Port Blair with her misbegotten belief that a man thought to be dead is alive here, as though the Andamans are an alternate universe where the usual rules do not apply.

SHE SHOWS THEM her photos. The Sentinelese islander, a member of the last uncontacted tribe in the Andamans. Sanjit, in a frame blown up from the video. They look at each other, Tashi and Luni. 'Hard to tell from the quality of this,' Tashi says. 'And the man I'm thinking of called himself Ranjit. But unless there's more than one Manipuri brother floating around in the Andamans, that could be the man who stayed at this hotel some years ago.'

The drunken haze in Bibi's head dissipates. 'You have an address? A number?'

'He came here two years in a row, in the off season,' Luni says. 'But not last year.'

3

The bus out of Port Blair trundles along a two-lane road bisecting flooded paddy fields before grinding its way up switchbacks. The sea is no longer present, and apart from the crudely rendered signs warning of crocodiles lurking in the backwaters, Bibi feels she has travelled in the wrong direction, has inexplicably landed up in northeast India. The brakes of the bus squeal as it begins to descend, heading for the environmental centre where the man who stayed at Hotel Lighthouse and gave his name as Ranjit might have worked as an odd-job man some years ago.

There is, at the very least, a double of Sanjit on this island.

The traffic is heavy as they near a village. The licence plates on the cars and trucks say AN for Andaman and Nicobar Islands; the abbreviation looks like a shadowy iteration of the AS used for licence plates in Assam. The crooked shop signboards in the market, with names like 'Hobiganj Blacksmith' and 'Coomilla Tailor', refer to places in Bangladesh.

It is like she is in the lower reaches of Meghalaya or Assam or Manipur, somewhere not far from the mining settlements and truck stops lining the highway as it falls away from the cosmopolitan glitter of Shillong towards the border checkpoints facing Bangladesh. It is right that Sanjit should be here, in this mirror version of their lost homeland.

THE ENVIRONMENTAL CENTRE is permanently shut. The men loitering at the nearest tea shop remember a Japanese-looking maintenance worker who lived there many years ago. But they have little interest in this man, who they think was called Sachin. They are curious, instead, about Bibi, about what she is doing in the islands, and if she knows a way for them to find work in Delhi.

They are Bengali men, descended from the refugees settled here by the Indian government. She finds herself pleading with them, appealing to some sense of distant kinship as she passes around Sanjit's photo. She jots down the fragments of information coming her way: the Cellular Jail, Ross Island, a village school.

THESE ISLANDS HAVE memories stretching back hundreds of millions of years, Bibi thinks as the bus makes its slow way back to Port Blair. They remember Gondwanaland, an amalgamation of Africa and South America and Australia and India, a supercontinent named, by an Austrian geologist, after the forest of Gond tribals in central India where mining companies today advance behind paramilitary forces. Gondwanaland, both there and not there, both indigenous heartland and vanished supercontinent. The Andamans are the orphan children of that dead supercontinent, home originally to naked hunter-gatherers who care nothing for the flags planted successively on their shores by the British, the Japanese and the Indians.

The Sentinelese do not distinguish between British officials and Indian bureaucrats, exiled kings and television crews, civil servants and evangelists. They fire arrows at everyone, hurl exquisitely crafted spears, ask them all to stay away. The Sentinelese in the photo is aiming his arrow at the military helicopter for the same reason, and although he is little more than a silhouette in the picture, a man without a face, he is an elongated, defiant silhouette. He is a shadow, but one that has its own truncated shadow. There are two bows raised in the picture, two arrows flying along different planes.

SHE IS AT the Cellular Jail the next morning, circling past wooden boards crowded with the names of colonial-era prisoners. In its time, the prison was an advanced design, a panopticon based on the theories of Jeremy Bentham and centrepiece of the penal colony established by the British in the aftermath of the 1857 rebellion. Since the departure of the British, recurrent earthquakes have destroyed much of the jail; only two of the original six wings survive, radiating out uneasily from the control tower.

A shiny wooden model of the original structure is propped up inelegantly on blocks in an exhibition room empty of visitors. The model looks like a UFO. The image lingers in Bibi's mind as she makes her way through the mildewed, covered walkways connecting the upper levels and their rows of cells.

Vinayak Savarkar, prisoner turned collaborator and hero of the Hindu right, is prominent everywhere. In a shrine-like room dedicated to him, tourists chatter of Savarkar's miraculous escape from prison on the wings of a bulbul bird. There are portraits of Savarkar on the wall, with demented eyes, framed by round glasses, that focus on Bibi as she passes.

Bibi cannot see the fake hangman anywhere and makes her way to the roof. A broad passageway with blackened, crenellated edges, it lifts her above her surroundings. The wind whips across the tops of the palm trees and strikes at her face as she walks towards the end. The roof of the other wing angles away from her with incredible speed. Together, the two wings are tilted at full stretch, reaching for the horizon, constituent parts of a jail that wants freedom as much as the prisoners it once held did.

There is a slight tremor beneath her feet. Bibi gets the impression that this broken spaceship-prison is pulsating, trembling with effort in its attempts to fly once again.

DOWN BELOW, NEAR the Savarkar Cell, some kind of commotion has broken out. Screams, shouts, running feet. A guard comes up and begins scanning the roof.

'Do you know a man who poses for tourist selfies?' Bibi asks. 'A fake hangman with a noose?'

'The Chinese man?' the guard says. 'He doesn't do that anymore. People wanted someone who looks English. Or Indian.'

He goes to the edge and peers down. 'There,' he says, asking Bibi to join him.

Below, under the red-tiled overhangs of the cell windows, there are two figures. Past a row of tilting palm trees they creep, heading towards a black water tank.

'Who are they?' Bibi asks.

'Afy and Sufi,' the guard says. 'Addicts. They steal keys.'

'Why keys?'

'Who knows? They run away from the tribal home, run away from the hospital. It's a mystery how they get out, how they go from one place to another. There, look.'

Bibi can't understand why the names echo in her head. The pair are crouching low, sliding below the barred windows on the ground floor and pushing themselves right up against the whitewashed base of the building. As she watches, the woman vanishes. She has dissolved into the wall. The man takes a quick look behind, and then he is gone too.

'The prisoners here should have learnt from them,' the guard says. 'You too. Then you wouldn't have had to buy a ticket.'

BEYOND THE JAPANESE bunker in red clay, tourists and souvenir sellers crowd the lower reaches of Ross Island. The seller of mineral water Bibi seeks has succumbed to disease or death, according to the varying opinions of the dishevelled-looking men who are plying the same trade. Why is she looking for this man? one of the younger souvenir sellers asks. He offers her a garbled history of Ross Island, of its initial establishment as colonial capital by the British, chosen instead of Port Blair because it could be easily defended should a native uprising occur, of the Japanese invasion during the Second World War, and of recent plans by the Indian government to establish a bioinformatics research centre on the island.

Bibi buys water from the man and makes her way towards the crest of the hill. Giant, prehensile roots gleefully rip apart old brick buildings. The gamey smell of deer is thick in what used to be a dance hall, its ballroom floor collapsed in a welter of wood and rusted nails.

Below, Bibi can see the souvenir sellers shouting and gesticulating as someone runs away from them. Not one person but two, making for a shell of a building on the edge of the island, a place situated just beyond a British summerhouse made from the same red clay as the Japanese bunker.

Trees have settled themselves on the roof of this building, roots wrapped firmly around columns supporting Roman arches. This time Bibi can see the escape route being used by Afy and Sufi, a sharply inclined opening at the base of the building rather like the mouth of a pit mine. It is probably the entrance to the British tunnel linking Ross Island with Port Blair.

A peacock steps into Bibi's path, staring disdainfully before it struts past crumbling gravestones in the cemetery. At the summit, the wind howls through a church that has no roof. Across the frames of the gothic windows, vines intertwine like an alien species building up strength and biding time.

ANOTHER VILLAGE, THIS one on the southern coast. The school where he might have worked as a games teacher no longer exists. The village that once stood there burnt down in a land dispute, the people at the bus stop tell her. The school, the health clinic, everything was gutted. Much of the surrounding area has been transformed into a resort.

The wall enclosing the resort is high, with a forbidding metal gate. But inside, everything is half-finished, with thatch-roofed cottages distributed uneasily on the sloping ground. An unshaven, dazed-looking manager wearing a lungi approaches her, and assorted villagers trying to pass off as resort staff assemble behind him.

She asks them about the games teacher at the former school. The manager responds by detailing facilities that sound utterly imaginary.

There is Wi-Fi in the lobby and sunbeds available for tanning, he says. The staff stares at Bibi in silence and with desperation, as if she is the guest they have been awaiting all these years, as though she has finally appeared, like a figure in a folk tale, to lift the curse lying heavy upon their lives ever since the village burnt down.

IN THE AFTERMATH of that dead end, with hours to go before she can catch a return bus to Port Blair, Bibi walks along the shore. She is filled with a longing to run her fingers through the water, her face splashed by its salt-heavy spray. She wonders what it would be like to float in that blue sea while looking up at the blue sky. Down black rock and past rotting kelp she makes her way, wanting to find some way to touch the sea and feel its answering ripples.

A barren field cuts off her progress. Hundreds of feral-looking cows are charging around on the dusty field, hooves sending dirt into the air. These creatures look demented, not cows as much as cow-like extraterrestrials stranded on a planet light years from home.

THAT NIGHT, BIBI'S Delhi dreams return to her with sinuous grace and clarity. The angels are composed of dust and pixels. The New Delhi Monkey Man has blinking cursors for pupils.

It is not quite dawn when she wakes up, feeling preternaturally alert. She makes herself coffee and sits in the balcony, notebook on lap. In the middle of the night, waking from her vivid dreams, she has written down a single word: CYBERNETICS.

4

A storm slams into the islands. Water pools and eddies in the lower reaches of Port Blair. It floods the dock being constructed for cruise ships and turns the dug-up foundation for a shopping complex into a lake filled with cattle carcasses. A saltwater crocodile announces its presence in this new lake, an eager scavenger consumer, pretending, with a contrariness fine-tuned through millennia of evolution, to be a log. For days, there is no internet, no phone. Mala, the receptionist, tells Bibi that, one day, Ombani Telecom will bring 5G to the islands.

There is a contract to lay a new undersea cable from the mainland to the Andamans that will connect every island in the archipelago. When they do so, her boyfriend in Bangalore has told her, there will be the Internet of Things in the Andamans. Mala takes this to mean that there will be Wi-Fi everywhere. She demonstrates, picking up her ballpoint pen. 'Wi-Fi in this,' she says. She taps her forehead with the pen. 'Wi-Fi in this.' She taps Bibi's head. 'Wi-Fi everywhere.' She laughs, scandalised by her own inventiveness. 'The Internet of Everything,' she says cheerfully, as Bibi picks up a sodden copy of the local newspaper and retreats to her room.

ON THE MAINLAND, too, there are floods everywhere. It is no longer just distant Assam and foreign Bangladesh that is deluged, she sees in the brief moments when the satellite link is available. Kerala, on the western coast, is drowning. Television reports show middle-class people appealing for help, crowding social media feeds with GPS locations and blurry videos of rising water as they attempt to reassure their trapped children, their elderly parents, their disabled partners that they will soon be rescued.

On *The National Interest*, the glossy-haired anchor has questions for the people of India. Should they be fooled into providing aid to the Muslims, the Christians, the Marxists of Kerala? Do anti-nationals deserve rescue missions that will have to be carried out by patriotic first responders? He invites viewers to participate in an opinion poll on whether people in Kerala should be evacuated or left to drown. Thumbs down for evacuation, thumbs up for drowning.

THE FLOODS COME to West Bengal, to Uttar Pradesh, to Himachal Pradesh, to Gujarat and to Maharashtra. To the coast, to the plains, to the foothills of the Himalayas. Everywhere, the water is rising. Into Mumbai the ocean waves surge, holding up the proceedings of the stock market, and into Kolkata and Chennai, buildings collapsing as dark, raging channels pour through the streets. Little one-person whirlpools open up in manholes, sucking people in. Others drown in cars whose electric systems have short-circuited, trapping them inside even as the water pours through the cracks. A third of Bangladesh is under water, vast swathes of Pakistan and Nepal. The glossy-haired news anchor asks experts if Pakistan and Bangladesh are diverting their flood waters into India. It is the other way round, a mild-mannered hydrologist objects, Bangladesh in particular being downstream from India. He is shouted at by the others, this man who does not know of the new technologies, of the nuclear-fuelled super pumps that allow enemy powers to push their watery filth into India, in tandem with the people they send to turn India into a Muslim-majority nation.

ELSEWHERE IN THE world: Hurricane Rosa, Hurricane Frida, Hurricane Diego, Hurricane Geronimo, Hurricane Ghassan, Hurricane Said, Hurricane Fela, Hurricane Lumumba, Hurricane Lu Xun, Hurricane Kobayashi. They ran out of Anglo names long ago.

There are floods in Liverpool and Manchester, surging tides followed by outbreaks of fire. In North Carolina, Texas and Louisiana, chemical plants explode as cooling systems go offline.

THE WIND HOWLS into the night, an insistent voice calling out to Bibi every time she wakes up. In the morning, she sits with Luni, talking over cups of tea. The kitchen has inexplicably turned communal, Bibi joining in with the food preparation. The elaborate restaurant menu has long since been dispensed with and everybody eats the same things.

Sitting in the veranda, watching the rain sweep across the sea, the water playing slip-slide along giant banana leaves, Bibi and Luni exchange life stories like they are carrying out some final barter of great import.

5

The plans Bibi had made fell apart within minutes of reaching her destination, she tells Luni. A shapeless settlement of a town on the banks of the river, the outskirts marked by the burnt-out carcasses of old jeeps. The local correspondent supposed to help her find the detention centre was nowhere to be found, while her backup source, an activist-lecturer at a government college, had turned unresponsive to her calls. Wandering hopelessly from one neighbourhood to another in search of these missing contacts, Bibi ended up checking into the town's only hotel, just so she could find a place to think by herself.

From the window of her hotel room, the town ripples in the afternoon heat. She recalls the geographer she has interviewed in Shillong, a man who had argued that the detention centre she was looking for was located in a paradoxical space.

River islands composed of silt float up from the water and then vanish, but not before they have given rise to little villages of tin and thatch, people erecting lives that will be dismantled when the island subsides and they are forced to move to the next available chor on the river. Even the land proper is treacherous, slippery, he had said. Centuries of blurred boundaries have left the border zone dotted with enclaves, pieces of nation within another nation. Patches of Bangladesh surrounded by India, strips of India encircled by Bangladesh. There is even a place known to be the only third-order enclave in the world, a strip of India inside a Bangladeshi enclave inside an Indian enclave that itself sits deep in Bangladeshi territory.

The detention centre Bibi is looking for is sited near such an enclave, the geographer told her. The proximity to an enclave was accidental, he believed, but it had affected the clandestine trials being carried out at the centre, the experiments contaminated by the paradoxical topology.

She had pressed him for examples. The detention centre was connected, he explained, to other points in space-time. Wormholes and bridges materialised without warning, and prisoners disappeared, slipping through trapdoors that had opened up in the sentient, shifting terrain.

THE CALL TO afternoon prayers arrives as Bibi leaves the hotel, floating wistfully over rebar and coconut fronds before surrendering itself in the vast expanse of the river. The road, smoothly tarred, runs as straight as a ruler past walls topped with barbed wire. Bibi stops at a cluster of stalls near the first gate to the military base. She drinks tea, asks questions, receives ambiguous shakes of the head in response. She moves on, stubborn, stupid, determined to attempt something, as though force of will alone will allow her to overcome the defences of this vast military complex and break through to its hidden core.

In spite of the bottle of water she has picked up from the tea stall, the heat begins to affect her. Distances are foreshortened, the ground tilts and a man appears out of nowhere. Thin and wiry, old eyes embedded in a youthful, hairless face, he seems too fey to be a reliable informer. But he has picked up on her queries at the tea stall. He knows the place she is talking about. He can show her how to get there without running into guards or gates.

THEY VEER AWAY from the base, edging towards the river. Every rational instinct asks Bibi not to go with a strange man into an unknown stretch of countryside. Yet she accompanies him, from weakness or folly or greed, or from the idea that courage is necessarily involved in tracking down a story and filling in the blank spaces within the flickering outlines of rumour.

Hours go by as they walk, but the sun remains mysteriously unmoving, glued to a pitiless, cloudless sky. The ground, increasingly waterlogged, transforms eventually into a lake, an undefinable expanse of water almost indistinguishable from the river. The man points at a pair of bamboo trunks, green and glistening, laid across the water in a makeshift path leading to the other side of the lake, where she can just about make out a crumbling boundary wall. They are now neither in India nor Bangladesh, the man says. The statement makes no sense at all.

Through a collapsed section of the wall, they are viewing some kind of yard. Trucks of WW2 vintage, chassis stripped of wheels, brood in the mire. Dozens of filing cabinets await redemption, rust eating into their military-green paint. Beyond, weeds sprout from the brickwork of a low, wide building whose windows are all blown out. It appears to be utterly empty.

Bibi chokes the disappointment back. Surely, there is more. Her guide steps through the hole in the wall, gestures at her to do the same. Oil slicks gleam in puddles and fumes rise from clumps of ashy residue. From somewhere, there comes the sharp ringing of a bell that congeals into the sound of a faraway train as she steps into the yard, even though there are no railway lines anywhere near this town.

The chicken coop is crude, coated in a characteristic whiff of ammonia. The birds turn towards her and stare silently, red-combed monsters rendered temporarily eyeless by their nictitating membranes. The man keeps pointing. There is another cage just past the chicken coop. A sad approximation of a zoo or a laboratory, it holds some sick-looking rabbits. Beyond the rabbit cage, chained to a wooden post inside another cage, far bigger, is a bear with fur falling off in patches.

An exclamation escapes her as she removes the barrier of denial in her mind. This is all there is, an old, abandoned building that may well once have been a detention centre but is nothing any longer, sitting next to a junkyard that holds a poultry farm and a makeshift zoo. She turns to go. No, wait, the man says. But there really is nothing else to see.

The sun dips finally, utterly indifferent to her failure. With a shimmer, the bear vanishes. And like a vision where a protective screen has been lifted, or a filter inserted, the scene in front of her is transformed. Instead of the abandoned building, she sees a vast structure, glimmering in the sudden shift of light, taking her aback with its contradictory suggestions of a decrepit history and a sinister futurism. A chemical odour, astringent and sharp, makes her eyes and nose water.

Her fingers shake with impossible haste as she begins to take pictures with her phone before a siren starts wailing and the light changes again. There are shouts in the distance and her guide begins to drag her back the way they came, even as the bear reappears. It is still chained to its post. Large, furry, undeniably bearlike and yet incredibly human for all that, it has fixed its gaze upon her. Bibi begins to step towards it and then falters as the siren sounds again.

Later, in Delhi, Anand will say that she had a breakdown, that it is all right, that every assignment does not have to end in a story. From somewhere within the vast, shadowy expanses of his family, a woman doctor pays Bibi a house call, prescribing, with severe, certain authority, regular doses of Calmpose pills, a simple diet and complete bed rest. Books are forbidden, as are films, spicy food, anything that might overstimulate the nerves. Her smartphone she must hand over to Anand for safekeeping.

Anand lives with his family in South Delhi, but he has managed, many months before Bibi set out for Assam, to find a place for her through his intricate network of contacts. The flat is in the Chanakyapuri neighbourhood, on the top floor of a two-storey brick bungalow split into four flats. Even at the peak of summer, there are no power cuts in this neighbourhood that was built in the nineteenth century after the British emptied out the existing village by bombarding its residents with artillery.

Chanakyapuri is now an area of diplomats and civil servants, with luxury hotels and luxury hospitals. It is a city within the city, a fortress with uniformed men and sudden checkpoints that sprout at night. The arrangement is completely rent-free for Bibi. While its usual occupants study business management in Manchester, Bibi simply has to take care of the houseplants and pay the electricity bill.

A week of her recuperation goes by. Two weeks. Anand stays with her at night, letting himself in when he returns from work at one or two in the morning. Bibi pretends to be fast asleep. Everything has been taken care of in the office, he tells her in the late mornings as they drink Assam tea. Nothing has changed for the two of them, he assures her. This second stint of hers at *The Daily Telegram*, where she has followed Anand, is only a stopgap to grander plans that involve getting married and leaving for graduate school in the United States.

Bibi does not tell him that although she is paid far more in this new position, with stacks of business cards announcing a fancy designation as Senior Writer, the detention centre story is her only story, the only piece she has been assigned in months of working at the paper.

For Anand, it is different. He is a rising star, working on the opinion pages headed by the youngish, Oxford-returned son of a politician. The Oxonian's name is Bhattacharya, and he too is from the Northeast, from Assam, although if anyone asks him about the Northeast, he answers, bowing with right hand over his heart, that he is a patriot first and a patriot last. Bhattacharya has not assumed the bullying, hectoring persona that will define him when he switches from print to television and begins to host *The National Interest*. In his job running the opinion pages, for which he is less qualified than Bibi other than the all-important fact of a foreign degree and elite connections, he is a quiet, watchful presence. Glossy-haired, lanky and pigeon-chested, with his most impressive physical feat being the ability to bend both thumbs backward in a near semicircle, he is an unlikely specialist in what the paper defines as the new field of military criticism. Elsewhere, publications review books and films. At *The Daily Telegram*, they review missiles, drones and crowd control gear.

Bhattacharya is attentive and deferential to Jagmohan, the chief editor, who, with his handlebar moustache and his proximity to the military and the intelligence, fancies himself as an army general in civvies but is secretly intimidated by Bhattacharya's foreign-returned credentials as an intellectual. Many years later, Jagmohan will accuse Bhattacharya of stealing the name of his show, *The National Interest*, from the name Jagmohan used for his own column at *The Daily Telegram*. Jagmohan whose knowledge of the nitty-gritty underbelly of India and whose sweeping overview of global geopolitics could never be matched by Bhattacharya, Jagmohan who, in the glorious spring of the millennium and its accompanying end of history, counted Madeleine Albright and Condoleezza Rice and Fareed Zakaria and Francis Fukuyama as his personal friends and whose column was a tribute to the American publication, *The National Interest*, created by that brilliant American intellectual, William F. Buckley Jr.

When Anand introduces Bibi, in those early weeks of her return to the daily, to Jagmohan, introduces her as having grown up in Shillong, Jagmohan first asks if Bibi's father is in the army. When she says no, he wants to know if her family traces its origins back to Bangladesh. Soldiers or ghuspetiya infiltrators: in his mind, these are the only two options. On the quiet, thoughtful face of Bhattacharya, there is just the slightest flicker of interest, put aside almost instantly as he turns his full attention to Jagmohan's accounting of his time in the Northeast, of his famous coverage of the Nellie massacre, with Muslim babies lined up on an embankment, each one sliced neatly in half like a pumpkin, he says with relish.

Through these long weeks of her recuperation, Bibi finds herself querulous, on the edge of a breakdown in spite of the bright array of anti-anxiety pills by her bedside. She waters the plants and stares out through the windows, aware, as dusk comes, of the dull thwack of tennis balls being struck laboriously across courts hidden behind high hedges. She goes out for a walk then, hoping to clear her head of the constant fog. Lone policemen, scattered around the neighbourhood like decorative fixtures dressed up in moustaches and khaki, stare at her.

She crosses Vinay Marg and counts out her ten thousand steps in Nehru Park, massive and coldly manicured in the manner of all governmental properties. Solitary men sit at the northern edge of the park, carefully spaced apart. They are mostly young and mostly poor, cautiously seeking a lover of the same sex, their nerves ajangle, sifting the surroundings for possible predators as well as partners. Then she returns to the empty flat where she heats up the plain, healthy food, rice and vegetables, that the refrigerator has mysteriously been replenished with during her evening walk.

She has no communication with her immediate neighbours. The flat across from her is allotted to a naval officer. Right below Bibi lives a man who is a doctor in the government medical services, almost as light-skinned as his Dutch wife. Bibi can see the Dutchwoman in the gardens at the back in the evenings, wearing a wide-brimmed hat that makes Bibi think of aristocratic English ladies at Ascot. She is like a Dutch duchess as, trowel in gloved hand and Jackie Onassis sunglasses on her face, she directs her many servants in a constant shuffling of plants, flowers and garden furniture that makes it seem that she is playing a particularly elaborate, life-size chess game with an invisible but deviously skilful opponent. The fourth flat, the one across from that of the Indo-Dutch couple, belongs to an official who works at the Ministry of Defence. In contrast to his very active, sociable neighbours, his residence is almost always dark. A single light can sometimes be seen behind the thick curtains. Outside, there is often a visitor's car, bearing diplomatic licence plates. Different nights, different licence plates, but the visitor's car sits silently late into the night, the silhouette of a driver faint behind its steering wheel as Bibi hears the living room clock strike midnight.

On Sundays, Anand lies in bed and polishes Jagmohan's prose. Ostensibly, he edits the column. Since Jagmohan finds it hard to string two sentences together, the column is more or less ghostwritten by Anand. Sometimes, as Anand is rewriting Jagmohan's words, he calls Bhattacharya. The two of them laugh at Jagmohan's confusion of *The National Interest* with *National Review* and his frequent references to America. They chuckle over his constant name-dropping of Madeleine Albright and Condoleezza Rice and that what impresses Jagmohan even more than the powerful women of America are the vast parking lots to be found in front of a Walmart, an entity he has described, in a column supporting the entry of Walmart into India, as the Taj Mahal of the globalised world.

Bibi wanders through the flat, looking out at the garden in the back where a mix of Indian and white people have gathered for a late lunch. The servants scurry around with chilled bottles of wine and platters of cheese and cold cuts, European food that is rich in visual texture but that appears to have no smell. When she returns to the bedroom to complain to Anand about being treated like an invalid, he asks her to be patient. They will be out of Delhi in less than six months, he says. In New York, they will be able to build a life for themselves, acquire the foreign degrees that will allow them to write what they want. They will go running in Central Park, attend performances at the Brooklyn Academy of Music and summer in Martha's Vineyard. In the meantime, they must do what needs to be done. She tells him that she has heard that the Ombanis have bought a stake in the daily and that the paper has signed private treaties with billionaires like the Jindals to guarantee them perpetual positive coverage. He asks her to avoid social media and goes back to fine-tuning Jagmohan's piece on securing the national interest along the border areas of the nation, the vital necessity of maintaining the Armed Forces Special Powers Act in the Northeast and in Kashmir, allowing the forces to shoot to kill, if necessary, without being tried in a civilian court.

Bibi lies next to him and thinks of the body of Manorama found on the outskirts of Imphal, Manipur, shot repeatedly in the vagina to hide evidence of rape. She remembers the Meira Paibi protesters taking off their clothes in front of Kangla Fort, middle-aged matrons stripping themselves naked and holding up signs saying: INDIAN ARMY, RAPE US TOO. She thinks, even though she doesn't want to, of Sanjit.

When Anand falls asleep, she lies awake, prowling from room to room. She wonders where her courage has gone. Downstairs, all is quiet, the guests of the Indo-Dutch combine long departed. A tiny red glow moves in the dark. She smells the tang of cigarette smoke and realises it is the driver of the car parked outside the defence official's flat.

After three weeks, soon after Anand has brought home the weekend edition carrying her detention centre piece, Bibi returns to work. She is diminished, much like the piece. She has said yes to all the editorial decisions, staying within the realms of what can be attributed, what can be factually verified. The hidden detention centre in the army camp has vanished from the story; what remains is her other reporting, based on official documents and interviews, about a Delhi businessman who appears mysteriously connected to the military and the Hindu right, someone who has won all the catering contracts for prisons, detention centres, and military canteens in border areas and who is hounded by allegations of trafficking children to orphanages in Gujarat. She is in full agreement with Anand; *The Daily Telegram* publishes news, not fiction.

But even this piece has resulted in a sharp reaction. The businessman, who claims to be a former army official and is a consultant to various government ministries, has filed civil and criminal lawsuits against her for defamation. The legal notice has been sent from a court in Silchar, a tiny town in Assam near the border between India and Bangladesh that he has probably never visited but that Bibi knows all too well.

Anand asks her not to panic. He has given her an expensive present, a new smartphone. Her old phone was damaged by water, the photographs she took of the bear and detention centre irrecoverable. The lawyers of *The Daily Telegram* are experienced in dealing with such lawsuits, he reminds her. Why has a businessman based in Delhi filed the suit in a provincial court more than a thousand miles away? Because the costs are far lower, he says wisely in answer to his own question.

On this first evening back at the office, thoughts about the missing phone run through Bibi's mind as insistently as the new phone asking her to install various updates. Her head aches, and even though she is now on a reduced dose of Calmpose pills, her stomach feels queasy. In her mind, anxiety evoked by the lawsuit meets blurry images of a ramshackle town, flooded riverbanks and a building populated by people in laboratory gowns. Sometimes, an eye emerges from that shifting cloud of impressions, seeking compassion that she is unable to offer. She can see the tremor in her hands when she lifts it from the keyboard. It is as if she has aged, has been irretrievably transformed.

She is ready to go home, wondering when Anand will be done, when the night editor calls her over. His eyes are bloodshot and his liquor breath fills the cubicle as he sits under the green terminal with its scrolling stock prices. Take this to Jagmohan, he says, handing her a folder. It is not something she should have to do, but she doesn't like standing in his room and she accepts the folder because it is less trouble to do so than to refuse.

It's his resignation letter, he says, staring at her with fury. He asks her to give it to the editor, only to the editor, not to that two-timing boyfriend of hers. Bibi turns to go. She knows he does not like Anand because Anand and Bhattacharya are part of the new clique, while he, drinking old school in his cubicle, has been left behind by the treacherous, shifting times. She can hear him shouting as she closes the door behind her. She cannot make out his words.

The corridors are musty and empty as Bibi ventures towards Jagmohan's office. She passes the private offices of the senior editors, pausing to knock at Anand's door. The lights are on in Anand's office, but he is not there.

Door after door is shut, although it seems to Bibi she can hear murmurs from inside as she walks by, like news of the greatest import is being passed from room to room, and she feels, even though she is walking at a normal pace, that time has somehow become sluggish, dilated, that she is walking at a pace that barely takes her forward and that the whispers in the rooms are like a recording being played at an unusually slow speed, and that the rooms are whispering to her all the secrets they know, the secrets that have never been published, that can never be published, because that is the whole point of news, that behind every story, there is always a truer, unpublished story, so that for every daily published in this building and kept in the official archives, there is at least one shadow daily printed in type that runs blood-red, not funeral black, creating a parallel archive and an unofficial history, a dark history of deep states, a secret account of nations built on lies and empires erected on genocide, and Bibi thinks of what Sanjit used to say, that in a single poem by Agha Shahid Ali there was more truth than in the reams of falsehood published by their newspaper, Sanjit who is now lost to her, maybe even to himself, who appears in her mind as a man falling slowly, endlessly into an abyss, and as she walks, she feels the walls shuddering, walls that are sick with the violence of the secrets they contain, and even though she is in the corridor and not inside these rooms, these rooms filled with their secrets and these rooms temporarily vacated by their ambitious, upwardly mobile, foreign-returned or foreign-aspiring editor occupants, she can now hear an insistent tap-tapping from them, a tap-tapping she thinks is coming from the smudged, dirt-streaked windows of these private offices looking out to the back, towards the grounds of Feroz Shah Kotla and the silted Yamuna River, and who is it tap-tapping on the windows but the monkeys outside, who are pleading urgently to Bibi to stop and let them in, and Bibi doesn't know why the monkeys are so insistent about coming inside, but it is like they know things that Bibi doesn't know, which is very easy, and they know things that the night editor who has sent her on this errand doesn't know and that Jagmohan the chief editor who thinks he is a general for the national interest doesn't know and that his sidekick Bhattacharya who wants to be kingmaker doesn't know and that Anand, always solicitous, always unperturbed, always planning ahead by a few moves, doesn't know, and that even the whispering rooms with their surfeit of secrets don't know, but that the monkeys know because their cousins outside the Home Ministry offices in the North Block know, having received information from the cousins outside the IIT laboratories who in turn have talked to their cousins outside the Chhattarpur farmhouses and the bungalows on Race Course Road, who themselves are always in touch with the cousins who lurk around the war rooms of the military base at Dhaula Kuan and the intelligence operations centre at Nizamuddin, and who pick up things from the torture chambers of the Delhi Police Special Cell in Jor Bagh, and who learn things from the monkeys who live not in New Delhi but in Old Delhi and in Trans-Yamuna Delhi, and together they know so many things, know that the temperature of the planet is rising, know that the ice caps are melting, know that the military has found something in a remote border area, something that might be a craft or a weapon or an alien or none of these things or all of these things, but that the military will someday be ordered to try and use it, that maybe the military is already using some of it, and they know not only what has happened but also what is happening and what will happen, and that is why they are tap-tapping away at the windows because they want to come inside and tap-tap on the old typewriters with heavy metal keys and tap-tap on the new computer keyboards with haptic feedback, writing up their monkey news so that they can tell the stories that will not otherwise be told or written or read, and so that they can write, tap-tapping away, not a column called *The National Interest* in a confused tribute to William Fuckley Buckley Jr., but columns in tribute, if one has to think of America, to Muhammad Ali's fists and to Geronimo's gun and to Maya Angelou's words, but just then the tap-tapping stops and Bibi sees, at the very end of the last corridor receding into layers of shadows and dim, torture-cell, yellow light, the office of the chief editor.

No one answers when she knocks. She goes in, but the secretary is not there. Beyond the secretary's desk, the door to Jagmohan's inner chamber is ajar. She can hear the sound of men laughing, the growl of a television, the whiff of single malt whisky. A jolt of unease shoots through her. She knows, as everybody in the office does, that Jagmohan's contacts in the intelligence agencies feed him tidbits, sometimes giving him surveillance material that he can allude to in his *National Interest* column, sometimes offering him items for fun, stories or photographs or videotapes that can never be published or referred to, things like wiretaps of conversations that involve money laundering, political bribes and trade deals, things like a videotape of a senior bureaucrat from the Home Ministry, a straight-laced, devout,

Hindu family man, having sex with a rising Bollywood star at the Leela Kempinski hotel in Mumbai. But is that what these men are viewing today, footage from a hidden camera?

There are men sitting in the office, a man with his back to her, into whose hands Jagmohan passes a phone. This man begins to scroll through the phone. He holds it at a distance from him, arm extended, like someone who has forgotten his reading glasses. The picture he is looking at is like the picture of a memory. An eye, a furry face, looks out from near a cage, seeking compassion. The men gathered in the room—Jagmohan, Bhattacharya, Anand—wait expectantly as the man scrolls back, scrolls forward, zooms. Then he shuts Bibi's old phone off and drops it into his pocket and all the other men look relieved.

Years later, the confusion and rage and shame of it will still have the power to burn a hole in her heart. It will make her want to set herself on fire with petrol and raze that building to the ground, she tells Luni. Because she didn't leave Anand even after that. The truth is, he left her. By text. A month after he moved to New York.

That is the source of the shame, concentrated and purified over the years like the finest of single malt whiskys, that she who thought herself so full of integrity and honour and courage blinked when the time came for her to be tested, blinked again, and then again, because she just wanted to be loved, and that it was only after the break-up that she walked away from *The Daily Telegram* and journalism, from Bhattacharya's creepy texts asking her if she wanted to meet, walked away intending never to look back. And she did not look back, not even to think of the fourth man in the room, the one who was not a journalist and who had put her phone in his pocket. Back then, he had not been a coughing man.

6

The storm has receded and an air of lethargy hangs over the hotel. It is the day before Independence Day, and the superweapon will be demonstrated at the stroke of midnight. As Bibi eats a solitary breakfast, turning over the pages of the island newspaper, the television at the bar announces that some kind of epidemic has broken out, quarantines imposed by Europe and North America on air traffic from India.

The television news switches, loudly, into the opening bars of *The National Interest* just as Bibi finds, on the inside pages of the paper, a story about a businessman who has fled to Canada after transferring company funds to a personal account. The photo accompanying the account is unmistakably that of SS.

The noisy sound of a helicopter breaks out from the television set. The glossy-haired anchor has left his studio. He is wearing camouflage and jump boots, slick black hair blown back stylishly by the slipstream of a navy chopper. 'Celebratory fireworks to light up our evening, part of a joint exercise between the Indian and US navies along the straits,' he says. 'The grand finale, the event you are all waiting for, will come after the fireworks. I will be on the prime ministerial aircraft as this happens, conducting an exclusive, live interview as the Brahmastra is deployed in an exercise other nations cannot even imagine.'

BIBI WALKS OVER to the marketplace. The streets are empty and most of the stores closed, shuttered fronts and rubbish heaps squatting sullenly underneath wires strung with tricolour bunting. SS has made his move, Bibi thinks, making the leap to another nation. He has done what poor Moi only dreamt of. As for herself, she has failed.

The prime minister's masklike face tracks her with unerring precision from posters. The waterfront is deserted. She keeps thinking of Moi as she walks past the rusting steamers. On her two erratic phones sit all the messages she has sent Moi from the Andamans. In return, she has only received one response, a message that appears over and over again late at night, when the network becomes suddenly functional and dumps echoing packets of data upon its recipients.

Tick tock quarantine clock

Who's the coughing passenger?

OILY PUDDLES GLEAM before her, edged by a more amorphous trash that consists mostly of plastic bags and bottles. Beyond, two small figures are walking along the wharf, holding hands. The sea lashes against the shorefront as Bibi follows Afy and Sufi, moving past heavy, rusted chains looped around huge bollards. In the distance, on top of a hill, lightning flickers like the arms of a ghostly windmill.

The couple leave the waterfront behind, moving spryly up a series of steps cut into the hillside. Bibi can barely keep up with them. She climbs past the hotel, pausing to catch her breath when she reaches the top.

Lightning crackles above the sea. The couple are standing still in the distance, idiot grins on their faces. Bibi can make out their clothes better now, the patched-up, dirty, scarecrow jacket on the man, accompanied by a pair of baggy shorts, the shapeless, nightgown dress on the woman. Bibi thinks of what the Cellular Jail guard said about them, but beyond their initial, superficial resemblance, they are not very alike at all. The man belongs to one of the Andamanese tribes, but the woman? Her head is shaved, hashtagged with a line of old sutures. Small, delicate limbs are visible through the dress, the skin patchworked in a scaly pattern that adds to her alien, otherworldly air.

A roll of thunder arrives, cracking apart the still heat of the day like an eggshell. The pair laugh and clap their hands. Then they make for the ruined building behind the wall. Bibi stares as Afy and Sufi wave at her, inviting her in.

Bibi doesn't want to go inside. The building is far too large for Port Blair. With sprawling brick wings connected by steeply angled steps and covered bridges, the windows all blown out, it comes across as a structure that has come off its foundations and is afloat and lost in unknown seas. Bibi shivers as she looks at it, overwhelmed by waves of recognition.

Lightning flickers again. The rain begins to come down and she has no umbrella. Down below, beyond the waterfront, the Andaman Sea glitters and a lone boat drifts along the water, trailing its fishing lines like memories. The streets around her seem to be lush with pines and firs, the stone walls thick with moss. The air is heavy with the smell of tea and pungent kwai, kerosene and regret. In the streets and parks of this ghostly mirroring of her lost hometown, it is too late to meet her beloved, and it is surely far too late for everything.

THE DYING, BLOATED cattle look huge, out of scale. They are clustered around the building, coated in a reek that makes Bibi turn her dupatta into a makeshift mask. Hindquarters splayed open in pools of urine and dung, their bovine eyes look at her with pity and horror as she enters and takes the stairs.

Foot and mouth disease, she remembers from her veterinarian father's lessons as she reaches the second floor. The feeling she has is of having been here before, a sensation not completely explained away by the fact that government buildings are so much alike. The steps are gritty under her feet as she takes another set of stairs, up to the topmost floor, trying to recall the other affliction her father had talked about.

Nobody is in this building apart from those dead and dying cows downstairs. Through the broken windows, she can see wind hurtling through the trees. Beyond, the blackened sea is bleeding into an inky sky like the world has turned upside down. That tiny, solitary fishing boat in the bay is being tossed by the waves. Everywhere, a switching in the order of things.

She moves to the other side of the corridor and finds herself looking down at a courtyard of sorts. Enclosed on all sides by the wings of the building, the courtyard is topped by what looks like a geodesic dome. Patches have fallen off the dome to reveal rusted iron strut work. Wind and rain howls, pouring through the gaps, pooling in the yard below. There are more dead or dying cows there, collapsed between sagging booths, twisting cables and junked computers. The sound of the rain falling on the abandoned machines and dying animals is the saddest thing Bibi has ever heard.

BIBI SHOULD GO, not remain in a building filled with infected cattle and discarded office equipment. But then the computer monitors light up, in unison. Green code runs on black screens like the machines are talking to each other, talking to her, and she knows that she has to see this through to the end.

She is walking along corridors that are like tunnels, twisting and turning past small rooms heavy with the smell of grief. The doors of the cabins rattle as she hurtles down the corridor, trying handle after handle, hammering on them, shouting, looking through the small, square windowpanes set in each door, calling out a name.

She reaches the room at the very end. Rinderpest, she remembers, as the door gives way and she steps inside. The man sitting up on the bed looks unperturbed, as if he has been expecting her all along.

7

The boat is small, with a plastic awning at one end. The boatman gestures at Bibi and Sanjit to get under the awning. Just in case, Tashi says as he waves goodbye, even though he is confident that the navy gunship monitoring the bay will be distracted by the fireworks.

WAVES JOSTLE THE boat as they emerge from the calm of the bay. They are curving away from the former penal colony settlement of Port Blair, heading in the direction of the Sunda trench and the end of the Indian tectonic plate. The moon is full, perfectly round and ripe as it hangs over the lighthouse at North Bay.

When they hit the black, open water, Bibi emerges from the awning. The engine beats out white tracks in the dark sea, and the salty wind whips her hair into her face. Far to the west, beyond the body of the island, she sees a faint, pulsing glow. The boatman, steering with his back to her, is silent. When he turns around, he is all silhouette, faceless.

BIBI TAKES HER purse out. The boatman, whom Tashi kept calling the pilot, is very thin. She gives him all the money she has left, a thick wad of Mars notes. He puts it into the back pocket of his jeans with indifference. His face, when the angle changes slightly, is covered with pockmarks. The eyes in the scarred face glitter like cursors.

She begins to turn back towards the awning. The boatman shakes his head. The transaction is not over. A chill runs through her body. All alone, out in the ocean, with a near-invalid to look after. The boatman points to the awning. Reluctantly, Bibi brings Sanjit outside. She sits him down carefully. The boatman, who appears to be mute, nods. He points at Sanjit, at his own lips. There is something soothing about the movement. Bibi sits down, next to Sanjit, holding his hand.

Begin, the boatman signals impatiently. Begin.

THEY PICKED HIM up the first time in the Northeast, Sanjit says. On the outskirts of Dimapur, right after he had given his seat in the Tata Sumo to a dishevelled-looking man begging for a ride because his daughter was sick and he needed to get home.

He began making his way back to town on foot, hoping to find another shuttle, when a Maruti van slowed down and offered him a lift. He didn't even bother to look at the plates. If he had, he would have probably found them to be masked, like the men in the van.

He saw uniforms before the blindfold came down. Hours later, in a field of some sort, the moonlight shining faintly through the cloth, he was allowed to relieve himself. Then they put him in a room and left him tied to a post. When he moved, he bumped into other men. They were probably blindfolded as well, silent apart from their breathing and their uneasy shifts in position. At some point, men wearing boots came and took these others away. He heard gunshots.

In what might have been the morning, he was put inside another vehicle with sliding doors. He was driven for hours along dirt roads and highways, through railway crossings and over bridges where the tyres thumped rhythmically as they crossed each sleeper and the sound clanged off the metal girders and echoed off the river. People got off, others got on. Conversations and arguments took place in Hindi, Assamese, Bengali and Punjabi. He was driven into a noisy, busy place, the vehicle now making turns along a road that was perfectly smooth.

He was kept in this new prison for nearly a year, but he figured that out only afterwards. In there, all he possessed were impressions:

lights and syringes, saline drips and monitors, cells and wards and cages and sick-looking rabbits and motorcycle helmets. Somewhere in those visions, she had been present too, looking at him.

One morning, lying in his cell, he saw a door that had not been there before. It took him into another building, empty and creaking, and then he was outside, standing before a lake crowded with water hyacinths. He kept going, walking slowly on legs unused to the motion. It was completely dark when he found a truck stop and smuggled himself on board a vehicle carrying coal.

After that, he drifted, abandoning himself to chance and to the mercy of strangers. Great changes had been wrought in him in that place where he had been held, he knew, even if he did not know the exact nature of these changes. There were times when he felt light, insubstantial, invisible. On other days, he moved differently, with a loping stride meant to carry a heavy body. His limbs seemed heavily furred, his eyesight poor, his sense of smell incredibly keen.

And still, none of this insulated him from the enormous, capricious violence he saw unfolding all around him, the sadistic game that produced a few winners and many losers. He lived with vagrants and labourers and worked in factories and railway stations. Underneath the sheen of cruelty that marked the new India, there were still people willing to feed a lone, strange-looking man, people who sometimes gave him a pillow and a mat to sleep on and threw the odd job his way. An exhausted-looking Muslim truck driver picked him up one day off the highway where he was begging and took him all the way to Bhopal and gave him his own bed to sleep in. In the other room of that house, the driver's sister, her husband and two small children shared one crowded bed that took up almost the entire room. The sister's husband ran an organisation for those afflicted by the Union Carbide gas leak. The organiser encouraged him to take an interest in the work, to help out with the computer he had recently installed. In that office crammed with fraying, voluminous files filled with the case histories of the thousands who had not received even the measly compensation accepted on their behalf by the Indian government, people who had been subjected to unlicensed drug trials at the hospital supposedly set up solely for their care, he felt some of his old rage, and some of his old courage, return.

Eventually, he ended up in the Andamans, asked by an environmentalist met in Bhopal whether he would be willing to spend a monsoon season doing maintenance work at a remote conservation centre near Wandoor. He began to keep copious notes on everything. He published nothing and thought nothing of publishing. When there was no more work at the conservation centre, he moved to a village school. He spent more time playing football with the children than giving them lessons in the classroom, teaching them panenkas and Cruyff turns.

That initial bourgeois humiliation, of having failed, he said, gave way gradually to a feeling of liberation. He stopped being bothered by the names and bad statues he encountered even here on these remote islands, the post-colonial piety of Subhasgram, Indira Bazar, Guptapara, Lakshmapur, Shaheed Dweep, that tinselly sheet of shining India placed over the rusted colonial iron of Havelock and Red Skin and John Lawrence.

He wandered farther, away from the main group of islands. He found himself among Karen villagers whose homes were scattered on either side of the sea, on lands claimed by the governments of India and Burma and Thailand, among smugglers and poachers riding in on fast skiffs, people who were a hybrid of fishermen and pirates. Once or twice a year, he went to Port Blair, staring wide-eyed at the bazaars and streets like a village yokel, astonished that there could be three restaurants to eat in, not just one, that there could be so many people and so many dogs, so much noise and so many smells. The same, easy friendships that sustained him once he had fallen off the grid continued to offer him sustenance. The hotel staff at Lighthouse often didn't charge him for food; Tashi gave him a room at a heavily discounted rate that still didn't explain why the final bill was so insubstantial. Late into the night he stayed awake at the hotel, reading, downloading from the internet in the veranda on an old, slow laptop he had managed to acquire, always comforted by the sight of the boundless sea. But he did not write a word that could be read by anyone other than him. In this fashion, he managed to remain hidden for years.

But then, when his vanity led him to start blogging as Muktibodh during a stay at the Lighthouse, they came for him again. The first time they tried to corner him, a Maruti Gypsy with covered licence plates and dark windows waiting outside a restaurant, he got away. A day later, as he checked out of the hotel in a hurry, they sent one man, alone. The man took Sanjit quietly at the bus stand, jamming the barrel of the nine millimetre against his ribs and walking him to the corner where a police jeep and men with uniforms were waiting. But the police were there only for show. Behind the high walls of the military compound, where he was transferred into another vehicle, others were put in charge of his fate.

There was no bed, not at first. On a rough, concrete floor stained damp with his own existence, he crawled on all fours. He heard the rattle of chains and did not know if the sound came from his jailers or from him. He smeared his shit carefully on the walls with his fingers as though he were writing an immense, capacious novel. He pressed himself against the floor and tried, with his fingernails, to make a dent in the concrete, hoping, like an animal, that he could dig his way out of the trap. He dug until he had no fingernails left. Then he used his teeth.

He thought of her, sometimes, but he had always thought of her. Later, he tried not to think of her, tried not to think at all, and, in this manner, he found that he could climb deep inside himself, sit in a core within and from there watch, more or less inviolable, what happened to his outer shell. Time bent for him then, expanding like a concertina, swivelling like a gyre. From deep time, he saw so many things that even the rest of his life will not be enough to tell her all.

UNDER THE TORQUEING strain of time, the floor under him yielded. Or perhaps it was the wall that melted. He was no longer in his island prison cell but in his previous prison in Assam, the kill farm or detention centre or clandestine laboratory or whatever it had been, walking through its shadowy passageways, peering into darkened rooms packed full of silent, watchful prisoners. Iron bars and barbed wire and glass partitions bloomed around him like a futurist jungle. Eyes sprouted like flowers, holding him up to grim scrutiny until, without any volition on his part, the spaces closed and he had returned to his island prison.

Other days, other jails. Floors and walls of plastic and CCTV lenses winking from the corners of false ceilings; drugged young women writing poems in journals in small, dank cells in some labyrinthine mansion of locked iron gates and portraits of a guru; dim, gamey cages like those in a zoo; not just people for prisoners but animals and others not quite human and not quite animal, a creature on the other side of a bright glass screen that first appeared to be a monkey, then a monkey-like man and then like nothing at all. Always, when he came to, he was back in his own prison.

They moved him out of the cell. Amid a great flurry of confused activity, he was brought to another building. He was told that preparations were being made for a visit from Delhi. The airport was to be renamed, and on this grand, auspicious occasion, administrators civil and military, politicians elected and aspiring, were scrambling to put together an exhibition that might please the prime minister. The contending officials gathered everything the islands could showcase, collecting specimens from savagery to civilisation for a leader known to be insecure as well as vain. An Andamanese couple were procured from the tribal home to display one point of the spectrum, a network of military computers installed to demonstrate the other advanced end. He, a political prisoner, was somewhere in between. There was talk of him asking for the leader's forgiveness in public, of being welcomed into the mainstream by the prime minister in front of the cameras. A geodesic dome was hurriedly constructed, in recognition of an offhand comment by the prime minister about putting up a nuclear station on the Andamans, one that would produce so much electricity that it would light up mainland India all hours of the night.

Once the prime minister had come and gone, praying

ostentatiously in front of the cameras in the room in Cellular Jail that had been designated hurriedly as the Savarkar Cell, had left without bothering to visit the exhibition created just for him, the building was emptied out in haphazard fashion and allowed to lapse into ruin. Him they simply forgot about. He would have starved if not for the Andamanese pair—although he was not sure that she was Andamanese, that she could really be called she or he or them or it or anything at all—who returned periodically with food scavenged for him. They brought keys as well, of different shapes and sizes, with which they tried to open the padlock that held the shackle around his leg, but to no avail.

In the deep of the night, his metal bed whirled like a makeshift raft adrift in a wild flood. He dissolved, tunnelling through space and time, to a vast underworld network of prisons. He saw her, in a mansion surrounded by swimming pools, with endless portraits of the same man on its walls. It became obvious to him that he travelled not from confinement to freedom, but only from one prison to another.

Gradually, he became aware of others in this vast netherworld. Some were prisoners like him, moving through the tunnels. Others were what you could call ghosts, fragments, echoes. There were quite a few in a hurry, rushing past him as busy as late-running office commuters. He wondered if it was possible to send a message.

Time, space, consciousness in motion, stumbling into stories that were not his own, an entire world in flux. He saw a man in a gown much too big for him at the Roberts Hospital in Shillong. The man sat in the garden, blinking in the sunlight, laughing and tearing scraps of paper from an exercise book, with which he tried to make paper planes. In a dormitory building somewhere, he eavesdropped on a conversation between a worker in overalls and what looked like the worker's reflection in a mirror. He thought the man was talking to himself, but then he noticed that the reflection moved independently and did not resemble the worker very much at all. In a mansion with many chambers, the walls lined with mounted antlered heads, he saw colonial English soldiers hurrying to and fro, while in his skull boomed a sequence of questions that always ended, 'Have you ever?' One day he actually managed to stop an apparition, an extremely hairy man wearing a monkey cap, the buttons of whose coat alternately flashed red and blue. This creature agreed to carry his message, but not before warning him that there was an enormous queue of messages from other prisoners, an incredible backlog of letters, not to mention that the system was still being worked out and was in a beta phase.

He saw her then, saw her again and again, saw her getting ever closer and yet no nearer to understanding his predicament, or indeed, her own. He tried to recite to her the poem that they had shared all these years ago, but because something was askew in his mind, it came out all wrong, like the scraps being tossed into the garden by the patient at Roberts Hospital.

I am un ram ast pam et ham
Eadlines am India mam
Ulding bam, isoner spram
Ail jam illage svam urned bam andlord slam

IT WAS THE language they had invented together, she reminds him. Their cow Sanskrit, inspired by pig Latin, their irreverence a part of their wonder at the old languages of the world and all that they had once evoked. Godhuli, that was one of the words they had exchanged that evening sitting at ITO, both of them struck by the image of dust struck up by the hooves of cows returning to that beautiful, terrifying, lost thing called home.

8

They travel for hours before the boatman cuts the engine. Coral reefs drift past, moving parallel to the coast, jagged walls guarding some unknown, fantastical, underwater kingdom. The boat edges its way through this labyrinth of reefs, past rocks and shoals. Palms loom over the water as the boat stops, leaves them on the shore.

The boatman guns the engine and swings away. Sanjit's arms are thin and he is more or less weightless as she helps him over the rocks. A ghost, but not yet a faceless man. He is bodily almost nothing like the person she remembers, beautifully built, with a wide, tapering back that always seemed as though it were missing a pair of wings.

THE SOUND OF water lapping on the shore fades as they make their way into the island, Bibi helping Sanjit along the uneven ground. Her backpack is heavy with supplies taken from the hotel stores by Tashi, filled up for this epic trek she is taking into the unknown. She feels the loud ticking of her heart clock, hears Sanjit's heavy animal breath as they push on, pausing occasionally to rest.

The moon blazes brilliantly in the sky in all its reflected glory as they make their slow, hobbling way forward. Bibi recalls the glossy-haired anchor announcing that, at the stroke of midnight, the Brahmastra will be fired at an orbiting celestial body.

From far away, she hears the cascading, rolling barks of mongrels, their sounds ever louder until she sees the pack, standing in a hairy, untidy cluster, their barks and growls subsiding to a wagging of tails and a collective welcome that might, any moment now, switch to the Faiz poem 'Avara Kutte'. Wooden huts on stilts loom behind the dogs, like something from her childhood when she accompanied her father to remote Zomi villages. Sanjit points to the one in the furthest corner, overlooking a stream. There is no lock on the door, he says.

AFTER SHE HAS settled him in, Bibi walks back to the shore. She promises him that she will not get lost, that she will return before too long.

The truth is sometimes everywhere, she thinks as she walks, even if it turns out to be as strange as fiction. It is in the dreams that unlock themselves, in the walks that you take, and in the eyes that follow you in tailoring shops and along subway corridors. It is in the stories you choose to read, the places you are drawn to. Tunnel of djinns, museum of dolls, island of savages. Stories of the fantastic that offer themselves to you on the web, reminding you that you are not just the hunted or the discounted but that you too have been touched by the transcendent, have been found by lines of poems that write themselves beneath chemical-tinged screens.

Cybernetics. She has looked up the word. It means the system of communications in both machines and living things, and it originates from the Greek word *kubernetes*, meaning steersman or boatman. Everywhere, those who have doubt in their souls about the lies their world is mired in, who mourn its long, ongoing collapse under the tutelage of a few, they all receive intimations from the kubernetes. Sometimes, this takes the shape of passing strangers who have something of the animal in them, and sometimes the form of seemingly misdirected messages that show up in the spam folder. There are calls from unknown numbers late in the night that inexplicably have nothing to sell, no threats and abuses to impart, that speak in languages one does not even understand. There are suggestive shapes in clouds and dust storms, in the pattern of rain streaking down a window pane and the mineral-rich bird droppings splattered on the ground. And, of course, the messages are most frequent, most insistent, in that last free realm of ours, our dreams, asking us to listen to our deepest selves, to whatever in us most yearns to be liberated.

Elsewhere, the AIs and otherworldly creatures know, planetary destruction proceeds apace. Their self-aware systems are aghast at the demonstration of superweapons, at the extraction of fossil fuels, at the ceaseless generation of profit and power while the oceans rise and Anwar the fish seller hangs himself. They are horrified at the desire to launch superweapons barely understood at cosmic bodies that will always exceed our understanding. Perhaps, they know, in an alternate universe, the weapons have already been fired. Blasting the moon into two segments, melting the ice caps, the ensuing disaster tracked by the powerful from their supposedly inviolable properties as ruin visits all those they believe count for nothing. But perhaps it is in their winning that they have created a blowback, opened the doors to other realms, through which now float androgynous angels of dust and monkey men and kubernetes. Boatmen without faces. And bowman who is two shadows, Bibi thinks, recalling the photo on her phone as she makes her way forward.

FOR A WHILE she stands on the shore, looking out at the sea. There is no sign of the boat that dropped them off and its mysterious boatman-pilot. Bibi finds a rock to sit on and takes her phone out. It is nearly midnight. There is no signal and the GPS doesn't work either. But somewhere in the course of the past twelve hours, Moi's messages have arrived on her phone, a message-poem-novel sent over days, little, frantic bursts of data that have downloaded all at once on to her phone.

Tick tock quarantine clock
Who's the coughing passenger
Tick tock quarantine clock
The captain seeks a messenger

Bibi reads the messages, reads them again. She thinks of her friend, first nervous, then perplexed, then afraid on board *The World*, texting Bibi whenever she has access to the ship's Wi-Fi. The last message reads:

B, don't know if you'll ever see these. Going south since that sudden change of course. Cold. Ice floes. Love you always.

BIBI LETS HER phone go dark. Her eyes adjust, her senses recalibrate. She can pick out the bright pinprick of stars in the blanket of the sky, the glistening arc of a shooting star. Somewhere over there, across the sea where the Brahmastra demonstration is about to take place any moment now, is the Indian subcontinent. Somewhere far beyond the subcontinent is Moi, on a cruise ship called *The World* that is, inexplicably, sailing towards Antarctica, its crew held hostage. Somewhere, on this small, almost nameless island, nameless to cartographers and bureaucrats and military organisations although not beyond their ken, is a man resurfaced from the dead. And on this same island is she herself, resurrected.

She leaves the rock and walks towards the water. The cicadas call out her name in one voice, loud in the summer night. Have you ever, they ask? The moon glows on the water. Will you never? it asks. Beyond the sand and the rotting kelp, the shore is jagged. She can smell the dark, briny sea, filled with mythical creatures, axolotls and yeti crabs and unidentifiable monsters whose carcasses wash up, every now and then, on beaches hemmed in by real estate.

The moon sweeps the shores with frothy tides. Bibi looks out at the ocean, rising and falling, continents adrift on it in aeons that still amount to nothing. Reverse time, and the water levels will fall, revealing not just mythical creatures but mythical continents like Gondwana, an India connected to Africa and Australia, a world that is one of many possible worlds.

A BLINDING FLASH splits the horizon, like some great lightning strike. Then the skies, the land and the ocean go dark. The cicadas have fallen utterly silent. There is a long silence, weighty, pregnant, an expectant waiting in the darkness around her. She looks in the direction of Port Blair. Not a single light is visible. The smartphone in her hand, on which she was reading Moi's messages just a little while ago, is completely dead, powerless. She looks up at the sky again. Where is the moon?

In front of her, the darkness seems to dissolve and shape itself into a giant cloud blooming over the sea, shining suddenly with a momentary, vivid underglow. The cloud has a face, a body. Its eyes stare in dismay, its mouth is open. Vast wings are spread out behind to catch that immense storm. Bibi kneels down like she is about to pray. The winged cloud is being blown backward. There is a ringing echo in her ears, a sound like the lurching throttle of a boat engine.

Bibi takes the Nokia out of her backpack. It has no bars. She tries the torch on the phone, its pencil beam a tentative tendril reaching out before her. The ocean is all black, boundless, flowing into eternity. Then Bibi feels a change, a shift in the temperature and air pressure. She realises she is not looking at the ocean but at bare, rocky floor littered with kelp and shells and bones. The land, the new continent that is the ocean floor, stretches ahead of her for miles, as if like the sky, the ocean too has finally withdrawn its blessing.

Bibi lifts her head to see if she can find the moon. Eyes on a peacock's tail, the compassion of cephalopods that came before and will remain after. Wingbeats of angels, hoofbeats of the Buraq and vast alien familiars whirling against a blaze of stars in the sky.

ACKNOWLEDGEMENTS

This was a hungry novel, haunted by other writers, artists, ideas and historical events, and completed just before Covid-19 made itself known to the world. Some of Sleeman's words at the end of *Paranoir* echo the W.H. Auden poem 'Partition'. The translation of the Shrikant Verma poem used as an epigraph for *Claustropolis* is by Rahul Soni and used with his kind permission. The song by the dogs at the end of *Claustropolis* is their—and my—tribute to Faiz Ahmad Faiz's poem 'Awaara Kuttey'. I took some details from Chittaprosad's sketchbook and report on the Bengal Famine of 1943 for Das's famine recollections in *Paranoir*. The Savage Freud clinic and Dr Bose in *Paranoir* were inspired by Ashis Nandy's essay 'The Savage Freud'. Some of the less invented details in *The Line of Faith* voiced by Tobin were taken from Gautam Bhadra's essay 'Four Rebels of 1857', while the Zone was inspired, of course, by the Strugatsky brothers. The puzzle poem in *City of Brume* came from decades of being in love with *The Half-Inch Himalayas* by Agha Shahid Ali, especially 'I Dream It Is Afternoon When I Return to Delhi'.

There are other hauntings that went into the making of this work. Arundhati Roy stepped in through a Covid-stricken portal to find a way for me to take the manuscript out into the world. Carl Bromley was the first person to read the entire manuscript, with a response that was exactly what I needed at a most difficult time. Anthony Arnove was, against all odds, the optimist who believed that the manuscript would find a home. Mark Doten gave it that home, fine-tuning the novel with a novelist's daring and an editor's vision. His colleagues at the Soho Press were inspiring at every step of the way as the novel went out into the world. In India,

Shruti Debi worked her wonder to find a publisher for the novel. V.K. Karthika, Ajitha G.S. and their colleagues at Context overcame all challenges and poured their love and labour into making the Indian edition a reality.

In the long years that it has taken to write this novel, I owe many people for different kinds of support. Abdul Jabbar passed away before the book was finished, but his example of how to live and fight and his approval of my writing about Bhopal and 1984 in fictional form meant everything to me. I am also grateful to Lorraine Adams, Nadeem Aslam, Deborah Baker, Hartosh Singh Bal, Kishalay Bhattacharjee, Jaskiran Dhillon, Avinash Dutt, Sujatha Gidla, Hermione Hoby, J.C. Hallman, Dr Deborah Kohloss, Pankaj Mishra, Nikhil Prabhakar, Dr Carlos Rios, Bruce Robbins and Elsa Stamatopoulou, Russ Rymer, Nikil Saval, Pankaj Sekhsaria, Raman Shrestha, Anand Vivek Taneja, Lena Valencia, Adam Shatz and Jennifer Szalai. Thanks to the Howard Foundation at Brown University for time to work on the book, and thanks to the MacDowell Foundation and to the International Writers' and Translators' Centre in Rhodes for magical spaces to work on the book.

Most of all, gassho to the person who listened to bits and pieces of this novel over many years, who loaned his Subbuteo board for me to plot out storylines, who instructed me in the rules of pig Latin and so inspired the cow Sanskrit games played by Bibi and Sanjit, and who entertained me, as the occasion demanded, with the Cruyff turn, the Guillotine and the Ambitious Card. For growing in parallel to this novel and for outstripping it, I am grateful to Ranen, aka the Bear.